RINGS OF PASSAGE

A Time Travel Novel with Richard III

BY KARLA TIPTON

Rings of Passage: A Time Travel Novel with Richard III

ISBN-13: 978-1493600243
ISBN-10: 1493600249

DEDICATION

To Kathie Weigel, who handed me
"Daughter of Time" by Josephine Tey
and said, "You *have* to read this."

ACKNOWLEDGMENTS

I owe a debt of gratitude to many people who assisted me on the long road to publication. Cara Bristol, who recommended my work to Staci Taylor of Lazy Day Publishing, has been a great friend through the years, personally and as my literary cheerleader. Ever since we worked together for the society section of a small local newspaper, we have shared career ups and downs, traded writing advice, and laughed a lot.

Thanks also to Kathie Weigel, who has gone through more fan crushes with me than I can count since we met in second grade, and "got me into" Richard III. Together we devoured novels and history books about his life, defended his reputation, and even incorporated him into a "dungeon" game scenario back when we were playing D&D – my first spark of inspiration for mixing up Richard's life story with fantasy and magic.

I want to thank Helen Maurer of the Richard III Society's American Branch, who patiently supplied me with the society's library books and articles necessary for conducting my research – back *before* there was an Internet, when it all had to be sent by snail mail.

I also am grateful for the help, inspiration and fellowship I have shared with many Richard III Society members in America and in England. I especially want to thank Gwen and Brian Waters of Gloucester, who welcomed me like an old friend when I visited England, even though we had never met before. In the many years since, they have provided friendship and encouragement.

I owe the sincerest thanks to the members of my Antelope Valley critique group, including Cara Bristol, Terri Shute and Margo McCall (as well as others who wish to remain anonymous), for patiently and tirelessly providing constructive criticism through countless rewrites of "Rings of Passage." Thanks also to my dear friend, True Carr, whose "fangirl" enthusiasm for my work inspires me to keep going.

Here's a shout out to the novelists whose work stoked my imagination and fueled my interest in Richard III: Josephine Tey, Sharon Kay Penman, Rosemary Hawley Jarman, Jean Plaidy, and John M. Ford, among others.

Thanks also to my cover artist, P.J. Friel, who made it possible for me to share with the world the image of Richard that I held in my mind.

Finally, I thank my family – my parents, Ted and Donna Tipton, and my sister, Darla Williams and her husband Tim, who have been immensely supportive of my writing career – ever since I was that nerdy teenager in my bedroom, punching out short stories on my typewriter.

CHAPTER ONE

Anise crashed into consciousness, her body battered against an unforgiving metal cage of some sort, a diabolical theme park ride, or...

What the hell? I'm wearing a suit of armor!

She tried to look at herself, but the helmet kept her from moving her head. Another lurch, another head bash, followed by another realization. This was no park ride.

Oh, my God. I'm riding a horse!

It was a big brute of a horse, too. Her legs straddled its back, as wide as a barrel.

How did I get here? The last thing she remembered before blacking out was being grabbed by some guy outside that gloomy farmhouse she'd inherited from her bio-dad, a man she'd never known. She could not think. She could only hang on for dear life.

The horse bucked, and somehow she did not fall off. Her gauntleted fingers were entwined in the animal's coarse mane, and should have broken like twigs. Yet, she was assisted by some power, some force coursing up her arm from her left hand, giving her strength.

Her head was pounding from her brains bashing around inside her skull. She saw only flashes of light through the narrow slits of the helmet, but she knew chaos ensued around her. The horse reared, knocking the breath from her lungs. The heavy armor on her back threatened to drag her to the ground. She fought for balance, and leaned into the fulcrum to stop herself from falling. She thanked God she'd had some equestrian training at school.

When the horse came down hard on its four feet and paused a moment, Anise managed to throw back her helm's visor.

A full-blown battle raged around her. Armored men on stampeding horses raced in all directions, viciously impaling their enemies with lethal precision. In horror, Anise watched a battleaxe hack into the skull of an unhorsed knight. His blood, bone and brains splattered in all directions.

She choked down the bile rising in her throat. *My God, this isn't some historical reenactment! It's real!*

The bodies of men and beasts were pounded and hewn to bits around her. Her horse reared again, its forelegs ripping through the air, nearly tossing her into the fray.

Somehow she hung on as her horse maneuvered out of harm's way…

…and into the oncoming path of a white-armored knight on a horse draped in battle colors of mulberry and blue.

His gallant figure seemed achingly familiar to her. Her heart exploded with overwhelming love for this man. She knew why she was here.

I have to save him!

At that moment, Anise dropped into a deep and blinding darkness.

CHAPTER TWO

BERKHAMSTED CASTLE, ENGLAND, 1485

As Richard the king lay awake within the velvet darkness of his curtained bed, he found his mind drifting. He fought sleep, for he found no solace in it. His thoughts wandered into territory inhabited by demons, lingering on foul details that turned his blood to ice.

It had happened years ago. With the Duke of Buckingham's sudden arrival at Gloucester, Richard had learned of the unspeakable events that had transpired in the Tower of London.

He now tried to shake off the memory. Hadn't he as much culpability in the matter as those who had carried out the abominable deed?

Though he'd never told his late wife of the horrific acts that had been undertaken in his name, Anne, his queen, had always forgiven him for his silence, knowing the burdens of a king required secrecy. His silent suffering dismayed her, but she gave him what consolation she could.

Now, in her absence, this memory of her tenderness was the only thing that comforted him at all.

He turned onto his back to gaze into the darkness. He loathed the night with its disturbing dreams. Only by imagining his dear wife, Anne, when she had been well and lying by his side, was he able to tumble into a fitful sleep. As dawn broke, he descended into dream.

The lady in mourning garb stood at the edge of the forest, her long dark hair hanging to her waist. When she called for him, he went to her, admiring of her pale skin and sad, blue eyes, and her beauty as radiant as an angel's.

Long they walked together until coming to an ancient stone church, deserted and unkept. Following her into the hallowed chapel, he joined her at the altar. When she looked at him, he saw tears mingled with pity. He turned to see why she wept.

Before them stood two stone coffins. The king had mourned many members of his family during his thirty-two years – a father, brothers, and uncles – yet great foreboding descended on him as he lowered his gaze to view these dead.

When he saw and realized who had been lost to him forever, the walls of the chapel crumbled down and buried him in ruins.

His own cry awakened him and he sat up, his heart pounding in his chest, his breathing ragged.

Richard fought to calm himself. *Only a dream, 'twas only a dream.*

Richard longed to banish the images from his mind. For in the dream, it was not his murdered nephews of the Tower who were lain out in their coffins.

Sweet Jesu, 'twas his son – his and Anne's only child, Edward – who lay there dead. And it was also she, his beloved queen. Not long ago, both mother and child had been lost to Richard. Some say it was God's punishment for the deaths of the princes. Richard's mother believed it was caused by the sorcerer's ring that Anne had refused to take off, forged a century earlier by the vanquished Welsh wizard Glendower.

Was this dark-haired woman of his dream a sorceress, too? What role would be played by the angel in black?

It was prophecy – that much was clear to Richard. Whoever she was, she would be his future. His ending. His fate. He felt it in his bones.

****

In the land Owain Glendower left behind, four score years had passed in blood and turmoil.

Drifting between life and death, existing neither on one plane nor the other, he slumbered so deeply it might have lasted through eternity.

While his countrymen died in a war between royal houses, the great Welsh wizard lingered, locked in an eerie balance between worlds. While the parade of souls passed by, Glendower merged with the universe and melded with the ether.

He slept. He listened. He waited.

At last, the summons came.

The ring stirred upon his insubstantial hand. Glendower's consciousness took form, gathering like droplets on the side of a chalice. His memory returned, and his mind sought for the source of his power. A keen yearning for life arose in him. Morton called, and his student would cater to the needs of his resurrected body. The heir of Cadwallader must have returned. And so the greatness that Glendower had sought for a century was within his grasp.

His spirit renewed, he descended into the vortex between worlds to seek his destiny on earth.

****

Anise awoke in a gale storm that ripped the breath from her. All she knew was chaos and fear.

Had she died? Was this Hell?

There were no flames. There was nothing but this mute tempest, as violent as the strongest hurricane, tossing her helplessly, propelling her soundlessly through space. Every revolution brought her nearer to the center, until she dropped into the storm's eye – and knew stillness at last.

A keen perception of things unseen replaced her missing senses.

She felt the presence of others, floating at the center of this soundless vacuum. Sentient beings with strange intents and purposes. Moving in and through the vortex, passing to destinations beyond. If she followed them, would they lead her from this storm?

In answer, one of these called to her, offering protection and escape. When she tried to follow, she was intercepted by another – this one reeking of dark purpose.

Secretive and craving.

Hungry.

It sought the magic she held within her – a golden ring of power.

The force advanced on her, trapping her like a hapless mouse in its jaws. Methodically, it consumed her, feeding on her soul, enveloping her mind until memory lapsed, sucking her life force dry, draining her of the power within – and the magic.

She struggled against it, fighting for her freedom. Somehow, she rallied, and gained. Its hold loosened. She'd had assistance from a friendly force – she did not recognize her champion. Yet the evil was driven away by this benevolent being. Desperate to survive, she escaped back into the gale…

…and was pitched from the darkness, falling hard upon the earth.

****

Anise awoke in darkness with her face against stone and the smell of damp vegetation in her nostrils. Something sharp gouged her ribs, and she ached with cold. Her hair was in her eyes, but when she tried to lift a hand to brush it away, she fell into fit of coughing that left her trembling. She did not try to move for a long time. She heard the wind rustle through the trees and small creatures scurrying through brush. How had she managed to run so far? The last she remembered, she had fallen in front of the farmhouse as she ran from her stalker.

Turning her head, she saw that it was night, but not a dark one. The moon loomed large above her. There was the silhouette of a rock outcropping beside her. She reached for it, and pulled herself into a sitting position. It was difficult, with this heavy weight on her arm. She realized it was her tote bag. Her shin smarted where she had fallen through the porch step of the farmhouse. Her head throbbed, the blood pounding in her ears, making her lose her sense of balance. She heard a stick breaking in two and a heavy footstep upon the forest floor.

Standing in a copse of trees several yards from her, Anise glimpsed the silhouette of a cloaked man.

"Keep away, you!" Her heels gouged into the dirt, but her knees buckled when she tried to stand. "I'll scream!"

The man remained where he was, as if startled by her presence. He was of medium height, but taut as whipcord and poised for action. There was something familiar about him, but it was not the man from the farmhouse. That guy had been much taller.

He advanced slowly, his hand hovering at his waist.

"Please don't shoot!" she begged.

"M'lady? Pray do not fear me."

Was this some kind of joke? Had one of the other actors followed her from the performing arts center?

"Joe, is that you? Are you trying to scare me? If it's you, just say so."

"I do not go by that name, lady. Come away from this unholy place. The spirits of the dead walk here."

Well, that cinched it. No way was this Joe. The timbre of his man's voice was different, and his accent unfamiliar. He spoke softly, but there was steel in his tone that told her he was accustomed to being obeyed.

As the man approached, the light of the crescent moon allowed enough illumination to glimpse his features.

"How came you to this place?" he asked. He knelt beside her, and Anise's heart raced. Her tears, never far from the surface, welled up with her anxiety.

With a shaky voice, she forced herself to say, "I don't know, but if it's so dangerous, why are you here?"

Her question seemed to unnerve him, and when she met his eyes, he whispered, "You were but a dream." He reached out to touch her hair, and when Anise flinched, he hastily drew back. Tears spilled down her face. His brow creased with concern. "Let me help you." He reached out again, this time pressing the back of his fingers against her forehead, as if feeling for fever.

Anise sensed she could trust him and was no longer afraid. "I'm not feeling very well. Could you take me home?" She shivered and closed her eyes. Her head throbbed, and she felt faint again.

She knew he would not hurt her, because she remembered him now. He was an honorable man, and his cause just. He was the white knight. As he picked her up, she passed out.

****

BERKHAMSTED CASTLE, ENGLAND, 1485

"I fear for you, Richard. I fear for your life."

The dark-haired man, his face lined prematurely around the eyes and corners of the mouth, smiled wistfully. "*Maman*, I fear too. But only that the realm will be disturbed yet again by battle and blood and betrayal. The least I fear for is myself."

Cecily, Duchess of York for most of the years of her life and a Holy Sister of the Order of the Benedictine for the past four, studied her son's lean, powerful frame, noting the hollowness under his eyes. Even though his duties were now mostly administrative, the muscular arms of a man trained for battle swelled beneath his finery. Yet Cecily recognized her son's fatigue. It revealed itself as the stoic expression she had seen on her own face, when forcing herself to a duty her heart did not endorse. The cold of the dawn was exaggerated by the dampness of her home. She saw him shiver involuntarily, as if from the chill that had fallen over his life since the death of his queen and their son, dampening his fervor, diminishing his urgency and his life.

And yet, he now had to face the threat of the imposter seeking the throne from across the Channel. Backed by French gold, the man calling himself the Earl of Richmond was putting his fleet together as they spoke.

"Will Tudor seek to invade the realm so soon?" she asked, pouring him a cup of mulled wine she had seasoned with special herbs, seeking to relax him.

He and his entourage of counselors and attendants had arrived at the castle early yesterday morn. The visit had begun strangely, with his discovery of the lady in the woods. Richard had carried the maid into the castle, his face twisted with a kind of worry Cecily had not seen since the queen died. The monks had taken over from there, and she had not checked on the lady's condition since.

She was too concerned about her son. The circles under his eyes told her he had not slept well last night. He'd sought her out before the dawn. "Tudor must move soon," he answered quietly, "or else he will lose those who have vowed to follow him."

Many times she had discussed strategy with his father, killed in battle nearly a quarter of a century ago. Now she discussed it with her only living son, Richard.

"We expect him in late summer," he said.

"Tudor cannot suspect what he is up against," said Cecily.

"No. I suspect not," said Richard, his tone laced with annoyance. "He shall soon discover we intend to settle his claim forthwith. I have no intentions of dallying with this one as with the others." He twisted the ring on his left hand.

Cecily forced herself to look away, biting her tongue lest she speak out – the ring was a topic he had forbidden her to broach.

Richard's anger, often a healthy sign for those in melancholy, relieved Cecily only briefly, for his forcefulness did not disguise the fatalism beneath. Her gaze turned back to his hands and the ring. He would not take it off. Yet if she could only persuade him to discard it, she was certain the evil humors he harbored would be dispelled.

Silently, she prayed for his deliverance, at the same time denying the futility of such a prayer. Her son was never one to veer from a path he had set his mind to. If he had to, in this fight with Tudor, he would go to his death. And while the knowledge that he had never lost a battle should have comforted her, she knew his time was different. Richard had never before gone into with so little to live for.

Cecily's blood ran cold. Nor had he ever done so with the curse of Owain Glendower's ring upon his soul.

****

Richard saw his mother staring at his hand. He wished she would just forget about the ring. It wasn't cursed. He was cursed.

"My son, I do so fear for you," the duchess repeated softly. The nun, her face still handsome beneath the black habit, stood to face him.

"Fear for my soul, *Maman*. I believe God hath already judged my decision to take the crown from my nephews. In the two years I have been king, even my existence has become a punishment as I watch those I love wither away, die, and leave me. I am but a younger you – watching your life's love taken from you, and then your children, one by one..."

He watched as his mother reflected on his words. Along with her husband at the battle of Sandal Castle, she had lost a brother and a son – his older brother, Edmund, only seventeen at the time. As the years swiftly followed, she lost her son, George, and cousins, Johnny Neville and Warwick. Then, alas, her son, Edward the King – and Edward's sons.

Richard felt a stab of guilt. Her grandchildren were near manhood when they were murdered. Of her twelve offspring, only three remained, Richard her youngest.

"There is yet England..." she said, absently.

But Richard interrupted with an ironic laugh. Quickly ashamed, for he never showed Cecily irreverence, he turned his back to her in a pretense of gazing out the window. Taking a breath, he continued, "England lies in a sorry state, *Maman*. Rumor indicts me of the foulest sins, causing me to wonder if damnation is my due. How can citizens of England trust my deeds when even I cannot? How can they have faith in my rule when even I do not? God has forsaken me. First my son's death, then Anne's..." Richard turned toward her again. "But you are right. I must do what I can for the realm, then tend to myself." He paused and took a long drink of wine. "It seems an eternity since she was taken from me," he whispered fervently. "Was it not significant that the heavens fell dark on the day she passed from this world? For me, the sun did not return. If God could only end *my* excruciating existence, I would be ever grateful." He tipped the glass up, finishing it.

Cecily's throat grew tight at his wretchedness, yet she whispered, "Richard! Say a prayer quickly!"

The king turned to look at her with bitterness in his eye, but upon seeing her countenance full of hurt and worry, forgot he was a king and looked at the floor at his mother's feet.

"I don't mean that, *Maman*." He crossed himself, his lips mouthing a prayer. "I have fits of maudlin. They pass." Absently, Richard again fumbled with the ring. "It's just that I cannot believe that I shall ever become used to a life alone."

Thinking of Anne brought to mind the woman in the woods – the woman of the dream he'd been having for so long. Before realizing what he did, he asked, "How is she? The lady I found yesterday morn?"

****

"I know not," she said simply. Again, that worry in his face. Lo, she had not seen that in him for some time. Now she knew she was not mistaken. Perhaps it was the time to speak of that which had weighed so heavily on her mind in these months since the queen's death.

He turned back to the window and looked out over the hilly countryside and the sun just peeking over its horizon.

Cecily said, "I wish to offer the king some advice – not as his subject nor as a tired old nun – but as his *Maman*. And as one who has known grief."

Richard turned to her with an affectionate smile, yet filled with sorrow. "I would that it helps me."

17

"Just now, I recalled how it was, losing your father. Not much time goes by that I do not remember it," she whispered. "Without him, my life was ever transformed. But it went on." She took a deep breath. "You must lay Anne to rest, Richard. Let her go or her ghost shall hasten you to your grave."

A dark shadow fell over his expression, and he turned away. "*Maman*, she haunts me. I cannot escape the memories."

Despite the pain that stabbed through her heart, she pressed on, her voice breaking, "Perhaps you are a younger me. If that is true, you can bear what is yours to suffer."

Richard glanced at her quickly and saw her tears. It stunned him to silence, and he allowed her to continue.

"I thought I could never go on without him. But I did. I found other things to live for. At last, I find solace in God."

"I have not your courage."

"You have more," she insisted. "Time does heal, Richard, if you let it."

Huskily he said, "But you had us, your children. Ned and George and Margaret and me. I have nothing."

Briskly, she brushed away the wetness on her cheek. "Have you forgotten your own children? John, who loves you dearly, and Katherine? Not heirs to the throne, of course – but of your flesh.

And you may have more. You must marry again. 'Tis the only thing to save you from this bitterness."

"There's no time to look for a wife now. For a king, it takes months, years..." he said hopelessly.

Cecily silently asked for forgiveness for what she was about to say. It was a sin against the Holy Father to even think of advising one to such a course of action. But there it was. And when it came to Richard, she was admittedly weak.

"There are other consolations. Perhaps you wouldn't have to marry. Take you a leman."

There. She'd said it. Cecily's heart ached at the thought that God might, instead, take her son on the battlefield, unshriven and heavy with the sin to which she had just urged him. But she let it go. She could not lose him, too.

"What of this woman you rescued?" she said. "I have seen your concern over her."

Richard's expression was one of shock. She knew he would react thus.

"*Maman!*"

"You are a man who needs to forget about your dead wife," she said harshly. "And you are my last son, grieving himself to an early grave. In his infinite wisdom and compassion, God will forgive you – and possibly me, as well." She drew herself up, knowing she would anger him with her next words. "You must forget about

Anne," she repeated. "And you must take off that ring, for it keeps her ever in your mind."

Richard's face twisted. "You know I cannot do that, *Maman*. I did promise her..."

A loud knock at the chamber door startled them both. When the monk entered and saw the king, he fell to the floor. "Your Grace. May I speak with Her Grace in confidence? 'Tis a matter of urgency."

Richard sighed in resignation and nodded his assent. He bid the clergyman to rise. The monk motioned Cecily into the corner. After exchanging a few hastily whispered sentences with the monk, she said to her son, "My services are required by one in distress, yet I cannot bear leaving it at this—"

His expression one of hurt, he said quietly, "You are needed, *Maman*."

Cecily gave him a meaningful look. "Think on what I have said," she whispered, before sweeping out with the agitated monk.

****

When Anise awoke again, she was in a stone room, its rough walls tinted golden with the sun. She lay on a feather bed, and the acrid smell of smoke from a nearby fire tickled her nostrils. The walls were covered with tapestries woven intricately into scenes of battle.

Where was she? Anise remembered her recent experiences in bits. She settled back on the pillow, her body still numb with sleep. She'd bashed her shin hard on the porch step when she fell, but the pain from that had gone, at least. She recalled running from the man in the house before she fell and hit her head. Whomever he was, he'd known her.

Her thumb rubbed against something encircling her index finger. Lifting her hand to her face, she looked at it. *A ring.* She had never worn much jewelry, except on stage, so it felt odd. It was a gold band, engraved with an indistinct design of a man holding something in his hands.

She had found the ring in the farmhouse that had been left to her by Matthew Fallon, the father she never knew.

Her mind cast back to that night Anise had moved out of her mother's home in Hollywood, vowing never to return. After they'd had that terrible fight – *and boy, could that woman shout, even if she was stuck in a wheelchair* – Anise had packed two suitcases, made plane reservations to Boston, and gave her mom one last chance to tell her the truth.

"So, who is Matthew Fallon, and why did he leave me a house in his will?"

"It's obviously a mistake. They've got the wrong Anise Wynford," hissed her mother.

"Now that's likely," Anise had said sarcastically, rolling her eyes. "He was one of your affairs, wasn't he? Was he my father?"

And her mother, with her immaculately styled platinum hair and her fallen facelift expression, glared at her through those expressive hazel eyes that had made her B-movie-famous for a dozen years.

Anise pressed her, "When I was seven, we moved away. We left Dad here, took a plane, and went to live in a big house."

"What of it? Tom and I separated for awhile. It happens."

Anise inhaled. Memories trickled back. "There was a boy. Older than me, with dark hair and blue eyes like mine. He called me 'sis.' And there was a man. Was he Matthew Fallon?" She asked again, "Was he my father?"

Her mom stared at her in stony silence.

"If you don't tell me, I'm going to find out for myself."

The former actress jerked her head around. "And just how are you going to do that, missy? You can't even say 'boo' to a mouse. How many panic attacks and psychiatrists have you been through over the years? I can't even keep track anymore."

"I wonder why that is? Maybe because you've always made me feel small. Because, to hear you tell it, I'm a poor excuse for a daughter and will never be able to live up to the glamorous movie star, Gwendolyn Gates."

Gwendolyn's hands gripped the arms of her wheelchair. Honest to God, for a moment Anise thought her mom was going to stand up for the first time in fifteen years. But Gwendolyn only lolled her head around on the wheelchair's headrest, moaning, "Look at me, look at me! How can you throw my career in my face like that, you ungrateful child? I was struck down at my pinnacle! *And it's all your fault!*"

Anise's chest constricted. Panic overwhelmed her – panic that had been preconditioned over the years by Gwendolyn's fits of blame. Anise burst into tears.

Forcing herself to stop, she vehemently wiped her eyes. "You're not doing this to me again, Mother." Anise pressed on, her voice shaking. "I've called Auntie Mabes. She's going to stay here with you, while I go to Boston to talk to this lawyer. If it turns out I really have inherited a house, I might just decide to live in it."

Gwendolyn laughed. The sound was derisive, and Anise hated it. "You're going to do this, you're going to do that. You're always *going* to… that's all I ever hear, and you've done none of it. Twenty-two years old and never even had a boyfriend."

"I made a vow not to treat men like you do." Anise's voice trembled. "My first time will be with a man I love."

Gwendolyn snorted. "Don't be naïve. You've read too many Shakespeare sonnets."

Anise ignored the dig. "And I *have* done something. Even with my condition, I made it through drama school, because Dad believed in me enough to leave me a trust fund. And now I find out he wasn't even my bio-dad – but he cared more about me than you ever did."

"Think about it, my girl. He may have put you through school – but you inherited your fine bone structure and talent from me. *That's* what matters."

Anise stood up. "This is what matters, Mother. I'm leaving."

And she left.

Matthew Fallon had been her father. The boy who had lived with them in the big house had been her half-brother, Dominic. Matthew died, and Dominic was missing. That's when the lawyer tracked down Anise.

Her property was in the small Massachusetts village of Williamstown – a summer stock theater town. The night the lawyer turned the keys to the farmhouse over to her was the night of the *Richard III* dress rehearsal.

It had been too much for one day. While on stage, reprising her role as Anne Neville, Anise had suffered a panic attack and ran out of the theater. She had not even bothered to get out of costume, a long black dress made to the pattern of a fifteenth century mourning gown.

Anise drove straight to the farmhouse. She needed answers – about the family she never knew. And about herself.

But all she found were more questions – and this ring. It had been hidden in a storeroom on the second floor. To slip it on her finger had seemed like the most natural thing in the world.

The man who had accosted her at the farmhouse must have been trying to take it from her. But the ring took her from him instead.

She could not remember much of anything after that.

Until she woke up in the woods. That's when the white knight had found her and brought her to this place.

The white knight. What made her think of him that way?

A sound interrupted her thoughts. A small, robed figure struggled with the creaky door, and rattled into the room with a tray. Setting the food and drink on a nearby table, he approached the bed and peered at her.

"Sweet Jesu!" he whispered, pushing back his cowl. "You are awake! Can you speak, m'lady?"

Through her confusion, Anise recognized the man as a priest or a monk. Yet, he spoke in a strangely affected accent. Where was she? Her throat was too parched to speak and, recognizing this, the monk hurried to the table and poured some liquid into a goblet. He held it to her lips, allowing her to swallow slowly. She choked at first, not expecting it to be wine. It was warm, spiced, and eased the tightness. She whispered, "I have to get home. The play opens tonight."

"Rest m'lady. Do not speak. May God be thanked, you have survived the devil's tricks. My name is Brother Benedict. You lost your way in the woods. 'Twas by God's blessing that His Grace discovered you. What can I do to comfort you? Do you have pain?"

"No – I'm fine. How did I get here?" Anise's eyelids started drooping. She was so sleepy.

"All in good time, m'lady. Just rest in the knowledge that you are truly safe here from the powers of evil. You are in the house of a great lady, who is in the service of God."

Anise's head throbbed and she felt sick to her stomach. The room went fuzzy again, and she never saw the monk's departure.

After what seemed like only a few minutes, Anise awoke in the darkness and realized she had slept into the night. Throwing off the bedcovers, she sat up. She felt physically sound, but disoriented. In her mind were confusing images of horses and fighting and blood. Had that been a dream? It left impressions too real to shake.

Her surroundings were no less bewildering. The window was high up on the wall. A basement room, perhaps? It could not be a hospital. It was too… "unsanitary" was the word that came to mind. She had no idea where she was. There was no place like this that she knew of in town. How far had she run to get away from her stalker?

God, this was opening night of *Richard III*. She had to get back.

Anise looked at her clothes and groaned. Good lord, she was still in her costume. Marilee really would go ballistic when she saw the condition it was in now, after she'd spent the night sleeping in it. A rush of adrenalin shot through her. *My tote bag! Where is it? My car keys…*

Frantically, she looked around the room and discovered the black bag lying on the floor beside the bed. With a sigh of relief, she yanked it up and began scrounging through it. Her hands fell on the two books, her acting edition of *Richard III* and the small journal she'd found in her father's farmhouse. She laid them on the bed. What she could not find was her wallet, cell phone, or keys. *Well, that's just great!*

Either they fell out in the woods or she'd been robbed by her stalker. She stuffed the books back in her bag and flung it over her shoulder.

I can't even call the director – not that he'd want to hear from me now. I'll never get another role after this.

The thought of her mother's smug satisfaction made her crumble inside, but she took a deep breath and forced herself to think about how to get out of here. Putting her bare feet on the stone floor, she scanned the area beside her bed, but did not see her shoes. Worse yet, there were no lamps.

What kind of place is this? If she did not know better, she might have thought she had gone back in time.

The fire in the hearth had burnt down, but still glowed slightly. She padded over the icy floor. There was a candle on the table, and she poked its wick into an ember. When the flame flared up, she went to the door and tried the handle. Well, at least she was not locked in. The wooden door was heavy, and creaked when she pulled it open. After peering both directions down the empty hallway, she slipped out.

CHAPTER THREE

Awaiting Cecily's return, Richard gazed through the narrow window, a cup of wine untouched in his hand. The fields were barely flecked with the dawn's light.

Deep down, he could not fool himself. He knew his mother spoke the truth when she said he should put his life with Anne in the past. Cecily had always known the source of his troubles. How often had she helped him solve complicated problems with her keen insight? She had been invaluable to his father, and Richard admired her for it. And yet Cecily could not realize how Anne's memory had seeped into every crevice of his being since her death. How could he seek a wife? Or a lover? Richard smiled at his mother's uncharacteristic suggestion. After all this time, would he even recall how to court a lady's affections? Unbidden, the memory of the lady in the woods came to him.

So like the lady in my dream.

He stared into his wine. Could he afford such a distraction right now? This battle with Henry

Tudor would be the one in which he would triumph absolutely or fail utterly. His success would depend much on presence of mind. And it had been so long since he sought womanly companionship, it would take all his time to relearn the art.

Had not that art been his brother Edward's undoing? In Ned's later years, it had certainly been his distinguishing flaw.

He recalled the day he'd discovered his brother's unquenchable carnal passions. On the brink of manhood himself, Richard had been new to his brother's court. Uncertain about some duty assigned him, he'd sought out the king in earnest to ask him about it. Unwittingly, he had walked in on them, Ned and his mistress. His brother was lying atop the coverlet naked and sated, encircled by the equally unashamed form of the harlot, Jane Shore, the goldsmith's wife. At his entrance, the woman hid her face by nuzzling her lover's neck while Ned merely grinned at him – as if inviting him to join in the sport. Richard had turned away abruptly.

Near the end, his brother the king let England languish and her people grow thin with over-taxation while he feasted and frolicked. His once-lean body waxed thick, and his once-stealthy mind grew slow with the attentions he paid to his female consorts.

Richard could not deny that the legacy of Edward's last years made his own rule all the more difficult now. Yet while two years had passed since his brother's death, he still missed him sorely.

As the king's eyes refocused on the pastoral scene below, he discovered it was quickly becoming populated with common folk making their way to their morning's labors.

They had lost trust in him, these people, as they never had done with Edward. Admittedly, it grew increasingly hard to win their belief after nearly thirty years of bloody conflict between the royal houses of York and Lancaster. Now, with the exception of the northerners, many citizens believed he had taken the crown wrongfully from his nephew, the young Edward V - Ned's son, the one born that same winter that Richard and his brother had languished in exile.

Many suspected Richard had killed the young prince for the throne.

Indeed, the sensitive Edward, along with his younger brother, Richard, Duke of York, were dead - not hidden at Pontefract, as the king wished people to believe, or exiled in France. The very thought of it stabbed through his conscience. The actions seeming right at the time appeared not so now. And after the loss of his own loved ones, this truth was harder to bear.

Richard stared at the heavy gold ring he wore. His mother liked to believe their misfortune was due to an evil talisman. Yet he knew the truth.

God had turned against him.

Chilled, Richard pulled away from the window and moved to a chair in the shadows, close to the spiced and half-watered wine his mother had prepared for him. As he swallowed the weakened mixture, it was not Ned nor his mother, but Anne who remained in his mind. He remembered her last words. Her voice almost inaudible, racked by death's rattle, came to him again in its smallest detail, as it had scores of times before: "Dearest, never forget how I loved you. You were my happiness, always."

How alone he had been since that day. Unbidden, he recalled the last night they had lain together. Even after twelve years of marriage, the urgency of their lovemaking had not diminished. His heart quickened as the memory became almost real, every detail intact. The silky caress of her hands. The tickling sensation of her hair against his neck. Their passionate consummation.

His celibacy had extended well beyond half a year now, since the time the wasting sickness had born down on Anne, and the physicians advised that he no longer share a bed with her for fear he would take the disease.

Not a woman since then had attracted his attention.

Until yesterday morn.

That lady had a fair aspect with fine, even features and hair the color of chestnut, nearly as dark as his own. Richard shook the thought from his mind. Thinking on a woman other than his wife seemed a betrayal. His queen had lain in the grave these many months, and still his grief was as fresh as newly turned earth. Sitting in the room's darkness, the widening hollow place in his heart pained him. Whether it was for Anne or out of simple loneliness, he did not know.

When he next looked up, the room had lightened with the quickening of the day, although his shadowed corner yet remained undisturbed by the sun's touch. Thick clouds massed in the sky, casting a pall over everything. How long had he been there, remembering? Richard shook his head, roughly combing his fingers through his hair in an attempt to shake loose the pictures filling his mind.

The bells of St. Peter's Church struck six – *so late!* – but the king did not move from his comfortable shadow.

The sound of the door to his bedchamber opening startled Richard from his reverie. He looked up, expecting his mother or one of his counselors come to urge him to the day's duties.

It was the lady from the woods.

Noiselessly, the slender woman slipped through the door, barefoot and wearing the black gown he had discovered her in. She did not yet see him seated in the shadows. He stared boldly, transfixed by the fall of hair that swept to her waist like a young girl's. Court ladies concealed their hair from all but their husbands.

She must have wandered from her room. The day was still new. This was the only reasonable explanation.

Peeking through a crack in the door into the corridor, she seemed quite agitated. Richard was intrigued. Was she hiding from someone?

She clenched her fists. "Where the hell am I?" she murmured.

Richard should have been provoked that his privacy had been disturbed. Lord knew he had little enough of it. But this puzzle fascinated him. Why did she seem so – *what was it?* – out of place?

A suspicion planted in him by his counselors took hold. Didn't Francis admonish him often about trusting too easily? She was not of the household, for no one in the castle knew her. Perhaps she had come to his room for some nefarious purpose. He could not rule out the possibility that her loyalties might lie with the Lancastrian cause.

The woman closed the door quietly and glanced furtively around the room. The light through the window had grown brighter with the sunrise, and Richard could see her face more clearly now. In her eyes he saw frustration – and fear. And while he knew he ought to look away, he could not help but stare at her long sheaf of silken hair and imagine how it would feel in his hands.

She spotted him in the corner and gasped. When he stood, she reached for the door and would have run out, but his words stopped her. "Fear not, m'lady. I won't call the monks down on you."

Richard could have commanded she stay, but doing such would have undermined the tiny bit of rapport they'd established in the woods. He wanted an answer to this puzzle: Was she a provocative innocent? Or a Tudor spy?

The woman stood poised by the door, staring back, her mouth open slightly – alluringly – in surprise.

"You do remember me? I discovered you in the forest."

The lady nodded, but behaved no differently when she saw his face and his royal apparel. Long accustomed to the courtesy paid a king, he was further taken aback by her failure to kneel. Certainly a spy, though disloyal, would adhere to convention for safety's sake.

She does not recognize me! The feeling that she was misplaced occurred to him again.

She took a breath, stepped forward and moved her lips as if to speak. She paused, as if she had thought better of it, and said, "I didn't mean to disturb you. I was just, I'm just..." Her eyes glanced over him and she appeared perplexed.

"Lost," he finished for her. Perhaps she suffered the delusions of fever. But the clarity of those flashing eyes certainly did not suggest illness. He took a step toward her. "Perhaps you are in need of a physician?"

She retreated toward the door. "No. I'm fine. But I have to get... back to town. I'm not sure how I even got here."

"Is your home far?" he asked gently. Being a northerner, Richard was unfamiliar with many of the small villages here in the South. Yet she was not dressed as one might expect a villager to be dressed. Although she spoke with a colloquial dialect, she carried herself well.

Certes, she must be nobly born.

He saw her eyes soften with tears at the word "home."

"If you do not want to be found, please take comfort here and await the return of my mother, Sister Cecily." He motioned to a nearby stool.

"Sister?"

"Yes. She has taken the veil." When this information did not seem to register, he said, "She is a Holy Sister. A nun."

The lady seemed startled, and licked her lips nervously. "Is this some kind of monastery? You see, I don't know where I am."

He thought her reaction a curious one, but as his eyes met hers, he found his suspicions evaporating. He could not tear his gaze away from hers. He kept his tone gentle. "Surely you know you are at the castle at Berkhamsted?"

Her mouth fell open. "Castle?"

"'Tis but a day's ride from London," he added.

A look of shock replaced confusion. She remained motionless for a long moment, before sinking onto the stool he had offered. She looked up at him plaintively.

"Might I be of service in some way?" he offered tentatively. Against all precaution, Richard found himself believing she was genuinely frightened. She could not be working for Tudor.

She shook her head. "Thanks, but I don't think so." Yet she made no move to go. She put her hands to her face to hide her tears.

Richard decided he should have her collected from his chambers and taken back to her room. Yet he found himself wishing her to stay. He surprised himself when he said, "I shall see to it that you are escorted home by a worthy squire." At her look of astonishment, he added, "Your safety is assured. My horsemen are armed."

Richard bit down on his words, suddenly embarrassed that he had let this sudden impulse to help her overcome his reason.

Yet he let stand the offer.

The woman seemed more bewildered than ever when she repeated, "Armed horsemen?"

He reached out and touched her shoulder. "All shall be well, fair lady." He wondered at his own boldness

Her forehead wrinkled, and she put a hand to her temple. "I'm so confused."

A wave of compassion washed over him. He said nothing, but patted her shoulder gently. He knew her not at all, yet could tell she was comforted by his presence. What an odd sensation, to comfort someone again after all these months. He marveled at the feelings it released in him.

The lady looked at him in gratitude and lifted her hand to his, closing her fingers around it. "I'm feeling a little better now."

He smiled, faintly relieved.

"What's your name?"

"Richard." He did not elaborate.

She squeezed his hand again. "Thank you, Richard."

He shifted his palm to her cheek and gently wiped away the dampness. Her mouth parted in surprise when his fingers pushed a strand of hair from her face. Though, it lasted but a moment, heat at that simple caress washed through his body, and he became lost in the sensation.

They both jumped at the sound of the door opening. Cecily stood there, observing them.

Richard's face flushed, as if he had been caught in a sinful act. Hastily he took a step toward his mother. "*Maman*, I am glad you've returned." How his voice shook! He took care to steady it. "This *demoiselle* needs your assistance."

His mother gazed at him with curiosity. At last, she said, "'Tis she I've been looking for, I believe. I never imagined she might be here." The look she gave Richard was one more of surprise than reproof. She turned her attention to the young lady, who was wiping her face with the back of her hand. "Are you the one Brother Benedict speaks of, who vanished under his care?"

Richard interrupted. "She doesn't need badgering by friars, *Maman*. She only wishes to go home."

Cecily's expression of surprise deepened, and she glanced at the woman, who nodded quickly.

Her son continued, "I've offered her an armed escort. Perhaps one of the household familiar with this locale might assist. What is the name of your village, m'lady?" He looked at the woman with whom he had shared an intimacy only a moment before. "You have the advantage over me – I do not know your name."

Cecily's eyebrows raised.

"Anise," answered the woman quietly, looking at her hands.

Richard gave his baffled mother an imploring look. "*Maman*, if you could…"

A knock came at the door. It was a royal page who said quietly, "I have a message for the king."

Cecily bade him enter, and Richard spoke with the boy a short distance away. "Inform Viscount Lovell I will be there in a moment."

He turned to Cecily and whispered, "I must go. You may continue this conference here. See that I am sent for when the lady requires escort home. I shall see that it is done."

The king offered Anise a reassuring smile, yet felt reluctant to leave. "My mother will look after you, so be easy in your mind."

Lady Anise gave him a dazed look.

With perplexed expression, Cecily nodded her assent. Richard kissed his mother's cheek and was gone.

****

WALES, 1485

The ancient stone walls glowed with light that had no source, rising eerily against the dark sky above them. Bishop Morton, clad in the black robes of his office, considered the petite graying woman who stood beside him, squinting in concentration. Her angular features stood out like granite against the light. A chill breeze swirled through the crumbling turrets of the old tower where they stood. Morton held a ring out before him.

Claustra clawibus egent et Owain Glendower portam eget.

Clawis suos animos habitens hanc portam ex morte inveni.

Tuus dominus in vitam sugat.

Rursum, Glendower! Suge! Suge!

The undefined light momentarily grew bright, and faded. Morton rubbed the ring so vigorously with a velvet cloth, it sparked. The woman placed a hand on his arm and hissed, "Are you certain the ring tested true?"

"Certain," he grumbled. He had forged six failures in his alchemy laboratory. Each failed ring carried weakened magical properties, but had not contained the power to call his master. When he'd finally got it right, he knew it.

"Then try again!" she said, impatiently.

He repeated the words. The light grew again, and faded.

"I don't understand," he muttered. "I've followed Owain's litany precisely. And yet, I might have misinterpreted it." He stepped away from the ceremonial circle and pulled some pieces of vellum from the pockets of his robe. He huddled close to the lantern, scanning the aged parchments. He ran his finger over the text, written in Glendower's extravagant hand.

Discovering an omitted word, he repeated it over in his mind, and rejoined his love. She watched him intently. When he met her eyes, his annoyance dissolved and he was warmed once more by their easy rapport.

Taking her hand so that their powers might be consolidated, Morton began the incantation once more. As he spoke the words, the evening's breeze was replaced by an unnatural wind originating within the stone walls of the tower and shooting up in a whirlwind through the roof. The torches on the walls flickered violently. The ring glowed crimson. Sharp pain swept up his arm from the ring, burning his flesh.

Lady Stanley gripped his other hand, but did not allow their pooled magic to fail. The sourceless light rose higher, blinding them. The wind rushed faster, forcing their eyes shut to its fury.

The conjurers were engulfed by their own magic.

****

Jack stood at a distance down the slope from the old Roman tower. He and his filly, Jennet, had been watching all night. The message from his lord had been to wait until dawn and report anything unusual that he saw. Near dawn, he heard fierce chanting and wailing that had more than once inspired him to prayers and almost turned him away from his duty.

He could not chase from memory the scene he had witnessed before at this tower. His master paid him well or he would not have come.

As of yet, he had *seen* nothing this night.

A hint of daylight spread itself across the sky. Jack knew that Satan found his door into the world at twilight and dawn, when the borders of the day were blurred. It was then that sorcerers called upon his powers. Jack had no illusions about this vigil. The warning was clear enough: stay away until there's something to report, then ride fast to the courier at the Welsh border. From there, the news will be taken by ship to Flanders —

— and to Henry Tudor himself.

Though he had been given no details, he knew he awaited the results of another of Lady Margaret's conjurations.

Native born to these parts of Lancashire, Jack had witnessed such sorcery before when he scouted the surrounding woods and looked upon Lord Stanley's Lathom Hall. There, Stanley's second wife, Margaret, the Countess of Richmond, remained while her husband served as steward of King Richard's royal household.

It had long been known that the lady practiced the Dark Arts. Yet the local ecclesiastics must have been well paid to keep their silence. The country folk kept their tongues as well – though sometimes there were grisly reminders of her night's work. They did fear the mistress of the Hall, who wore always a countenance of steel, but mostly people respected her. Many a time had she warded off plague from their village with her burnt offerings. And did she not make a potion for his sister, who had nearly died from the milk sickness after bearing that stillborn babe?

It had been that very night of his sister's distress that Jack had discovered the lady here, just inside the ruined tower, working her spells. So frantic was he to save Mary's life that he had run first to Lathom before going for the priest. They'd told him at the door that Lady Margaret was not there. But Jack managed to persuade one of her lord's retainers to tell him where she might be found.

"She is at the tower – but *beware!*"

Jack would never forget the ungodly acts he'd witnessed there. The Lady Margaret had made blood sacrifices that night. The memory of it still brought him sleeplack.

He never knew how long he had shaken with fear outside the door, unable to move, his back tight against the wall of the tower. But when the Lady Margaret had discovered him, she had not been angry. Somehow, he'd remembered the reason he was there – *Mary* – and babbled to the lady about the milk sickness. He must have also told her where he lived, for within a few hours of his dazed return, a potion had arrived from Lathom Hall.

Mary lived.

Though he knew it was a payment for his silence, Jack could not hold it against the Mistress of the Hall. Nor was he surprised when the lord asked Jack to do him some service from time to time.

On this night, evil is nigh, he thought grimly. For Lady Margaret had brought along a formidable assistant.

It was said when a man of God acted as a disciple of the Devil, the most powerful sorcery of all could be wrought. Jack shuddered and pressed against Jennet for protection.

The man who'd accompanied Lady Margaret to the deserted tower had worn the robes of a bishop.

Jack saw the hint of light reflecting from the structure's roof. The next thing he knew, Jennet reared wildly. A light brighter than a thousand suns blinded him, but he managed to hold onto the frightened horse, who was struggling to get free. Staggering from the tower, he led the panicked beast into a copse of trees. His sight returned, but the great light still raged beyond the woods. Jennet was skittish, so Jack guided her farther away from the tower. After calming his horse at last, he climbed on her back and rode in haste toward Wales.

CHAPTER FOUR

Anise's words caught in her throat as she watched the man in nobleman's costume sweep from the room. "King?" she murmured. Had she heard right? The man who'd found her in the woods called himself... She put two and two together. *King Richard?*

She could almost feel the warmth of his hand still touching her cheek, making her heart beat erratically. Although she knew it when she saw it on stage, she had never before experienced what drama coaches call "chemistry." *Intense, like I knew exactly what he was feeling.*

What she *should* be feeling was panic. How far had she wandered from the farmhouse? Was this a mental asylum? Or some designated historic landmark where docents staged reenactments? *Maybe I can get a job.*

She noticed the duchess, now sitting in Richard's place, giving her an odd look.

"Anise? Is that what you said your name was?"

Why did everybody here speak with that funny accent? Cecily had pronounced her name with the same strange annunciation as Richard had, placing the emphasis on the first syllable. This accent sounded even more foreign to her West Coast ears than the Massachusetts one she had grown accustomed to in the past few months.

An answer was expected from her. Well, she could play along. She'd had plenty of practice recently. "Yes, Your Grace."

"My son likes you, my dear. Very much. You should feel grateful for that. And you like him, as well?"

Anise blushed. "I do, mistress. But I need to go home. My director's going to kill me as it is, and…"

Cecily's eyes widened. "Someone wants to take your life? For what reason?"

Anise was startled. Her words had alarmed the woman. So much so, that she could practically feel it crackling in the space between them. "No one really wants to *kill* me. I'm just saying he'll be upset because he doesn't know where I am."

The duchess breathed in relief. Why the extreme reaction? It was as if the woman had never heard that figure of speech before. Anise began to wonder if she *had* fallen back in time. *But that's ludicrous!*

"My son would be most aggrieved should you be in any danger," said Cecily. "Earlier today, he asked after you."

Anise's heart leapt at that bit of news. *He asked after me?* Yet this preoccupation with Richard was not getting her any closer to home. Her lip trembled, but she fought the tears. "Can you tell me please...where's your little girl's room?"

Cecily gave her that confounded look again. "There are no children in this castle. Pray tell, what do you mean?"

Anise could not take much more of this. "I understand getting into a role, really I do. But I need to use the bathroom."

An expression of comprehension crossed Cecily's face. "Do you mean the privee? Certes, I shall show you."

Relief flooded through Anise. "Thank you!" *The world hasn't gone crazy after all.*

But when the duchess led her down the corridor to a tiny room with a slat for a toilet seat and the unmistakable odor of an outhouse, she felt the blood drain from her face. Rather than allow the duchess see her break down, she entered the dark, vile-smelling chamber and closed

the door. At first she clung to the wall, but started shaking so badly, she had to sink down on the edge of the wooden plank or else tumble into the pit.

Had she gone insane? The alternative was too unbelievable to contemplate.

In the first place there was Richard, done up in medieval costume – first in the woods and then here, answering to the title of "king." Second, this castle had no electricity – only candles. The duchess-turned-nun did not understand common slang. And finally, this unsanitary hole-in-the-floor served as a restroom. If this had been a real tourist attraction, Anise knew there'd be proper bathrooms.

Had something incredible happened when she hit her head on the porch steps? She had never experienced a dream this real. *Maybe I'm lying in the hospital unconscious!* Anise pinched herself, and it hurt.

There was no getting around it. She was not in the twenty-first century and this was not Massachusetts. *I'm stark-raving mad. It's the only explanation.*

And if it was not that, then she *had* somehow gotten thrown back in time to the reign of King Richard.

Anise took a deep breath. If it were true, what the hell was she going to do?

For an instant she thought maybe Richard would help. He *had* offered.

Oh, yeah, right. He'd been nice to her for, like, a millisecond. That certainly would not last if she told him she had been born in the nineties – the *nineteen* nineties.

She did not even know which King Richard he was. The Lionhearted? Richard the second? The *third?* Was he the same power-hungry king who plotted and schemed and killed his poor nephews? The *same* King Richard who Shakespeare's most famous play was about? *That* Richard was supposed to have been a hunchback. This one was not crippled *or* deceitful.

She remembered why the play was called "The *Tragedy* of Richard III."

Richard dies.

Well, she could not stay in this stinking closet forever. If it were true that she had gone back in time – *and I'm not committing to that idea just yet* – then she'd have to come up with some game plan. And fast.

Anise relieved herself, and emerged from the privee. She returned to the room where Cecily waited. "What year is it?" she asked in a tentative voice. *This is absurd.*

Startled, the duchess replied, "'Tis fourteen hundred and eighty five, from the year of our Lord."

That's just great. "What month?"

"Why, May, of course."

Hadn't the Battle of Bosworth, where Richard would have traded his kingdom for a horse, taken place in August? Her arm tightened on the handbag slung over her shoulder. She really needed to look at that play again when she got the chance. There must be details in there that would help her. *Help me do what, exactly?*

Well, she'd have to think of something.

Anise did her best to recall what she knew of English history, mostly learned in her high school British Lit class. When Richard was killed, Henry Tudor took the throne, and the period known as the Middle Ages came to an end. Henry's son, Henry VIII married a lot of women, insisted on divorcing one, and set off the Protestant Reformation. Then his daughter Elizabeth's royal navy defeated the Spanish Armada, transforming England into a world power. The queen ended up lending her name to the era of Shakespeare.

Was it purely coincidence that Anise had come here, to the same time period in which she was playing a part on the stage? And who had been stalking her at the farmhouse? Did *he* have something to do with all this? The last memory she had of the twenty-first century was of the stranger grabbing her shoulder.

He wasn't a stranger. He knew my name!

Had he traveled to this century, too? Or had he brought her here? If so, she had to find him. How else would she get back to her own time?

52

I haven't a clue what he looks like! What chance is there of finding him?

And yet she *was* dealing with impossibilities here. Maybe *he* would find *her.*

"You're miles away, lady. You must be tired and hungry," said Cecily, startling Anise from her reverie. "We can discuss these matters later." The nun stood up and reached for her hand. But when Anise went to take it, Cecily stared as if she'd seen a ghost.

"What is it, mistress?" stuttered Anise.

Cecily slowly sank back down into her chair. "Nay, I've changed my mind. I think we shall talk now." She stared at Anise's hand, and into her eyes as if trying to read something there. "You say your name is Anise. What is your father's name?"

Startled by Cecily's sudden frostiness, Anise answered in a dutiful tone, "Wynford. I am Lady Anise Wynford."

"My son found you near a pagan altar. How came you to be there?"

Anise swallowed hard. She was getting an idea of what this line of questioning was leading to. Next to treason, she knew the worst thing anyone could be suspected of in medieval times was witchcraft. There was nothing to do but bluff it. To buy time, she spilled the tears that had been threatening since she'd gone into the privee. "I have no memory of it, Your Grace. I... I..." She was going to have to come up with a cover story fast. *Why not use this to her advantage?* "I was searching for someone. I must have gotten lost in the woods and fainted."

Cecily's eyes narrowed. "Who were you searching for?"

"A man. A… friend."

The nun raised an eyebrow. "A lover, perhaps? What's his name?"

Anise's face went hot. "Not a lover!" *That at least was the truth.* "I don't know who he was." *That was the truth, too. Now a lie:* "He found me on the road, and when I told him I remembered nothing of my circumstances, he said he knew me. He told me my name and said he would take me home. Somehow we got separated."

Anise tried to wipe the tears, but the duchess would not let go of her wrist.

"Where did you get that ring?" Cecily asked firmly.

Ring? Anise realized she was wearing it on the hand Cecily held in an iron grip. As the duchess stared at it, Anise could almost feel the woman's suspicion.

Anise hesitated, and decided to play dumb. "I know nothing about it, m'lady. I've always worn it, as long as I can recall."

Cecily pulled Anise's hand toward her, examining the ring more closely.

"Why does it upset you?" Anise ventured.

The nun paused before answering, "It is so remarkably like one the king wears – except that the engraving on this one is worn almost beyond recognition."

The *king* wore a ring like this? Anise realized her mouth was hanging open, but it was too late to hide her surprise.

"You have no idea where you got it?"

Anise could literally feel Cecily's wave of suspicion washing over her. That was the second time – *no, third time* – she'd sensed the woman's emotions. *What is going on here?* "I speak truth, m'lady," she mumbled. She had no choice but to feign ignorance. "D-do you think it's *stolen*?" Even before Cecily's face had relaxed, Anise knew she was in the clear. Her performance had been taken at face value.

"No – perhaps not," said Cecily, looking at her appraisingly and releasing her arm.

Anise exhaled in silent relief and rubbed her wrist. She recognized a close call when she saw it. "How had – His Grace – received his ring, mistress?"

"'Tis too long a tale for telling now," she replied, getting to her feet. "Come with me."

Anise followed the straight-backed nun through the corridor, her mind racing. *How the hell could Richard be wearing a ring like the one from that farmhouse? What in God's name was going on?*

****

Richard sat at the dark wood writing table reserved for his administrative work when he visited his mother's residence. A multitude of letters and documents lay before him. Having dispensed of the mundane matters filling his morning, the attending few members of his Privy Council filed out ceremoniously. Scanning over a parchment he held before him, he pinched the bridge of his nose.

Francis, Viscount Lovell, observed his sovereign's expression. As the king's secretary – and his friend – he knew he should insist that Richard take time to rest. Dickon had suffered from sleeplack for so long, he scarcely resembled the man Francis had known two years ago. There was a bone weariness about him that made him seem far older than his score and twelve years. And it had worsened in the last few months, since the death of his queen.

Richard had taken to carrying his familiar bed from castle to castle – and at times to the field – yet even that did little to secure him more than a couple hours of sleep a night.

Once the room had been cleared of council members, Francis would have a chance to persuade Dickon to lay aside his work for today. But the steward of the king's household, Thomas,

Lord Stanley, had other ideas. "Your Grace, if I may…"

Richard looked up from the document. "Yes, Thomas?"

"There is a trifling matter that, if you could attend to soon, would greatly ease my mind. It has to do with that property dispute at my estates in Lancashire. I've placed the letters at your right hand – yes, there. If you could just attach your signet, Your Grace, the argument might be settled."

Richard scanned the sheets, but not closely, and endorsed them. Francis held back the cautionary words that came to his tongue. Obviously, the king had not read the documents, but trusted Stanley's recommendation. Francis shot a glance toward the steward and noted the smug expression as he surveyed the signature. Stanley paid no mind to the secretary's displeasure. The king turned his attention to other matters.

"If I may be excused, Your Grace?" requested the steward succinctly. The king did not look up. "Certes, Thomas."

When Stanley had exited, Francis shook his head in frustration. Richard worked on, ignoring the fatigue that so obviously wracked his body and impaired his judgment.

Damn these troublesome times! Dickon deserved better than Stanley.

The physician, Hobbys, continually voiced concern over the king's health. He had told Francis in confidence that he was fearful of Richard's exposure to the consumption, the wasting sickness that had taken the frail Queen Anne, so weakened by the grief of her son's death. If only Dickon could find some distraction from the worrisome burden of his realm. If only he could get some peace.

But worrying for his king's health and mind in silence did no good. The time was long overdue for him to voice it.

"Dickon—"

Richard did not hear him, so deep was he in concentration – or exhaustion.

"Dickon, please..."

Richard looked up. He immediately recognized Francis' look of concern and sighed softly, as if he knew what his friend was about to say. "You are a true friend, Francis. And I can see that you are about to bid me to rest."

Francis could only nod, his eyes imploring. Richard smiled sadly. "Even if I could make the time, it wouldn't matter. I can only sleep when exhaustion overcomes me. It's what my life's become, and sleep's no solace. But no difference – much of my life has been thus, especially lately... I am quite used to it."

But Francis knew when Richard's bout of sleeplack had originated. And Stanley had been in the thick of it. It had been within weeks of Edward IV's death. Richard had assumed the Lord Protectorship of his brother's son and heir, and was administering the office's duties.

That's when Dickon had learned of the plot.

Stanley was in league with the widowed queen's in-laws, the Woodvilles, and the bishops Morton and Rotherham, who were planning to assassinate Richard. Yet the worst blow was the discovery that Dickon's longtime friend, Lord Hastings, had been involved in the intrigue. Richard had spared most of the plotters – putting Stanley under special detention, briefly imprisoning Rotherdam in the Tower, sending Morton to Brecknock to be warded over by the Duke of Buckingham. But so stricken was he by the unexpected betrayal of one so trusted, that he ordered Hastings to be sent to the block without even a trial.

Dickon's remorse at his rash decision had haunted him ever since.

Thus he had taken his loss of sleep as deserved punishment for his error in judgment, and dismissed Francis' concern by changing the subject. "You are troubled about our Lord Stanley?"

Francis exhaled softly. Dickon had easily followed the path his mind had taken. There was little Francis could hide from his friend of twenty years. "If I may ask, Dickon, what was the urgent matter…?"

"That?" The king shrugged. "A dispute between Thomas and an adjoining property owner. 'Twas nothing. A trifle."

The secretary stopped himself from questioning Richard's conscientiousness, yet could not help but be concerned over his sovereign's dismissive attitude. In younger days, Dickon treated every matter that came before him with sober deliberation, as if he considered every citizen of the realm as important as the lord he served.

The viscount's thoughts returned to the smug expression on Stanley's face. The question of the steward's loyalty had remained unanswered for years. And the king refused to address the issue. Francis feared that the resolution might come on the battlefield at the most crucial of moments.

Was Thomas Stanley true to the king? No one could be sure.

Richard had certainly made it worth his while to remain so. Since Dickon had taken the throne, Stanley had been gifted with the castle and lordship of Kymbellton and other land grants, plus had been made the constable of England with an annuity of a hundred pounds. His brother, Sir William Stanley, had been appointed Chief Justice of North Wales and made constable of the castle and captain of the town of Caernarvon.

Lord Stanley commanded large armies that would pose a great danger if he turned against the king. And what chance did the steward stand of denying his wife's ambitions? Lady Margaret Stanley was Tudor's mother. She had already entered into negotiations with the late king's widow, Elizabeth Woodville, on her son Henry's behalf, and the dowager queen – who longed to see *one* of her children on the throne – had promised her daughter Elizabeth's hand should Henry triumph over Richard.

When Margaret's intrigues had been discovered, she had been placed immediately in the custody of her husband – a dubious watchdog, in Francis' opinion.

"I doubt Stanley's motives," said Francis. "'Tis he who is in Lady Stanley's custody, not the reverse."

The king was deep in thought. At last he spoke, "Yes – I believe that is so. Still, he has not digressed since his involvement in the plot on my life. 'Tis my hope the better part of the man shall prevail. "

Francis bit back a scoffing remark about Stanley's better part.

"It always prevailed for my brother," Richard added, his tone carrying inflections of love, loss, and frustration as he spoke of Edward. Yet memory of the late king appeared to lend Dickon strength: Francis saw the familiar light of naive faith come into the king's eyes. Such belief in one whose life had seen so much treachery seemed incongruous.

It had been Edward's bad planning that had caused the present deplorable state of affairs.

At first, Edward had proved an able king and general, inspiring his men in battle while committing to memory each name, to be called forth at a moment's notice. Yes, he had certainly been one to win loyalty. But once he had brought peace to the land, Edward had forgotten his own loyalties. Had he been thinking with his wits rather than his gender, he might not have married Elizabeth Woodville, thus leashing her grappling brood upon England and dividing it into factions. Why had he never attempted to dissolve the pre-marriage contract he had made with the Lady Eleanor Butler, still in force when he'd married Elizabeth? Even knowing that the truth must eventually come out? And knowing that the promised betrothal negated his marriage to Elizabeth?

And barring that, why couldn't the king have remarried the queen after Lady Butler had died, thus making at least some of his children by her his legitimate heirs, so that Richard would not be forced to take the throne as the next legitimate Plantagenet in line for it?

Francis had never once believed the fabrications about Richard putting to death his nephews. He could only fume at Edward's ineptness and lack of foresight. He might have been a brilliant politician and general, but the memory of his skill would be short-lived and overshadowed by the shambles in which he left his country and his family.

Of that family, only Richard – and the aged Duchess York – survived in England. So 'twas Dickon who must carry the weight of the Yorkist claim and preserve their legacy for posterity.

Richard, who scarcely slept two hours a night.

Richard, who acted as if he did not realize what costs Thomas Stanley might, in the end, exact.

The viscount forced his gaze to the floor. He should not doubt the judgment of his childhood friend from Middleham. Out of that group warded over and trained in arms by Anne's father, Warwick – brothers Richard and George Plantagenet; Northumberland's heir Robert Percy, and himself – Richard had always been the even-tempered one.

The king certainly realized the threat Stanley would be should he turn traitor.

Perhaps it was the impending, but necessary, battle with the crown-hungry Tudor that was making Francis uneasy. Not fear of death: Francis had faced that harsh lesson too many times to tremble in its face. No – his dread was of the battle's aftermath, no matter the outcome. After such treachery against him, how would Richard choose to govern England? How else but without mercy?

And if he lost...

With Richard nearly dead on his feet, Francis' confidence had little to bolster it.

Francis' words carried urgency. "You must not give Stanley the chance to be persuaded to the other side's cause by his wife. You cannot permit him to leave before this battle. I know he shall request it."

"So do I," said Richard simply. "Yet I cannot force him to remain."

Startled by the answer, Francis mouthed the word, "Why?"

Richard smiled ruefully. "I must know if I am worth his loyalty."

****

Cecily watched her mysterious ward dine heartily on white bread, cheese, and wine, and wondered why she avoided the kidney pies. She vowed to get to the bottom of this woman's strange tale. If Lady Anise was to be the one to bring Richard to his senses, Cecily must set it in motion.

Anise drained her wine glass.

"We must talk," said Cecily, pulling her stool closer. "This friend you mentioned. Who is he?"

"I told you, mistress. I know not."

The story sounded contrived to Cecily, but she pressed on. "How did you know you could trust him?"

"I don't know why. I was alone and frightened. I had to trust someone. And there was something familiar about him."

The duchess sighed. It was no use. If this girl was keeping a secret, she held it dear. "Do you want to find this… friend?"

"Very much, Your Grace."

"I shall see to it that this part of the countryside is searched thoroughly. If he is here, he shall be discovered. I only ask for a small favor in return."

Anise rubbed her temple as if it pained her – or as if she were buying time to conjure up a story. Nevertheless, it gave Cecily the opportunity to get a better look at the ring.

Cecily recalled the strange tale Richard had told her of it.

"They may contain some magic," the Duke of Buckingham had insisted when he'd gifted her son and his wife with a set of the two identical gold bands at Gloucester, a stop on their Royal Progress after the coronation. Buckingham, the king's "faithful" adviser – who not long after proved himself a traitor – had

*said, "I've only just discovered these in the dungeons
of* Brecknock, no doubt the work of a sorcerer –
*perhaps of Merlin, himself. May they serve as a pledge
of my loyalty and bring good fortune to your reign."*

Yet naught but ill luck had come to Richard
after that day.

Brecknock had been Buckingham's castle in
Wales where, along with Bishop Morton, the
Duke had helped carry out the plots woven by
Elizabeth Woodville and the Lady Stanley to
benefit Tudor. Richard and Anne had accepted
the rings shortly before the Rebellion, when
Buckingham was caught and beheaded.

Cecily remembered Richard's wrath, how he
had wanted to destroy the rings because they had
been the gift of a traitor. Yet Anne had prevented
it. When Cecily had asked why his queen would
do such a thing, Richard had explained with
some embarrassment. Cecily could almost
imagine Anne's sweet voice, as her son repeated
her admonition: "Should we throw away good
magic, if there be some, because the man who
gave it to us turned traitor? If we should do that
with all gifts, what possessions would be left to
us? Perhaps the rings are charmed to prevent
sickness or to ensure fruitfulness? I do so much
want another child. Suppose this is our only
chance? Are we to toss that away?" Anne, who
had trusted her husband fervently, would not

budge on this, keeping the ring on her finger always. At last the king relented. He even made a promise to her – as long as the queen wore hers, so would Richard wear his.

If any magic resides in those rings, it is there to do harm, not good, thought Cecily. Their luck and lives had disintegrated, thereafter. Anne had gone to her grave with it around her finger. Richard might or might not believe that it contained some magic. But he ignored his mother's pleadings, and wore his still.

As long as Anne wore hers...

The engraving on Anise's ring was much more weathered than Richard's, as if her ring was many years older. In fact, so smooth were some of the lines that the image appeared indiscernible in places. This could not be Anne's, since Cecily had seen the ring interred with the dead queen at Westminster. This was a *third* ring. How many were there?

Anise caught Cecily staring at her hand. "What is it you want from me? The ring?"

Cecily smiled faintly. "Yes – in a way. As it stands now, we have no reason to trust what you say. You are given lodging in my home because of my charity and the king's favor. Of your family I know naught. Treachery surrounds my son these days, and if you remain, you, too, might fall under suspicion – if someone said a word against you."

Anise's eyes grew wide. "What are you going to tell the king?"

Certes, the Lady Anise Wynford catches on fast. Cecily shrugged. "I would not tell him anything. And I might offer you protection against those who might."

Anise's face flickered with mixed emotions. Cecily saw uncertainty and doubt, as well as a fragility not unlike the late queen's. This, she suspected, is what had caught her son's attention. When she had walked in on them in his rooms, Cecily had not been as surprised at the embrace as at Richard's heated expression. Whatever had led up to that moment, Anise had touched his heart in a place that had been sealed off since Anne's death.

"Duchess, will you honor your promise to help me look for the man who knew me?"

"If you do as I ask, I swear I shall see to it you are given all the assistance you need."

Anise's breathing quickened. "What do you want me to do?"

Cecily knew she was taking a chance. Yet the duchess believed, as strongly as she believed in God, that Richard would not prevail in the coming strife – not with his desperate mood and that cursed ring on his hand. Could this woman – perhaps a Lancastrian agent, perhaps a witch – be trusted to attempt the near impossible task Cecily had in mind? She stared directly into the woman's eyes appraisingly. They were sincere, but veiled, innocent, but provocative. Anise had appeared from nowhere and concealed much, certes. And yet Cecily did not believe she was a spy. Nor a witch. And she had gained the interest of her son. Sweet Jesu, if this woman could interest the king in life again, it would be the cream on the cake. If there was a chance Richard could find redemption at her touch...

Cecily silently sent a prayer heavenward, asking God to forgive her this deceit. "I think we can help one another – I worry about my son, you see."

"What are you suggesting?" the woman asked.

Cecily took a deep breath. "I want you to get close enough to Richard to exchange rings."

****

The windstorm subsided. As Morton and Margaret clung to one another, the last of their magic's fury died. The two conjurers watched, mystified at what they had wrought. An ethereal mist swirled beneath the cracked ceiling of the crumbling Roman tower where they stood.

At last they had rubbed power out of Morton's ring, but it had not brought them, as they had expected, the physical manifestation of Owain Glendower.

The cloud overhead seethed with its prodigious presence.

Morton, exhausted from the sorcery, caught his accomplice's eye and grasped her arm with apprehension. "I know not what demon we have called, mistress dear, but this is not what was supposed to happen."

Margaret cast her eyes at the amorphous cloud gathered against the lightening dawn sky and pressed closer to the bishop. "How could we have gone wrong? We followed the text exactly. Could Owain Glendower have erred?"

At that, a thunderous roar abused their ears. The skies overhead darkened. Words of fury ripped through the air. "Glendower... never... errs!"

Might it truly be he, trapped in the ether, still a prisoner of death? Lightning flashed in answer, propelling the two sorcerers into each other's arms.

"'Tis he," whispered Morton. "'Tis Owain – in that mist!"

The voice burst forth once again. "We struck a bargain, my acolyte. Your life for mine. Your life has been lived far beyond your years. Now return me to mine!"

Fear and wonderment swept over Morton. He could scarcely bear to hear the tormented voice of his master, coexisting between the two worlds of the living and the dead.

"Release me from this cursed state!" Glendower demanded.

Morton moved away from his accomplice to stand beneath the turbulent center of the mist. "Owain! Is that you, in sooth?" he asked, his voice tremulous.

The voice rumbled its affirmation.

'Twas the great wizard indeed! Morton felt a hand on his arm.

"Address him with deference," urged Margaret. "Even in this state, he might aid my son's cause, if we can harness his power!"

Incredulous, Morton turned to her. "Harness Glendower? Be you mad, mistress? We were supposed to call him forth in corporeal form, not... not *this*. We shall be lucky if he does not exact revenge for our failure."

"I thought he was your mentor?" But her words were lost as that unholy roar rolled over them once more, a tremendous gale blasting them where they stood, and forcing them to take refuge once more in one another's arms.

The spirit of Owain Glendower was not amused.

CHAPTER FIVE

The fire cast a gentle glow over the room. Anise sat on the bed, gazing at the fall of Satan playing across the tapestry on the wall, her thoughts as tangled as the threads weaving pictures through wool.

She traced the ring's design with her thumb. The engraving was so worn that it was almost indistinguishable. The ring was roughly made, not a jeweler's work. Why had it been among her father's possessions? And how was it possible that the king wore one like it?

At the thought of Richard, her heart leapt. She forced away the feeling. This was not the place.

Or the time.

Time – did that have something to do with it? Anise certainly was not a physicist, but she'd seen as many time travel movies as the next person. Wouldn't the same object from two different centuries cause a paradox that created great instability in the universe?

That did not explain how she got to the fifteenth century.

Complicating matters was Cecily's plot. The duchess must have truly believed there was a curse, for what other reason would there be for her to want Anise to get close to Richard?

Close to Richard. Anise flushed. Only by accident had she gotten close to the king in the first place.

Staring at the ring on her finger, she considered the facts. She'd found it in her father's house – could he have known its secret? Not that it helped – Matthew Fallon was dead.

The whole preposterous situation made her head hurt. Anise reached for her tote bag. Rummaging for the aspirin bottle, she also pulled out the two books: Shakespeare's play and the journal from her father's house. It would be a miracle if it actually contained information she could use, but it was certainly worth a shot.

Lighting a candle in the hearth, she placed it on a wooden table by the bed and opened the journal. The handwriting did not look familiar.

April 2, 1997

Gwenny told him the truth last night. He took it better than I thought. But to get him to agree to a divorce? I'll believe it when I see it. Wynford won't give up easily. Dominic's mine – Wynford can't touch him. He'll fight for Annie, though. Legally, he's the father. I only pray that he considers what's best for the girl.

Annie? Had he been referring to her, Anise?

We could be long gone – vanished from the face of the earth. Nineteenth century London, Sixteenth century France. Considering all we know of history, we could invest our money on a sure bet and live like royalty. But Gwenny won't leave. She won't give up her bloody career. I love the woman, but she's infuriating. Our daughter is at stake. Why won't she come to her senses? If Wynford wins in court, there's no choice but to use the ring and disappear.

The diary fell out of her hand to the floor. *A magic ring? A magic time travel ring?* "Damn you and your secrets, Mother," she whispered hotly. "I'm stuck in the fifteenth century and it's all your fault!"

Her only hope was to figure out how it worked. Anise closed her eyes. In her mind, she pictured her apartment and rubbed the ring. *Nothing.* She imagined the farmhouse. *Still nothing.*

"Abracadabra, twenty-first century!"

Nothing.

"That's just perfect."

She thought about her conundrum until her temples throbbed. The man who had been stalking her at the farmhouse had something to do with all this – she knew it. Anise remembered what the lawyer had said about Dominic, her missing brother. Was it possible he had gone to his father's house?

It was a stretch, but what if had been he who'd called her name? What if he'd gone there to find her? Her stomach tumbled over itself as a thought struck her.

What if he was looking for the ring?

He had grabbed her shoulder just as she had blacked out. Was it possible he'd hitched a ride on her trip through time? Was it possible he had followed her to the fifteenth century? Talk about impossibilities. And even if he was here, she had no idea what he looked like except for her childhood memory of a boy with dark hair and blue eyes.

Anise retrieved the diary from the floor. Maybe there was something more. She paged through slowly, scanning for any mention of the ring. A snapshot fell onto her lap. She picked it up and the breath left her lungs.

It was Mother – and Matthew, the handsome Irishman. Beside the six-year-old girl – *that's me!* – stood a young boy who looked like his father – *Dominic.* The picture was taken in front of the old farmhouse.

My family.

But here she was, stuck in a time centuries before they were born. Centuries before *she* was born.

Alone.

If she ever needed someone to talk to, now was it.

In her mind, she saw Richard's concerned face. But that's impossible. Confide in a king? What was she thinking?

Tears spilled down her face. *Damn you, Mother.* Anise pulled the blankets up around her ears and cried herself to sleep.

****

Henry Tudor, the slight-framed Earl of Richmond, sat astride his gray-and-white horse on the shores of France, staring across the channel waters toward his homeland. A chill headwind blew in from the sea. The night was not dark. Stars spilled across the sky above him, shining with a certainty he had never in his life felt. It was an evening as clear as his mind was cluttered with the past, the present, the future.

He cursed his cousin Richard, who, though just a few years his elder, had been fighting and winning battles beside King Edward since he was seventeen.

Richard had been consequential in that sovereign's battle at Barnet, where Warwick's attempt to return the Lancastrian's Mad Harry to the throne was quashed forever with the Kingmaker's death. And he'd been there at the Battle of Tewkesbury, when the deposed queen

Marguerite d'Anjou was captured and her son Edouard, the Lancastrian hope, was slain – some say by Richard's own hand.

Soon there would be another battle. Henry's fight. The fight that would vindicate his claim to the throne – or not.

He heard the sound of horses approaching, and his stomach fluttered a little. Though always kindly treated, he had been the prisoner of one sort or another for most of his twenty-nine years. He never knew when it might happen again and was always on the alert.

But the moonlight illuminated the flat coast as if it were daylight and, though still far away, he soon recognized his Uncle Jasper, his dead father's brother, astride his huge roan charger. Beside him on a smaller horse was his knight of the body, Gaspard.

When Jasper rode up, Henry asked, "What news? Have you heard from Reynold?" Though he preferred French, the language of courtiers, he spoke in Welsh so Gaspard would not understand. "Has the summoning been successful?"

But Jasper, long of face and thick of dark mane despite his advancing age, shook his head. "Not a word."

Gaspard understood "word" and took it upon himself to nod furiously at the same time. "Oui monsieur, we have word from Good King

Charles and generosity toward your campaign," volunteered the knight in broken English. "The word is—"

Before Gaspard could finish, Henry barked, "Silence! I am to be addressed as Your Grace – not monsieur. Do you not realize you are addressing a king?" Hadn't he, after all, surrounded himself with all the amenities of a sovereign visiting at the court of King Charles, thanks to the benevolence of that good monarch?

"Pardon, Your Grace," murmured Gaspard, as Jasper looked at his nephew with a critical eye.

Although Henry loved Jasper as the only father he had ever really known, he ignored his uncle's displeasure.

Henry had not always been the Lancastrian consideration for king. No – it was not until the disappearance of Edward IV's sons that they'd thought of Henry Tudor, descended not only from Edward III, but also of Charles VI of France, the great-great-grandfather of that Charles who sat as that country's king.

Now that Henry was to be King of England, he did not want anyone to forget it.

Under the watchful eyes of his uncle and the chastised ones of his uncle's knight, Henry held back a smile as he thought of the missing Prince of Wales and his brother.

Disappearance! Hah! He shifted his gaze toward the sea in grim satisfaction. Dead, they were, these two years past. He knew it as a certainty.

He turned to his uncle. "What news is this we have of Charles' generosity?"

Jasper grunted, annoyance obvious in his tone and in the look he cast toward Gaspard. "Generosity be a strange name for it, Henry," he said in English. "Our cause may be harmed as much as helped by this kind of generosity."

The fear in Henry's stomach returned. "The two thousand men he promised. He's not delivering?"

"He's delivering, certes. His eldest sister, the Lady of Beaujeu, is filling the quota with two thousand felons from the jails of Normandy. They've been offered their freedom in exchange for putting up a good fight for thee against Richard. Quite a vote of confidence on their part, I would say," muttered his uncle sarcastically.

But it was relief, not dismay, that swept over Henry. "Then he's making good his word. They should make fierce fighters, those who desire their freedom so much."

"Aye," answered Jasper. "But how loyal, once their feet touch ground outside their prisons?"

For an hour, his uncle stood with him at the shore, talking of strategies and what chances they had against Richard. At last he gave up urging his nephew to join the discussion and returned with Gaspard to their residence.

Henry could not yet leave. His mind was across the sea. The summoning must succeed, for if it did not... He forced the thought of defeat from his mind.

Failure was not in the cards. Bishop Morton's prophecy, read from the tarot deck two autumns ago, had made that clear.

Shortly afterward, the pieces fell into place.

With the persuasive suggestion of his mother, Margaret Beaufort Tudor, now the wife of Thomas, Lord Stanley, it had been arranged that Henry would marry Edward IV's daughter, Bess – assuming his campaign against Richard succeeded.

Henry fidgeted on his horse. *When* it succeeded!

Shortly thereafter, Henry had won the support of France's King Charles. This spring, the sovereign had pledged an advance of forty thousand livres and a French fleet of ships, despite England's traditional stance as France's hated adversary. Now there was the realized promise of two thousand men to aid his cause.

To Henry, even this seemed not enough. He was, after all, launching his attack against Richard – the man who had stopped Warwick, who had ended the careers of numerous

Lancastrians – and a fearless general who had not lost a battle.

Henry had never fought. Though learned in arts, languages, and *politesse*, he had during his varied captivities received precious little training in the arts of war.

Doubts swirled around him like the breeze of the cool night. Despite the support he was promised, despite Morton's prophecy, Henry was afraid.

It was his uncertainty that had brought him down to this shore. Henry longed desperately for word from across the waters. If all had gone well in Wales – if his mother and Bishop Morton's plan had gone as expected – Henry would soon receive news from her indefatigable servant, Reynold Bray.

Only then would he know his chances for becoming king.

****

There was no way she was going to put a bite of that cooked swan in her mouth. With a vehement shake of her head, Anise refused the plate being pushed toward her. Her dining companions – especially the nobleman with whom she had been pressed into sharing her trencher – stared openly at her discourteous behavior. Bad enough everyone knew her as the lady found lying alone in the woods on a pagan altar. Now she was an ungrateful guest, as well.

Seated at one of the long trestle tables in the great hall, her awkwardness became obvious as the long processions of servants – the cupbearer, the pantler with the bread and butter, the butler and his assistants with the wine and ale – began bringing the food, course after course after course, hour after hour after hour. Her fumbling over medieval dining protocol and her refusal to eat called even more attention to her situation. Most of the food she'd managed to choke down. Some of it was even good. There was peppery roast beef and baked trout so heavily spiced, she did not object when her companion took the larger share. And she figured the batter-fried apples would not make her sick.

But broiled swan? There was no way.

Eating with only a knife and her fingertips, she shared her food from a single trencher of stale bread with the king's steward, Lord Stanley. She followed her dining companion's obsessive habit of frequent hand-cleansing in a basin of rose-scented water – a rather poor substitute in this filthy environment for the small bottle of hand sanitizer she was used to.

The only bright spot in this whole dinner mess was watching Richard. Clothed in fine velvet and seated beside his mother, the king forced himself to join in the conversations around him. Anise could tell his mind was elsewhere and on the rare occasions he smiled at someone's jest, Anise knew how it pained him to force good humor.

Once his dark eyes caught and held her gaze – and Anise's heart nearly stopped. To hide the color rushing to her face, she feigned a sudden interest in her green almond soup.

Lord Stanley never ceased staring at her. As was the custom – the man tending to the needs of the woman – Stanley broke the bread, cut the meat, and passed the wine, watching her scrupulously and keeping her on edge the whole meal. She forced a smile as he filled her goblet. The wine was sour, but it took the edge off her anxiety.

Thomas, Lord Stanley, was a character Anise remembered well from the play. He was a man well-versed in the art of betrayal and was Richard's final traitor.

Conversation fell off as everyone relaxed after the meal. As the servers presented the "subtlety," a confection of spun sugar molded into a hunting scene, Stanley asked the question she'd been dreading, "Lady Wynford – we are all curious at how you have come to Berkhamsted. Tell us how you came to be found upon an unholy stone altar?"

There was not a sound to be heard. Anise's tongue froze in her mouth. Stanley's eyes bored into hers until he forced her stare downward. She felt Richard's gaze.

Anise formed her answer in Shakespearian English. "I remember not how I came to be there, m'lord." Her voice shook. "'Tis is as much a mystery to me as to you, and I wish we could speak of aught else."

Stanley was not after idle chat.

"If you were the victim of a sorcerer's enchantment, m'lady, you owe it to His Grace to identify the conjurer."

Cecily stood. "My Lord Stanley. The lady's ordeal has left her shaken. Please don't insist that she relive it."

Disappointed whispers filled the room. Anise wanted to thank the duchess, but could not speak. She managed a weak smile of gratitude. It was answered by a nearly imperceptible nod. She could feel Cecily's immense satisfaction at stifling Stanley.

Anise was too afraid to look at Richard. She felt sick at the thought of his scrutiny. Her stomach roiled from the spicy food and sour wine. *I have to get out of here!* She rose unsteadily, palms gripping the table to keep her balance.

Stanley stared, fascinated at her reaction.

"I-I feel…" Anise fled the great hall without finishing her sentence.

****

Glendower ached for the passions and pleasures of the physical world thrumming around him. To exist in this limbo between men and ghosts was intolerable. But as the hours wore on, his anger eroded to vexation and finally to annoyance, as he realized his only hope for immortality lay with the man who had been his hapless student in life, Bishop John Morton.

As morning waxed into afternoon, Morton, by turns, had begged his master for mercy, swore profane oaths at the gods for their disfavor – and heaped all blame for the turn of events upon his companion, the witch, who stood patiently by his side for the whole of his tirade. "Master, speak to me, I beg thee! Spare me your wrath. I know not what has gone wrong, but the fault lies not with me – I have done all that you asked…"

His student's fear piqued him. What had Morton to be frightened of? In his piteous state, Glendower was powerless. Yet silence would accomplish nothing. Time wore on and the spirit of the great wizard grew impatient.

"You need not scream at me. I can hear you."

Morton's shock was palatable. "You are not angry?"

"Anger interferes with reason, and 'tis reason conjoined with magic that shall free me."

Raising his arms toward the broken roof of the tower and the cloud of ether that was his master, Morton cried, "This time I shall not fail. Only say what must be done to bring you forth into the world, and I shall make it so."

Morton had always been more of a performer than a proficient. In that long ago time before his mortal death, the wizard had placed too much reliance on his student's skill – now Glendower's fate rested solely with him. Perhaps, all was not lost. The formula for the ring was incorruptible, if the ring was forged with precision.

Drawing upon its power, the wizard focused his concentration on the gold circlet the bishop wore – the material mate to the one Glendower held as an astral manifestation within his soul. Directing his will, the wizard traced the magic within the alloy. Morton's emotions unfolded before him, and Glendower knew the ring's power held true.

"John Morton, the ring of life everlasting was forged in strength by your own hand. Seize its power and call me forth!"

"I cannot, Master," came Morton's disconsolate reply.

The ethereal wizard released an otherworldly sigh. Morton was hopeless. Yet he had not failed entirely, having brought Glendower to the threshold of life.

Glendower knew his discovery of the Philosopher's stone was the crowning achievement of his life, even transcending his reign as Owain IV of Wales and his struggle for Welsh independence from the cursed English. His formula had been derived from simple ingredients – sulfur, mercury and salt. The essential secret lay in the balance of opposites.

Each ring conferred magical abilities upon the bearer. But by embedding the Philosopher's stone within the ring's alloy, two rings of equal power could be conjoined to achieve immortality, marrying the material world with the ethereal, the physical body with the spiritual, building a pathway from death to eternal life.

'Twas on this conjunction that Glendower's resurrection depended.

"How shall we proceed, Master?"

"The fault does not lie with the ring, but with the bridge between worlds. All is not in balance."

Morton flinched, as if caught in a lie.

Glendower sensed Morton's discomfiture. There was more to this than he was saying. "Tell me the truth, John Morton, or you shall know my wrath at last!"

With a whimper, the bishop fell to his knees. "I have failed you, my master – many times over – but this last time is the most grievous of all. I have a collection of rings in my laboratory, all failures. I saved them, for I thought they might not be entirely devoid of magic – but I did not consider how their existence would affect the balance. My foolishness has caused this calamity!"

A fool he was, indeed, but Morton could not be blamed for this. "Get to your feet, man," grumbled Glendower. "Your useless trinkets are not the cause of my imprisonment."

Morton rose, his head wagging in confusion.

In Morton's confession, Glendower discerned the missing clue. "There is a third ring – but it is not one of yours."

Morton gaped. "I don't understand."

"Another ring exists. An equal to yours and mine. 'Tis the only answer."

"What does it mean, Master?"

The witch stepped forward. "It means that another has answered our call in Glendower's stead. They have come into this world in his place, trapping Glendower beyond our reach."

Shocked by her audacity, Morton blathered, "Pardon the Lady Stanley. She—"

"I can speak for myself!" she proclaimed in a sharp tone. "Master Owain, am I not correct?"

Glendower understood immediately that Morton's mistress had far more knowledge of the ways of magic than his student. "On my journey here, I encountered an entity of immense power. I did not comprehend, at the time, that it was because she wore the ring."

"A *sorceress?*" Lady Stanley was not pleased.

"Certes," replied Glendower.

Morton stared in disbelief. "I destroyed the scroll, Master! Since she cannot know your formula, is it possible that a mere woman forged a ring of immortality by her own skill?"

"The skill of the mage does not depend upon gender!" protested Lady Stanley with such wrath, Morton drew back. "Take you into account the great Rhiannon, whose feats of magic are unsurpassed in the legends of Wales."

With this statement, Lady Stanley earned Glendower's respect. "'Tis true – there have lived very few wizards who have commanded the power held by the Welsh witch. However, I do not believe this sorceress forged the ring herself. I think she came by it otherwise."

"But how?" asked Morton. "If only two rings such as these exist in the world?"

"It can only be this: my tomb has fallen to ruin and my corporeal body is dust. The ring has surfaced in a distant age beyond ours and has come into the possession of she who bears it now."

"But, Master, your body lies undisturbed in a secret crypt in Sycharth. I visited it myself only days ago!"

"In the lands of shades and angels, time has no dominion. That the ring is worn by another proves my quest for immortality shall fail and so will Cymru's struggle for freedom. If this remains so, the prophecy will not be fulfilled – and you shall never be anointed archbishop by the rightful king, for the heir of Wales shall never wear the crown."

"The rightful king? Refer you to Henry Tudor, my son?" cried Lady Stanley. "The crown is his birthright, which he claims in the name of the usurped Lancastrian king!"

"He shall never prevail so long as the balance between the heavens and earth held by the ring remains cloven. While she who wears the gold as matter, and I possess its magic in spirit, we are both trapped – she out of time and me between worlds."

"Then find her!" cried the Lady Stanley. "And marry her! For it seems to me that is the only way to solve this dilemma."

Glendower considered her words. *A marriage.* His respect grew for the Lady Stanley. "'Tis not beyond the realm of possibility."

Morton's eyes were wide with wonder as he looked upon her. "Margaret, you are a genius!"

Lady Stanley turned to Morton, her affection renewed. Glendower sensed their bond and his amorphous heart ached. How he yearned for the pleasures of the flesh.

And now he might have found a way to achieve it. "I shall wed the sorceress. As the union is consummated in the marriage bed, so shall the rings join as one – and I shall at last gain immortality."

Morton raised his arms to Glendower. "Henry Tudor will defeat Richard, Wales shall be freed, and the prophecy shall come to pass."

"We must find this woman – this interloper!" cried Lady Stanley.

"She might be anywhere in the world – in France or Egypt or China – how can we find her?"

"Even now I am able to sense the being whom I encountered in the vortex," churned Glendower uneasily. "The woman is in England – not more than eighty leagues to the south and east."

"That is not far from London," stated Morton.

"She is at court," Lady Stanley announced without doubt. "My husband is there, too – with that tyrant, King Richard."

"Your husband shall deliver her to me immediately," commanded Glendower. "I look forward to our wedding night – it will be *most* satisfying."

****

Anise stared up yet another stone stairway and sighed miserably. All she wanted to do was get to her room.

Once she had escaped the great hall and the dozens of curious eyes, she felt better – if only she could get to her bed. The last hour she'd searched the corridors for any clue to guide her the right direction. She came upon a stairway and peered into its murky depths. No torches lit the passage, but it *did* look kind of familiar. She started to go up – but stopped at the sound of a footstep.

Someone was following her. Her pulse quickened. She bolted up the stairs – up and up, into the darkness. Twenty steps and a landing. Another twenty-three steps and a landing. More steps. At the top, her way was blocked by a wooden door.

Her pursuer was not far behind. She held her breath and tried the door – the knob turned. She closed the door behind her.

A fire burned in the hearth. Had it been the room's owner following her? All her fears might have stemmed from something entirely innocent. If he came in, how would she explain herself?

Anise froze at the sound of someone at the door, her blood pounding in her ears. She heard receding footsteps and she trembled with relief. She thought it best to remain here awhile before trying to find her way to the main corridor. As her eyes adjusted to the firelight, she noticed small details of the room, and realized it looked a trifle… familiar.

Oh, God! She had to get out of here. These were the king's apartments!

She grasped the door handle and yanked – and her heart nearly stopped. Dropping into a curtsey, she lost her balance and collapsed to the floor. The king grasped her shoulders firmly and pulled her up.

Anise stared into his dark eyes, her words frozen on her tongue. "Y-Your Grace..! I-I'm..."

"You're lost," Richard finished. "I know." The corner of his mouth twitched.

Anise flushed when his eyes ran over her. He released her, satisfied she could stand on her own.

"Again." She knew she must be white as a sheet, but clamped down on her fear, scarcely believing he was not angry.

He smiled tiredly.

"I wasn't feeling well, Your Grace. And when everyone looked at me in the Great Hall..." *Quit stammering, you fool!* "I-I couldn't breathe. I had to get out of there." Anise felt the tears building. She took a breath and managed to push them back. "I heard someone following me. I was frightened, Your Grace. I ran up this stairway, into your room. If I'd known it was you..."

Richard's expression clouded, as though he did not believe her.

"I don't blame you for not trusting me," she said miserably. With the back of her hand, she wiped away the one tear that had slid down her cheek. *I'm not going to cry, dammit.*

Her words seemed to trouble him. "You misunderstand me, m'lady. I fear what you say must be true – someone was following you. I did not come to my rooms by the stairs, but by another way." He paused. "I am disconcerted only by this knowledge – not because I harbor any suspicions, for I do believe you speak truthfully."

Richard stared at her so intently that Anise looked away, her heart in her throat, her face hot. Why was he so kind to her? *More to the point, why did make her so breathless?*

His expression softened. "You're as pale as a shade, m'lady. Sit by the fire." It was an order, not a request. Anise found a chair by the hearth. He left for a moment and she heard the sound of liquid being poured. The king placed a cup in her hands. "Drink this. *Maman* tells me 'tis a balm to the nerves." After a moment, he added, "That you found my rooms 'twas fortunate. Many at court are not kindly disposed toward me, or my guests. It might have gone ill, should you have wandered to other parts of the castle."

He stood very close to her now, gazing at her with an expression she could not read. When Anise met his eyes, she could barely speak, somehow managing, "Thank you, Your Grace."

She remembered how he had gripped her shoulders before realizing who she was. He was a warrior. He could be dangerous. But the intensity she saw in his eyes now was not violence.

It was passion.

Her heart pattered erratically. She swallowed some of the wine, but the alcohol stoked the heat building inside her.

"I shall see that you are escorted safely to your rooms. And I will make inquiries." His velvet voice and lilting accent only seduced her more. Anise started to get up. Richard placed his hand on her shoulder, his face softened with concern. "You need not go – rest awhile. Finish the wine. It will give us time to talk. *Maman* reminded me of my offer of help. We will put forth a search for this man who claims he knows your birth."

So he *had* paid heed to her plight. Even amidst his own troubles. Anise nodded and dropped her gaze, as was proper when addressing the king. "Thank you, Your Grace. I appreciate your concern. I believe the man is my brother. He said his name is Dominic."

But she could not keep her eyes from searching his. Unbidden, their first encounter came to her mind and she blushed. Quickly, she averted her gaze, hoping he would not read her thoughts in her eyes. When she looked up at him again, however, she knew that he had.

Surely, he would think her wanton! Not only had she come to his rooms, but she'd accepted his offer of help. What was the fifteenth century protocol for such behavior? Did he expect favors in return?

Anise jumped to her feet, the wine in her cup sloshing over the sides as she set it down hard. She blathered, "Thank you so much for your kindness – I-I know I deserve it not, behaving as I did when last we met – I-I apologize, Your Grace. I never meant to…" Anise swallowed nervously "maybe I should… just… leave." She turned toward the door, at that moment wanting only to escape the embarrassment of the situation and caring not at all if she was dooming herself to wandering the corridors of the castle all night with a stalker at her heels.

Richard touched her arm and gently drew her around to face him. He bent his head low to gaze into her eyes. His smile was shy. "You were upset and grateful for my assistance – please don't apologize. I understand loss better than you know – especially the loss of a brother. To have consoled you also consoles me." His expression softened. "On that morn, I was haunted by my own bereavements." The timbre of his voice, so filled with pain, reverberated through her. "I want you to know – you helped me that day."

His honesty startled her. Pleasure that she had helped him – that he was grateful for it – rushed through her. Anise took an unsteady breath. "My heart is filled with gladness that I might have made your loss easier to bear, Your Grace." Without thinking, she placed her hand on his shoulder and pressed her cheek to his.

With a gasp, she drew back. "Your Grace, I'm—"

Richard smiled. "Don't."

Anise gazed enthralled at his expression of amusement.

"Tell me about him," said the king softly. "Tell me about Dominic."

Anise looked away. Suddenly, she felt ashamed to be lying to him – but saw no other way around it. "I-I do not remember much, Your Grace," she started, mentally gathering the details she'd used to convince Cecily. "I have remembered a bit more since you found me in the woods. Dominic's hair is dark like mine—like ours." She flushed at the reference. "He is of a good heart, and I am much distressed I didn't know who he was." That was as close to the true facts as she could reasonably come. From here on out, the truth was negotiable.

Richard had drawn so close, Anise could feel his breath. She cast her gaze downward, afraid to look in his eyes – afraid he would know she was lying. "I-I didn't know about Dominic's existence until he told me. He had come from Ireland to find my father. But my father is dead."

"He found you instead."

"Although I don't remember any of it, when Dominic found me on the road, he told me I'd welcomed him home." Anise had come up with a fabricated story she thought sounded plausible –

but had not yet worked out all the details. She fell back on the improvisation skills she'd learned in drama school. "There were those in our household who accused him of wrongful acts against my father. They drove him away. He went into hiding, but after hearing I had gone to find him, he came looking for me. When he came upon me traveling, I did not know him – I don't know why. At first, I believed he meant to rob me – but after a time, I knew he spoke the truth. I don't know how I knew that, either. He promised to take me home, but on our way, we were attacked by highwaymen and," she faltered, "and the next thing I remember, you were carrying me into the castle."

Richard's fingers grazed her chin. He turned her face upwards and their eyes met. "If your family will not help, are there no others who might? No… betrothed?"

Anise swallowed. "None that Dominic has told me of, Your Grace." She could not break the lock his gaze had with hers. "And no one I remember."

After a long pause, the king said, "Should your search take you to the north, you might travel with me – with my retinue – until our paths diverge. Along the way, I could send out some of my retainers to search the nearby villages, should your search carry you that direction, of course."

Anise breathed deep. "I accept your offer, Your Grace. For I believe the trail does lead north." It was a bald-faced lie. But it would please Cecily, whose support she required if she were to remain above suspicion.

Pleasure crossed Richard's face. "Then I am glad for it." His voice grew husky. His eyes never left hers. Anise nearly stopped breathing when he placed his hands on her shoulders. "Sweet Jesu, you are beautiful." He drew her face to his.

His lips touched hers with great tenderness, at first – then grew in urgency. Anise's heart contracted as she lost herself in his embrace, her senses reeling.

A knock on the door startled them both. With reluctance, Richard parted from her. After a long look – *was it surprise?* – he answered it. A squire stood waiting for his king's command.

"Please take m'lady to her apartments," said Richard quietly.

Anise curtseyed, "Thank you, Your Grace."

The king lifted one of her hands and touched the back of it with his lips. Anise's eyes met his once more. The heat in them warmed her all the way to her rooms.

CHAPTER SIX

Anise sat astride the gentle dappled mare provided to her for the trip north, scarcely believing this was the morning of her third day in the fifteenth century. It was clear and pleasant, and the verdant slopes surrounding Berkhamsted seemed to glow. A light breeze carried the scent of farmlands, ripe with green growth and animal manure. Beyond the outer curtain walls of goose-egg-sized bricks and mortar, fields of grain prevailed, dotted with the locals who worked them. It surprised her how compact the castle and its grounds were – she'd always imagined them larger.

As she waited for Cecily, the unfamiliar combination of men shouting marching orders, the snorting of horse and jangling of harness, and the general disorder of a large medieval assemblage preparing for a journey, emphasized her sense of displacement.

Yesterday had been fraught with preparation for the trip. Cecily came to her room with a retinue of attendants with clothing to be altered to Anise's size. Once she had her wardrobe, the rest of the day was filled with devotions and dinner. Each time she thought she might get an opportunity for some privacy to read her father's diary, there was a lady-in-waiting or a monk or the duchess at her door with one more task needing completion.

Anise had to be careful. If anyone found the diary or the photograph – or even one of the items in her tote bag – Cecily's offer of protection would not make much difference in the face of undeniable accusations of sorcery.

At last she had to admit defeat – there would be no privacy for her that day – and fell into an exhausted sleep, not waking until roused by a knock on her door and a breakfast tray.

Anise's horse whinnied, yanking her attention back to the moment as cartloads of supplies and barrels rolled past her toward the wagons.

The castle's bailey swarmed like a hive, as the king, his counselors and their men readied for the departure from his mother's residence. Cecily had filled Anise in on the route. From Berkhamsted they would travel to the castle at Kenilworth, then onto Nottingham, Richard's stronghold in the Midlands. There he planned to await news of Henry Tudor. Because of her familiarity with Shakespeare's play, Anise knew

Nottingham was the last place the king would be before the battle.

Her heart tugged, and her fingers found her lips as she remembered Richard's kiss.

The first leg of the journey – to Kenilworth, near the town of Coventry – required a day's ride. Cecily would be accompanying the entourage there and had requested Anise to be her lady-in-waiting. It would be the first opportunity to look for Dominic – a venture into which Anise had placed much hope.

The May day grew lighter and warmer as the morning wore on. Anise's gaze fell upon Lord Stanley shouting orders at a hapless page. She recalled Stanley's uneasy company on her first night in the Great Hall, when she had to share dinner with him. Fortunately, Cecily had seated her with a much less caustic companion for succeeding meals.

Watching him gallop his black stallion arrogantly through the crowd, Anise's face flushed hot at the memory of his probing questions. She had already discerned that the other women in the castle disliked him as much as she did.

Stanley guided his horse toward Francis Lovell, another of Richard's counselors, who was mounted on a gray mare. The night before, Cecily had introduced her to Richard's right hand man.

While he'd been curious about the strange circumstances surrounding Anise's arrival at the castle, he had not queried her endlessly like Stanley. Shortly after speaking with her, he left the Great Hall to dine privately with the king, who had been taking meals in his chambers.

Anise considered Lovell's expression as he watched Stanley's approach. Had Lovell's eyes clouded at Stanley's smirk? She thought that it had.

Anise felt woozy. She grabbed her horse's mane to steady herself. What was it with these dizzy spells? She reeled from a feeling of... of *doubt* – far stronger than what she'd experienced moment ago. Raising her head, she looked straight into Lovell's eyes – and discovered that *he* was the source. Somehow it was Lovell's emotions she was feeling. Nausea swept over her. She could not stop staring at Lovell, even while his contempt of Stanley engulfed her as completely as an ocean tide.

Clutching her horse's neck, Anise swayed in the saddle.

"Lady Anise – are you unwell?" It was Richard. "Langdon – get Hobbys! The lady is ill!"

The rush of adrenaline at Richard's voice brought her around. As Francis got caught up in the drama of his king, his intense feelings about Stanley diminished, and Anise's dizziness evaporated.

"I'm better now," she insisted. "The sun's heat and the excitement is all 'twas. She straightened in the saddle. "Please, Your Grace. No doctor."

Mounted on his gray horse, Richard rode toward her. He wore a purple doublet, hose – and unconvinced expression. "You are no fonder of physicians than myself, I see." He considered her closely to ascertain whether she spoke the truth. Satisfied, he nodded to his squire. "I shall look after her until my mother arrives – but make sure Hobbys remains close by."

Anise cast her eyes downward. "Thank you, Your Grace." At the rate her pulse was racing, she surely would need a doctor.

When she looked up, she could not avoid Richard's glance. "Your decision to accept my offer does please your king," he said quietly. "Would that my knights may find your brother, Dominic."

Anise's gaze traveled to his lips – and she flushed when she realized he knew where she was looking. She felt a wave of pleasure. Was it only hers – *or his, too?* Anise's breath caught in her lungs.

Richard's face remained expressionless. "Have you traveled much?"

She shook her head, keeping her eyes focused on her hands gripping the saddle horn.

He did not seem to mind her lack of speech. "The journey is not a hard one. We should arrive at Kenilworth this night, if all goes well. After a week, we'll depart for Nottingham." He took a deep breath of fresh morning air – and his eyes clouded. "Sweet Jesu, how I once enjoyed a journey! That was long ago."

Anise sneaked a peak at Richard from the corner of her eye and noticed how weary he was. The duties of king weighed heavily on this man who was only thirty-two. In the fifteenth century, Richard was considered middle aged. But Anise knew the king would never see his next birthday.

She ignored the ache that had grown steadily in her heart since they had met. "Do you not still enjoy traveling, Your Grace?"

He offered a faint smile. "My destinations are not ones of my choosing. Nottingham Castle I prefer least of all. 'Twas there that we..." He hesitated. "Anne was with me there when we heard our son was dead."

Anise felt his grief as acutely as if it were her own. She longed to comfort him, but did not dare show it before such an audience. "Please, Your Grace, do not remind the heavens of unlucky times, so that better ones might follow."

His face relaxed. "You are wise, Lady Anise. The past is gone and dwelling on it never returns those we have lost. The journey ahead must be our chief concern."

A cry rose at the head of the retinue and men and horses formed a marching order. "Are we leaving?" she asked.

He followed her glance and nodded curtly. "I must take leave of you." His eyes found hers once more. "We shall speak again soon, lady. Find me later and we shall travel together for a time."

In stunned silence, Anise watched him gallop away.

****

Astride their mounts, Lord Stanley stood with Francis Lovell, as retainers struggled by with supplies and gear to load on the wagons. Francis studied Stanley's face. "Journeys recall to my mind endings – do they to you, Thomas?"

Stanley noticed the sour look dogging the viscount's expression. Lovell's irritation with him was obvious. He pretended he did not notice. "Indeed, my friend, it may in fact signify a beginning. Once this battle is over, peace might at last return to the realm."

Stanley smiled inwardly. He knew his words would aggravate Francis' already piqued humor. They had never been friends, but Lovell disliked him even more since he'd been caught participating in that embarrassing plot against Richard, who had not been king at that time, but merely Lord Protector of his brother's son, Edward V.

He should have throttled Margaret for involving him. How he had ever let his wife and that incompetent bishop talk him into such an ill-advised plan? He knew the answer to that. At that time, his heart was still devoted to the cold-hearted bitch – a bitter memory.

And yet, the thought of Margaret and Morton, together, pained him. He pushed down the feeling.

This time, the plan would work. Stanley had more to gain under rule by Henry Tudor than he'd ever had under Richard. Although Margaret was Henry's mother, this had naught to do with her.

His wife may have hatched this scheme, but it hinged upon Stanley's role, and therefore would succeed.

It amused Stanley greatly his role in that failed plot incurred no harm to his place in the King's household. Afterward, Richard had granted him large land grants and titles, believing that it would quench Stanley's desire for power.

Lovell was not so convinced. The viscount, Richard's friend and staunchest supporter, did not dismiss the lord's transgression so easily – and remained acutely suspicious. Stanley had to be very careful around him.

It would not do for Lovell to hear sarcasm in his voice or see the ambivalence in his face. Stanley sought around for another topic. His eyes fell upon Lady Wynford. The commotion the king made over her fit of swoon seemed to discomfit Lovell.

"What think thee of the lady, Francis? Has the king at last taken a mistress? Has His Grace spoken of it to you, his closest friend?"

Lovell retorted, "The king has not taken a mistress and will not. He yet grieves abominably for his queen, may her soul rest with the Lord in Heaven."

"Francis, do you think Richard is unnatural among men? Even kings, with the weight of the realm upon them, must have needs of carnal comfort. What other preoccupation might otherwise ease a troubled mind so completely?"

Francis could not disagree. "You are right, of course."

"And so, what think you of the lady?" Stanley did, in fact, want Lovell's opinion – for when he had recognized Morton's ring on her hand, it startled him. Margaret *must* be behind it all. What was she scheming now?

"I only met her but once, briefly. She seems, almost – foreign. English, she is – and yet, not. 'Tis quite strange."

Stanley nodded toward where Anise stood with the king. "Certes, she has engaged the attentions of the king."

"Indeed," agreed the viscount. "I have not seen him speak so intently to a lady for many months – excepting of course, the duchess, his mother. Now that you mention it, I worry at his incaution. For what know we of her?"

Stanley now regretted his query. Should Lovell decide to ask Richard about the lady, it might interfere with Margaret's plans – if, in fact, this was one. It did but irk Stanley that his erstwhile wife had once more gone behind his back. Did she not understand the danger in which she cast him, in such proximity to the king?

Might Lady Wynford be an aspiring sorceress sent here to work some fell magic on Richard? Certes, it must be, for where else had she obtained that ring? Lady Stanley had sent her – but who was this strange woman, that his always distrustful wife should invest her with such power?

He had wasted no time in sending a messenger to his wife with a description of the new lady at court. Had Stanley less at stake, it would please him if the Lady Wynford turned out to be one of Margaret's few mistakes in intrigue. If he heard nothing back within the week, he might be forced to action. Stanley's eyes swept over the lady's assets, and he smiled at the thought.

The concern in Lovell's voice brought Stanley back to the conversation. "I am decided – I shall ask him."

Stanley looked Lovell in the eye. "That may prove ill. He is pious. If he has taken a mistress, its notice might undo him. If any man deserves a nightly diversion, 'tis he, certes."

Francis considered this. "Maybe discretion would be best." He seemed surprised at Stanley's concern. "Thank you for the advice."

Stanley smiled.

****

Anise watched the king advance to the front of the retinue, veering slightly from his path to speak to a woman arriving in a large-wheeled, horse-drawn chariot – and felt a twinge of jealousy. When Richard rode away, the woman in the vehicle hailed to her. It was the duchess. Feeling foolish, Anise reined up.

"Give your horse to one of these young squires and attend me, Lady Wynford. I have need of you," called Cecily over the cacophony. Richard's mother was no longer attired in a veil and wimple, and instead wore a simple, but fine, traveling dress and black hood. Anise turned her horse over to one of the teenage squires and climbed into the chariot.

"These chariots wrack the nerves, but 'tis beyond my years to manage one of those beasts, though I sat a horse with the best of them in my youth." Cecily considered Anise seriously. "Begin the journey with me. You may ride later with my son – I insist upon that. At last, I think, we might be on our way."

As she said it, the chariot grinded into motion. The entourage lurched along in steady, if bumpy, advancement.

Anise wondered if Cecily was reconsidering whether to trust her. The king might be drawn to her, but anyone of rank might easily convince him she was untrustworthy – Stanley, perhaps, who had his own agenda, or Lovell, who was obviously very protective of the king. Her presence at Richard's court was precarious, at best.

Only Cecily might intervene on her behalf – and she, too, had her own particular reasons. If Anise defied her, she'd lose her only line of defense.

The duchess proceeded carefully. "We have made our bargain and vowed not to ask one another for explanations – and yet I feel I owe one. You desire only to find your brother – not a difficult request to oblige for a household as powerful as the king's. I have no right to demand your services in return for simple Christian charity and assistance, and yet I have done so. I denote fear in your stance, but be at ease, lady. I wish not to bring troubles upon your head. 'Tis only that with so many enemies in our midst, those of us close to the king must be careful. I watch you with my son and all suspicion flees."

Anise was taken aback. "Thank you, m'lady."

Cecily nodded. "That said, we must now discuss the plot we've cooked. I should not rest easily, should harm befall you. I give you this chance to back out and abandon Richard to his fate without risk to your own. Help finding your brother shall go forth, as planned."

Anise knew she should jump at the chance for an escape from the intrigue surrounding the king's court. She'd agreed to swap rings with Richard only to secure the duchess' protection – and had no intention of giving up the only thing that might return her to her own time. But what if Richard was truly cursed and she could save him?

God, what was she thinking?

Still – could it hurt to play along a little while longer?

Before she knew she had decided, the words slipped out, "I do know the risks, m'lady. But if you think 'tis for his benefit, I will commit to your plan without question. I, too, am concerned for Rich— I mean, His Grace."

The duchess' expression softened. "That I do believe, m'lady, now that you speak these words to me. I am a daughter of God and trust His plan for each of us. Yet I cannot sit by and do nothing when the chance presents itself. And you, my dear Lady Anise, may be the only chance Richard has."

Anise nodded. "I'll try."

"There is more to tell. Richard will not even consider his difficulties are caused by enchantment. He thinks that God is displeased with him," Cecily hesitated, as if unsure of her words, "that God is displeased he seized the crown from his nephew. But Richard had no choice, once Edward was revealed to be Elizabeth Woodville's bastard. 'Twas not Richard's fault he was the next in succession. 'Twas not even his desire to be king – and yet his subjects were glad for it. His ascension saved us all from the grasping Woodvilles as well as a minority king. Yet Richard insists his wife and son have been taken from him because of this misdeed." After a long pause, she added quietly, "Richard believes 'tis God's displeasure. I believe 'tis the black arts.

What I fear," the duchess' eyes widened as she lifted Anise's hand, "is that the ring you wear is as cursed as the one Richard has and even if we do succeed, we shall yet fail to save him."

Anise stared at Cecily and then at her hand. Besides being a ring of passage through time, was it also cursed? Is that why her life – why the lives of her entire family – were so messed up?

The duchess sighed at her reaction. "You hadn't thought of that, I see. But take some heart in this: the engraving on your ring is smooth with age. If it carries a curse, perhaps the years have worn away its potency. This is a desperate hope, I know. But what else can I believe? Your strange arrival with the ring seems a portent I cannot ignore."

"You think Richard's going to die if I don't help him?" The words were out of her mouth before she'd considered them.

Cecily frowned but did not answer. She did not have to; Anise knew she was right. She *felt* it.

"It may be that your ring is not cursed. Or that its powers are different – protective, perhaps. You have survived much these past days. You survived the evil of that pagan place where many disappeared, never to be seen again."

The fear pouring from Cecily was unmistakable. Anise's senses reeled – the very same thing had happened when staring at Francis Lovell! What was going on? Had coming here made Anise telepathic?

Wrapped up in her own distress, the duchess did not notice Anise's reaction. "The rings were made by the Welsh wizard, Owain Glendower, a master of the black arts. I grew up hearing many stories of him, for his Welsh rebellion caused great strife during the lives of my parents. The traitor was crowned as Wales' king. More than three score and ten years have passed since his death, yet he is spoken of in that land as if he lives still. If this is true – if he has found some way to immortality, then we are all in danger – you and my son most of all, who wear his evil creations."

Anise grabbed Cecily's arm to stay aright. She was going to faint if this did not stop. She fumbled for the ring on her finger and yanked it off. Coming back to herself, Anise blinked.

She knew the ring's secret. *Empathy!*

Cecily looked at her, startled. "M'lady?"

Anise stared at the ring in her palm. "It's… I'm all right."

Cecily studied her. "I blame you not for wishing to be free of it. I've warned Richard, but he forbids my speaking of it. I would try to accomplish this thing myself, but he would never allow me to handle the ring without suspicion." She gazed upon Anise knowingly. "You, he would not suspect. I see how he looks at you. He is – unguarded."

Unguarded? Her heart raced as she remembered his mouth on hers. Had she such an effect on Richard that he'd allow her unquestioned access to him? Anise's face went hot. *To his body?*

She *was* attracted to Richard – but was there more to it? Did she want entry to his heart?

Was it possible she could even win that? Not only the body, but the *heart*, of a king? That he might actually want her, Anise, whose existence was so insubstantial that her own mother believed a strong enough gust of wind could blow it away?

Anise closed her eyes. God knew, she wanted Richard – she could not deny it. Is this what love felt like? Was this heady feeling the whole reason her mother had so many affairs?

Of all men, why must Anise fall for this one? Besides living in a century so totally unlike her own, he was doomed. History had already written his fate. In a couple of months, Richard would die. There was no way she could alter that.

Could she?

With the image of Richard's face – and future – clear in her mind, Anise knew what she had to do. She slipped the ring onto her finger. "I don't care about the danger. I'll do whatever I can to help His Grace."

Cecily's flood of relief washed over her.

****

It felt good to be moving again. Richard took a deep breath of the fresh country air and spurred his horse forward. His gray, Roget, was not as fine a beast as White Surrey, but was even-tempered and quick. Riding him was sheer pleasure.

As he trotted at the fore of the retinue, the king could almost forget about his troubles. The trees bloomed sweetly, and the heather swept across the fields in a sheaf of purple flowers. A chorus of birds sang unhindered by the disturbance brought upon it by the men and horse of his household trudging through. At this moment, the thought of merry England embroiled in another skirmish between York and Lancaster seemed impossible.

And yet, with Henry Tudor even now making preparation to embark from the shores of France, it was inevitable.

At the thought of the Pretender, Richard considered those riding with him. Who might be the next to desert him? Certes, not Francis, who was his closest ally and comrade. He could not imagine the viscount betraying him. And yet, neither had he suspected the Duke of Buckingham until it was too late. Stanley might bolt at any moment – Richard had no illusions there. Was it not just a matter of time?

Richard had no luck holding the loyalty of men as Edward had done. For the hundredth time, he wondered why. He had not until now considered asking his mother this. He wondered what she thought of him. Did she compare

Richard to his brother and determine he did not measure up? Did she fault him for his errors in judgment?

Richard heard the wheels of Cecily's chariot crunching on the road to his back. In sooth, he knew Cecily's heart to be true, not bitter. The duchess had supported all the men in her family who had claimed England for Yorkist rule. This not only included himself and Edward, but also their father, the Duke of York, who had died trying to gain the throne. Each had made dreadful mistakes along the way. To all had she willingly pledged her faith.

Cecily came with him now, as he was the last of her male children, and perhaps it would be the end of the road for them and the Yorkist cause. For what if Tudor prevailed? Was it not possible?

The Rose of Raby – that was how Cecily Neville had been known in her youth, so beauteous was she. Yet now she was an old woman who must be carried along by chariot, too great in age to ride – and she had been a fine horsewoman. Age had crept up with insidious stealth. Soon she, too, would be lost. Strange, how one's family slips away one by one.

Unbidden as always, memories of Edward rushed to mind. Richard could not remember his brother without a hollow feeling of loss. How he longed for Ned's presence, his light heart and his companionship. Though the gulf in their ages was wide, Richard had found no friend so dear as Ned. Even his beloved Anne had not been so close to him as his brother.

'Twas not always true between royal brothers. Odder still was that he and Edward had not achieved that closeness until adulthood.

It was a loyalty forged that frigid winter across the Channel in Bruges, where they sought exile with their sister, Margaret, and her husband, Charles the Bold, after the Earl of Warwick's

surprise attack against Edward in the first years of his reign. There Richard learned that the brother he'd looked up to, who was ten years his senior, considered him as confidant and worthy of strong affection.

That bitter winter night had held no promise for Edward or the Yorkist cause. All but their staunchest supporters had gone over to the other side, joining Warwick to rule England through the manipulation of poor, mad King Harry. Set aside years ago because of his ineptness, the old king had been reinstated to the throne, becoming Warwick's puppet. Meanwhile, the exiled Yorkists' debts had run so high with the merchants, that some now turned them away.

The inn had been nearly deserted, their cups nearly drained. Both were at the end of their endurance, neither could bear more charity from their sister and the Duke. Richard sought distraction wherever he could find it, and was grateful that some friends remained true to him. As he stared into his drink, he thought of his conversation that day with his old friend William Caxton, formerly the governor of the English merchants in Burgundy, and now in his sister's employ.

He glanced up at Ned, noting the deep furrows in his forehead. "Do you know of this new science, printing?" he asked, seeking to draw his brother's attention momentarily away from their sorry plight. "Master Caxton tells me of a German who makes his livelihood printing books with a method that employs no scribes. They do print many pages at once, and quickly, too. He sells the books to anyone with gold enough to buy. Will's enthusiasm overflowed with his telling of it. He does believe he can open a shop in London and do well with it."

But Ned only swirled the liquid at the bottom of his cup, nodding absently at Richard's words. "Have ye numbered those who've gone to our cousin, Warwick's, side? Those we counted on, I mean?"

Richard sighed. There was no distracting Ned that night. "This I fear to do," he said, "for my anger may grow so great I could not control it. How these men in good conscience could turn from you..." Wrath rose within him as he thought on it.

The corner of Edward's mouth twitched up slightly. "Conscience may have little to do with it, certes. But count how many, Dickon. And among them, Johnny Neville, the cousin we do both still love—"

"Warwick's brother," added Richard grimly.

"Yes – but what of our own brother? What think you of George? Gone to Warwick's cause!"

Richard smiled sadly. Warwick had approached him, too, hoping to turn both brothers against Edward. Yet Richard never considered turning against Ned, whom he so loved. It rent his soul that George could be so easily won, and he still held out hope his errant brother would change his mind. "I cannot believe he will stay long. He hopes only for the crown in your stead. When he sees he will not get it from our cousin…"

"Perhaps, perhaps," Edward nodded, growing silent for a long stretch. "Yet what I do arrive at, brother, is maybe we will not succeed. I think only too often of our father…"

"No, Ned – do not!" Richard whispered fiercely, setting his cup down hard. And yet he, too, thought often of their dead sire. The Duke of York had wrenched the crown away from the feeble-minded King Henry, only to discover the people had not wanted him. When he was killed fighting for his cause, their brother Edmund died with him. Harry's vengeful queen Marguerite d'Anjou ordered their heads to be spiked atop Micklegate Bar, the south gate into York, as a mockery to the Duke's title. When Edward took the crown in their father's name, he had remains of their kin solemnly interred. Yet neither Edward nor Richard could forgive the Lancastrians this atrocity.

"'Tis thee who descend rightly to the throne, directly through Lionel's blood!" Richard said hotly. "Our cause is just! We must not give up!"

Ned had seemed startled by Richard's fury. "I did not think to cease fighting," he said quietly. "It just may be that I fear for the future of my son..."

Edward's queen had just borne his heir, should he ever be returned to the throne. And while Richard had not approved of Elizabeth Woodville – a widow with two grown sons and Lancastrian ties – he could never turn against his brother because of it, as had Warwick.

When Ned next spoke, Richard heard his brother's soul naked in his words. "My first son has been born, and I have not yet laid eyes on him." His voice was thick. "He cowers with his mother in a church's sanctuary with my daughters, waiting for me. And I am here, helpless, powerless. Not much of a king." An ironic smile passed over his face. "And yet you remain."

"Yes," Richard had answered. "My heart allows no other choice. My allegiance lies with only one king, you, my brother. You must believe that we shall overcome this obstacle. Our cousin cannot remain in power long. The love of the people lies with you."

Edward had gazed at him a long time, his expression sad. "Ah, Dickon. Do you know that you are but the one person in this tempestuous world that I can count on? While I may never trust anyone else for the rest of my life, God has granted me your undying faith."

"It is undying." He had looked into his empty cup and said softly, "And I trust you with my life, too, brother."

Edward sighed. "And do you know that I am afraid? Do you know that your life may not be safe with me? That I'm not in control? That I cannot be certain of our future?"

But Richard hadn't any doubt. "My life is safe with you. You cannot convince me otherwise."

Ned had gripped his arm, as if he had not believed what he heard. His voice fell low. "And I believe my life is safe with you." He paused, and then: "'Twas Edmund who was the last to hear those words from me. When he died, so did a part of me. But you have helped fill that void. Believe me, Dickon. You have."

It was then that Richard realized he was more than the king's youngest brother. He was his friend.

Before long, fortune again turned in the direction of Edward and his small band of supporters. At last, a disappointed George had seen through Warwick's empty promises of power, and so he rejoined his brother's cause.

Together Edward and Richard gathered troops and recaptured London. Within two weeks the Kingmaker and his brother, Johnny Neville, were dead on the field at Barnet. Within a month, the old king was imprisoned in the Tower and Queen Marguerite was captured with her troops at Tewkesbury, trying to escape over the River Severn to Wales. Her son, Prince Edouard, the Lancastrian hope for the crown, was dead.

Through it all, Edward and Richard had forged a lifelong bond.

"Your thoughts must be deep, Your Grace."

Richard had not heard the hoofsteps of Lady Anise's horse come up beside him. Roused from his reverie, he turned toward her. The sight of her dark eyes and delicate features lightened his heart, and he felt some of the tenseness drain from him. "'Tis true, m'lady. My mind had wandered to days past and people lost. It has been disobedient of late and travels there often."

She nodded, still keeping her eyes averted, as was proper, and a soft smile lit her face. "Mine own mind also, er, has a mind of its own." The lady laughed at her tongue-twisted words. "What I meant, Your Grace, was—"

"Never mind!" he snorted, and they both laughed.

After a pause to catch their breaths, he ventured, "I am glad you decided to ride with me awhile, lady. I did not know if you would."

Her face radiated at his comment. "Somehow your mother has fallen asleep in that awful chariot. I couldn't bear it any longer. I thought my head would be shaken from my shoulders," adding hastily, "Your Grace." Her voice fell quiet, almost too low for him to hear over the noise of the entourage. "Talking with you makes me feel better."

"Are you thinking of your family?" he asked, recalling too late that she had said she could not remember them.

He was surprised when she nodded. "I wonder if I should ever see my brother again." There was pain in her voice. "Even if I never remember him, it's something just to know I'm not alone."

Richard felt a stab of grief. *Yes. That was it. To know you are not alone.* He swallowed the lump in his throat. "I was thinking of my brother, Edward, just then, when you rode up."

Anise gazed at him directly, as was not proper, and yet his heart skipped a beat at the emotion in her eyes. "You have lost so many," she said. "How do you bear it… Your Grace?"

He could not stand her formality and urged his horse closer, leaning toward her so that none of his retainers would hear. "Call me by my name, Anise. As you did at the first."

She hesitated, but nodded, saying quietly, "Richard."

He felt a quickening of his pulse and answered her question, "I cannot bear the loneliness sometimes. There are friends who mean well. They offer advice. All are gone from me who would offer comfort." Her gaze was turned down again and so he studied the sweep of her forehead, memorizing her high cheekbones, her long lashes and delicate nose. "And yet, perhaps, not all," he said after a moment, but he did not think she heard him.

She did not speak for long minutes, before she said, "'Tis worse than death to be so alone. And yet, at the same time, so hard to get close to anyone."

Her words echoed that which was in his soul. "Our thoughts ride down the same road," he said. "Mayhaps t'would do us both good to travel together for a while."

She glanced up quickly again, her eyes filled with longing that said, *yes, we could.* But Richard would not know her response, for a squire rode up hastily beside them. "Your Grace, we must halt. A wheel has broken on one of supply wagons. And the Duchess Cecily, your mother, does ask for you."

Nodding in acknowledgement to the man, Richard turned to Anise. "I must go."

Her eyes were averted from him again, and he could not see her face, though he heard her say, "Goodbye, Richard."

The note in her voice was indefinable to him and he loathed to part from her. Someone else called him.

"Your Grace!"

With one more glance at Anise, he turned his horse and rode away.

CHAPTER SEVEN

Still no word from his mother.

As he sat in the main hall of the residence King Charles had provided for him in Rouen, Henry Tudor felt his tensions rise to a fever pitch. The interminable waiting of this last fortnight had nearly driven him to madness and certainly to distraction. Waiting was something he understood innately – and hated passionately. All those years of biding his time in the household of Lord Herbert, waiting for his Uncle Jasper to return, waiting until he could stand it no more. A virtual prisoner, held there in safekeeping by the Yorkist kings, bought by the Herberts and raised by his foster parents to be married to their homely daughter Maud, who clung to him like a trellis rose. How glad he was that *that* had never taken place!

But waiting, knowing that his destiny lay elsewhere – just as he was waiting now.

Henry scowled at Gaspard, who stood before him at the dais he had ordered to be made for him, in light of his future kingship. Of late, he had been dressing in the role of a monarch, wearing a doublet made of the finest damask cloth, his silk hose new and dyed black, and his rich velvet robes so long they touched the floor.

But all this had not eased his mind. Or the agony of waiting. Would he ever know how it went? The King of France – and especially the king's eldest sister, who had taken the reins of the government in Charles' minority – expected the Tudors to be gearing up for Henry's foray against Richard. And so, he and Jasper were at Rouen, at the mouth of the Seine River, putting into some order the fleet of ships and the wretched French troops put at their disposal. His uncle carried on diligently, placing little stock in Margaret and Morton's machinations. Jasper had no doubt that with good planning they could win. Henry knew his uncle scoffed at his hoped-for supernatural assistance.

Still Henry was paralyzed with the waiting. How could he, without word, plan his next move against his cousin, Richard, the usurper? Why had he heard nothing? The desperation in his heart threatened to show through his demeanor – and he could not let that happen! He must not show his fear. He must not let Jasper know that even he, Henry, did not much believe in his chances against his cousin – even if he did have God on his side. Not unless his mother succeeded.

Within moments of these thoughts, Jasper, dressed as always in the garb of a soldier rather than a lord, swept into the hall. He brought with him the chill night air – and a half-bearded man, his clothes still damp from the seawater, looking around him in wonder, as if he could not believe he had attained his destination.

Jasper pushed him down into the kneeling position of respect before his nephew. "Tell His Grace what news you have. Come on, man."

Still gasping for breath after his strenuous journey, the man hesitated before answering, and looked in amazement at the group of people who awaited his words.

His eyes fell on Henry. "My Earl of Richmond, I am commissioned to present to Your Grace this message from the man called Master Reynold Bray."

Tension pounding at his brain, Henry impatiently leaned forward in his chair. "Yes, man, yes. Go on!"

"The Master Bray says that Your Lady Mother and the Good Bishop Morton have succeeded in their efforts and that you should proceed with your plans."

Relief flooded over Henry and he sent a thankful prayer heavenward that he was sitting down. *Success! Ah, success! My Dearest Mother, though I have not known you these many years, your efforts on my behalf have proven your worth to me! You shall ever be treated with honor and respect at my court, when I take my rightful place as King of England.*

Once the shock of the news – for which he had seemed to have waited an eternity – had worn off, a rare smile lit his face. Henry noticed that even his uncle, so often serious, was laughing and bidding the messenger to rise, though deep down Henry wondered if it might be a show on Jasper's part for Henry's benefit.

Henry motioned for his servants and spoke to the bringer of good tidings. "You are welcome here, my fellow." And to the others: "Treat this man as my honored guest. Provide him with a feast, for he is foremost in my favor this day."

Ignoring the superstition about jinxing the future by speaking of it, Henry cried, "Uncle, get that man's name! I shall find a place for him in my government when I am King!"

****

The ride to the castle at Kenilworth was a hard one for Anise. The weather was dry and hot, the trail dusty. She stayed on her dappled mare as long as she could, because bumping along in the crude chariot was a torture. But riding long distances astride a horse was an acquired skill that Anise had experienced, but never mastered.

For the last third of the journey, she gave it up and retired to the chariot with Cecily.

After eight long hours of traveling, the procession came over a rise in the ground and the great fortress of Kenilworth loomed before them. Anise inhaled sharply.

Here was a castle. So much larger than Cecily's residence, its very appearance cried a warning to those who dared ride to its gates. Anise pushed down her anxiety. What was there to be afraid of? The king led this procession. Anise tried to calm her nerves by studying the structure they were approaching.

As did almost all ancient castles, it stood on a rise overlooking the villages and farms surrounding it. Encircling it was a wide lake, or mere, as they called it, which increased its inaccessibility to enemies.

Unlike Berkhamsted, Kenilworth was built of the roughly-hewn bricks that she had always seen in pictures of castles. As they rode up to the bold structure in the lengthening shadows of late afternoon, a premonitory chill ran over her.

The procession passed matter-of-factly through the outer curtain wall, and over a bridge leading into the inner court. A massive keep rose starkly to the right. When the spiked gates came down behind them, Anise felt trapped.

After many greetings and conversation in the main hall of the castle, the ladies were shown to their rooms. Cecily recommended that Damsel Juliann be freed from her duties so she might attend Anise for the duration of her visit, and whispered to Anise that she would find Juliann affectionate and trustworthy.

As she and the duchess parted ways, Anise was led deep into the fortress. A member of the household staff named Mabel lit their way up frighteningly uneven stairs that seemed to spiral forever. Kenilworth was not as ancient as Berkhamsted, as evidenced by the magnificent sectioned glass windows, yet a sense of isolation descended upon Anise.

When they attained the second landing, she was well out of breath, which drew a scornful look from the wiry Mabel. They stood in a rough hewn foyer.

"Beyond that door are your apartments. Your trunk of belongings will soon arrive," said Mabel. "Dame Juliann shall attend you. Even now she arranges for your supper to be brought up."

After the woman had gone, Anise reached impulsively into the familiar tote bag she clutched by her side for reassurance that the play and the diary were still there. She leaned on the heavy wooden door to her room and went in. When her eyes adjusted to the light, she found it better than expected.

Although smaller than the room she'd had at Berkhamsted – which she learned later was used for the sick or dying – this one seemed almost cozy. Covering the walls were intricately-woven tapestries depicting the martyrdom of some saint, his face twisted in agony from the flames of the pyre licking his feet. There was one window, covered over with a thick shade, and a small fireplace set into the wall. The dark wood of her canopied bed was covered in carvings and the thick curtains designed to keep her body heat in and the cold out.

The room was cold and she was tired. Nothing would suit her better than a nap. She stripped down to her chemise and pulled back the covers. She was tired of thinking, tired of rationalizing, tired of plotting. As she was about to crawl in, there came a light knock on the door. She assumed it was her dinner. Drawing on her cloak to hide her state of undress, she answered it.

It was Lord Stanley.

Before she could slam the door in his face, he pushed his way in. Draped in clothing finer even than what she'd seen Richard wearing, the king's steward stared at her with a ravenous smile. His eyes seemed to see right through her cloak.

Anise pulled it closer around her.

In one deft movement he grabbed her left arm. Though she yanked back, he pulled her closer, grabbed her hand and studied it. "'Tis the ring!" When she cried out, he caught her other arm and held her fast, despite her struggles. "Has Margaret sent you here? Are you checking up on me? The bitch is intolerable! I do her bidding while she cuckolds me with that fornicating bishop. As further insult, she sends you!"

Stanley tossed her from him with such fury that Anise fell to the floor. The cloak, which had been shaken loose, fell open.

Stanley leered. "What's this?"

Anise shivered and tried to cover herself.

Stanley pulled her to her feet, his hands slipping beneath her wrap to caress her breast through the chemise. Feeling sick at his touch, Anise broke away.

"Suppose I took Margaret's little spy here on the floor. That would give you something to report, wouldn't it, *Lady* Wynford?" He sneered, grabbing her arm and leaning closer. Anise punched him in the chest, to no effect. He took a step back, laughing as she backed away.

"Get out, you bastard! I don't know who you mean."

Stanley's expression sobered and he appeared thoughtful. "Perhaps she sent you to bed the king. Is that it?"

Anise caught her breath. First Cecily, now Stanley. How many plots were there that involved her seducing the king?

Now that he'd revealed so much, Anise decided she'd better play along – or who knew what he'd do?

"Why don't you ask Margaret yourself? Now leave me alone, Lord Stanley." Her attempt at anger disintegrated into gasping. "Or I'll report you."

He laughed again. "I would not have bedded you, in sooth. 'Twas only but a way to prove your allegiance to my scheming wife. I know exactly why you have been sent. 'Tis all going according to plan."

Stanley crossed the short distance between them and put his palm to her cheek, his hot breath on her face. "That's not to say I would not have liked to."

Before she could pull away, Stanley turned on his heel and slammed out the door.

Her knees weak, she stumbled to the bed. When Juliann brought her supper, Anise was huddled under the blankets. She was grateful to see a friendly face. "Thanks, but I don't feel good."

Juliann persisted, "'Tis most likely the sun-sickness coming upon you after the long journey. You need to take nourishment, mistress. Have some wine, at least."

Maybe alcohol would calm her nerves. Anise sat up as Juliann handed her a pewter goblet. As she drank the spiced concoction, she relaxed a bit

– and wondered if she should mention the confrontation with the king's steward. She decided not to.

The alcohol did nothing to stimulate her appetite. When she crawled beneath the covers shivering, Juliann put a hand to Anise's forehead.

"'Tis not the sun-sickness at all, m'lady," said Juliann in a concerned voice. "I must fetch the duchess." To Anise's relief, the woman left.

When she woke up, Anise's throat was sore and she burned with fever. Cecily sat by her bedside, pressing a damp cloth to her head. As the fever persisted through the night and into the next day, Anise drifted in and out of consciousness, but her rest was plagued with nightmares about the brother she could not find and the father she never knew – all the while, her mother berating her for being a silly little girl.

On the afternoon of the second day, the duchess insisted that the doctor be brought in. When Anise awakened to find him approaching with the cure for all ills – leeches – she swatted at him weakly until he backed off. "Get those things away from me!"

"She must be bled!" Hobbys stated firmly, coming closer.

"No, please…" Anise collapsed into dry sobs.

Cecily hesitated before placing her hand on the doctor's arm. "Come back in a while – I shall make her see the sense in it."

After Hobbys had gone, Anise tried to take matters into her own hands. Her body could not fight the fever without nutrition. "Bring me some broth," she implored Cecily – but the duchess shook her head in refusal. Anise despaired; apparently, the old wives' tale of "starving a fever" had taken hold by the fifteenth century.

"There may be something better." Cecily left.

A short time later, she returned with a flagon of hot tea. "Drink this. 'Twill banish the sweats. 'Tis the monks' remedy of willow bark."

Anise drank and the hot liquid eased her aching throat. Willow bark. Why did that sound familiar? She groaned. *How could I be so stupid?*

Cecily leaned over her. "What is it, my dear?"

"My tote bag." What did they call them in medieval times? "My leather bag. Can you bring me my bag?"

Juliann nodded from across the room. "I know what she dost speak of, Your Grace." The maid found Anise's bag in the wardrobe and brought it to her. When it was in her arms, Anise hugged it. She had every remedy known to modern man in this thing. Unzipping the pocket where she kept the pills, she found the bottle of aspirin.But the effort of scrounging in the bag had exhausted her. Still, she did not dare let them see what she doing. With her hand in her bag, she struggled with the tamper proof lid and managed to extract two aspirin.

The two ladies stared as she put the pills in her mouth and swallowed them with the tea.

"What is that, m'lady?" Cecily appeared alarmed. She tried to look into Anise's bag.

But Anise held onto it; she took it under the covers. "It's my own remedy. I forgot I had it. It will help."

By the third day, Anise realized the aspirin would not be enough. She was getting weaker as the hours went by and lamented the partial prescription of antibiotics sitting in her bathroom cupboard at home. She'd finally convinced Juliann to bring her some broth. It felt like she was being provided her last meal.

The doctor came back. The situation was getting desperate. What medieval crud had she caught?

Hobbys approached her with his barbaric leeches. Anise stared at him as the obvious occurred to her. "Do I have the plague?"

His eyes widened at her question.

Oh, God, it was! Didn't it start in the throat? "The Black Death! Do I have it? Am I going to die?"

He shook his head. "Speak not of such things, m'lady – 'twill bring the evil upon us."

"Well, is it?" Panic rushed through her.

He shook his head with vehemence. "No. 'Tis not la Peste, but Swamp Fever."

Anise groaned in relief. She rasped, "How do we bring it down?"

"Leeches, m'lady. 'Tis the only thing to drain the ill humors from you."

"No way!" She had to think. *What would you do, Mother?* Anise's immediate answer to that was, *probably let me die.* But then an image niggled at the edge of her memory. Spots all over her body. Being so hot, so thirsty. Seeing rag dolls everywhere, on the bed, on the walls – hallucinations from fever. Where was her mom? In her mind's eye, she saw a man in a plaid shirt, the arms rolled up.

He was putting her in the bath. Anise shivered. A *cold* bath.

She remembered the photo from the journal. The man was Matthew Fallon. Her father.

"No leeches," she repeated to the doctor. "Where is the duchess?"

"I am here, lady," said Cecily, coming to the bedside.

"Bring a tub of water. The coldest water you can find."

The duchess looked at the doctor. "'Tis the fever talking."

"No, please. I want a bath. A cold bath." Anise knew they would not listen to her – knew they'd let this fever kill her before doing what she asked.

Juliann also heard the request. She immediately took Anise's hand. "A cold bath! M'lady would surely catch her death!"

Cecily shushed her. "Say a prayer quickly." Anise caught the glance between them. Her life really *was* in danger.

The duchess' eyes went to Anise's hand resting on the covers – she was looking at the ring. Cecily thought it was what had made her ill.

"If that's what it is, then it doesn't matter. If it's black magic, then I'm going to die, anyway – so please do as I ask? I know what I'm doing."

Cecily frowned, but nodded at Juliann. The maid released a small gasp, and ran from the room. An hour later, two men clothed in the king's colors carried an iron tub into the room and lowered it to the stone floor.

As pitcher after pitcher of water was poured into it, the tallest one spoke. "Here 'tis, the coldest water from the castle's cellar."

On the way out, the other man asked Juliann, "Who be this lady that the king should urge such haste upon us?"

Anise did not hear the answer as she put her legs over the side of the bed and tentatively got to her feet. After the men left, with Juliann's assistance, she pulled off her clammy gown. She gasped when she got into the water, unprepared for the shock of cold.

She held her breath until she got used to it.

It felt good. For the first time in days, her flesh did not feel like it was on fire. Cecily and Juliann watched wordlessly as Anise gathered up her hair with one hand and settled into the water up to her neck.

This was going to work. She felt better already.

When Anise stood up after being in the tub for a while, Juliann toweled her off. She climbed back into the bed, snuggling under the covers. The fever broke a half hour later.

****

Francis Lovell stood in the shadows beyond the sickroom, waiting. He had been drawn there by the rumors of the curious cold bath called for by the Lady Wynford. Mystery shrouded this woman and everything she did. Francis wanted to hear the story directly from Juliann.

He smiled at the thought of his buxom mistress. Juliann had won his affection with kindness and humility. His own wife was as cold to him as a Yorkshire night, caring only for her life at Westminster Palace where she used her position as a noble's wife to attract the ardor of younger lovers.

Francis had sworn off women.

Then he'd met Juliann. She had been the duchess' attendant for many years when Cecily resided at Baynard's Castle. Juliann's plump beauty and demure ways, so different from his wife, captivated Francis immediately.

For months, Francis ignored her, avoided her, denied how he felt – until at last, he could do naught else but acknowledge it. In a self-induced fever, he confessed to her his love. To his amazement, she whispered that she returned his affection, and they became lovers.

The thought of her warmed his heart by day, as her body occasionally warmed his bed by night. He was glad to be back in her company, however temporarily.

For the past few years, they had been much separated, since the duchess took the veil and moved away from London. His heart had ached tremendously for Juliann, and he often made the day's ride to Berkhamsted to see her. How often he had wished during those long trips that somehow they could be married – but of course, it was impossible. Divorce from his wife would never by granted by the Church, which only allowed such a breach of the marriage covenant under the strictest conditions.

But soon he and Juliann found out their situation could be worse. When she was sent to Kenilworth, their trysts dwindled to a few times a year. They were forced into separate lives altogether.

Still, their affection did not wane. Each time their paths chanced to cross, their love was miraculously renewed. Francis never again took another woman to his bed.

The door to the sickroom opened. Juliann stood there. She did not see Francis hiding in the shadows. Removing her headdress, he saw her pinned-up swath of auburn hair twisted at her nape and longed to release it. Juliann leaned against the stone wall and closed her eyes, as if exhausted.

When Francis startled her with his touch, she gasped – and smiled when she saw it was him. He pulled her into the shadows and massaged her shoulders.

He kissed her behind the ear. "M'lady is very warm."

She gave him access to her throat and Francis ran his lips over it. "The room must be kept warm for the lady, who is so ill. The fire is stoked to a blaze. The worst is over now. She will live."

Francis said nothing, ministering to her with his affection. She would tell him what he needed to know. He did not need to ask. Their minds were as one.

"'Tis incredible, but Her Grace, the duchess, remained with the lady nearly as long as I have. Lady Anise is a worthy and good woman. Though she suffers, she asks nothing from us. She sent Hobbys away and refused to be bled –

not that I blame her. Then she cured herself – with some remedy from her black bag and the cold bath. 'Twas only moments ago that the fever broke."

Francis embraced Juliann around the waist from behind and pulled her against him. "When the king learned of her illness, he insisted the bath be drawn and taken to her rooms as she requested. I thought it odd – like something a witch would do. Is she that, Juliann? Did she cure herself with sorcery?"

Juliann spun to face him. "How could you suggest such a thing? Did I not say that she is worthy and good? Did I not say that the duchess stayed by her side?"

Francis could not endure Juliann's displeasure when they saw one another so seldom. "'Twas but a jest, my sweet." He removed the pins from her hair, allowing it to fall around her shoulders, He smiled at her beauty.

Juliann laughed. "Now look what you've—" But as Francis had covered her mouth with his own, she could not finish her sentence.

****

By the time Anise had awakened, daylight had been replaced by night. The fire in the hearth reflected upon the walls and softly illuminated the tapestries that in the low light looked more like paintings than woven threads. The bed curtains were open, and there was a candle on a table beside her. Beneath the covers, her hand clutched the tote bag that contained all her secrets.

With a soft footfall, Cecily stepped into view. She wore her black nun's habit and held a rosary.

"You are much improved," said the duchess.

Anise nodded.

"You must be hungry. I shall send for some broth."

Anise did not want her to leave. She wondered about the rosary. "Have you been praying?"

The duchess smiled. "Certes, my dear. I am a nun. I ask God to restore your health."

A lump rose in Anise's throat. "Everyone is so kind – especially you."

Cecily sat down on the bed, her expression serene. "Please know I pray for you not because I believe you are my son's last hope. I do so because, in these past days, I have grown fond of you, Anise. I wanted to tell you that before I go."

Anise's heart sank. "Go?"

"In a few days' time, I return to Berkhamsted. I am an old woman and long for my home. I shall leave Dame Juliann behind to attend you. She will accompany you to Nottingham. Do not worry, dear. Before I go, I shall remind the king of your search for your brother – although I do not believe he has forgotten. Then, when you are well, you might try to accomplish our mission, if God wills it."

Beneath the covers, Anise rubbed her thumb over the ring to ensure it was still there. "Does His Grace know that I've been ill?"

Cecily smiled. "'Twas the king who saw to fulfilling your summons without question, even to me. The news of your recovery has spread through the castle." She paused. "And my son has told me how relieved he is that by God's grace you are well again. He wants to see you. He asked to be sent for as soon as you are able."

Anise could not speak. Tears threatened. "I'm much better, m'lady." There was understanding in the duchess' eyes. "I would like to see him soon, too – at His Grace's convenience, of course."

A look of compassion passed over Cecily's face. "I'll send for your supper. Once you have eaten, Richard shall be sent for."

"Thank you," Anise whispered.

****

After her meal, Anise tried to stay awake, but the crackling of the flames in the hearth and a full stomach lulled her to slumber. When she opened her eyes, she caught a glimpse of a shadow on the wall.

"Is that you, Madam?" Her words were thick with drowsiness.

The figure in the room moved into view and she came fully awake. "Your Grace!" she sat up in the bed. "I did not expect for you to come so soon."

Richard was richly dressed in a jeweled doublet of purple velvet and black hose that disappeared at the ankles into pointed shoes. The rings on his hands glimmered in the firelight.

He smiled nervously. "I came as soon as I heard you were better. I hope... you do not mind?"

Anise's mouth went dry.

"My mother informed me of your recovery. Did she say how grateful I was for it?"

Startled, Anise did not know how to answer. She sensed his strong attraction for her through the ring, and was taken aback. "Where... where is the duchess?"

"She has retreated to the chapel. Damsel Juliann is beyond the door. Are you in need of her?"

Anise shook her head. "I-I..."

Richard seemed embarrassed, seemed to be searching for the right words. "I know 'tis improper to come into a lady's bedroom unescorted. 'Tis not usually my way to flagrantly take advantage of my position. But, well... I-I wanted to see you – I mean, see for myself that you are better. You do not mind?"

Anise smiled. "No – I'm happy that you're here." Goose bumps covered her arms. This was fever of another kind.

He approached the bed. "I am glad." His voice was soft. He found her hand, which was resting at her side, and held it tenderly. Anise could not take her eyes off his face. But Richard gazed only at his hand holding hers. "'Your call for the bath – my household cannot stop talking of it. Are you a healer?"

Her voice came out in a hoarse whisper. "I-I witnessed it in my travels… in another country… far away."

"'Tis a miracle." The king raised the back of her hand to his lips. "I was so worried."

His eyes found hers, and she saw the relief in them.

The floodgates of his emotions fell open, and Anise could not tell where her affection for him ended and his for her began. Her mouth fell open, but she could not speak. Richard whispered, "Say nothing." He sat on the bed and leaned toward her, and Anise welcomed his lips on hers. She rested her hand on his shoulder as his mouth devoured her, falling backward into forever as their doubled passion blissfully engulfed her.

Then it was over. Richard rolled his affection up inside himself. "Forgive me. I should not." His words were abrupt. He straightened, began to get up. "I have no right."

Anise's hand was still on his shoulder. She would not let him go. "I do not mind, Your Grace. I—I..." The words caught in her throat. "Please – stay."

Surprise lit the king's face, and the tenseness around his mouth relaxed. He took her hand from his shoulder and held it between his. "Jesu, sweet lady. What 'tis it I'm feeling?"

His confusion mingled with her desire. Their eyes met. She longed for him to take her in his arms.

Richard squeezed her fingers. "Tell me of your life. Mine is an open book, but yours is a sweet mystery that I long to unravel."

Anise's breathing quickened. How could she tell him of her life? He would never believe her. "I-I cannot tell you," she whispered. "I do not remember much... yet."

Richard considered her for a long while. Had she offended him with her refusal? Seeming to make some decision, he kissed her hand – but stopped with an incredulous look.

Oh, God – he's seen the ring! She almost pulled her hand away, but did not. How would that look? She stared, stunned to silence, as he ran his thumb over the face of the ring, comparing it with the one on his own hand, and at last found her eyes.

"Where did you get this?" His voice was soft – but it was Richard the King speaking, not Richard, the man who desired her.

She forced the words through her dry mouth. "I was wearing it when my brother found me – but I don't know anything about it."

His face hardened. Anise was sure he did not believe her. But as he looked upon her, his expression relaxed as if he'd read her mind. He held his own hand up so she could see. The ring he wore on the third finger of his left hand was identical to hers. On its face, she could clearly make out the figure of a man holding a sphere and scepter.

"There was but one other person who had a ring such as this. Anne, my queen. 'Tis buried with her."

There was a revelatory light in his eyes. Anise could not make out what emotion he was feeling, but it was strong. Her analysis went no further, for he brushed a loose strand from her eyes and ran his palm over her hair until her heart raced with longing.

"So much are we alike, dark one, that I wonder at it. Both of us have lost brothers. Both wear similar rings." He paused, his voice thick. "Both of us are a stranger to our own times, and out of place in the world."

Anise quivered at how close he had come to the truth. Was his ring giving him the same kind of insight she had? She should look away – but could not, so lost was she in his eyes.

The next words he said almost under his breath, "Has destiny led us to this moment, Anise?"

She was stunned. The thought had not occurred to her. Had fate brought them together for a reason? Was there a sense to all this she could not see?

"I was drawn to you from the moment I found you in the woods," he whispered. "We must discover the reason for this – connection." He spoke urgently. "We will find your brother. He might have the answer."

Anise froze at the mention of Dominic. Their moment was gone. She wanted him to take her in his arms, but he did not. Richard got to his feet. Anise caught his hand but could not say the thing she wanted to – that everything would be all right. Because it would not. She knew what destiny had in store for him.

CHAPTER EIGHT

"Are you mad? If we tell him about this, he shall never sail!" Morton stared at the pinch-faced woman seated beside him. "Henry must believe all is well, or he'll never challenge Richard."

With a glare, Margaret got up and stood before the hearth of her private, paneled rooms at her husband's residence, Lathom Hall. "But all is not well," she said as much to the fire as to him. "Your so-called Great Glendower is powerless. Should my son sail now, his troops might well be obliterated by the king's army. I cannot risk his life. I will not. He is our only hope," she paused, "and he is my only son."

Morton searched for the words to end this disagreement, but could find none. He went to the lady, smoothing his palm over the taut arch of her shoulder, but her posture was unbending. With both hands, he massaged the muscles. "Dearest one, we must ride this momentum. If Richard remains on the throne another year, we might never be able to dislodge him. The rumors we've so diligently spread shall die down and the citizens will support him. No matter how big an army Henry raises, it will never be enough. Do you wish our efforts to have been in vain? Think of our efforts, Margaret."

Lady Stanley began to relax beneath his touch, her ire waning. She turned to face him, laying her head upon his chest.

"But my son…"

"He shall prevail," said Morton. "Jasper is an able commander. And your husband shall bring the woman with the ring to us. In two days' time, Owain shall regain his lost power. Success will be ours. "

Margaret stiffened. "Do not call Thomas my 'husband.' 'Tis in name only. He is inept and weak. 'Twill be a miracle if he does not botch this."

"Give him more credit, my love. He is a capable man." Morton experienced a deep satisfaction at her pronouncement, but could afford to be generous. He kissed her neck and drew her close. When she tilted her face toward his, he lovingly traced the worry lines at the corner of her mouth. "Stanley and Glendower shall prevail. When the battle ensues, Henry cannot lose, though he doubts it himself. Should he suspect a problem on our end, he shall never leave France." His voice fell to a whisper, "Promise me you won't alert him." Their lips met, and Morton felt the iron-willed Margaret melt beneath his passion. They parted, and he looked into her eyes. "Promise."

"Yes, *yes*."

Morton smiled and pulled her to him once more.

****

The king closed his eyes, pinching the area between them with his fingers, attempting to massage away the headache settled there. He had worked through the day until well past dusk, trying to drive the significance of this date from his mind. At mid-morning, the discussion with his counselors over the best method to disseminate news of Henry Tudor's landing stretched overlong and grew tiresome. All concurred that the Pretender's uncle, Jasper Tudor – the true commander of the forces – would sail the fleet to Wales, his home country and full of rebels supporting their fellow Welshmen's cause. By late afternoon, the king and his counselors determined the placement of the Royal forces, with Francis Lovell to go to the south coast to monitor the organization of the navy. Richard was sorry his friend's departure would need to be soon.

Evening saw the conference break for supper and devotions, yet the king toiled on. He accepted wine and a few bites of food at his desk as he wrote to those commanding and supplying forces for the battle. Nothing must go amiss nor any potential supporter overlooked. Tudor, the thorn in his side, must be plucked out and Richard's reign made peaceful.

With this battle, it must be finished – forever. The king was tired of pain, tired of grief. One more betrayal would undo him.

But Richard could not go on at this pace – not with this pain lodged in his brow. He sealed the letter, now dried, and drank deep from his goblet. His limbs had grown stiff in the room's evening chill. The fire had gone out and he had not even noticed. He took another swallow. The wine warmed him. Still he could not chase the day's ghosts from his mind. Would he never forget? Did he want to?

He thought of Anise. At prayer that morning, she had seemed fully recovered from the fever. He asked his mother of this, as she made preparation for her return to Berkhamsted, and she reassured him the lady was indeed well. Cecily's words came with a knowing smile. She touched her cheek to his in farewell, as was her usual manner. He saw with surprise that her eyes were brighter than usual and he gave her a gentle hug.

"Godspeed, *Maman*. We shall be together again soon."

The duchess blinked. "Remember Richard, always have you been my dearest. May God keep you safe." She kissed his forehead and was gone.

The meeting had underscored the pain today held for him.

Yet he had one thing to be thankful for – death had spared Anise. Her presence in his castle soothed him. He recalled her lips on his.

He remembered with regret how he had pulled away from her and how they had parted.

The ache in his forehead echoed through his heart. He poured more wine from the flask and drank.

Guilt had prevented him from taking her, though he'd wanted to. In the months since Anne's death, he had set aside that which his flesh craved. He refused to seek refuge in the arms of another woman. Would that not betray Anne's memory more than all else?

And yet, it had been all he could think of since finding Lady Anise in the woods.

Richard recalled his mother's shocking advice – to lay his wife's ghost to rest and love again.

But without the possibility of marriage, would a union with Anise be anything more than the selfish satisfaction of carnal desires? All he could offer her was the life of a concubine. To marry a woman of common birth, as his brother had, would serve only to remind everyone of the bitter legacy of the Woodville brood. He would not do that to England. His first loyalty must be to the kingdom. To see his beloved land torn apart once more by factions taking sides against an inappropriate queen was unconscionable. Should Richard marry again, it must be beneficial to his country. A sovereign did not have the luxury of acting on emotion.

He could not treat Lady Anise with such unworthiness.

Richard took another swallow of wine. His headache had retreated, a pleasant fuzziness taking its place.

The room no longer seemed cold, though the night had worn on. As futile as it seemed, Richard knew he should try to sleep. He doubted whether he could shake the ghosts of this anniversary from his mind. His memory's sprites would call for him in his nightmares.

As he stood considering, a knock came at the door. "Dickon, 'tis Francis." The door creaked open. "Are you busy?"

Richard shook off his reverie. "Come in. I thought I should retire – though I doubt I will find much solace there."

Francis appeared uneasy. "Pray, do not seek it in Lady Wynford's bed."

Richard wondered at his friend's motives for such a bold statement. "Why would you think her my bedmate?" As he said it, he felt his face flush.

"You give yourself away, Dickon. I have seen it. We have all seen it – when you speak to her, when you look at her. Do you think that your visit to her sickbed went unnoticed?"

This angered him. "I was concerned for her. I committed no indiscretion. Think you that I would take to bed a woman barely recovered from the fever?"

"Of course not," Francis answered quickly. "But you cannot deny your attentiveness toward her. She is the first woman since the queen at whom you have even glanced. Dickon, 'tis in your eyes, even as we speak."

Why should this upset him? Why could he not simply admit it? Richard stared into his goblet. "'Tis true. I do care. Why does it matter?"

Francis' posture relaxed, glad to have at last gotten at the truth. "We know nothing of her."

The king sighed. "Fate has brought her to me, Francis. Though you may not believe it, we are much alike. Anne's memory does not haunt me so much since Anise has come – she brings comfort to my heart."

"Fate? Richard, you never believed in such—"

"We wear identical rings." He showed Francis his hand. "Anne wore one like mine. The Lady Wynford wears one, too."

Francis gazed askance. "Does that not make you suspicious? Who presented you and Anne with those rings? Buckingham! Does your good mother not believe them cursed? This woman is obviously a spy or a witch – why have you not thrown her from the castle? You did not treat your brother's harlot, Jane Shore, with as much charity when she was accused of sorcery! She sat imprisoned for weeks!" Francis threw up his hands. "Since her trick with the cold water, there has been talk of sorcery. Juliann tells me the lady took a fever remedy that she would not let anyone see. And at prayer this morning, I watched her. She repeats none of the litany. She moves her mouth, so those who are nearby believe she prays – but she speaks not one word! I tell you, Richard, she is up to no good."

Richard grew angry. The wine made it easier to voice. "I trust the lady because she has done nothing to deserve mistrust. The ring, I cannot explain. But this idle gossip you repeat to me is profane. Are you forgetting how cruel rumors have damaged my own reputation and hinder my ability to rule?"

Francis flinched at the king's words, but Richard had not yet spent his rage. "The lady has done nothing wrong but save herself – she learned some healing arts in her travels. Have you not noticed her odd manner of speech? Whether or not I choose to take her to my bed is none of your concern. Do not interfere – nor plague me further with gossip. You may go."

Francis' face went white, but he hesitated only a moment before asking, "How many times must you be betrayed before you stop trusting the wrong people?" With that, he was gone.

The confrontation made Richard shake with fury – then regret. Francis's reminder of how many times he'd been betrayed – and how many of those traitors, once friends, he'd been forced to put to death – splayed his soul open to the one image he'd repressed all day: the face of his son, cold in death – not newly dead, and peaceful – but lying in his dark grave, the flesh falling from his once-beloved face, empty sockets where laughing gray eyes once were. It was God's punishment for Richard's unconscionable acts since his brother's death.

Richard could not shake it. He took a long pull from the flask. One year ago today he had first conjured up that horrible image representing his life.

****

Anise's eyes flew open, her sleep disturbed. She could not see through the darkness, but sensed something.

Something sinister.

She glanced through the bed curtains, which she'd left slightly parted, and called for Juliann, who slept nearby – before she remembered she was not here. The maid had caught Anise's flu. Mabel refused Anise's help, and Juliann was being tended to elsewhere. Anise offered to do without an attendant for a few nights so Juliann received the benefit of an extra pair of hands.

Anise touched the ring anxiously, immediately sensing its power. A strange vibration crept up her arm, as if the ring was reacting to something – or someone – nearby. Anise could not see anything in this darkness. Lighting a candle was out of the question; she dared not move.

A shimmer on the wall formed into a glowing mist. The steady volt of energy made her arm go numb. Anise stared in horror as the mist crept toward her.

The memory returned with a shock – floating in that place absent of sight and sound, lost somewhere in time. She'd had only a sliver of awareness, more like intuition – and even that had ebbed as she was smothered, absorbed – devoured. Anise shuddered. *It was coming for her again!*

The mist halted a few feet from the bed. "You are the one."

Anise's mind boggled. *It was speaking to her?*

"Give me the ring, and you shall be spared."

"I remember you," she whispered. "Leave me alone!"

"Do what I say, and you shall be returned to your own time."

She shook her head.

"If you help me, I'll help you."

"I don't believe you." Anise was stalling. She touched the ring, trying to gauge the truth with her intuition. *It's lying!*

The mist knew what she'd done and boiled angrily. "Hand it over!"

Anise inched backward on the bed. She'd never be able to save Richard if she gave this... this *thing*... the ring! "Keep away from me!"

The mist laughed. "It matters not that you come willingly. I shall have it – if not now, then when you become my bride. I am pleased you are so lovely, so... virginal."

Repulsed at the thought, Anise braced for its icy touch.

A knock sounded on her door. The mist evaporated.

Her body clammy with fear, Anise exhaled, relief surging through her. The knock came again, and she leapt from her bed, pulling on her robe. Even Lord Stanley was preferable to that horror.

Unbolting the door, she peered through the crack. "Who is it?"

"'Tis I. Richard." His voice was unsteady, his words slurred. He held a flask. Anise let him in.

"'Tis late, I know," he apologized, his hand reaching for the wall to steady himself. "And I am... not myself." He entered the room and fell into a chair near the hearth. "Might I tarry here a few moments, m'lady?"

He was drunk. It did not matter. He was here – with her. His presence set her stomach fluttering. A shiver ran through her, and she pulled the edges of her robe together.

The king leaned toward the glowing embers, his elbows on his knees. Searching for something to occupy herself, she retrieved one of the irons and poked at a log. She could feel how closely he watched her.

"Please," he said, motioning her to a nearby chair. "I am in my cups, but mean no harm." He dropped his gaze to the floor. "On the way to my chambers, my mind wandered far from my path. I found myself here. Did I wake you?"

Anise sat down gingerly, found her voice. "Your Grace—" she faltered. The hour of the night, the fright from the specter's visitation – Richard's nearness – left her off balance. Now, through the ring, she sensed his despair. *And something else.* She meant to look away, to lessen the power of the ring – but she could not tear her gaze from his face.

Richard felt her stare, turned toward her.

Anise's heart pounded. *God, he shakes me up.* "I'm glad you have come, Your Grace. I've just awakened from a bad dream."

"Call me Richard."

She swallowed hard, forcing herself to conversation. "I can tell you are uneasy. What disturbs you so… Richard?" Her voice shook.

He averted his gaze to stare into the fire. "The date is one I care not to mark, yet my mind will linger on nothing else."

Anise did not know her history as well as she'd thought – had no idea what today's date might mean. Nor could she bring herself to ask.

Richard supplied her with the answer anyway: "On this day last year, I visited my son's grave for the first time."

Anise took a breath. "Your Grace, I'm…"

"Word of his death had come to us much sooner – but when I saw where he lay deep within the ground, I truly comprehended that he was gone. We had been separated much." The words caught in his throat. "I imagined his sweet face, so very dear to me, encased in cold stone, ravaged by decay. I will never forget what my mind conjured up at that moment. That was the day I realized how I had doomed those that I loved." He fell silent.

She felt the rawness of his emotions as if they were her own. When she could not bear it any longer, his pain drew her. Unable to stop herself, she got up and went to him. Touching his broad, straight shoulder with her hand, she mused on Shakespeare's portrayal of him, crippled and grotesque. How had the playwright gotten it so wrong?

Richard's gaze was fixed on the fire. "My decision to become king, to depose my nephew, Edward, has brought only despair. And so I've incurred God's wrath. For what else could it mean? I've lost my son and my wife. My reign signifies the end of many hopes, loyalties – lives. Blood stains my hands, I cannot deny. I've have betrayed all my brother stood for. I've become that which I hate most – a traitor, like all the rest." He shook his head. "Had I not insisted upon the invalidity of Edward's marriage, upon the bastardy of his heirs. Had I only turned the realm over to the Woodvilles, perhaps my family might have survived – and Ned's sons..." His voice trailed off.

Anise's hand remained on his shoulder. She did not know what to say. From that first horrible day, when she realized she was lost in time, Richard had offered his compassion when he had not needed to. Yet he gave it gladly. His forthrightness, his honesty, touched her. In return, she empathized with the tragedy of his life – of how keenly he clung to his duty, although he was reviled by his citizens, now and forever.

Historians wrote how he'd killed his nephews in cold blood to seize the crown. Anise knew that it could not be true. Despite what he seemed to be confessing to, Richard would never have committed such an act of betrayal to his brother's memory.

Anise's heart twisted with his pain. She loved him. She'd tried not to, but there was no denying it.

"You weren't the cause of their deaths," she whispered, embracing him. "Their blood is not on your hands. You might be a king, but you're not God – only He knows the reasons. You could never have killed your brother's sons. The history books have played a cruel trick on you, Your Grace."

The battle drew near. A king that no one, even through history, would ever truly know, would fall to his death beneath a traitor's ax. With a gasp, she released him and stepped away, tears running down her face. She heard him rise – and he was behind her. He took her arms and gently turned her to face him in the firelight.

His expression relaxed as he looked into her eyes. Concern for her drew him from his misery. Anise could take little consolation from this. How could she, knowing what was going to happen to him?

He ran his fingers over her cheek, wiping her tears. "Do you cry for me?"

Anise's breath caught in her lungs. "You're suffering and I wish you weren't."

"What did you mean by the 'history books'?"

Anise could only answer with more sobs.

The king wrapped her in his arms, held her close, smoothed her hair. "I am not worthy of your sorrow."

She caught her breath. "Richard."

"Anise," he whispered, bending her name to his medieval tongue. His emotions, amplified through Glendower's ring, washed over her until she could not tell his desire from her own. He claimed her mouth, pitching her into a sensuous whirlpool.

With a moan, she looped her hands behind his neck and opened her mouth at his demand. Their tongues collided and danced, sending tendrils of sensation through her body. They kissed until breathless, and when at last they parted, Richard gazed into her face so lustily that Anise's insides throbbed with need. Lifting her into his arms with ease, the king carried her to the bed and lay beside her. He smoothed his hand over her cheek, and captured her mouth again, his lips caressing hers first gently, then hungrily. She fell back into the bliss of having him so close, touching her with such intimacy, feeling the energy surging between them, succumbing to the pleasure.

Richard pulled away abruptly. She opened her eyes to find him sitting on the edge of the bed, the firelight illuminating his taut expression. "I am not my brother – I will not force myself on you."

"Richard," she breathed. "You're not."

"Certes, how I want you," he exhaled heatedly. He turned to face her. "The truth of the thing is this: I can never make you my wife. And I will not lead you into this sin."

Even on the brink of sex, he was gallant. He did not know how little time he had left. Anise did not want to think of that. What she wanted was Richard. Her inexperience unnerved her. She felt the prickle of tears behind her eyes. She would not cry – not now. Not when she wanted him so badly.

Not when she knew her tears would stop him.

There was no way – not when she knew this might be their only chance. "Don't worry for my soul. This is my decision, too."

"Anise."

She urged him to lie back. "Come to me." She wove her fingers through his hair and kissed him.

He wrapped her in his arms, his lips pressed to her ear. "This feeling overwhelms me. I cannot fight it."

Magnified by the ring's powers, Anise floundered in emotion. "Then don't."

Richard groaned helplessly at her words, ran his hands over her thin gown, exploring her body, cupping her breasts, caressing her hips tenderly. His lowered his mouth to her stomach, lingering there, savoring the intimacy. When he got up, Anise nearly protested – before realizing what he was doing. Breathlessly, she watched him undress, his body a lean silhouette against the firelight. White heat coursed through her at the sight of his naked approach, his member rigid with anticipation of her. When he pulled her against his firm body and parted her knees, Anise repositioned herself beneath him. He gazed at her from beneath hooded eyes. "Wait – are you a maiden?"

Anise's face went hot. She nodded.

Richard kissed her, urging her mouth open with his tongue, consuming her lips. His hand worked between their bodies, diving lower to slide his fingers into her slick center. As he massaged her core, Anise moaned at the pleasure ripping through her.

Richard took her to the brink of ecstasy before shifting atop her, entering her with a firm but gentle shove. She cried out in surprise at the sensation of his manhood filling her – her own self explorations had not been so bold.

"Be brave, my sweet – I shan't go on 'til you're ready." His words were rife with restraint, but he could not honor them. With a groan, he thrust into her a moment later. In his urgency, his hands caressed her breasts. When he captured her lips, Anise opened to him above and below, matching the rhythm of his need. As he spoke her name, white heat ripped through her, and what had been discomfort became pleasure. She reveled in his tender caresses and the moist touch of his mouth against her skin. But soon the searing heat of their passion swept even that from her mind and their bodies became one. Through a whirlpool of emotion, she heard Richard's feral cry, and the rush of their combined passion carried them to ecstasy.

****

Richard slumbered beside her in the darkness, but Anise could not sleep. Their night of lovemaking done, she was loathe to give up this bliss to sleep.

Listening to the steady rhythm of Richard's breathing, Anise realized she'd given him another gift: relief from the insomnia she'd heard people whisper of. Reaching over to caress his cheek, his hair, his shoulder – she could hardly believe what had happened. She was no longer a virgin. She'd made love with a king – a king who wanted her. She wondered what her mother would have to say about that.

She loved Richard so much, it was incredible. As she thought of the joy they'd experienced together, tears prickled behind her eyes. It could not last, could it? History was non-negotiable.

Or was it? Anise found his hand through the blankets. There it was – the ring. Was Cecily right? Did Glendower's creation somehow work against Richard? The one on her hand had power. If she thought she'd been imagining it, the appearance of that unholy mist had cured that misconception.

But what powers did Richard's ring have? Not the same gift of empathy, surely – or he could have easily seen through the lies of those who'd betrayed him.

If Cecily was right – if the ring Richard wore was cursed – perhaps Anise could alter history. For if Richard could discern who was loyal and who was not, he would have the advantage.

This might be her only chance. She had promised the duchess.

If this really worked – if Richard won the battle at Bosworth instead of Henry Tudor, what would the future be like? Would the world she went back to – if she ever saw it again – be totally different? What would it be like without Henry Tudor's son, Henry VIII's, break from Catholicism, or the legacy of Elizabeth I and the defeat of the Spanish Armada, which transformed England into a superpower of the Renaissance?

Would the reality she grew up in never exist because she loved a king?

As she lay beside Richard, his warm skin touching hers, his words of tenderness echoing in her ears, she made her decision. The thought of him lying dead on a battlefield froze her soul. If she could stop it, she would. If giving Richard an edge over his enemy would help him, she must do it.

Making the exchange was easy. His ring slipped from his hand easily. The one she returned to his finger went on just the same, magically adjusting to fit him.

She missed her ring immediately. The world of emotions closed to her again. She considered what Richard's unlucky ring would do to her life. Anise touched her lips to Richard's forehead and never looked back.

She slept. When she opened drowsy eyes into the light of the morning, Anise was alone.

CHAPTER NINE

Though just after dawn, the king already paced the floor in his study. He felt more refreshed than he had in months. He had a slight headache – the after effects of too much wine – but it did not compare to how he usually felt after a night of insomnia.

It had been the sound sleep that follows lovemaking – there was no substitute.

His conscience panged and he stopped pacing. A woman without a dowry might marry well if her maidenhead was intact. Yet the king had taken this from her without a proposal. All he offered was protection – and that only in the near term. The image of Anise and the light in her eyes clung to the edges of his memory. They had both been a bundle of nerves, it being the first time he had been with a woman in a year; and Anise, but a maiden. Even now, he shivered to remember the taking of her virginity. As he recalled her touch and her words, his desire for her blazed within him. His pulse raced thinking about it. He longed to feel her moving beneath him once more. Had he it to do over, Richard would have again chosen to bed her.

The thought of Anise being with another man did not please him. Yet it was all but impossible for him to take her to wife – especially now, after what she'd done while he'd slept.

"Why, Anise? Why did you take the ring and leave this one in its place?" His words echoed in the silence of the morning.

Had she done it as a gesture of love to stand for a promise never made? Or was she, as Francis suggested, a Lancastrian spy? Had she played him for a fool from the moment she'd wandered into his room at Berkhamsted? Was she here on behalf of Henry Tudor, to distract him from the battle by taking him to her bed?

Wouldn't switching rings only call attention to her subterfuge?

Another possibility occurred to him. This thought sent a shudder through his soul. Repulsed at the idea, he sank dejectedly into the chair at his writing table.

Had Francis been right? Was Anise a witch?

According to his mother, the ring had been forged by the wizard, Owain Glendower. What if Anise wanted that ring for herself? Remembering what he'd seen in her eyes and how she'd called his name, Richard could not believe it was so. Yet what if she had cast an enchantment on him? Perhaps his affection for her was an illusion. Maybe she did not care for him at all, but viewed him with contempt.

He looked again at the ring. She had to know he'd recognize the difference. Why would she risk allowing him to know she had a duplicate by wearing it? None of this made sense.

Yet her deception pierced him. He had taken comfort in her, but now feared the falseness of her heart. Still, he could not shake the longing he had to once again feel her body entwined with his. God help him, he loved her. He refused to believe it was witchcraft.

His thoughts swirled with speculation – but that's what it was… conjecture. Her actions did not necessarily signify a betrayal or witchcraft. Did Anise not deserve the benefit of the doubt?

Still, he would not confront her about the ring forthright. Richard determined to wait and see what she did next.

****

A page stood at the Lord Stanley's door, announcing the arrival of a young man in country livery. This missive had been forever in coming.

"Jack, good fellow. 'Tis good to see a face from home. Come in." Stanley grasped the man's shoulder and pulled him into his room, bolting the door behind him. The steward did not stand on ceremony. "What word have you from my wife?"

"Here, m'lord." Jack nervously pulled a letter from within his doublet. "She hath told me to return with your answer."

Stanley grunted and threw a sour look Jack's way, as if that would be his answer. He tore open the parchment.

My dearest husband,

Your correspondence regarding the Lady Anise of Wynford and her adornment has been most welcome. After conferring with the Good Bishop on the matter of which you wrote, he Requests Urgently your conveyance of Lady Wynford to Lathom – as soon as possible. Our plans have been thwarted for now, but Master Glen sees no reason that his marriage to the Lady Wynford should not proceed by month's end.

Yours ever in obedience,
Margaret.

Scoffing at his wife's salutations, Stanley was not at all put off by her cryptic tone, but discerned his wife's meaning immediately. Lady Wynford had overstepped with the ring. Margaret wanted her – and the ring – returned to her. Apparently the lady knew too much.

Stanley smiled to think his wife had miscalculated, and considered the punishment in store for Lady Anise: marriage to a grizzled old sorcerer risen from the grave after a hundred years.

So a return to the living aroused a craving in Owain Glendower for a wife? This did not surprise Stanley. The flesh is a powerful master. His thoughts returned to Margaret.

He would have given her the world; all she wanted was an errand boy. Now she expected him to escort the virginal bride to Lathom. He hoped the lady's purity was not a requirement for the wedding night. To bestow such virginal flesh upon a shriveled old wizard... why, 'twas a waste. Stanley remembered how it felt running his hands over her velvet skin.

Besides having a fair wench in his bed, Stanley might find other uses for Anise. If the lady could command the ring, perhaps the two of them could use it for their own mutual benefit – he to grab more power without Margaret's interference and she to avoid betrothal to an old man. Stanley had no doubt he could prevent Glendower from ever claiming his bride.

He looked forward to persuading Anise to his plan, remembering her fiery refusal of him. His loins tightened. He *would* convince her.

Once Anise was conquered, Stanley would have power over Margaret – and how delicious to have outwitted his wife at her own game.

He looked up to find Jack watching him, waiting patiently for an answer. "Tell Lady Stanley I shall fulfill her request as soon as I can."

Jack nodded and was gone.

Before the door was closed, Stanley received another visitor.

"What have you seen?" he demanded of the gnomish servant standing there.

"Only the king himself, m'lord. Leaving the chambers of the lady at dawn, looking very refreshed after spending the night there." He grinned.

Stanley guffawed and slapped the man's back. "Well done!" He pulled a coin from a leather pouch on the table and gave it to the knave.

Closing the door after his spy, Stanley reveled in this turn of events. Old Glendower shan't like the idea that his betrothed was the king's concubine. Better yet, Stanley would not be blamed for bedding her first.

He strode to the hearth, tossed in the parchment and watched it burn.

****

"This be too much, Dickon."

Richard looked up from his writing at Francis, who stood before him, face stricken with grief.

"The fever hath taken Juliann." Lovell's face was drawn. He had not slept.

"I am sorry. You were close to her." Richard sensed his friend's sadness – almost as if it were his own.

"I-I loved her, Dickon." Francis' voice was ragged.

"Let us pray that the fever does not take other lives," said Richard quietly. "What did Hobbys say?"

Francis nodded. "He did what he could. He believes these might be isolated cases."

"She was a kind gentlewoman. Her family hath been loyal to York. My mother told me Juliann tended to Lady Anise with much devotion." He paused. "Has she been told?"

His friend tensed. "'Tis why I am come."

Richard knew Francis' worry, his grief – and fear, also. He looked into Francis' eyes and saw that it was the truth. Where had this knowledge come from?

"My doubts about the lady are known to you." Francis braced for Richard's reaction, but the king only stared at him, dumbfounded by the emotions he was feeling – emotions that were not his own.

The viscount continued uneasily, "What if Juliann had information about Lady Anise she'd rather not have generally known? T'would be to her benefit if Juliann died from the fever."

The king forced his concentration to what Francis was saying – and realized his friend's fear was rooted in the loss of his lover. Did Francis think the same thing would happen to Richard? He reined in his anger. "I know you suffer, Francis. I even know *how* you suffer. But what Juliann would have seen, so did my mother. Cecily does not think Anise is a danger or she would have told me." Richard realized his words were disingenuous; he suspected Anise as well, though he was reserving judgment – for now.

Francis's fear lessened at hearing this logic.

Richard felt it.

His friend had been afraid for him – but perhaps he had been a little afraid of his reaction, as well. T'would be little wonder, considering how he'd treated Francis the evening before. "I should not have behaved thus last night," said Richard quietly. "The wine muddled my head. Woe the day I treat my friends worse than my enemies."

The viscount's expression relaxed. Richard felt relief.

Francis' relief! 'Twas as if I was reading his mind!

"Dickon, do not think ill of me," interjected the viscount. "I have a plan. I swear 'tis not sorrow over Juliann, but concern for you at the bottom of this."

"I know that," said Richard. "What is this plan?"

"An observer to report to us. Juliann would never have agreed, yet whosoever attends Lady Anise in her place may not object, if we choose her well."

Richard gleaned Francis' meaning. "A damsel to watch the lady – is this what you suggest? To discern whether her actions reveal her to be a traitor?"

The viscount nodded. "A traitor – or a witch. I know of one lady who would do it with discretion, but I shan't go behind your back. You must give your consent."

The king took a breath and considered. He did not like the idea of spying on Anise – but what if Francis was right?

Richard's responsibility to England came before all else. He could not allow his emotions over a woman cloud his judgment. Was that not what Edward had done, so many times, leaving the kingdom in a shambles?

"You have my permission."

As the viscount nodded and left, Richard felt Francis' sense of satisfaction wash over him.

It was true then – he *had* read his friend's mind. With comprehension, the king stared in dismay at his hand. It had to be the ring.

****

Anise stood by the hearth in her room, studying the ring by firelight. Upon close inspection, its dissimilarities from Matthew's ring were apparent – this engraving was clearer.

There's no way Richard would not notice. What would he think? That she had tricked him into bed to get his ring? She felt sick. Of course he would – it was the obvious answer. The "why" hardly mattered; she'd deceived him.

At the time, it had seemed the right thing to do – switching the rings. Yet she might have ruined everything. Richard might never trust her again. Not only that, but without Matthew's ring, Anise might never get back to the twenty-first century.

She sank down on the bed and put her head in her hands. What had she been thinking? Why hadn't she found out more about this ring before acting?

The answer was obvious: because the opportunity presented itself.

Still, she should have looked for answers sooner. What she needed to know might have been in her possession the entire time.

Scrabbling beneath the mattress, she found her leather tote, which she'd kept carefully hidden. If anyone ever discovered her possessions, she'd be dead meat. Not only were there dates in her father's journal she'd have to explain, but having a book called "The Tragedy of Richard III" would not go over all that well, either. She pulled out the journal.

Opening the book, she began scanning for references to the ring. Only, all she found were references to herself.

April 6, 1997

Wynford, the fool! He's going to sue for custody. He can't let us be. He's going to ruin our lives if he can. And Gwen – she refuses to leave. She says she can talk sense into him. I'm living in a hotel. I can't even visit Anise. This has to end. If I thought I could get away with it, Wynford would be a dead man.

Anise closed her eyes. Why couldn't she remember more of her life in the old house? Why had her mother kept it all so hush-hush? Anise might have had more of a chance to reclaim her memories if they had talked about her childhood sometimes.

The diary fell shut. *Why did you deny me my own past, Mother?*

As she sat by the fire, Anise riffled over the flashes of memory she'd had of Matthew and Dominic and the few things she could recall about her life in the farmhouse, forgetting all about the ring and Richard.

Anise was pulled back into the moment when there was a tap on the door. She threw the book in her tote bag and shoved it under the mattress.

It was Mabel, head of the household staff. Her face taut with crying, she glared at Anise.

With a bad feeling, Anise forced herself to ask, "How is Juliann?"

Mabel frowned. "The fever hath triumphed, m'lady. Death hath taken Juliann. She is with God."

Anise was speechless. *Juliann, dead? From the flu?* Tears filled her eyes so quickly she could not stop them. If only they'd permitted her to look after Juliann! She could have used aspirin and another cold bath to fight the fever.

Mabel considered her. "You were not at devotions this morning. A prayer from one who benefited from Juliann's care was too much to ask?"

Anise heard the disapproval in Mabel's voice. "Of course I prayed for her."

"A Requiem Mass for Juliann is planned for the morrow," the maidservant said abruptly. "I am here to let you know that Alice will be attending you and remain with you henceforth."

After Mabel left, Anise thought about Mabel's manner with disquiet. Who else wondered why she had not gone to church? Had Richard noticed? Cold fear crept over her.

CHAPTER TEN

"'Tis time for the funeral, m'lady," said the damsel Alice. "Shall I retrieve your gown of mourning from the wardrobe?"

They had just returned from dinner, from which the king was again absent. Anise shared her trencher with Alice, who'd said little more than a few words to her since morning devotions.

Anise had dared not miss the pre-dawn prayers. She'd risen with all the other ladies before five to attend "Lauds" in the chapel, spending more than an hour on her knees moving her mouth to the Latin litany. She hoped no one noticed she did not know the words.

And she could not tell by empathy anymore – now that she no longer wore the ring, the world of others' emotions was closed off. Life in medieval times seemed more frightening than ever, especially with Cecily gone...

...and Juliann dead.

Anise shook her head. "I shall get the gown, Alice. Would you mind retrieving some wine for me?" she asked, hoping the maidservant would leave.

But the eyes of the fair-haired woman never stopped watching.

Alice had a quiet, observant manner, unlike Juliann, whose irrepressible temperament made her easy to know. And from the moment the damsel took her place with Anise, she had attended her ever-so-closely.

As much as Anise wanted to speak to the king since their encounter, there was no way – especially under Alice's watchful eye. The king had been absent from meals and at prayers. Anise had only caught a glimpse of him at the chapel, where he sat on the upper level reserved for only family and dignitaries. Though his own vantage point was good, he had not once looked her direction, intent only on his devotions.

But she certainly felt observed from other quarters. Besides Alice, Anise also caught Francis Lovell's glance and felt the burning stare of Thomas Stanley. Once, their eyes met across the chapel and Anise saw the corners of the lord's mouth turn up, sending a shiver of disgust through her.

As Anise rifled through the gowns in the wardrobe, it did not escape her notice that Alice had not moved. "Please. The wine. I must soothe my nerves before the Mass or I shall never get through it."

Alice reluctantly retreated to the outer room. Anise knew she had no time to lose. She rushed to the bed, removed the two books from her bag under the mattress and hurried back to the wardrobe to put them into the pockets of her black gown – the dress she was to have worn in the play back in her own time.

As she was pulling the dress from the hook, Alice returned. "Let me help you."

Anise escaped with the garment over her arm, and laid it on the bed. "Help me undress, Alice." She began unfastening her laces.

"Yes, m'lady." Annoyance was evident in her voice.

Once the gown she was wearing was off, Anise piled it into the damsel's arms. "Hang this up for me?" As she did this, Anise pulled on the black dress quickly, avoiding Alice's help – and her eyes. "If you could assist me with the ties, and then, please, pour me some of that wine?"

The woman stared at Anise, who realized – without help of the empathic ring – that Alice was looking for her to make a mistake. Anise was increased since Juliann's death. How was she ever going to find another opportunity to read her father's journal?

"There is no time for wine, m'lady," said Alice. "We must go or be late."

Anise hoped – *no, prayed* – that Richard would be at the chapel.

****

Lord Stanley signed the parchment, rolled it up and sealed it with his wax signet. With a terse smile and a gold coin from his pouch, he handed it to the knave who had served him so well the day before. He would now use that particular piece of information to drive his plan.

"Master Jennings should recognize my seal," said Stanley. "But see to it personally that this goes only into his hands."

The constable at Nottingham castle had been of great assistance to him in the past – provided the price was right. Stanley doubted not he would be useful this time, as well. A bit more insurance could not hurt, however. "Make sure Master Jennings understands this to be a matter of urgency. Tell him the whole country might be at risk if he fails – that the king needs this done. Do not forget to mention that he will be paid handsomely," he saw the look in the gnomish man's eye, "as will you yourself, when you return with his answer."

****

Anise and her attendant arrived early at the chapel, where members of the household were gathering for the Requiem service. *There must have been some way I could have saved her.*

Juliann had been well loved. Members of the household, staff and some of the noble ladies were attending.

Anise and Alice stood at the front of the chapel near Julian's coffin. Tears ran down Alice's face. Trying to comfort her, Anise reached out to touch her arm – but received such a glare she pulled back.

As she looked at the coarsely constructed pine box, Anise swallowed the lump in her throat. She could not help but feel guilty over Juliann's death. The maid had caught the fever from her, and she had not even tried to slip her some aspirin.

Anise shivered in the cold air of the stone church. The robed priest stood before them. *Why didn't he begin?* There was a commotion to the left. Anise stood on her toes to see. A dozen of the king's royal retainers joined others who had gathered in the nave.

Anise's chest constricted. Richard had come to pay his last respects to the woman who had helped save Anise's life. Within moments, Richard would be within sight, maybe even within speaking distance!

The drawn face of Francis Lovell appeared in the procession. He and several others filed into the pew beside hers. When their eyes met, Anise could see his were full of loathing for her.

He obviously blamed her for Juliann's death, too. But Francis Lovell was the king's right hand man – why was he so broken up over the loss of a lady-in-waiting?

Then it occurred to her: *Francis and Juliann? Uh-oh.*

Richard was there, too – not five feet away. He stood beside Francis, the grief for his friend revealed in his expression. Anise ached for him. She tried to read his feelings – but could not. The ring she wore did not give her that power. Richard was wearing...

What if she sent him a message? Would it work?

Anise reached deep inside herself, pouring out her heart. *I love you, Richard.*

The king lifted his gaze and caught her eye. Surprise transformed his expression. But the ceremony began and he had no choice but to turn away. Anise's heart sank as she forced herself to pay attention to the service and mouth along with the endless litany.

When the mass ended, the royal procession filed out. Richard never looked at her again. Her chance to speak to him was gone.

Richard was not at supper. Anise hoped for a message – but none came. She spent her evening with Alice in the company of other ladies of noble birth, who embroidered pillows and sang songs that Anise did not know the words to. Her out-of-placeness became more obvious every minute.

Alice never left her side when retiring to their rooms after Vespers. Anise never got to read the journal or look at her copy of "Richard III," that had, in the back pages, an encapsulated biography of Richard and his final days. Any little clue she could glean might help her prevent his death at Bosworth Field.

It was a slim hope. Alice never left the room as they made ready to bed down for the night. At this rate, Anise might never see the king again, let alone save him.

****

Lady Stanley made her way up the treacherous stairs to the crumbled top of the ruined tower, her laced garments cutting into her ribs, making it hard to breathe. She had ridden from Lathom Hall with her best servant, Jack, in the misty dawn, but left him tending the horses at the edge of the wood.

The mist that was Owain Glendower churned before her in the crisp air of the overcast morning. "What news?" it bellowed.

Margaret was more annoyed than disturbed by the wizard's loud demand. She had learned the cloud had no bite behind its bark. "I hath heard from my husband. He said he would bring the woman here as soon as he was able. I doubt not that he will. Then we can get on with it, at last."

The cloud swirled. "How soon? This vaporous state is a curse. I want the world again. I want bones, flesh, blood."

Margaret replied in a bored tone. "Lord Stanley must be discreet."

"I desire my betrothed – she is a chaste maid. I have seen her."

Lady Stanley worried about Glendower's obsession for this mysterious maiden with the ring, and harbored grave concerns about whether the wizard would toss aside her son's claim to the throne to run after his lithesome bride.

Glendower sensed this immediately. "You cannot hide your doubt from me. How dare you question my wisdom?"

Margaret was caught off guard. Glendower knew her thoughts. Was he a mind reader, as well as a wizard? Still, she would not be bullied by a cloud of mist. "My son, Henry Tudor, whom you promised to help – shall you uphold his cause?"

The cloud rumbled. "I was sovereign over this land once. Henry Tudor is a Welshman, therefore I shall see to it that Henry Tudor rules. Your son is my kin. Victory over England is victory for Wales – and for me."

"You are both of the same, great Welsh bloodline." Margaret knew it was true: Henry's grandfather Owen Tudor told her he was a distant cousin to Glendower. If only her son had inherited the wizard's powers.

Her thoughts turned inward. *Of all my husbands, 'twas only Edmund Tudor that I'd truly loved. The rest were merely necessary.*

"And John Morton? Do you love him?" Again, the mist had known her thoughts.

Margaret stumbled over her words. "W-we share the same purpose."

After a hesitation, Glendower said, "I thought not. I am like you. I marry for necessity. The wench is comely, to be sure, but I expect little in the way of other comforts. As for you, Margaret, we are of the same mind, you and I – are we not?"

Margaret's mind reeled. It was the first time the wizard had spoken her name. "Our minds are both shrewd," she agreed. *What was he getting at?*

"Shrewd, yes. But intelligent – fascinated with intrigue." Glendower drew out the last word seductively. "You could learn from me, and I from you."

Margaret knew she must remain calm at this turn of events, but his words thrummed through her.

"Our combined skills in sorcery would be formidable," he continued.

This turn of events was not one she had expected. To form an alliance with such a man – at least, when he became a man again – would place unlimited powers at her disposal! Compared to Morton, there was no contest.

Yet what of Morton? And of her husband, Thomas? And Glendower's bride-to-be, who must marry him to free the wizard from his unearthly form. "There are obstacles."

"You are concerned about my betrothed, but do not fear. Once the marriage is consummated, her existence is no longer necessary. Obstacles can be dealt with."

Margaret smiled. "Where do we begin?"

****

It was the sun, not Alice, that woke Anise the next morning. Her maidservant was nowhere in sight. Searching her rooms quickly, Anise discovered she was, indeed, alone.

She dressed herself in the black gown, fastening the laces as well as she could without assistance, and drew "The Tragedy of Richard III" from the pocket.

She got into bed and yanked the bed curtains closed. If ever discovered, this little book with its garish cover art would surely brand her as a traitor and witch. It depicted Richard in battle – losing.

She leafed to the back, where she found "Historical Background and Sources." She studied the diagram of the battlefield and memorized it the best she could. *Richard there, Tudor there, Stanley between them.*

Next she scanned the text: "August 7: Henry Tudor lands at Milford Haven, Wales, claiming to be descended from Cadwallader, the mythical king of Wales. In fact, his Welsh bloodlines originate from a union between Henry V's widowed French queen and Owen Tudor, a member of her household who was a cousin of the rebel, Owain Glendower."

Glendower – who forged the rings!

"I need more info on the battle," she murmured to herself, reading down the page. "Here—"

"On August 22, the battle ensued. As Richard and his small group of supporters charged for Henry Tudor's standard, Lord Stanley and his men swept upon his rear. Surrounded and unhorsed, Richard III died wielding his ax."

Anise swallowed hard as she read what was in store for Richard. She knew if she gave the king this information, the battle itself need never happen. His troops could be waiting for Tudor to land. They could drive him back before he ever got off the ship!

All Anise had to do was to show him these pages.

And convince him I'm from the future.

Even if he did believe her about *that* – which was highly doubtful – there's no way she'd escape being called a traitor if he ever read what Shakespeare wrote about him, describing him as a mass murderer and a hunchback.

She got an idea. She *could* do some damage control.

Grasping the dozen or so pages of the historical section, Anise carefully tore them from the binding and shoved them into her pocket. All she had to do now was burn the play, with its plastic-coated twenty-first century cover and Shakespeare's damning verses.

Too late!

Anise heard the door open. She shoved the book underneath the mattress just as Alice yanked open the bed curtains.

"What are you doing?" she asked.

"Did you think you would frighten the sleep out of me?" said Anise smoothly. "As you see, I am awake and dressed."

Annoyance crossed Alice's face. "I'm sorry, m'lady. I thought you might be ill. You sleep with the bed curtains parted, usually."

Anise released a breath.

"I went to answer a summons from the king. He has sent someone to deliver to you a message. He awaits outside."

Her heart pounding, Anise followed Alice to the outer apartment. Before her stood Viscount Lovell.

She curtseyed and looked at him in question.

Francis nodded at Alice, and she retreated into the other room. "I bring a message from His Grace," he said.

How much had Richard told this man? Did he know about the ring? Did he know they'd slept together? Anise trembled, but did not dare let Francis know she was afraid. She nodded.

In a terse voice, Francis said, "You are to accompany His Grace's personal entourage to the town of Coventry, to attend the Corpus Christi celebrations." Anise's heart leapt into her throat when he added, "The king has many questions for you."

Her mouth dry, she muttered, "Thank you, Viscount Lovell."

Through a muddle of emotions, Anise remembered to curtsey again. After a long, probing stare, he left.

What would the king ask her? What answers would she give?

CHAPTER ELEVEN

Francis Lovell paced his room, anger outweighing grief. Because of *that* woman, he'd lost Juliann. He stalked to the table by the fireplace and poured more of the unwatered wine. It had tasted sour at the beginning of the evening. Now he did not even notice.

Alice had learned nothing more of the Lady Anise. He did not doubt the vigilance of his spy – she was Juliann's sister. But he knew Anise was hiding something. Mostly likely, it was her practice of witchcraft. For how else had she managed to enchant the king? Richard never lost his head over a woman.

That was not entirely true. Richard had acted the fool when he fought with his brother, George, over Anne Neville. George, who was wed to Anne's sister, Isabel, had forbidden Richard to marry the recently widowed Anne, over whom he claimed guardianship – even though Anne had *wanted* to marry Richard, and Edward the King had given his permission. George had not wanted to lose Anne's half of the lands inherited by the two sisters from their father, Warwick. George hid Anne against her will until Richard came after him, threatened him and, at last, rescued Anne. In exchange for the woman he loved, Richard had handed over the inheritance to George to do with what he would.

Even Edward had been shocked at the lengths to which Richard went for Anne.

But that was not the end of it. Always short on patience, Richard again acted without care, marrying Anne – his first cousin – without waiting for the proper dispensation from the Pope to arrive from Rome. It was a needless risk for the gain of a few months of matrimony and could have resulted in Richard's excommunication.

Francis took another swallow of wine. Perhaps Richard was more like his impulsive brother than either of them wanted to admit. He had certainly fallen hard for this woman. Asking her to accompany him to the Corpus Christi celebrations to interrogate her was highly indiscreet.

He had only been a duke when courting Anne. Now he was a king. This time, there was too much to lose.

A knock on the door disturbed his thoughts. Unsteady on his feet, he went to answer it.

"Stanley. Come in."

"I have news about Lady Wynford."

Although he did not trust Stanley by a long shot, they had discussed Anise before. "I'm listening."

"I had a conversation with the king – about his need for female companionship."

Francis nodded. "I have talked to him about this, too." It was a conversation that played over in his mind often. "He has an interest in the lady you mention, but tells me he has not approached her."

The corners of the lord's mouth turned up. "You have not spoken to him recently, then. He was seen leaving the rooms of that very same lady at daybreak – two days ago."

Francis stared at Stanley. That had been the very night he had warned Richard against her. "How know you this?" He sat down heavily in a nearby chair.

"I was suspicious of her motives and had her watched. 'Twas for the king's good," said Stanley, defending his actions. "The king stayed in her room the entire night."

"Richard is not like his brother." Despite what had just been running through his mind, Francis knew the king's feelings ran deep. He did not bed women indiscriminately for pleasure.

But Francis had seen the state Richard was in over this woman. He had no choice but to believe what Stanley said was true. "This is not good."

"In this case, you are right," agreed Stanley. "There is too much about this woman we do not know. She is not as innocent as she would have us believe."

Against his better judgment, Francis filled Stanley in on his suspicions: how Anise had survived a fever that Juliann had not, how she did not repeat the litany during prayer, how she did not know the words to songs everyone knew. He said nothing about the identical rings, though. Francis did not trust the steward that far.

Even without the evidence of the rings, Stanley agreed with Francis' conclusion. "Sorcery. That must be it. He is under her spell. If that is true, we must act."

Francis nodded. The next words out of his mouth made him sick. "We must not tell Dickon."

****

The manor house belonging to the lord mayor of Coventry was large and fine, with its high, timber-framed roof and many glazed windows facing onto the main street.

The king sat in front of the largest window with his personal servants, members of the mayor's family, and Anise, seated in the chair next to his. By her side was her attendant, one of the king's choosing, rather than Juliann's sister.

It was still early morning. All spectators, inside and out, eagerly watched for the first wagon of the procession in celebration of Corpus Christi.

"We have forty-two wagons this year," said the mayor, "representing each of our guilds. Not as many as York, to be sure, but still very good. Each wagon will be stopping right out there." The balding man pointed through the window at several banners hanging together, marked with the arms of the city. "Then they go on to the next station. The shipwrights and mariners guild is first, with Noah's Ark. Here they are now."

The wagon ambled into view, carrying its cast: Noah with his white beard and an assortment of exaggerated "animals" wearing oversized and elaborately-made heads and covered with fur. Cheers and shouting from the crowd outside broke out when the animals started fighting with one another. Richard chuckled when Noah triumphed and the wagon moved on.

That was a surprise; Richard had not expected to enjoy this. These celebrations reminded him so much of Anne. As Duke and Duchess of Gloucester – and once as king and queen – they had been members of the Corpus Christi Guild in York, the city nearest their hearts and their home of Middleham Castle. Every year, they had participated in York's festivities, the grandest in all of England.

Today he smiled at the memory without dwelling on Anne's loss. What had changed? Richard looked around the room. His two attendants were talking to the maidservant and laughing at the procession outside, while the others had gone to other windows for a better view.

His eyes fell on Anise.

She fidgeted in her chair, forcing a nervous smile at the amusements out in the street, yet never saying a word.

She wore black in honor of Juliann, her pale face standing out against the dark attire. Her raven hair had been twisted up and hidden inside her headdress. Richard remembered her hair heavy in his hands as he pulled her to him, her breath warm against his throat.

Richard fought back the memory. He ran his finger over the face of the ring – a tool with which he had quickly become adept. Though he knew it had been made by sorcery, he could not ignore its usefulness. He had prayed for guidance, but of course God had not answered. So he continued to use the instrument delivered into his hands. Now he would use it to discover the reason why.

He studied Anise and found uneasiness, apprehension, bafflement.

Uncertainty. She caught his gaze. *Fear.*

They had traveled to Coventry separately the night before and had said nothing to one another since arriving at the lord mayor's house.

At the moment, all eyes were turned to what was happening down on the street: the vintner's guild was turning water into wine. Richard, having analyzed his impressions, remarked casually, "You have never before seen Corpus Christi festivities? From whence might you hail, that one of the most popular holidays in Christendom is not celebrated there?"

Anise's mouth fell open. Her fear increased. So his assessment was accurate. She was afraid of being found out. What was she hiding?

She did not speak, but looked askance at the ring. Why the surprise? She had used it, too, to read his emotions. Had she not? His mind raced. If she had come by the ring accidentally and had not understood its potential, maybe she never realized that sorcery was behind her feelings for him. Could she truly be as innocent as she acted?

That was wishful thinking. She knew more of her past than she was telling, Richard was certain. Only a direct question would provide the answer.

Now was not the time. On this day, among these people, Richard must not allow anything to appear out of the ordinary.

He must discover Anise's truth, but in private.

He leaned toward her. "Come to me tonight, using all discretion."

Anise's eyes widened – and she nodded once.

Richard knew she was afraid. Soon enough, he would know why.

****

As he stood staring at the door of Lady Anise's apartments, his hand poised to turn the knob, Francis Lovell seethed. Had he known that Dickon had taken this woman to his bed, he would not have encouraged the king's plan go with her to Coventry for questioning, away from Francis' advice and counsel. Dickon had deceived him because of a woman.

Francis heard a footstep behind him. "Alice!"

"I got your message," she said in a whisper. "What do you intend to do?"

He guided her inside and closed the door behind them. "To find what we can to discredit her. Her motives are suspect, and I fear she will be the death of the king, if this continues."

The damsel's eyes grew wide. "Yet I have searched and found nothing."

Francis opened the wardrobe. "We must look again!"

Looking over his shoulder, he found her mirroring some realization. "What is it?"

"The bed," she said, taking a step that direction. "This morning she concealed herself from me behind the bed curtain. I think she was hiding something."

Francis was there before her, rummaging through the blankets, groping beneath the mattress. His hand hit upon something hard and square. He pulled it out. "What...?" His voice shook. "What kind of witchery be this?"

It was a book, but the binding was smooth and unnatural. The cover was stained with reds and yellows, Satan's colors. Examining it closer, he could make out drawings of mounted men going to battle – and a knight falling from his horse. Francis had never seen anything like it. With a rush of fear, he realized that he might easily become entranced by this evil thing. When he forced his eyes from it, they met those of Alice, who stood beside him, white-faced. "Only the dark arts could have produced a thing such as this."

Taking a deep breath, he held onto Alice's arm to steady them and started for the door. He could not keep his eyes from the book and looked at it again. For the first time he comprehended the strange lettering emblazoned above the colors and his heart nearly stopped.

It read, "The Tragedy of Richard III."

****

Anise sat alone in the office provided for the king during his stay at the lord mayor's home. It was late. The celebrations had gone on nearly to midnight, breaking only to eat. She was exhausted.

Since morning, Richard had only offered her polite small talk. In her head, she had rehearsed what she'd tell him. How could a medieval man believe such a thing if she could hardly believe it herself?

After retiring to her room upstairs, thinking she'd escaped interrogation for the day, Richard's man escorted her to this office.

Like a lamb to the slaughter. Only lambs did not know what was coming; she'd prepared all day. Nervous perspiration prickled beneath her heavy gown.

When Richard entered the room, he was alone. The door closed behind him and Anise felt trapped. He came to where she sat, but she was afraid to look at him. Her heart thumped so hard she thought it would explode. She stared at her hands.

"Look at me." His voice was quiet, reasonable, dangerously seductive. She was still afraid. If their eyes met, he'd know for sure everything she'd told him was a lie. All the air left her lungs.

"Look at me." His words were now clipped.

Anise knew she did not dare disobey. She found his eyes and a sob caught in her throat. His gaze, full of fiery passion a few nights ago, had turned cold. Yet she could still see the sadness that had drawn her to him.

He studied her. Anise remembered what it was like to wear the ring. His expression relaxed. "You have not betrayed me." It was more of a statement than a question.

Anise swallowed hard. "I love you." Her voice shook. "I could never betray you."

His short laugh startled her. "One does not necessarily guarantee the other."

She was still frightened – but relieved. *He doesn't think I betrayed him.*

"I feel your affection," he said softly. "'Tis this ring..." his eyes bored into hers, "is it not?"

Her tongue would not work. She nodded.

"Why did you take my ring – the one I see there on your hand – and give me this one? You did do that, did you not?"

She nodded again. Anise fought the tears pushing behind her eyes. She would not cry.

"Tell me, why did you do that without my consent? It has tainted my memory of our night together."

The words stabbed through Anise's heart.

All her rehearsing had not prepared her for this moment. The easy way out was to tell him Cecily had asked her to do it. He'd know she was not lying. But he might know she was holding something back: the truth about herself and what she knew about his fate.

And how she hoped to save him.

"I wanted you to have this power."

"Tell me what this ring is," he said intensely.

"It lets you know what others feel. I thought if you had it, you'd know who to trust – that it would give you a chance of winning the battle with Tudor."

Richard inhaled sharply. "You believe I will not vanquish him?" He left her and sat down at his writing table where he remained silent for a long while. His next words were nearly inaudible. "Are you a witch? Is that why you have the ring? Do you know the future?"

Anise sought his eyes. "I'm not a witch. I found the ring."

"Your memories are returning, are they?" There was steel in his voice. "Where did you find it?"

She opened her mouth, but hesitated. She knew hardly anything about the ring, except it had belonged to a father she could barely remember. She knew the ring had carried her into Richard's arms, and her whole life had changed.

His eyes burned into hers, and Anise felt sick. How could she tell him she was from a world that would not exist for five hundred years in a country that had not been discovered yet?

What would he do if she lied?

His impatience broke through his impassive demeanor. "Well?"

"I found it in… in my father's house – after he died. When I put it on, something happened – I became confused and got lost in the woods. When you found me, I thought all of it was a dream."

She'd said nothing but the truth, but Richard appeared skeptical.

"What of this man you said was your brother? Are you not still looking for him? Is there a brother?"

She nodded.

"Have you asked after him here?"

Anise looked at the floor. "Finding him is impossible. I've almost given up."

"If you no longer search for your brother, why then do you remain at my court?"

Their eyes met. "You know why."

"England is on the brink of attack. I shall make arrangements for you to return home, for your own safety. You do remember where it is? "

Unsure how to answer, she nodded.

"There's more, is there not?"

Anise bit her lip. The risk was great no matter what she did. And yet, to save his life, she must tell him all she knew. No escaping it this time.

The ring would inform him she spoke the truth. That was the best she could hope for.

Richard got up and came to her. He took her arms and pulled her up to face him, his manner not altogether gentle. "I must know." He released her. "Continue."

Her mouth went dry, but she forced herself to go on. "I know what I'm about to say seems impossible. It'll sound like witchcraft. But it's not. The ring... you'll know I'm not lying."

She met his eyes and saw a willingness there to believe her. Words tumbled out without forethought. "I'm not of this time. I'm from the future. I was born in the year nineteen hundred and ninety-one. I..." She stopped when she saw the look on the king's face.

"*Nineteen and ninety-one?*" He was astounded. "Nearly five hundred years from this day you were *born*?"

Anise did not look away from his burning gaze.

The muscles in his neck tensed. "This is madness. An impossibility. But the sorcery in this ring says you're telling the truth." He briskly pulled it off his finger. "What enchantment have you worked on me to make me believe in this power of empathy? May God and England forgive me, that you have shown me to be a fool!"

Anise heard the pain through the anger of his voice. She brushed off the tears on her face. "I'm telling the truth! I've stayed at court because I know for a fact that Henry Tudor wins at Bosworth. I know! Because to me, it's history. And I want to help you. I don't want you to die!" Surprise crossed his face. Anise thought there might still be a chance that he'd believe her.

The door burst open. Stanley and two armed men stood there. Francis Lovell pushed through to the front. He stared at her, full of hatred. Turning to Richard, he pointed to Anise and said, "Treason." The king looked at her with a hard expression.

Her knees went weak when she saw the viscount hold out the book of Shakespeare.

As Richard took it from him, Francis repeated, more quietly this time, as if to soften the blow. "'Tis treason, Dickon."

CHAPTER TWELVE

"He dreams of being archbishop, the peacock!" laughed Margaret. The thick mist swirled above her, silhouetted against the night sky through the broken ceiling. "He recalls a prophecy, made for him when still a child. He repeats it to me often. You should see the longing in his eyes!"

Her words echoed against the tower's stone walls as Morton, recognizing the sarcasm in her voice, listened from the crumbled stairs below. He knew she was not talking to herself – that she was speaking to his master. *Margaret. I thought you loved me.*

Glendower's deep voice made answer, "'Twas my own prophecy! He came to me as a boy. Archbishop, he shall be."

"You know this for certain?" Astonishment rang in Lady Stanley's voice. "Then John Morton must surely become cleverer than he is now."

Morton slid down the wall to sit on the steps. He buried his face in his hands. *How could you both betray me thus?*

"He is not a fool, madam. Certes, you know that. Only – he is not a good wizard."

Lady Stanley's voice lightened. "Not as you are, Owain. Power suits you."

The statement, as sweet from her lips as warm mead, tore the bishop's heart. 'Twas the honeyed tone he had believed she saved for him.

"Intrigue suits him well," insisted Glendower. "He shall wear the red robes."

"Not under the reign of Richard Plantagenet."

The cloud churned overhead.

"John must be left to his own devices now," said Margaret coldly. "Send him away, and I'll see to it that Henry rewards him for his loyalty. We have more important concerns."

How could she be so callous? Had he not struggled for years on her son's behalf? Had he not proved his love for her, even under threat of death and exile? How could she turn on him after all they had been through together? All for the power that a disembodied wizard might offer her, in the happenstance he ever again walked this earth?

Her cruelty had not yet played out. "I have tired of him. His intellectual abilities pale in comparison to your own. I covet your companionship, Owain Glendower."

The words tore Morton's heart.

"We cannot send John away; I need him," said Glendower with determination. "The Bishop of Ely must perform the wedding ceremony. No one else must know about me."

Morton's despair shifted to anger and he formed a hard resolve. *We shall see who is clever.* He had a plan.

Margaret was not pleased. "Mightn't we wrest the ring from the wench's finger? Why go through all this?"

"The ring I hold within this cloud of vapor leaves me without solid form while Lady Wynford walks the earth. The science of alchemy hinges on balance – and that works against me now. Two rings might exist on the same plane only through consummation of the spiritual with the physical. Until I wed her – and bed her – I shall remain a mist." Glendower's voice contained a mixture of anxiety and anticipation. "This ceremony is the last service I'll require of John before releasing him from his debt to me."

"And then you will get rid of her?"

"When the two rings have joined."

Morton smiled. He had read Stanley's last message. Lady Wynford had become King Richard's lover. Margaret had not yet informed Glendower of this, apparently.

"Will you kill her?" Margaret's tone held no mercy. "I have discovered that permanent solutions are the best kind."

Margaret was not the least bit squeamish. Morton knew this firsthand. More than one of her acts of human sacrifice had been excessively bloody.

"Do you so casually pronounce death on an innocent girl?"

Lady Stanley snorted. "Innocence holds no sway with me. Power is what matters. Besides, she's not so innocent as you believe, and will not enter your marriage bed as a virgin."

Glendower roared.

Margaret smiled, her aim achieved. "Death is too good for that wench, robbing you as she has."

The ancient stone tower shuddered. Morton grew afraid. What did Margaret think she could accomplish by this?

"What happened?" Glendower's own thunder nearly drowned out his words. "Tell me!"

Morton felt the stones behind him shake. He stumbled down the stairs to save himself as Margaret screamed, "She is the king's lover!"

When he was outside the walls, Morton looked up at the sky. The full moon was blotted out by the dense cloud. The bishop ignored the pain in his chest and dove into the black woods, terrified of being crushed when the tower fell.

By the time he reached his horse a few moments later, the moon shone in the sky once more. The tower stood. Peace reigned.

Morton leaned against his dappled mare, catching his breath and trying to figure out what to do next.

****

Francis Lovell felt a sense of satisfaction sweep over him as he watched Dickon turn his back to the treacherous wench and stare in amazement at the shiny little book with his name on it. It was not until one of the viscount's men grabbed her arms and began to drag her from the room that the king interceded.

"She is not to be harmed," he said, his voice low but stern. He looked first at Stanley then at Francis, summing them up. "And she is not to be imprisoned until my order commands it. Keep her confined to her quarters." He paused and looked at the book thoughtfully. "I shall examine the evidence."

Francis saw the woman struggle against her captors.

"Richard..." she said, trying to catch the king's attention. Such a breach of manners, in the presence of others, to call the king other than His Grace. The viscount snorted. Dickon would never stand for that.

But the king surprised him. Though he spoke not a word to her, he at last turned to the Lady Anise as she was being pulled from the room.

Their eyes met for an instant, and Dickon's gaze was not filled with anger, but only regret and pain. In that moment, Francis understood the depths of what he had done. Unreasonably – for the truth of her guilt was obvious – he prayed that he'd had acted rightly.

As the woman was taken from the house, the men-at-arms also exited the lord mayor's house. The viscount looked on with pity as Richard stared wonderingly at the tiny tome. Francis had caused the king more pain. Had he threatened their friendship as well?

"Dickon..." he started, uncertainly.

Richard spun toward him, his dark eyes flashing. "So – you have accomplished your aim. Do you also realize you have rent my heart?"

Francis swallowed the lump in his throat, but would not allow Richard, in his fury, to ignore the facts. "Is it not better that we know now than later, Dickon? This book was indeed found beneath her mattress. What arts could have produced such a thing, but witchcraft?"

The king was leafing through the pages. "A printer, such as Caxton, might have created it. See – the lettering is odd. It may be the product of another kingdom."

The viscount sighed. "And so, 'tis only by coincidence, that your name is emblazoned on its cover? Dickon, I think not."

Closing the book, the king looked at him again, hardness in his glance. "That you believe such, my friend, is obvious. But I will not have the lady ill-treated until we know the origins of this," he waved the book, "and what its text tells us. She shall be confined in her rooms – nothing more – until we know."

Taking a deep breath, Francis knew the time had come. He forced the words out. "Dickon – I... I know... of your... intimacy with the lady." Half expecting the king to demand how he knew, the viscount continued quickly, his voice as assertive as he could muster. "I believe it would be better if she were sent ahead to the castle at Nottingham. You shall be following in just a few days. In that time, you would then be able to gather the information you need, without her presence nearby..."

But Richard finished the sentence abruptly, "To tempt me?" The king shook his head and sighed. "You, too, lose faith in me, though you admit it not, even to yourself." His voice and manner seemed more resigned to what had happened, and Francis was thankful for it. "But I suppose you are right. Tell Stanley he shall escort her to Nottingham tonight."

"Stanley!" Francis was surprised. "Think you not that t'would be safer that I see the lady north?" It had been Stanley's suggestion that the woman be taken to Nottingham. Could Francis have foolishly become entangled in one of the lord's machinations?

Richard's gaze was unfathomable, but Francis took it as friendship when, sadly, the king said, "I do not wish to be alone tonight."

The viscount realized he could not leave Dickon. Is this what Stanley had hoped for?

****

Feeling hollow inside, Anise stood outside the house with the regiment of men and horses who awaited orders. Stanley emerged from the house first. He studied her from a short distance away. Francis Lovell joined him. She caught their words on the breeze.

"I accompany the lady to Nottingham tonight," said Stanley. "His Grace insists she be made comfortable in her own quarters and suffer no ill treatment."

"It is for the best," said Francis. "We have effectively removed the witch from the king's bed – I do not wish Dickon to make matters worse somehow and turn more people against him. I recall the fate of the unfortunate Hastings, dispatched so quickly, and without a trial."

Stanley said grimly. "Those of us in the king's household would all do well to remember that."

"I shall be staying with the king tonight – he requires my counsel," said Francis. "Those of us who are loyal to Richard have no need to fear."

Stanley laughed, "Luck to you then, my friend."

The two nobles parted, and a squire led the viscount's horse toward the stables. Lord Stanley approached Anise, the light of the full moon revealing the satisfied expression on his face. Thinking she could not hear him, he said, "She shall be well-handled under my care."

****

Two knights-of-the-body attended the king and Francis Lovell, disrobing them of their silk shirts and hose, gowning them for the night and setting a livery of wine and bread. After pulling the pallet from beneath the bed and lighting the fire, they left.

The king watched them go, and sat down by the fire. "I cannot bear their transparent thoughts. They suspect me of atrocious crimes, they see me as a witch's pawn. Their perception of me as their sovereign worsens. What it comes down to is their doubting my ability to rule."

Francis, standing before the hearth, caught Richard's glance and wondered at the steel in it.

"I cannot believe you have done this thing to me." There was accusation in the king's voice.

Francis' chest tightened. So Dickon blamed him.

"To take from me the only joy I've known for months. I cannot dispel this bitterness, Francis. I feel that you – my truest friend since boyhood – have betrayed me, though you believe you have not. Tell me – how knowst you that I've lain with Anise?"

Stanley. Francis could not say it. To tell Dickon it was Stanley who had led him down this path, to admit that he had been manipulated by the most untrustworthy lord in the king's service, was not easy.

Sweet Jesu, but what if Stanley had planted the book beneath the mattress! T'would have been easy to accomplish. Was it not rumored by some that the Lady Stanley, his wife, practiced sorcery?

Francis rued his involvement in Stanley's plot. How could he let him know he acted with such disregard for Richard's feelings?

As Francis watched, the king turned his ring 'round and 'round on his finger, he found himself lying, "'Twas servant's gossip. I tracked down the man who saw you leave her room at dawn."

The king's eyes narrowed as he absorbed this information. "Because you believe that Anise is responsible for Juliann's death, you searched her room?"

Unnerved by the king's icy manner, Francis nodded and sat down. "We found the book."

Richard stared through him, as if he were transparent. "Lord Stanley knew nothing of this before you asked for his help?"

Francis forced himself to speak past the lump in his throat – and past the truth. "No."

Richard turned toward the flames and bowed his head, as if in grief. Francis remained silent. After long minutes, the king still did not speak. The fire began to die.

Francis took up an iron rod and poked the embers to life again.

"She is doomed because I love her. It is the way God has for punishing me," said Richard, his voice as stark as bleached bones.

The viscount turned to Richard, who stared into the flames. He kneeled abruptly before the king. "You have done nothing wrong!" he whispered fervently, believing it himself and wanting Richard to. "I should not worship you so if I thought it to be true."

The king smiled ruefully. "Friends once as dear to me as you have often told me this, then acted otherwise. Yet I hear in your voice such raw conviction that I am convinced of your sincerity. You are of two minds, tonight – and I am a fool." After a moment of silence, he proclaimed, "Come up off your knees. We are alone tonight and equals."

Francis got up, mystified at Dickon's odd behavior. Were they still friends?

"Listen and I shall tell you something I've told none other."

Francis recalled Stanley's words about Hastings – and anxiety nagged at the edge of his mind. He sat down near the king. Richard poured the wine and thrust a cup into Francis' hand. "Drink. I see the fear in your eyes. There's no point hiding it. You, too, are wondering if I am fit to rule. Perhaps you will be able to answer that for me, when I'm done."

"While you live, I follow none other."

Richard smiled. "Speak not what you may live to regret, my friend. No matter. Let us confront the first accusation, the crimes against my brother's sons. You know, as well as everyone else, apparently, that they are dead. And so the question remains, in the minds of the populous, did I order them killed to ensure they would not arise later on to challenge my place on the throne?"

"Of course you didn't!" insisted Francis. "Why do you constantly torment yourself, Dickon?"

Richard ignored this and pointed to his bed. "You know I suffer sleeplack. You see me take this bed with me wherever I go, for 'tis the only one in which I can find the slightest amount of rest. Know you why I suffer insomnia? Think you that it is just because of the worries of being king?"

The viscount could not keep the sadness from his words. "'Tis because of all the deaths. Edward, your brother, the queen, your son – crowded into such a short time. And all the betrayals—" Francis swallowed hard at those last words.

Richard shook his head slowly. "No, friend. All that comes as a result of the first betrayal – my own. The royal bastards are dead because of me."

Francis' head spun with the wine and the words. His voice broke. "You... you ordered it done?"

"No," said the king shortly. "But I am responsible for it."

The viscount could barely ask. "How?"

Richard sighed. "The sleeplack began when Stillington first told me of Edward's secret marriage. I agonized for days, sleeping not at all. But for Anne, I think I would have lost my reason. She counseled me. She did not want me to be king, but she realized that Prince Edward, being now proved a bastard, was not a fit ruler. There was nothing to do but let the truth out and take the crown." The king looked directly into Francis' eyes, his own flashing with fervor. "I wanted it. I could rule rightly. Had I not proved it to be so as Governor of the North? I could lay these factions to rest, disperse the grasping

Woodvilles. England would have peace! That is what I wanted."

Francis nodded, pushing back the emotion welling in his eyes. "I know, Dickon. I have seen."

"So I made the decision. And still, I could not sleep. For what should now happen to Edward's sons?"

Richard buried his face in his hands. "Francis, I cannot deny the thought crossed my mind. How could it not? Had not every displaced king before this died at the hands of the usurper? Did my own brother not kill the saintly King Harry, insane though he might have been? Yet I could not bear it. Kill Edward's sons? It was not bear it. Kill Edward's sons? It was beyond my abilities to order it, and yet, through the actions of kings before me, I would have been advised to do just that."

Francis swallowed hard and grasped the king's arm. "I knew you could not have done it," he whispered.

Dickon raised his head. "But still, I could not sleep. I asked Anne. Thinking of our son, she said I should let Edward and Richard rejoin their mother and sisters in sanctuary. That she herself would not be able to bear it if her children were locked away from her. That Elizabeth Woodville, for the first time in her life the victim, must be grieving terribly." The king smiled. "Anne's heart was tender. But, of course, her advice was impossible."

Richard refilled his companion's empty cup. Francis' nerves had calmed, yet he welcomed the wine. As he watched the king drink, he was frightened not by his revelations, but by his behavior – and comprehended the damage done by the loss of the Lady Anise. In this state, could the king even face Henry Tudor?

"At the time, I believed God had guided me down the path to becoming king," he said. "Certes, 'twas divine intervention, to secure, at last, England's shattered peace. I did so believe it. And that night after speaking to Anne, I turned to prayer, kneeling before the crucifix and candles in our room, where at last I fell to the floor in exhaustion." He stood and walked to the hearth, staring into the flames.

"'Twas then the dream came to me," whispered the king. So low did he speak, that Francis went to him, in order to hear the words. "I stood in the royal apartments in the Tower at London. Edward's sons were grown before me. But his eldest son, named for him, was no more different from Ned in stature and manner than if it were he, himself, returned to me as I loved him best." His voice cracking, Richard continued, "In this vision – for at the time I believed it to be sent by God – these sons of my brother had thrived under my guidance. They bore me no grudge.

They said they loved me. But what they did next," the king paused, swallowing hard, "what they did next still burns in my mind as if Satan put it there to taunt me for my foolishness. The lords bastard – with young Edward grown into this great golden giant so much like his father – kneeled before me and pledged their fealty."

Unable to continue, Richard stared into the fire. Beside him, Francis stood unmoving. "When I awakened at dawn, I believed that God had at last answered my prayers. I ordered that the lords bastard should be confined to the royal apartments, away from the all others. When I returned from the Progress after my coronation, I would see that they were properly supervised."

"But we never saw them again," whispered Francis.

"They were dead," Richard stated softly. "So you see, 'twas long before this that I first served a sorcerer's evil."

There was a long pause before he added, "On progress, Harry – Buckingham – came to me. You remember what a state he was in? He told me they were murdered. I suspected those who believed they were serving my purposes. I even suspected him. But when we were alone, he told me. And though it seemed he didn't say everything he knew, from the horror on his face as he recounted what he found, I knew it hadn't been Buckingham who'd ordered the deed."

Richard took a deep breath, as if gathering strength to continue. "Buckingham did not come alone. The attendants who were with him when they found my nephews were equally convincing. This was no story conjured by the duke." Richard turned to Francis, his eyes filled with pain. "No human could have done what was done to my nephews, Francis. They were charred beyond recognition, burnt, as if on a pyre. But by all accounts, there was nothing else in the apartments revealing a fire."

Francis sat down, his knees shaking. The wine, hastily finished, sat sour on his stomach. Richard's tale sat heavy on his mind. *Charred beyond recognition.*

But the king had not finished. "What next they told me turned my blood to ice," he whispered. "Their bodies, so burnt, lay directly at the spot they kneeled for their prayers. It was then that I knew my vision had not come from God. 'Twas then I realized that all along, some evil controlled my dreams and my actions." He turned to Francis. "That God had forsaken me."

The viscount was too overwhelmed by the account to listen clearly to what followed. But the king did not stop. "What could I do? The evil was done. Dickon and Edward were dead. My whole being screamed with the guilt I knew was mine to bear. I forced myself to make decisions. I tried to get Harry to discuss it, to advise me. With no explanation for the state of their bodies, said I, they could not be displayed publicly, as when Old King Harry died of a *sudden illness.* Their disappearance would have to go unexplained. I knew I would get the blame. But what else was there to do? As I pondered this question, Harry became overwrought. He admitted to me that he had already buried the bodies beneath a staircase in the Tower."

His head numb, his whole being ill, Francis murmured, "'Tis why no one ever knew what became of them these two years."

The king nodded. "When I suggested he return to London, Buckingham nearly swooned. So I sent him and his attendants to Brecknock. I trusted that Harry would pay well to keep them silent. I discovered later he had them murdered. When rumors began spreading, I realized before anyone else that he had betrayed me, planning that aborted rebellion. I wondered again if it had been he who had killed them. But I could only remember the horror in his voice and on his face as he told me what he'd seen. Though he used their deaths to his advantage, Harry had not done the deed. And to this day, I know not who did."

Francis was shaking his head in disbelief when Richard turned to him again. "No one else but me – and the murderer – lives to describe the horror of their deaths. You are the only other to know the truth."

The viscount realized what Richard had done. Knowing such a terrible truth about a king put his life at risk. The least little hint that he'd turned traitor and Dickon would have cause for permanently silencing him.

Richard watched him absorb the implications in silence. At last he said, "Perhaps you can tell me now if I am fit to rule?"

CHAPTER THIRTEEN

The moonlit road was uneven, disrupting the horse's gait. Anise's feet hurt. Her shoulders hurt. Her rear hurt. Her eyes were puffy from crying. Despite the king's orders not to mistreat her, Stanley's men had seen to it her feet were bound tightly to the stirrups on either side of the horse, although her hands had been left free so that she could hang onto the saddle. She, Stanley, and his men had trudged for hours toward Nottingham Castle. The whole time, the scene at the lord mayor's house replayed relentlessly through Anise's mind.

The king had turned his back on her. "I shall examine the evidence," he'd said, his voice cold and dangerously quiet. Anise's stomach had dropped to the floor when she saw his eyes, filled with angry hurt. For the first time, she feared for her life.

Recalling the conversation she'd overheard between Stanley and Francis, Anise realized that Hastings was the one in the play beheaded as a traitor. Would she be next? Unbidden, Richard's line from Shakespeare echoed from another lifetime: "I am so far in blood that sin will pluck on sin. Tear-falling pity dwells not in this eye."

By taking her to Nottingham, was Stanley saving her from the king's wrath?

Stanley. She watched the broad backed man riding ahead of her. What reason might he have for wanting to keep her alive?

The journey seemed endless. Anise slid deeper into contemplation, her mind numb with shock and her limbs with cold. As the sun flickered over the horizon, she saw an immense stone fortress towering atop a great rock, lording over the countryside. One glance told her it would be no easy feat to escape from there. Fear gripped her soul.

Dawn broke. Stanley, his men, and his prisoner followed the steep road toward the castle. She was exhausted and would have been thankful to lie on hard ground if it meant she could sleep. The ride to the top was long, and when the lathered horses reached the summit, the sun was high overhead.

They rode to the enormous spiked doors. Anise could not escape the oppressive feeling of doom.

****

The torchlight flickered against the stone walls. Morton, disguised as a goldsmith, crept to the shrouded corner of his laboratory at Brecknock Castle. The familiar pungent smell of damp earth reminded him of his failures. How he had loathed that odor by the time he'd achieved his one success.

Scanning the shambles of his work area, he saw most of his tools and materials were gone. Thieves, no doubt.

He prayed that the items he had come for had not been stolen, too. Morton cursed his luck. He'd had no choice but to leave them behind after Buckingham's rebellion had failed and the duke beheaded. The bishop had fled Henry Stafford's without a moment to spare. Had he not sailed for Flanders, he would have shared the luckless duke's fate and been dead these last two years.

Bracing the torch in a sconce, Morton found the familiar section of wall. As he reached for the scarred brick that concealed the hole, his eye fell on his ring – the mate to Glendower's, with the power to raise the dead.

He rued the day he had resurrected that old devil.

Morton wriggled the brick free and thrust in his hand. His fingers closed over a leather pouch. He smiled; his plan might go forth, after all. Glendower and Margaret would make no fool of him!

He replaced the stone and he spilled the contents of the bag into his palm. Holding the gold circlets beneath the torch, he examined them. There was one ring, in form and design identical to that which he wore on his left hand. Then two. And three. But no more?

He felt the pouch. Two rings missing! Morton shrugged. No matter. They were merely trinkets – if they possessed magic, it was weak, useless. And he needed only one. He dropped the rings back into the bag and he hid it within his clothing. He grabbed the torch and made for the exit.

Footsteps!

They descended the narrow steps, his only escape. Dropping the torch, he retreated into the corner. If he were found out – *and how could he escape?* – he would be imprisoned and executed by the king's men who now occupied the castle. As he moved further into the bowels of the undercroft, his eyes adjusted to the darkness, feeling along the wall for a nook or crevice. He found one at last and crawled in, but it was not quite big enough to conceal him.

Morton sensed his own impending doom as the footsteps moved closer. There were at least three of them, and when they came upon the burning torch, one cried out. Swords were drawn. It would not be long before they found him now. He wondered what death would feel like.

Glendower was right, he thought bitterly. He was as inept a wizard as ever lived, to have forged a great ring of power and yet not have the skill to call upon it to save his own life.

The men came forth with a cautious but steady gait. Morton squeezed into the hidey hole, but knew it was futile.

In desperation, he put the ring to his lips, seeking its power with his will. *"Munimen abusque adversarius,"* he whispered. He tried to concentrate, but his mind flitted between images of places he had visited and people he had known.

Although Morton had come to this cursed dungeon to forward his plan to get even with Margaret, he ached at the thought of never seeing her again.

He could not sustain such painful thoughts, knowing death approached with every footstep, so his mind settled at last on the memory of his beloved home in Flanders. Provided on behalf of Henry Tudor's supporters, it had been a most comfortable residence before Margaret aided his return to England.

He did so enjoy the creature comforts.

In his mind's eye, Morton transported himself there, and imagined a great fire in the hearth, a book on his lap and a cup of wine in his hand.

The footsteps and the jangle of chain mail drew nearer. The light from their torches nearly touched him. Morton doubted he would be captured and imprisoned – most likely, they'd run him through first, and then rob his corpse.

Torchlight washed over him. One of the men cried, "Over here!" Morton mouthed the last rites to save his soul. As he spoke the litany, his vision of Flanders returned. The knight drew his sword and rushed him. Bishop John Morton closed his eyes and prepared to die.

A vacuum stole his breath. A moment later, his blood froze, wind whistling past his ears. All went black.

****

Richard performed what was expected of him as king at the Corpus Christi celebrations, worked tirelessly on government business during his last days at Kenilworth, and arranged every detail of the journey north to Nottingham. Although he had settled into life at the castle and toiled incessantly over the paperwork piled before him, still he could not obliterate Anise's deceit from his mind.

How could he? The evidence lay right there before him – as it had for the week since being thrust into his hands. Francis recommended the king should examine it before arriving at Nottingham. But Richard had not. Instead, he'd looked at it once the day it was given to him – but had thrown it down in frustration. He had not been able to bring himself to pick it up again since.

Nor was Francis here to press him. The morning after he told Francis what he knew of the lords' bastard's deaths, the king had sent him on his scheduled mission to the Royal Navy in Southampton to prepare for Tudor's attack.

Francis' actions had not amounted to betrayal, in truth. But he'd lied to his king about Stanley's involvement. As Richard considered this, Anise's ring seemed to beckon to him from his finger. Francis had never again mentioned the ring that had first convinced him Anise was a witch. But the king had learned its uses. After Stanley's men forced her from the room at the lord mayor's, the king had returned the ring to his hand.

Francis had lied to him. Still he could not fathom that. 'Twas but one step more to complete betrayal. At one time, Richard had counted on his friend's loyalty. Now he trusted no one. So he had told Francis about Edward's sons. It was dangerous information to possess – for one contemplating treason. Francis knew the king's justice could be swift. He would think twice about lying again.

And what of Anise? The powers bestowed upon him by the ring proved she did not lie. And yet her fantastic assertions were impossible. No one but a witch would make such claims. What had she hoped to gain with her trickery? The sting of her deceit still pained him. Once again, he had put trust in one unworthy of it. And this one he had loved.

He realized now he should not have immediately sent her north to Nottingham. If he had confronted her after that first night of her house arrest, he was certain she would have revealed all her secrets. Now he was at Nottingham, too – and yet he could not even bring himself to ask where she was kept.

He no longer had his anger to shield him. If he went to her now, he would be vulnerable to her enchantments – if what Francis believed was true, that she was a witch. Besides, since her betrayal, he could not bear the pain of looking upon her.

Yet, he might not need to confront her in person, if he could learn the truth through other means.

With a sigh of resignation, Richard opened the book lying before him on the writing desk. If he could read it, he might understand.

He leafed through the pages. The craftsmanship of the book was remarkable, with its unnatural shine and color. The parchment was strangely smooth, without the usual ragged edges. Instead of being writ by a scribe, it was printed, as were the books that came from Master Caxton's shop in Westminster. The king recalled fondly how his old friend had dedicated the "Order of Chivalry" to him while he was still Richard of Gloucester.

Could a book be the result of sorcery? Only Caxton could say. And so the king wrote a letter urgently summoning the aging printer to come immediately to Nottingham – if, at his great age, he was able to make the trip.

Looking through the pages randomly, the king managed to read words here and there, but the letters were difficult and strange. Although he recognized it as English, it was not the written language as he knew it. He felt again as a young child, learning his Latin and French letters. Now, as then, he threw it down with impatience. But he was determined. He picked up the book again and forced himself to consider the oddly shaped words.

"Richard III." 'Twas one of the things he could read, his name. That was particularly frustrating – knowing it was a book about him and not knowing what it contained. He continued to work his way through some of it. At the beginning, there were other names he knew: his brothers Edward IV and George, Duke of Clarence. Elizabeth Woodville. His nephews, the lords bastard. Marguerite d'Anjou. Even his own dear Anne. There were his supporters, the Duke of Norfolk, Sir Richard Ratcliffe, Sir William Catesby. There were those of whose loyalty he was not sure – Lord Stanley and Francis Lovell.

And there were those who had already paid the price of treason – Anthony Woodville, the Duke of Buckingham, Lord Hastings.

His life was played out upon these incomprehensible pages, and here were the characters who had acted in it.

He turned the page. There, in a box, he read, "Act I." And his name again, the title. Since deciphering the names, he found that the strangely formed letters were becoming familiar to him. Now he attempted to read the words above his name, and found that he could: "The Tragedy of."

Disquiet descended upon him. "The Tragedy of Richard III." He certainly had never thought of his life in those terms, and yet, had it not been a tragedy?

What had seemed impossible before now occurred to him.

What Anise had said, about knowing his fate – could it be true? Since she had made that outrageous assertion, he had dismissed her as mad. He had been angry with himself for being taken in by her. He had told himself the ring was a deception. But he had never considered her utterances as anything but a crazy, desperate attempt to escape punishment.

The king turned to the next page. "Scene I. London. A street. Enter Richard, Duke of Gloucester."

He felt a hollowness in his gut. 'Twas coming easier now. All it took was a little practice. Then, his name again. The next line, he read out loud, with hesitation. "Now is the... winter of our discontent..."

****

Dominic stood on the veranda of the old house, staring helplessly into the dark trees. Dampness settled over the night. He did not notice.

I was so close!

Since that night fifteen years ago, when he had fled with his father, Matthew, from the room where Tom Wynford lay dead, Dominic had never seen his sister again – until the other night. Since the murder, his father had been a broken man, unable to live with what had happened.

Gwendolyn Gates had ruined all their lives when she'd hid the ring.

Gwendolyn did not really want Anise – but when Wynford had discovered her infidelity, she went back to him, and refused Matthew his daughter. After Wynford died, Gwendolyn, bitter and paralyzed from a stray bullet, accused her lover of the murder to save herself.

If Dominic and his father could have used the ring to flee to an earlier century, they could have lived on the fortune Matthew had amassed across the centuries. But without the advantage of time travel, they were forced to stay put in this century, assuming new identities to escape the law. Even so, Matthew had stashed away enough money during his lifetime to fund his son's education. Dominic managed to complete university in Dublin and earn his medical degree.

When Matthew died, Dominic returned to Williamstown. He tracked down the estate lawyer, who told him Anise had no memory of the farmhouse, nor of her biological father and brother. Anise was six when Wynford died. She knew nothing of the ring when she happened upon it in the farmhouse. It must have been fate that led her to it.

The night Dominic found Anise – he lost her in the same moment. He reached out and caught hold of her shoulder, but she ran from him, afraid. She stumbled down the porch steps, and tripped into the past, God knew where.

On the porch, Dominic paced, anxious for his sister. There was nothing he could do but wait and hope Anise found her way back.

CHAPTER FOURTEEN

Anise awakened with a sneeze. Lying on a thin, straw mattress, she sat up in the early dawn and shivered. Although June, the morning held a chill. She looked around at her tiny room with its sparse furnishings. There was a small hearth, but no attendant here to start her a fire. She was out of wood anyway, and no one had thought to bring her more.

Anise knew she was unkempt, her dark hair snarled in unwashed tangles. She had sobbed for a week; her face was no doubt a wreck. The black costume dress she had worn to Richard's time was shabby and torn.

Her tears had run out days ago. What use was crying when there was no hope?

Upon their arrival, Stanley had unceremoniously tossed her into the cold cell.

"Didn't His Grace tell you I should have comfortable quarters?" she'd asked.

The lord laughed. "These are the most comfortable quarters in Nottingham – for traitors."

In desperation, Anise put on her sweetest stage voice. "My lord, I overheard you tell the viscount that I should be kept away from the king for my own safety. Please – show me some kindness now? This place is horrible."

A faint smile passed over Stanley's face. He pulled her beyond the sight of his men in the corridor. "I do not give kindness freely," he murmured, "but I might be persuaded to barter." He rubbed the inside of her arm.

Anise repressed the urge to spit in his face. "I wouldn't go to bed with you if my life depended on it!"

Stanley laughed again. "And it might, at that. Certes, it just might." With a swoosh of his cloak, he departed, locking the door behind him.

No matter how much she cried, no one came to her except for the gaunt man who gave her food twice a day. Unlike the room, the fare was decent – usually bread, cheese, and spiced wine. After a few days, she lost her appetite entirely, and was only able to eat enough to keep from starving.

She braced herself for a visit from Richard. She knew he was due at Nottingham. According to history, it was from this castle that he left to do battle with Henry Tudor.

In her mind, she rehearsed their meeting, scripting what she would say in the best possible scenario, when he came asking forgiveness for his suspicion, and accepting her wild tale of being from the future.

At other times, she imagined the worst. The king coming to her, ridiculing all she told him as a desperate attempt to escape her punishment for being a traitor and a sorceress. Like that ruthless killer in Shakespeare's play, he'd sentence her to death on the spot. Then he'd drag her to the castle square and have her secured to a wooden stake before a gathering crowd, to be burned alive.

Anise tried to imagine what death by fire would feel like – flames licking past her ankles, charring her skin; the smell of burning flesh, and finally the intense, searing pain, and then the darkness.

These thoughts descended upon her at night, replaying through her mind as if preparing her for the worst. Gazing around her prison room for the hundredth time, she saw no escape. Death would come for her. There would be no eluding it.

Yet Richard did not come to forgive nor condemn her. Anise saw no one but the man who delivered her food. She might rot in this cell. The king had deserted her, but she prayed he might somehow survive the battle. His fate haunted her, as she imagined him dead, his body battered and mutilated on the battlefield.

For many days, she forgot about Matthew's diary.

When she did remember, it did not seem to matter. She stood on the threshold of doom. What good would it do now to learn more about the ring? She could not go home – she did not have the means. The ring was on Richard's hand. And in a short time, Richard would not have it either – soon the king and his magic would be lost to the world forever.

Yet this waiting was unbearable. She turned to Matthew's journal to relieve the boredom. And because she understood she might be dragged out and killed at any moment, she started at the end. What the hell? Why not see how it all turned out?

The last entry was not in her father's handwriting.

April 23, 1997
My Dear Sister,
Father and I don't want to abandon you, but we have no choice. He's going to be blamed for Tom Wynford's murder – but the gentle soul who is our father would never survive prison. Please understand. We have to go on the run. We'll return for you when it's safe.

We love you,
Dom

Matthew had killed Tom Wynford? Her breath caught in her throat. She had loved her stepdad. It did not surprise Anise that Gwendolyn had kept this from her – but shouldn't Anise have remembered *something* about it?

She thumbed back through the entries. She learned more about her mother than she ever had living with her. Gwendolyn had grown tired of her husband. She spent months on the East Coast, acting on Broadway, hobnobbing with the famous. Matthew had been a gifted playwright – her mother had performed in one of his plays during summer stock. As they spent consecutive summers together in Williamstown, they fell in love. Then Anise was born.

Why couldn't you tell me the truth, Mother? Now it hardly matters at all.

Matthew wrote about his childhood in London. It was from these entries that Anise learned of the ring's history. His father, Stephen, had been an archaeologist in the employ of a treasure hunter. They excavated the ring in Wales, and Stephen was given it as partial payment for his services. In cryptic language, Matthew wrote how they used it to "travel." Anise understood exactly what *that* meant.

Time travel.

Lying on the dirty mattress in her cell, Anise pondered this new information. Even with these fresh clues, the long buried memories of her childhood eluded her. The little daylight she had through the window faded, leaving her in darkness. Night came and she never noticed.

****

"Do you not like my gift, Your Grace?" said William Caxton, standing before the king in his office at Nottingham. The sixty-five-year-old master printer watched Richard turn the pages of Caxton's latest text, his own translation of Sir Thomas Malory's "Morte d'Arthur."

Richard Plantagenet had been Caxton's friend since the exiled Duke of York's son was a sickly child of nine. They strengthened the friendship later when Richard and his brother, Edward the King, sought refuge with their sister, Margaret, in Burgundy ten years later.

Caxton suspected the king was distracted by this urgent business which had caused Richard to summon the printer from his cozy Westminster shop. Yet why did His Grace look so closely at certain pages in the new text, as if examining their quality?

Caxton did not want to appear impolite, but he longed to be seated. "Your Grace? I loathe to interrupt your concentration, but my journey was a tiring one for an old man. Might I request your leave to…?"

The king looked up to see him gazing covetously at a stool by the hearth. "Sweet Jesu, my friend! I think only of my own concerns. Pray, sit down! It was good of you to come."

Gratefully, the printer eased his aching frame onto the seat by the fire. "One doesn't often ignore a summons by the king, Your Grace."

"Did my messenger not tell you that you should come only if you were well?" asked Richard with concern.

"Yes," said Caxton, with a nod, "but I thought it must be more important than your eagerness to see the Malory."

The king smiled. "It is a beautiful work, William. I did not mean for you to think I didn't like it."

His feelings assuaged, Caxton acknowledged the compliment. "You are kind, Your Grace."

Richard made up for neglected amenities by tasking his attendant to bring wine and food. Once the livery was before them, he dispatched the servant promptly and turned to his guest. "My friend, you seem well for a fellow who labors most hard, while others his age rest – but you are thinner than I remember."

Caxton was touched by the king's concern. "'Tis true, Your Grace. Sometimes I work through the night and don't take meals as I should. It has been some time since we last met."

Richard's face clouded. "You no doubt wonder why I summoned you." The king drew forth a small book and brought it Caxton, who sat with his cup, enjoying the fire's warmth. "'Tis your opinion I require."

Setting down his drink, Caxton accepted into his hands what he saw to be an astonishing book. Its smooth binding and cover entranced him – the colors were so vivid! Even the Italian printers could not produce such an exquisite work. He must know how it was done.

Seeing the incredulous look on Caxton's face, the king said, "'Tis extraordinary. Now look inside."

When he opened the book, the printer was stunned. The pages were not ragged, but remarkably pliable and thin. There were no ink smears, not a one. He examined the text and found it to be English – but with such odd lettering!

His eyes skimmed over the sentences. As an expert translator of Latin and French, Caxton quickly discovered how to read the strange print. And what he read disturbed him. "This is treasonous."

"Yes – but you must read it from the beginning, as I have. Then I will explain."

As the king sat at his desk, deep in thought, Caxton did as Richard requested. An hour later, he read the last page. "I have finished, Your Grace. Pray tell me the rest."

Richard joined him by the fire. Caxton listened thoughtfully as the king told him about Anise, in whose possession the book had been discovered. He showed him the ring and described what he knew of its powers. He told Caxton how Anise insisted she had been born in a year that had not yet come to pass, and had come here from the future. How was that possible? Yet the ring's powers of empathy verified she spoke the truth. But was it truth? Or was it an enchantment?

The longer Richard spoke of the mysterious Lady Anise, the more Caxton believed the king had been enchanted – yet not by sorcery. Caxton knew Richard well, and began to understand the King's passion for this woman. Richard may be expressing anger, but beneath this outrage dwelled the pain of betrayal.

The king spoke tersely. "I must know if this book was made by witchcraft."

Caxton was surprised. "Witchcraft? Certainly not. I see only superior methods of printing and bookbinding in this exquisite tome. Though where in the world these techniques are to be discovered, I do not know. Nor have I seen our language rendered in such a way. 'Tis almost a mutation. 'Tis what happened to Latin – words changed in meaning and spelling over the centuries."

Comprehension passed over Richard's face as he pondered these words. "But what of the tale itself? Are Henry Tudor's supporters behind this plot? To destroy my reputation and any remaining faith my citizens have in me?"

Caxton considered what Richard had told him about Anise. Could her explanation be plausible? The facts seemed to add up: the language, so transformed; the book, with its advanced techniques; the magic ring allowing insight into a person's soul.

The last must be proved to him. "Your Grace. Might I try the ring?"

Richard looked at him in surprise, but handed Caxton the ring. The printer slipped it on – and was startled as his senses blossomed and he interpreted his surroundings with acuity.

When he looked at the king, he felt Richard's anger, frustration, and curiosity. "You are angry. You know you are taking it out on me, but are doing your best to repress this. Something prevents you from dealing with the woman whom you believe a traitor. You also wonder if the ring will bestow its power on me – ah, but that feeling is now gone." The old printer pulled the ring from his hand and gave it back. "Are those impressions correct?"

Nodding, Richard put the ring on. "Your facility with it startles me."

"Perhaps it is my age."

"Yes... perhaps." The king, thoughtful, looked into the fire.

Caxton took a deep breath. There was only one way to say this: "Have you considered what the Lady Anise tells you might be true?"

Richard frowned. "That she is from a future time? Utter nonsense!"

His joints protesting, Caxton got up. Sweet Jesu, he'd sat there too long! He went to stand by Richard. "Your Grace, it does seem impossible, and yet there are details in this work by... what's his name?" Caxton glanced at the book. "William Shakespeare. These details would be unremarked upon by a scribe of today, yet would be used by an author writing history to evoke a past era. Yet this is not a history, but a work of poetic art. No historian writes as this man does."

"I had noticed," whispered the king, "how I am depicted as one of the devil's emissaries."

Caxton nodded. "As conquerors typically depict those they have defeated. History is written by the winners."

"This is how I am to be remembered?" Richard asked bleakly. "A caricature of evil, appalling to look upon, who murders his kin and kills children without remorse?"

Caxton tread softly. "You are speaking of the lords bastard. I have heard the rumors – but Master Shakespeare seems to know a great deal about it."

Richard again stared into the fire. "Master Shakespeare is right. They are dead. And though I did not order it done, the blame is mine."

Caxton said nothing. So it was true. He had suspected, although could not believe Richard Plantagenet would murder his brother's sons. When they were in exile in Bruges, Caxton had witnessed the ardor with which the younger brother served the eldest, Edward the King. For Richard, Loyalte Me Lie – *Loyalty Binds Me* – his chosen credo, was not limited by the boundary of death.

After a long silence, the king spoke. "Do you believe this book contains tidings of what will soon be? That the battle shall be fought at a field near Market Bosworth? That Henry Tudor will be victorious?" Richard weighed his words. "That I am the last Plantagenet king?"

Caxton sighed. "About those exact facts, I know not, Your Grace. I only know what I can surmise about this book and about this ring. I have seen much in my life, living on the Continent as I have. I have witnessed such advances in the science of man that I never thought possible. And though none of it compares to what I have experienced here today,

I have come to believe that there is much about the world concealed from us. It cannot all be put down to witchcraft."

Richard scowled. "If she does come from the future, what could it be but sorcery? Surely such a thing is not science?"

Caxton suspected there was more behind this vehement belief that Anise was a witch than he knew – but he could guess.

Richard paced as he thought aloud. "If the lady speaks truth, if Master Shakespeare's poetry is prophecy – it means that because of Stanley's treachery, I am soon to die. It portends that he who is the most unworthy of the crown, Henry Tudor, descended through bastard blood, shall rule England in my place. It means that my decision to seize the throne from Edward's bastards will have been for naught. If I had not acted on Stillington's word, then Edward V would be alive – and king! A bastard would be king, but one more worthy than Tudor. If I accept this book as truth, I acknowledge that my bad judgment shall result in historians and poets through the ages casting me in the role of a monster, and portraying my life as a tragedy." Richard appeared stricken. "And perhaps they would be right. Yet, I cannot accept it. I will hear no more of this foolishness from you. Leave me now."

Caxton had no choice but to do as the king ordered. He left.

Richard's realization was a cruel one – but the printer could not dismiss it. For when he had worn the ring, "The Tragedy of Richard III" had lain on his lap. Caxton had gleaned the truth of the book, and knew for certain it foretold the future.

Yet there was one more piece to this puzzle that he must discover, and she was imprisoned somewhere within the castle walls.

****

"Bishop Morton, you know I am surprised to see you. I thought you were in England with my mother." Henry Tudor's expression registered concern. He was playacting his role as king to the hilt.

Although Morton had spent little time with Margaret's son, his resemblance to his mother was striking – so much so, it pained the wizard as he recalled her betrayal.

"I have certain abilities enabling me to travel swiftly, without horse or ship, Your Grace." The bishop glanced uncomfortably at the other members of Henry's court. "Might we speak alone?"

With a flamboyant wave, the room cleared of all but one man who stood across the room, observing them. Henry said, "That is my uncle, Jasper Tudor, who is in my confidence."

"Jasper Tudor? We met long ago," stated Morton. "I hear the tales of his military prowess – and his loyalty."

Henry motioned for his uncle to join them. Jasper recognized Morton. "How many years has it been, Bishop?"

But Henry interrupted, "You have proven your loyalty, as well, Bishop Morton. Your warning two years ago kept me from falling into Richard's hands, enabling me to escape to France. When the kingdom is returned to rightful hands, you shall be generously repaid. Still, your presence now concerns me. Did my mother send you? Is something wrong?"

Morton bent this moment to his advantage. "A complication has arisen. The Lady Stanley begged me not to tell you. She feared..." he purposely hesitated, "she feared you would postpone your invasion if you knew the truth. But I thought you should be told. Unbeknownst to her, I have come."

Henry Tudor's face went white, then red. When he stood, his kingly poise stayed behind in the makeshift throne. "Mother thinks I'm afraid!"

Jasper urged Henry to take his seat and not panic. He spun toward Morton with a hiss. "What is this about?"

Morton addressed him calmly. "I bring you news about Glendower. Treat me with civility, and I shall tell you."

Henry whispered urgently to his uncle. Jasper looked around for an attendant, but found them gone. With a grunt, he retrieved a nearby chair for the bishop.

Henry asked, "What is this news?"

Although he'd rehearsed every word, Morton pretended to weigh each one with great consideration. "Glendower's resurrection was not entirely successful. He has been called back in spirit, but not in corporeal form. As he exists now, he will be ineffectual to your campaign."

Henry gasped. But Jasper became angry – not at Morton, but at his nephew. "I told you we cannot count on sorcery to secure this battle. Here is the proof of it. We can win without the help of wizards!"

Henry shook his head. "We will not! My cousin, Richard, has never lost a battle. The launch must be called off!"

Morton thoroughly enjoyed this little display, but pretended not to notice. "You shall have the assistance of one magician." He held up his hand. "This ring gives me supernatural abilities. It is built with Glendower's magic and is powerful and true. Your mother might not believe in you, but I shall help you prevail, Henry Tudor. God and Bishop John Morton are on your side."

Henry was still beside himself. "I do not believe—"

Jasper snapped, "Collect yourself, nephew. You look no more like a king now than you did on the day I rescued you from Pembroke, fourteen years ago. Behave as a sovereign, if that indeed is what you hope to be!" Jasper's eyes flashing with contempt, he turned to Morton. "What can this ring do? How can it help us?"

The bishop suppressed a smile. "He who wears it is able to travel – with magic. If our young – king – here, wears it, it will keep him from harm's way. If he learns to use it with proficiency, he might visit the enemy camp, gain information, and return to his tent within seconds. Perhaps he might even murder Richard Plantagenet in his bed. 'Tis possible. If His Grace wears this ring in battle, he will not die."

Morton saw Henry's eyes widen. The young man had clung dearly to his father's title, Earl of Richmond, but had been controlled by others his entire life. He desperately craved the power of kings. Royal, though bastard, blood burned unfulfilled in his veins. He would gladly go to fight – if he knew he could not die. All this, Morton knew.

Jasper did not believe him. But using the ring's second sight, Morton knew the uncle would not interfere. A transformation had come over Henry and he spoke with surety. "What price shall you name for this ring, Bishop Morton?"

Morton smiled. "You misunderstand. 'Tis only that I believe your cause to be just. Have I not already proved my loyalty, as you pointed out? I ask only that, when you defeat your cousin, I am granted the honor of serving you, Your Grace."

Henry's eyes were fixed on the ring. "I must have it." He turned to his uncle. "When do we launch?"

Jasper appeared startled by his nephew's fresh resolve. "We shall be ready in a month's time. We set out no longer than a fortnight after that."

Henry looked at Morton. "I must have the ring now. I must learn its powers."

"You may not have it yet," said Morton, his words bold to the ears of one who already considered himself King of England. "I need it for a while longer. There is business in England which must be attended to." His prelate's robes swept the floor as he turned his back on the self-proclaimed monarch. "You shall have it in due time."

Henry got to his feet. "I have not given you leave to go. I demand the ring now!"

But the bishop had already vanished into the howling vortex.

CHAPTER FIFTEEN

Anise watched the dab of sunlight creep across the stone wall.

For a week and a half, her existence had been reduced to lying on the mattress, her body sluggish from inactivity, her mind numb with boredom. She'd finished the diary and still had gained no memories of her father or her brother.

She'd given up on Richard, too – but refused to believe he hated her. In her mind, she relived the night they'd made love. Hadn't he cared for her then? But the comfort in that notion vanished whenever she remembered that he was going to die – and die soon.

Anise sank into a depression that required no thought.

One day, she heard voices beyond the door when it was not mealtime. She recognized the sounds of arguing and sat up.

Maybe she had given up on Richard prematurely. She prayed it was him.

The door bolt lifted and someone came into her cell. Anise released a breath when she saw the man was old and thin – perhaps he was another poor soul who would be locked up with her. At least she would not be alone.

But no, the elderly man wouldn't be staying. She heard her keeper – the one who brought her meals – grumble, "You got but a few minutes, Master Caxton. Lord Stanley says she ain't to have visitors."

The door slammed. The man sighed.

With her hopes dashed again, Anise started to cry, the first time in a week. Or was that a month? She looked at her visitor and forced back the tears. Crying was not going to help.

The old man stood in the center of the room, looking uncomfortable. "I shan't be allowed to stay long."

Perhaps he had information about what was going on outside her prison. "Have you news of Richard?"

He gazed upon her with sympathy. "My name is William Caxton. I have spoken to the king."

Anise could barely ask. "He's not dead – yet?"

"So you *are* the Lady Anise, then? The woman of mystery."

She nodded. "That's me. A mystery even to myself."

Caxton said carefully, "I have just now left Richard. He is well, but troubled, m'lady – troubled about *you*."

Anise's heart leapt into her throat, and she gasped, "He's here? He hasn't forgotten about me?" Swallowing hard, she stared at the old man.

Caxton seemed uncertain how to continue. "His Grace summoned me to Nottingham to ask me for advice. I am a printer. He needed my expertise – about a book."

The name "Caxton" clicked in her mind – of course, England's first printer. Her blood froze when she realized what he'd said. "He read the Shakespeare." Anise covered her mouth with her hands. "Dear God, oh, dear God."

Caxton stated quietly, "Richard believes it's treason."

She choked. "He must hate me."

The old printer did not hesitate. "Not at all. In his heart, he holds you dear."

Tears flowed down Anise's face. She wiped them away. "Then why hasn't he come?"

Caxton sighed. "His Grace suffers terribly. Though he knows what he *should* do, he cannot bring himself to publicly accuse you. Yet if he chooses to believe your incredible story, he must accept the deaths that followed in the wake of his seizing the throne have been for nothing."

The man's thorough understanding of the situation stunned her. "How is it you know so much?"

Caxton whispered, "Because I have worn the ring. I have seen the truth."

Speech abandoned her.

"His Grace showed me the book you claim to have brought from the future. He wanted to know if it was made by sorcery."

Anise's mouth went dry. Her nightmares of being burned alive flashed in her mind.

"I was astounded by many of the book's qualities." He paused for a long moment. "I told him these things might be possible with advances in the printing sciences. Then the king insisted that I read Master Shakespeare's tale."

Anise could barely breathe, let alone speak.

Caxton shook his head. "What a shock it was, m'lady. At first I, too, believed it treasonous: the enemy's attempt to turn the citizens against their king. But I am also a translator by profession. The strange lettering, the unorthodox spellings, the poetry of the words. It made me wonder why someone who wanted people to believe these things had included so many blatant untruths? His Grace has been seen in public all his life. He has no crookback nor withered arm. Would that then not cast doubt upon all the rest of it?"

Anise stared at the old printer. If he kept talking this way, he would end up sharing a cell with her.

"Then His Grace described your insistence that you came from a year far distant in the future." Caxton's voice dropped. "He said he was compelled to believe what you told him."

"Because of the ring," she whispered.

Caxton nodded. "Then he gave it to me, so I could know its power. When I put it on, Master Shakespeare's book was lying in my lap – and I knew beyond a doubt it came from the future."

Anise inhaled sharply. "Did you tell him that?"

"Richard insists this 'truth' is an illusion, although in his heart, I think he knows. How can he be blamed for it? To learn one's actions will come to nothing, after so many had lost their lives? 'Tis a hard truth to bear."

"What's he going to do?"

He shook his head. "I don't know."

Disheartened, Anise sighed. "Thank you for telling me."

But Caxton was not done. "His Grace has been my friend since he was a child. I lived in Bruges for many years. For awhile I was in the employ of his sister, the Duchess of Burgundy. Richard and I grew close during the time he and his brothers were exiled there. I love him dearly." He seemed to weigh his next words. "You know what is to happen, do you not? Because, for you, it has already happened. Tell me then – is he to die?"

Tears prickled behind her eyes again. Anise could not speak, so she nodded.

Caxton looked stricken. "I'll go now."

What had just happened sank in. "You believe me?"

Caxton gazed at her, his eyes bright. "I can only believe my own senses. I knew the truth when I wore the ring, and I know it still. Yes, I believe you." He reached for her hands. "I know one other thing. At first I did not think I should tell you, but now I must – His Grace does love you."

Anise stared at him. Might there still be hope?

There was a sound at the door. "I must go," said Caxton.

"Stop, please." Anise rummaged through the pockets of her bedraggled gown and retrieved the pages of history she had torn from Shakespeare's play. As the bolt was drawn, she shoved them into Caxton's hands. "Take these to Richard – it's his future. He should know what's going to happen. If he would agree to see me, I could explain everything!"

The printer quickly folded the pages and hid them in his clothes. "I will do my best, Anise. I cannot guarantee he'll read this."

"If he won't see you, take them to his mother at Berkhamsted. Tell her they're from me."

"I will," he promised.

"Time's up," said her warden, who stared at them through the door.

Caxton turned to her. "The future of printing – it is assured, then?"

Feeling the first bit of hope she'd had since being arrested, Anise smiled. "Yes, Master Caxton – your invention will make its mark."

****

When Thomas, Lord Stanley, passed Caxton on the stairs, he recognized him immediately. He was here to consult with the king about the book, no doubt.

Richard's agonizing over the Lady Anise quite amused Stanley. The king would come to the conclusion she was a traitor. Or a witch. How could he not? It was a circumstance that would play right into Stanley's hands – as Margaret had intended.

She was wily, his wife. The lord did not doubt it had been her – or perhaps that snake, Morton – who'd arranged for the book to be found in Anise's room. It fell right in with Stanley's plan to transport her to his estates at Lancashire, where Glendower waited to marry her. As it turned out, Stanley might have already been able to complete this task – but for some plans of his own he hoped to accomplish first.

Anise had been a prisoner for a fortnight. That ought to be long enough. Stanley ordered that she be escorted to quarters more fitting to her station, where she was allowed a bath, a decent meal and a damsel to attend her.

By this hour, she ought to be settling in for the night.

Stanley knocked at the door of her new apartments. When her attendant let him in, he summarily dismissed her.

Anise stood by the fire, her alluring curves draped in a maroon gown, her hair tumbling loosely down her back.

When she heard his footfall behind her, Anise turned. She was beautiful, her face radiant. Then her expression crumpled. Stanley comprehended all: she had been expecting Richard.

His resolve hardened. All the better. Yet she must believe he feels kindly toward her.

Stanley said smoothly, "You must wonder why you have been brought here. I wish it were good tidings, but I cannot lie to you."

Her voice shook. "What tidings?"

"Upon the king's order, you are to be executed come dawn."

Her eyes grew wide and Stanley repressed a smile. When she swayed, he closed the distance between them and caught her. Holding her next to him sent a thrill to his loins. He dare not reveal his intentions yet. By morning, he hoped to have control over both Anise and the ring. "You nearly fell. Allow me to help."

Anise pushed him away. "I'm going to be killed without a trial?"

Stanley had anticipated the question. "A tribunal of judges examined the evidence. The conclusion is irrefutable."

After the many days in captivity, Anise's face had thinned, throwing her cheekbones into sharp relief. Her eyes now filled with fear and her lip trembled. Stanley wanted to capture that mouth for his own. How he desired her!

Her voice shook. "How am I to die?"

"Perhaps you should sit down, lady," said Stanley, approaching her. "Let me pour you some wine."

Anise backed away. "Just tell me."

Stanley shrugged. "His Grace has decided that he cannot subject a woman to the traitor's death – drawing and quartering. Mercifully, you shall be sent to the block. Your end will be quick."

At this, Anise sank onto a stool by the hearth. Stanley could barely make out what she said: "Beheading."

Stanley pulled up a seat. It took all his muster to repress his desire. "I can help you, if you let me."

When she turned, her face registered surprise at his closeness. "How?"

Stanley could not bear that her mouth should be within reach but he could not claim it – yet. He looked at the fire. "I did help you once before."

"When you tossed me in that filthy cell?" For a moment, her anger overrode her fear.

Stanley's patience wore thin. Still, he controlled himself. "I transported you beyond the king's reach when he might have executed you immediately. M'lady – I do not believe you are guilty. I think Lovell planted the book in your room to make you appear guilty, and so get you away from Richard."

Anise looked astonished; Stanley saw his advantage. He placed his hands on her shoulders. "Allow me to help you." Consumed by desire, he pressed his mouth to hers. As she struggled, his manhood stirred. Stanley persisted, and she folded beneath him, bending to his will, giving him leave to crush her against him. "You shall not regret this," he breathed in her ear. He slid his lips down her throat toward the v-neck of her gown. "I shall ensure you do not die."

He slipped a hand inside her bodice and caressed a breast. *Sweet Jesu, she would be his!*

Stanley's guard had slipped and in that moment, Anise knocked him away and scrambled to her feet. By the time he had recovered from his surprise, she was across the room.

Anise stared at him with hatred. "Your terms are unacceptable. I already told you I'd rather die than sleep with you."

His face hot with humiliation, Stanley's fury gripped him. *I will take her now. She will have no choice in the matter.* Her eyes widened as he took a step toward her. He stopped in his tracks.

That would not work! If he took her forcefully, she would never agree to join forces with him against Margaret.

Stanley took a breath. The night was yet young. Anise believed her life would end at sunrise. A few more hours of thinking about death would set her priorities in order.

He could wait.

Stanley smiled. "You need time to think about my offer. I understand. Expect me before dawn."

****

Pacing in his office, the king recalled the expression on Master Caxton's face when Richard had turned him away for the second time. After their confrontation this afternoon, Richard did not want to hear more of the same. He made sure the old printer had escort to London, but he refused to talk to him.

If the king believed what Caxton thought possible, then Richard was doomed to burn in Hell for all eternity. How would God be able to forgive him? How could he forgive himself? He would not deserve forgiveness.

Anise, from the future? It was impossible. A book foretelling Richard's death and Henry Tudor's victory?

Richard dared not believe it.

He dared not.

And so, his advice obtained and rejected, the king sent Caxton away. The time had come for Richard to face the inevitable.

Though he loved her, Anise must stand accused of witchcraft.

As he made his decision, a knock sounded on the door. A page answered it and a messenger entered, bowed low before his sovereign, and handed Richard a parchment. After bidding the boy to rise, the king opened the missive.

It was from Caxton.

"To His Grace. Know that I rue our disagreement. Know also that, in the event that you should need me for any reason, I will return. For you and no other shall remain my sovereign lord. Yet I cannot depart without making a request on behalf of the lady who so occupies your thoughts. Give her audience before her fate is decided. You will regret your decision otherwise, for I know you, my friend. Your loyal servant, Caxton."

The king dismissed his servants. Standing before the hearth, he pondered Caxton's note. The old printer had visited Anise. He had done what Richard could not – to seek impossible answers to impossible questions.

Yet Richard had faced the impossible before. Certain defeats on the battlefield had turned to victory. Too, he had stood up to unbearable truths and yet had borne them. The deaths of his father, his brother, his son, his wife. Through all these, Richard Plantagenet had endured.

What was the specter of his own death in comparison? On numerous times he had confronted that wraith and triumphed.

Richard braced himself. Caxton was right. It would not be wise to make a decision without knowing. It would be foolhardy and he would live to regret it.

Just as he had regretted his refusal to face in person those who had betrayed him, especially Buckingham – who might have confessed what he knew about the grisly deaths of the Princes had Richard given him audience at the end.

But what if this impossibility proved true? Would admitting the last two years of his blood-soaked reign had been for nothing be easier to endure than deciding Anise's fate without all the facts?

The king crumpled the paper and threw it into the fire. "I cannot," he whispered aloud. "Sweet Jesu, I cannot."

****

Dread crept into Anise's every muscle as she sat staring into the dark. Perspiration prickled beneath her arms. It was hard to breath as she imagined her own death. Would she feel pain as the ax sliced through her spine? Would Richard watch her die? She had no answer to these questions. She did not even know how she would react. Plead for mercy or go to her death with courage?

Afterward, would existence be the soul-dead limbo she had experienced when traveling through time? She suspected that it would be, caught in that place, insentient, surrounded by other lost souls.

There *was* a way out of this.

Stanley.

The thought repulsed her. She might sleep with him – and then be sent to her death. Stanley would laugh: he had never meant to save her. She would die with shame seared into every inch of her body. And Richard, with the power of empathy through the ring, would know what she had done.

That was one betrayal she would *not* commit.

Death it must be then.

She smoothed her hand over the velvet of the gown she wore, and felt queasy. Anise refused to die in clothes Stanley had given her.

From the garderobe, she pulled the tattered black costume she'd worn to the fifteenth century. She called for Maud to bring her a needle and thread.

For what remained of the night, Anise occupied her mind with repairs.

After the rips were mended, Maud helped her scrub the away the dirt. Anise donned it to her attendant's approval. If the damsel knew of the fate awaiting Anise, she never mentioned it.

Dawn drew near, and the knock came.

Stanley stood on the other side of the door, ready to deal. He ordered Maud out, and cast a critical eye to Anise's apparel. "You throw off finery for rags?"

Her usual anxiety was gone, her voice steely. "I intend to die in my own clothes."

He frowned. "You refuse my generous offer?"

Anise exhaled slowly. "I won't betray Richard." She turned her back to him.

"Has not His Grace betrayed *you*? You are going to the block without a trial." Stanley sounded smug as he took a step toward her. "Give me the pleasure of your body, and I allow you to live. My retainers are waiting outside with horses, to enable our escape. Do this one thing and you shall be free."

Anise heard him move nearer. She braced for his touch. When it did not come immediately, she turned to find his face inches from hers. Her voice did not shake as she told him, "Death is preferable to being indebted to you."

The words were barely out when her jaw rocked with pain. Stanley wrapped his arms around her. Anise shoved him away. He caught her again, crushing her against him, his hot breath in her ear. "Time's up, witch." He dragged her to the bed, pushed open the curtains and flung her onto the mattress. He anchored her body with his. Anise struggled, but could not move.

She glared at him. "Get off me!"

"I'm having you," he ground out. "And the ring, too." He pressed his mouth on hers, forcing his tongue between her teeth.

Repulsed, Anise bit down. With a cry, Stanley punched her again. She almost passed out, but jerked to lucidity when she felt him grab her skirts and yank them up. Anise screamed as he forced her legs opened with his knee. When he reached to loosen his hose, she pushed her advantage and almost got away, but Stanley caught her and wrested her back down onto the bed. She struggled futilely as he poised his manhood between her legs. When she opened her mouth, he covered it with his hand, muffling her cry.

A moment later, the weight of his body lifted as Stanley was wrenched off her. There were shouts. Anise sat up in time to catch a glimpse of him through the bed curtains as he was dragged from the room by two men. A cold draft on her legs reminded her about her state of undress and she pushed her skirts down.

Anise's heart pounded in her chest as the truth sank in. She'd almost been raped.

A man's voice: "Confine the blackguard to his quarters. I'll get to him later. Wait outside."

It sounded like…Was it…?

Footsteps approached the bed. A hand grasped the edge of the curtains and pulled them back.

Anise saw the ring. "Richard?" Relief swept through her when he reached for her. The king helped her to her feet, his dark eyes filled with concern.

Though he had denied her, though he had imprisoned her, though he had sentenced her to death, there was no one else in the world she wanted to see more.

Wordlessly, Richard guided her to a chair. His voice was terse, but tempered with worry. "Has he harmed you?"

She shook her head. "Almost – if you hadn't come when you did…" Her sentence trailed off.

His gaze was intense. "Thank God I found you in time."

Dawn's light filtered through the window. Anise realized what time it was. "Am I going to die now?"

Richard brushed her cheek. "I should never have let it get this far…"

Her voice quivered. "Then I'm not to be executed?"

"Is that what he told you?" he asked hotly.

Anise nodded.

Richard's eyes flashed. "I would never do such a thing to any woman, especially not you. Not even for treason."

Weak with relief, she breathed, "Caxton found you?"

Richard averted his eyes. "I did not see him. He has left for London."

"Then he didn't give you the pages of history I gave him?"

His demeanor was sad. "You stand by this story about being from the future – about knowing what happens to me?"

"Yes, Richard – because it's the truth."

"I read that book. There was no 'history' – no proper discourse on the sequence of events. Only artifice and lies."

"Because when you read it, those pages weren't there. I ripped them out. I was going to burn the play, because I knew if you read it, you'd think I..."

"Was a witch?" He smiled ruefully. "Or a traitor?"

Anise's mouth went dry. "I'm not either."

Richard took a step back and nodded. "So you say." He turned to gaze into the fire.

Anise did not care what he thought of her. She had to tell him what was going to happen. Her voice was low as she began. "Henry Tudor's fleet will land at Milford Haven on the coast of Wales sometime in August. He will receive no resistance from the Welsh. The battle..."

Richard spun to face her. "I will not hear this!"

"Listen!" she said louder. "The battle was fought near a place called Market Bosworth. Don't rely on Northumberland – he's going to back out of the fight. Don't trust Lord Stanley, either – you probably know this, but he's going to betray you – and so will his brother. They went over to Henry's side, Richard – and you died!"

Anise stared at him, wondering if her words sank in. She saw that they had. He'd heard her! Thank God, he'd heard her.

He did not break her gaze. "You speak as if it already happened."

"It has, for me. You have to believe me. If you trust nothing else I say, believe this – I want you to live."

Richard's face was unreadable. He walked toward the door as if to leave. Anise felt the wall come down between them. "Do not fear for your life. I have destroyed the book. It shall be as if it never existed. An armed escort will take you wherever you want to go. I will deal with Stanley."

Anise's heart broke as she watched him leave. If history played out as written, he would die.

CHAPTER SIXTEEN

Lady Stanley paced the hall where a few moments earlier she had been sitting peacefully among her ladies and their embroidery. It was empty now, except for her and Morton. "It's not safe for you to be out wandering. People think you are in Flanders. If anyone should see you..."

Morton repressed a scowl. He knew Margaret had no true concern for him. "I've been to Wales, raising support for Henry." It was a lie.

Lady Stanley seemed satisfied with this report. "If my son lands too soon, he will need all the men he can get."

Morton was surprised. "Your husband hasn't yet delivered the bride?"

Margaret shook her head. "He has not come. I know not the reason, unless the king has discovered Thomas' treachery."

"Maybe Stanley has plans of his own." That ought not to sit well with her.

Margaret's eyes widened. "He wouldn't betray Henry!"

Morton said nothing.

Lady Stanley lifted her chin. "I have taken matters into my own hands – I've sent Thomas's son for him. He will listen to his son."

Morton could not hide his irritation. This could spoil his plans. "Which son, lady?"

"His firstborn. George, Lord Strange."

"How much have you told him?"

"He knows nothing about what we're doing," said Margaret. "But he'll convince Thomas his place is here."

Morton paced. "What if the king interrogates Strange about his father? Do you think he's figured things out?"

Margaret shook her head. "He knows nothing," she caught her breath, "only that his father and his uncle are loyal to my son – but he shall never reveal that!"

The bishop threw up his hands. "Should Richard learn this, Thomas Stanley will never be allowed to come home, let alone bring Owain's bride!" *Sweet Jesu, without the bride, my plans for revenge will never see fruition!*

Margaret snorted. "Bride! More like the king's harlot. But I did not tell thee – Thomas has seen to it she has been arrested and put in his charge. Why is he not here yet?" Through the ring, Morton sensed her distress. It was time for concern when Lady Stanley's plans went awry.

His mind raced. "We must contrive an alternative plan."

Margaret turned to him in relief. She needed him at last. Morton smiled – but not out of love.

****

The king could barely control his rage as he hastened to Stanley's quarters. That his steward had so injured Anise rent Richard's soul. 'Twas doubly hard knowing he had trusted the lady to Stanley's charge.

If he had not decided to act on Caxton's advice, Anise would have fallen victim to the lord's lechery. Richard would not remain in residence at Nottingham with Stanley here.

Two men-at-arms stood at either side of Stanley's door. They bowed as Richard approached.

Stanley stood in the center of the room, scowling. He spun to face the king. They studied one another silently. Richard touched his ring and knew Stanley's deceit.

"Thomas, Lord Stanley, I hereby declare you to have acted dishonorably in your position as steward of the Royal Household. Your soul and your name have been besmirched with this shameful act – and I, as your sovereign and liege lord, are shamed with thee." Richard could not suppress his fury. "Your attack on Lady Wynford is an attack upon me. Is this how you regard all your duties to the crown?"

Stanley's face contorted. He was angry at being caught – not remorseful for what he'd done.

"She bewitched me." Stanley's voice was cold – yet his lust was still roused for Anise. "She enchanted me so that I would desire her. I had no choice but to take her to bed."

Richard dared not show his rage. "You would not admit the truth to the Holy Mother, let alone me."

Stanley's eyes burned. "What will you do? Send me to the block without a trial?"

Richard felt the blunt edge of these words – and did not care. But his voice he kept steady. "Indeed, I would."

The steward's eyes widened.

"But I shall not – yet. However, you cannot remain at Nottingham. I want you gone, Stanley – back to your estates until you are sent word to come and defend king and crown."

The king sensed Stanley's relief. He did not trust him, but was put in the position of relying on his support. What if Anise's tale of madness were true?

It cannot be true, the king told himself. *It is impossible.*

"You do intend to remain loyal to the crown, do you not? Anything else is treason."

The steward forced a smile. "I am your servant, Your Grace."

"Then you will forgive me – and understand why I take measures ensuring that loyalty?"

Stanley's smile faded. "What mean you?"

Richard nodded to his men. One departed, returning a few minutes later with a man in noble dress.

The steward's face fell.

"Your son, George," the king said simply. "Lord Strange shall remain under guard with my retinue until our confrontation with Tudor is decided. Your eldest son's life depends upon you, Stanley. Are we understood?"

Stanley's face went red – but he nodded. "I do."

As he was leaving, Richard turned. "I want you and your men gone by dawn."

****

Though almost daybreak, Anise had not slept a wink. Still occupying the room Stanley had arranged for her, she was too numb to cry. She paced the room. Maud stuck by her, doing her best to comfort Anise, but fretting whether she would be held responsible for Stanley's getting into the room in the first place.

Anise's relief that she was not going to die by the king's order wore off quickly after Richard told her he was sending her away.

She would live, but he would not. In despair, she realized there was nothing else she could do to save him. Within weeks, Richard would lie dead on the battlefield. And if she did not get the ring back – and even if she did – she might be calling the fifteenth century home for good.

She must see Richard one more time. It would be one more chance to convince him not to go to Bosworth.

There was a knock.

Maud jumped from her chair. "What if it be His Grace, mistress?"

Anise forced herself to be calm. "Just answer it!"

The damsel opened the door a crack. "Go away. The lady is indisposed until sunrise." Maud squealed when a group of armed men burst through. The men were clothed in the king's colors and wore Richard's white boar emblem.

The leader stepped out from the rest while Maud fluttered beside him, casting worried glances at Anise. "My name is John Harper, retainer to the king. He has sent us as escort. We shall accompany you to whatever destination you name. His Grace orders that you depart Nottingham before daybreak."

Anise realized she would not meet Richard again. She'd not get the ring back and she could not save him. What could she do? Where would she go?

Then she knew.

Anise stuffed her few belongings into a small trunk and addressed the knight. "Take me to Duchess Cecily at Berkhamsted."

****

Through the window of his office, Richard watched Stanley and his regiment recede from view as the sun's rays shone on the village of Nottingham below. Though glad to be rid of Stanley, Richard paced, the weight of the kingdom on his mind.

How he longed for Francis' company. He wanted to discuss these turns of events with an adviser who was also a friend. Despite Francis' recent disloyalty, Richard still trusted him. But the viscount would be in Southampton for another month preparing the Navy against Tudor.

The king had been angry with Francis for trusting Stanley. But had Richard not done the same? And yet, neither did he trust Anise, who loved him but did not lie – or so the ring informed him.

Still – how could he believe her words foretelling his destruction?

"Henry Tudor's fleet will land... Don't rely on Northumberland... Don't trust Lord Stanley... If you trust nothing else – I want you to live."

Richard longed for her presence.

Having seen Anise and knowing she cared for him, it tormented him she was so close, and yet he could not go to her. He wanted to wrap her in his arms, to carry her to his bed, to let her know that he loved her.

He loved her.

Richard yearned to lie with her, to join his body and soul with hers.

When he'd found Stanley forcing himself on Anise, Richard had wanted to kill him.

The king loved Anise – but he could not believe her story.

A knock came. It was a squire with his breakfast and a vessel of wine. Richard nodded to the servant to pour and sat reluctantly to sup, his thoughts heavy.

Anise gave him hope and despair. She gave him a future but stripped him of his past. She gave him life and death. If he accepted her love, he loathed himself. Sending her away smote him to the heart. Keeping her with him did the same.

To keep her safe, he must live without her.

Preparations for the battle would be all that kept Anise from his mind. God be thanked such concerns were plentiful.

A ruckus outside disturbed his meal. Beyond the door, his men-at-arms held a rough-shorn knave who seemed familiar. Richard demanded to know the reason for the commotion.

The captain came forward. "Pardon us, Your Grace. This man admits to being an accomplice in some act against Your Grace – but he will not disclose what it is to us. He is a stableman at Kenilworth, but 'twas here at Nottingham that he came forth, asking for audience with you." The man cast an inquisitive glance at the captive. "He sayeth his conscience bothered him."

A few laughs ensued among the men. Richard did not join in. His eyes narrowed at the fellow. His attuned senses detected guilt, remorse – and fear. The king stood and motioned the prisoner forward. "Release him unto me."

The knave was released. With fear, he took a few steps toward Richard.

The captain held out a cloth pouch. "There is this evidence, Your Grace."

Richard took it. "Leave him to me."

Acknowledging the dismissal, those in the room made hasty retreat.

The king stared at the scruffy man, who had fallen to the floor in deference. "Rise," said Richard, taking his seat.

The knave stood, his tongue frozen.

"What is your name?" asked Richard, in a tone that brooked no deceit, yet was not entirely unkind.

The man's voice shook. "Dick Hawley, Your Grace."

"Tell me what you know. Do not be afraid. I shall not go hard on you if you admit the truth. Who has deceived me?"

Richard sensed the rogue's relief.

"Lord Stanley, Your Grace. 'Twas Lord Stanley."

That, at least, was no surprise. Richard held up the bag. "And what's in here?"

"A letter, Your Grace. Mostly burned. I saw Lord Stanley put it in the fire – at Kenilworth, Your Grace."

"How did you come to see this?"

"I-I watched through a crack in his door, Your Grace."

"Were you working for Lord Stanley?"

"He paid me a gold sovereign, Your Grace," he said, as if this explained everything.

"Do you know what's in the letter?"

The man's face turned red. "I cannot read, Your Grace."

Richard's patience wore thin, but he did not let it show. "What service did you perform for Lord Stanley?"

Hawley looked at his feet. "I... I carried a message from Kenilworth to Master Jennings, the constable here, Your Grace."

The king considered the man. The ring informed him Hawley knew more than he was saying. "What else?"

Hawley fell to his knees and bowed his head. "That I could be so untrue to Your Grace torments me."

Richard pitied the man. What price was loyalty when a gold coin could buy bread for his family? What harm was a small service performed for Lord Stanley to eke out some comfort from the world? But to feel the sting of conscience, and throw himself on the mercy of his wronged king – that was an honorable man, and Richard could not hold it against him.

The king sighed. "You performed another service for Lord Stanley."

Hawley stared at the floor, unable to meet his sovereign's eyes. "I told him you spent the night with the Lady Wynford."

Richard closed his eyes. It was as he had suspected. Hawley told Stanley – and Stanley informed Francis. He opened the cloth pouch and withdrew a charred parchment. Half of the letter had burned away, but he learned enough.

Richard forced his eyes from the words to the messenger, grounding out, "You have eased your conscience. Get out of my sight."

Hawley scrambled to his feet and ran.

CHAPTER SEVENTEEN

Richard held forth in his office and refused to see anyone but those with information about Anise. So far he had learned, from questioning the constable of the castle, that Stanley had imprisoned her for weeks in a filthy cell. He also discovered that Stanley had departed Nottingham before dawn with a woman riding by his side, her ankles bound to the stirrups.

Stanley had taken her against her will – and it was all Richard's fault. Instead of protecting her, he had banished her from his presence. His blood chilled at the thought of her at Stanley's mercy. But what chilled him most was that Stanley was within his rights.

For the dozenth time, the king read the remains of letter —

Bring to Lancashir
nise of Wynford
ward of Thomas, Lord
tract of betrothal to
Master Glen awaits his bride.

—and could glean only that Anise was a ward of Thomas, Lord Stanley, that she had been pre-contracted in marriage to a Master Glen, that her presence was required in Lancashire and that Stanley must return the runaway bride to his estate.

Stanley had manipulated the situation for his own benefit, to break down Anise's resistance, to seize an opportunity to be alone with her to take advantage. This infuriated Richard, yet there was nothing he could do to save the lady from her fate.

If he had known the truth sooner, he might have appeared publicly with Anise, protecting her by his favor – for who would have opposed the king? Richard might have sought dispensation to break the pre-contract or—

The king shook his head in frustration. Such delusions were madness. Stanley had played him for a fool, and Richard had walked right into it. Now he must accept the fact that there was nothing he could do for Anise.

It struck Richard that his brother, Edward, had been politically embarrassed more than once because of a woman, which had had a negative impact on his ability to govern.

In this, Richard had believed he and his brother to be very different. In this, Richard had been wrong.

Edward had been in love with many women who'd paved their way to his bed with lies.

But Richard could not ignore Anise's lies.

Who was the man Anise had been looking for when Richard had found her in the woods? Was Dominic really her brother? Or had she concocted the story to escape her marriage to Master Glen? Was she lying about the ring, too? And the book? And her unbelievable story about being from the twenty-first century?

As Richard stared at the ring, someone knocked.

"Who disturbs me?"

"'Tis Sir Thomas, Your Grace. I have Lady Anise's attendant who was with her when she was taken."

Richard went to the door and flung it open. Sir Thomas, a knight Richard recalled from his ranks, stood with a woman whose face was as white as bleached bone.

Sir Thomas led her into the room. She was visibly trembling.

"Why did you not come to me before this?" demanded Richard.

The woman looked like she might faint. Thomas answered, "We caught her attempting to escape to the village, Your Grace. I did bring her directly here when I learned she had waited on Lady Anise. Her name is Maud."

Richard's considered her. "What know you about Anise, madam?"

Maud opened her mouth to speak, but nothing came out.

"Sit her down," said the king. Sir Thomas guided her to a chair. "Tell us what happened or it will not go well for you."

Maud summoned the courage to look at Richard. "I-I was with her, Your Grace."

"When Stanley's men came?"

She nodded. "I tried to-to keep her from going, but her mind was set, Your Grace. I could not stop her."

Richard's ire increased. He demanded, "Stop her from what? What do you mean?"

Maud again swallowed with difficulty. "I could not prevent her from going with him. I tried. She ordered me to pack her trunk and she left!" cried the woman.

He felt as if his chest had been kicked in. "She went with him by choice? Is that what you're telling me?"

Maud nodded as the king paced. Coming to a dead stop, he faced her. "What did you say?"

Thomas pulled Maud to her feet. "Answer His Grace!"

Richard's eyes burned into hers. "Repeat what you said."

Maud's voice shook as she murmured, "The lady and Lord Stanley were lovers, Your Grace."

Richard saw red. He saw Maud crumpled on the floor, sobbing. He stared at his hands. Sweet Jesu, he had struck the woman!

Sir Thomas was staring askance. Richard turned to his knight and said raggedly, "This woman lies. Get her out of here. Make her tell you everything. Then go after Stanley. I'm putting you in charge."

"Yes, Your Grace." The knight dragged the weeping Maud to her feet. As he was about to leave, he looked at his king.

Quietly, Richard said, "See that the Lady Anise is safe. Bring her back to me."

Sir Thomas nodded and was gone.

****

Cecily Neville was glad to hear she had a guest. Even more pleased was she to discover it to be her old friend, Master Caxton. Her devotions finished for the morning, the duchess went to the sitting room at Berkhamsted where she received guests. Will looked thinner and considerably older than when she had seen him last – but then, didn't they all?

Caxton grinned when she came into the room. "A fine welcome to you, madam. You look well indeed!"

Cecily could not help but smile. How good to have company!

"Master Will! How kind of you to come from London to see me. Have you a new printing?"

The old printer was obviously pleased she asked after his craft. "Indeed I do. Indeed," he nodded, indicating a large pack on the floor.

The duchess recalled his back trouble and said, "Sit down, Will. We shall get to know one another again."

Grateful, Caxton settled into a chair by the hearth.

Cecily sat across from him. "Tell me – what news is there of London?"

He sighed. "The city is busier and more crowded than ever. I am often glad for my decision to keep shop in Westminster instead." Caxton grew serious. "Yet I come not from London, madam. I bring news from Nottingham."

Cecily was surprised. "So far north! What business had you there? Did you see Richard?"

"'Twas he who summoned me there. There are doings of great import occurring at His Grace's court. Richard is troubled."

The duchess whispered, "I have had no word from Richard of this."

Caxton frowned and reached for his pack. Fumbling within it for a bit, he withdrew some crumpled parchments. "Before I show you these, I must ask you – know you a lady by the name of Anise?"

Apprehensive at the mention of that lady, Cecily nodded. Had Anise tried to switch rings with Richard? Had she been caught?

"The king," Caxton hesitated. "Your son is... enamored... of this lady. He..."

Cecily stood and walked to the narrow window. She knew what Caxton wanted to tell her. She decided to make it easy on him. Her gaze fixed on the fields below, she asked, "Did Richard take her as his mistress?"

"Yes."

Cecily's heart lifted. There was a chance that Anise had gotten that ring off Richard's finger – and gave him a reason to embrace life once more, as well.

She turned to Caxton, suppressing the hope that had sprung to her heart. "Tell me."

"I know he loves her," said the old man. "There is more to it than that."

The duchess returned to her chair. "You said Richard is troubled." Cecily had known there would be risk when she knowingly sent a woman about whom she had known nothing into her son's midst.

"'Tis complicated. I'm hoping when you read these, you'll understand. Anise asked me to give them to you." Caxton handed her the pages.

Cecily smoothed the papers on her lap. "What odd parchment." When Caxton said nothing, the duchess examined the text. "Such strange letters. What language is this, Will?"

"Look closer," he said. "'Tis our own tongue."

And she did look closer. Cecily saw one word she recognized. "Richard," she read aloud.

When she looked at Caxton, she saw him nodding. "This tale is a strange one and will take long to unravel, madam. There is the matter of the ring."

Cecily's mouth fell open.

Caxton raised an eyebrow. "You know of it."

"I do."

"Then we may yet save his life."

****

Anise cursed to herself. Here she was again, chained to a miserable horse, trudging through the night, staring at Stanley's back... All because she was too stupid to see the man's ruse.

How could she have taken for granted those men wearing Richard's colors were Richard's men. How gullible she was.

She cursed herself again.

It was only a small addition to the number of insults tossed at her by Stanley after he finally believed her about the ring. At least she had not slipped up that time.

After she had been escorted out of the castle, Anise had been startled when one of Richard's men grabbed her and forced his foul fist into her mouth so she could not scream. In moments, they had gagged her and tied her to the horse. She had not even time to wonder at Richard's motives when Stanley appeared before her, grinning triumphantly.

"Little fool," he hissed. "I understand Richard Plantagenet twice as well as you think you do. Come dawn, he will be wondering if his decision to send you away was right. By noon, he would have come for you. You really believed he would expel you into the night? Most harlots know their men better than that."

The rag in her mouth did not allow her to retort, yet his words stabbed through her heart. Stanley was right. How could she have thought Richard would do that?

Agonized, but too exhausted to cry, Anise trudged behind Stanley. As they rode into a copse of trees, beyond the sight of those watching from the castle perched high above them on its great rock, he reined his mount to a halt. A half dozen of his men also stopped.

"Move on," he cried to the majority of his men at arms. "To Lathom, all of you!"

Anise's stomach tightened. She had postponed considering what Stanley's intentions were in abducting her. Now there was no denying it. He would finish what he started.

"Get her down!" he ordered. "Bring her to me."

Roughly Anise was untied, pulled from the horse and dragged before Stanley, who had dismounted and stood a ways beyond the road.

"Remove the gag."

One of the men ripped the cloth from between her teeth, but Anise could not speak because her mouth was so dry.

"Bring a flask!"

A moment later, a soldier put a flask to her lips and poured warm ale down her throat. She choked as it ran down her mouth and over her dress.

"Leave us. All of you," Stanley demanded. "Ride up the road, beyond my sight."

Anise looked at each one, her eyes pleading, but they avoided her gaze. Not one would oppose his master's will.

Anise stared at the ground as their horses galloped away. When they were alone, Stanley approached. She looked at him to find him studying her, but made no other move. At last, he pulled a cloth from his belt. Anise held her ground as he wiped the ale from her chin.

"I bring to the table another bargain." His voice was matter-of-fact.

Anise glared. "Why don't you just get it over with?"

"Because I would rather have you willingly."

"Forget it."

"You should listen to what I have to say before tossing away your life."

Anise swallowed hard. "I would rather die than..."

Stanley rolled his eyes. "Yes, I know. Listen – what I tell you will interest you. I have not gone through the trouble of this abduction simply to ravish you. You are caught up in machinations I suspect you know nothing about. Once you hear what I have to say, you will be ready to deal."

"So tell me." Anything that postponed Stanley's touching her was a bonus.

"First of all, I know you are my wife's agent. She has revealed to me by letter that she knows who you are."

He had accused her of that before, but Anise had no idea what he was talking about. Who was Lord Stanley's wife?

Then it came to her: "Margaret," she said aloud. *Of course! But how did Margaret Tudor Stanley know who she was?*

"Margaret – and you are her apprentice. Don't deny you are a witch. The book proves it."

Where was all this leading?

"You also can't deny you know about the ring."

This startled Anise. "What do you know about—"

"Did you steal it? Is that why Margaret wants you back so desperately?"

Anise's mind whirled. What did all this mean and how could she use it? She stalled. "Is that where you're taking me? To Margaret?"

Stanley smiled. "She and the great wizard have plans for you and that ring. He wants to marry you. Perhaps the idea of taking up with me is more appealing than sharing a dead man's bed?"

His words found their mark. "M-marry... a...?"

"Dead man," said Stanley, finishing her sentence with a satisfied look on his face.

"Who are you talking about?"

"Glendower, of course."

Glendower! The Welsh wizard who had made the rings? "He's alive?"

Then she remembered the dream she'd had before Richard came to her room and made love to her that night. She recalled the energy that had paralyzed her body, the cold hand reaching toward her, the ghostly mist demanding the ring...

Glendower.

"They weren't exactly successful, Margaret and that idiot bishop. They managed to call the old fright back from the dead – only now he wants a wife. Damned if I know why he wants you, but it has something to do with that ring. Once he gets it, I doubt you'll survive much beyond the wedding night. Such a waste."

At these words, Anise felt sick. Her legs felt like water and she stumbled. With a deft move, Stanley swept her up in his arms. "You and I and the ring together could accomplish so much. Once we put Tudor on the throne, we can get rid of my wife and Morton and Glendower. Margaret's son will be beholden to me and she'll look like a failure to him, while I will be his champion. My place in the new kingdom will be assured," he whispered. "Share it with me. I promise to not demand your body at first."

Anise stared at him. "What?" *He was being sincere!*

"We could get to know one another and you would come to my bed in your own time. Everything I have will be yours – all you have to do is teach me how to use the ring."

It took a moment, but when what he was saying sank in, Anise laughed. She could not stop. Stanley scowled. He caught hold of her shoulders and shook her.

"Stop it! Damn you!"

With her head being shaken off her shoulders, Anise's laughter died. Was she crazy? Stanley was a nutcase. Best to go along with whatever he said. But she'd have to bring all her acting abilities to the fore to make this sound believable.

Anise smiled. "It was wrong of me to laugh. I should thank you for your honesty. I was laughing at myself."

Stanley's anger dried up. "What do you mean?"

"I did steal the ring, thinking what I had already learned from the Lady Margaret would allow me to unlock its powers. But after days – weeks even – of working on it, I have only exhausted myself. I wish I could avoid the fate in store for me with Glendower, but I can't lie to you. Even if I did take you up on your offer, I couldn't ensure Henry Tudor would gain the throne. I am as ignorant of this ring's magic as ever."

With a cry, Stanley threw her away from him in disgust, and she stumbled and fell, hitting her head on a rock. Through a muzzy head, she felt Stanley wrap his arms around her and any moment expected to feel him between her legs again. As she struggled against him, he instead dragged her to her feet and toward the horses, all the while cursing hotly in her ear.

"Did you think I would want you anyway? Without the ring? And then let you tell Margaret everything? To the devil with you, wench! The dead man can have you."

He lifted her onto her horse, and tied her legs together snugly beneath its belly. "This beast will be all you feel between your thighs today, sweet lady."

"That's a relief," she said loudly enough him to hear. And with her arms hugging the horse's neck as she held on for dear life, Anise set off at a gallop to her wedding.

CHAPTER EIGHTEEN

With each pitch of the sea, Henry Tudor's stomach threatened to heave. Men swarmed all about the deck, manipulating the sails, sweating and raising a stench that Henry feared could make him as ill as he'd been when they had first set to sea five days ago. Henry went to the side of the ship and gulped the ocean air into his lungs. Surrounding him on all sides was the never-ending expanse of the sea. He stared hard in the direction of England. Would his feet ever touch land again?

No one knew his weakness. No one but Uncle Jasper. Yet it was his uncle who had summoned him to the deck from Henry's safe haven below.

"Get thee above, nephew. How can thy men have confidence in a commander they never see?" Jasper had bellowed.

Henry had obeyed. As much as he hated the week's sail from France to his homeland, he must not shake the confidence of his soldiers.

Their loyalty was somewhat questionable anyway.

His true supporters were only a handful compared to the two thousand French mercenaries King Charles had mustered from the jails of Normandy with an offer of freedom for their services. At first, Henry had high hopes for them. Though his own confinement had been much easier than theirs, he understood the frustrations of prison. What man would not fight hard for his freedom?

Then he saw the motley troops: savage, but contemptuous; well-armed, but untrained; numerous, but undisciplined.

And he knew of the Welsh hatred for the French. Though Henry might be loved in Wales, would his countrymen fight for him beside the despised Frenchmen?

After Bishop Morton had come to him, Henry had been certain these obstacles would not prevent his victory. He knew of his mother's abilities. And with the power of Morton's ring upon his finger and the Great Welsh Prince, Owain Glendower at his side, how could he fail?

But Henry had not heard from Morton. He had received no instructions from his mother. Uncle Jasper insisted that to postpone their invasion any longer would be to lose Henry's cause forever. And so, with their French fleet of fifteen ships, they had set to sea from the Seine.

Long ago he had sensed his destiny within him. Henry did not look back.

And yet, all was uncertainty, and Henry was a cautious man. The fear growing in his stomach replaced his seasickness, and he gulped more air. At least the weather had been with them on this voyage.

Henry knew he should reveal himself as a capable commander, make a show of confidence and strength – and yet, he could not. The capable voice of Jasper Tudor carried across the ship. The men trusted his uncle implicitly. He was a fine general and strategist. Henry could never hope to think in military terms.

Not like his cousin Richard.

The ocean splashed against the ship, tossing it gently as Henry pondered this. He squinted through the sea mist toward his homeland. Would he ever be welcomed there?

Then he saw it, ever so slightly, through the fog. The dark brown crags of the coast.

Wales.

His heart leapt. He had so longed for it, these many years! How long had it been? Fifteen?

A cry welled up in him. "Land! Land! England lies before us! Land!" Before he could repeat his cry, his men took it up and the words resounded across the deck. "Land!"

Suddenly, he felt a closeness with his shipmates – *his men* – that he had never experienced before. Hearing a step behind him, he forced his eyes from the vision of Wales and turned to see those who so heartily shared his excitement.

Jasper stood there, a grin stretching his weathered face. "Our victory lies close at hand."

From behind his uncle, Bishop John Morton stepped forward, resolution evident in his expression. "Your Grace," he said in greeting. "I have come."

In disbelief, Henry nodded to Morton, and realized the sickness in his stomach had subsided. He turned again toward his homeland and felt the certainty of his destiny rise inside him, as inexplicably as it had numerous times throughout his life.

"Certes, victory is at hand!" he cried. "England will have no choice but to welcome me! My own country shall at last be mine own!"

Loud cheers rose up from those working on deck and Henry's joy nearly overwhelmed him. His men had heard – and had approved.

****

Margaret's first look at Anise was not heartening. The girl had been confined without amenities since her arrival in one of the lower rooms of the ruined tower, and had about her a bruised look and a wan complexion. Still, her young flesh would appeal to an old man's lust. As she peered through the crack in the door at the luckless woman shivering in the corner, Margaret considered her own situation.

Lady Anise was a formidable rival for Margaret, a faded beauty who was more than fifty years old. It would be foolish to rule out the possibility that Glendower would renege on his promise to kill his bride once the marriage had been consummated, Lady Stanley realized.

Margaret must be careful to keep all her options open. There was a coldness in John Morton's attentions toward her that indicated he had discovered her betrayal. She suspected it was Morton's hatred of Richard – and not his love for her – that kept him loyal to her son.

At least they still had this in common – Henry Tudor's cause must come first.

Margaret knew she could only gain power through the men around her – an undeniable truth even for women with royal blood flowing through their veins, as it did run through hers. There had been exceptions, but even Eleanor of Aquitaine, the strong-willed queen of Henry II, spent much of her life in close confinement.

And so, without a male consort, Margaret knew she could never gain the position she desired. If Glendower chose the king's tender mistress over Margaret, then she must scramble to the top by some other route – at least until her son was on the throne.

Now that Morton had found her out, he was no longer an option. She wondered if he knew everything – that she had never truly loved him at all.

Margaret thought of Stanley, her husband, and scowled. She had married Thomas to consolidate their properties and power. Lord Stanley controlled the great territories of Lancashire. When he confessed his feelings, she had been fascinated at his desire for her. Once married, however, she shunned his bed. Although she controlled him easily, she could not tolerate his embarrassing attentions. And now Margaret could not count on Thomas accepting her back into his life after being cuckolded by a bishop. He had not even spoken to her since his return to Lathom.

Her thoughts turned to Glendower. Uniting with the great wizard would ensure infinite power for both herself and her son. Being half Welsh, with royal blood running through his veins, Henry could rightly claim descent from Cadwallader himself. With Glendower's counsel and wizardry, Henry might rule as the great King Arthur once had.

Margaret must find out more about this wench who so captivated the hard-won attentions of Richard Plantagenet.

Margaret noted the look of surprise given her by Anise when she stepped through the doorway. "I am Lady Stanley."

"I know," the woman said in a flat tone. "Your husband has told me much about you. None of it good."

This annoyed Margaret. Thomas was a simpleton. Why should he reveal anything at all to this woman? "What has he told you?"

When Anise smirked, Margaret realized the wench had information she needed to know. Never underestimate the enemy.

"Thomas and I are lovers," Anise said shortly.

Margaret had not expected this. She tried not to care, but realized her options were down by one more.

Anise held up her hand to show the ring. "We are learning how to use this – together. Once Glendower and I are married, I'll have power equal to his. Thomas cares for nothing but to defeat you. Together we intend to fight for King Richard."

Margaret was stunned. Glendower had not let on that Anise would have power after the wedding. But why not? The concept made perfect sense. And Thomas – had he truly turned against Henry? He had switched sides so many times, how would once more make a difference? And yet, she could not ask him forthright; she could not let him know she knew!

Was the Lady Wynford bluffing? Margaret could not tell. Anise had her facts straight. To make matters worse, the lady knew she had caught Margaret by surprise.

Without another word, Lady Stanley abandoned the room, her hopes for power fading.

****

Dafydd ap Llwyd cursed as he forced himself up the stairs of his mill. The day was warm – as warm and dry as the summer was long. It had been a difficult season, for the farms and his business. Without the rains, the stream powering his mill ran low. He had to adjust the wedges every time, lowering the wheel to make the most of the currents God gave him. Now the hoist was stuck. No doubt it was the broken pulley.

Attaining the top floor, Dafydd stopped to catch his breath and considered the problem. Yesterday morn, the winds had picked up. Today they blew just as sure. Should a storm come in tonight, the stream would rise, and his adjustments to the wheel today would have been for naught.

Yet he would still have to fix the pulley. Dafydd sighed. It was nearly sunset. What chance was there that a storm would blow in by tomorrow?

Putting off his task, he went to the window facing the sea and stared out, examining the sky. He grunted. No storm in sight. Back to the pulley. As he was about to turn away, a speck atop the water caught his eye. He squinted, focusing his gaze. More specks. And more.

As they drew closer, his heart raced. It could not be. But it was. French ships.

Invasion!

He did not want to believe the word that lodged in his mind. Anger rushed through him, as it would have through any Welshman with an inbred hatred of the French. He must alert the village. Thank God in Heaven that night was falling.

Dafydd's exhaustion evaporated as he raced down the mill stairs. With hands trembling, he somehow managed to light a torch. He ran with rare purpose through the gloam toward the ancient chapel atop the crest of St. Anne's Head a half mile away.

His heart was near to bursting by the time he had crossed the distance to the deserted chapel. With only a slight hesitation, he looked up at the structure towering twenty feet above him. He entered, crossing himself and whispering, "No evil can reside in this place, in this house of God."

It made him feel calmer. He turned to the task before him.

The light from the torch illuminated the stones of the chapel and he made his way to the crumbling stairs that led to the top. Mustering his courage, Dafydd went up.

He thought about the French ships and his duty to his countrymen. In no time, he reached the rooftop and stood once more in the night. The breeze blew sure and cool off the sea, but he did not allow his mind to linger on the storm it carried in. In the darkness, the ships were visible no longer – yet he felt their presence.

In front of him was a timber frame with an iron pitch pot hanging at its center. When he put the torch to it, the flame guttered at first, and burst into a steady blaze.

The beacon could be seen from miles away – even across the mouth of the Milford Haven at N'angle. Once his signal was sighted, the next beacon in the line would be lit, until every village across South Wales would know of the invasion. The French would be repelled.

His duty done, Dafydd gulped the sea air. He ran down the stairs, thinking of nothing else but the safety of his family.

****

Jasper Tudor shivered as he set foot once more onto the shores of his beloved Wales. The sunset cast an orange glaze over the land he knew so well, throwing its cliffs into relief so sharp it rent his heart. He paid no heed to the ships with their disembarking troops. Jasper felt Wales' holy presence surrounding him as he sucked in its salt air.

Home. More than a dozen years it had been since he had rescued Henry from his comfortable prison at Pembroke Castle – once Jasper's residence. But unlike Henry, the elder Tudor had lived and breathed the air of Wales all his life, sharing his love of the land with his countrymen, reveling in the life of a Welshmen, lording as a fair and popular governor over his beloved lands as the Earl of Pembroke. Henry had lived in Wales, yes – but only within the walls of a castle until he was twelve years old. The child did not care when he left his home country behind – but it had smote Jasper to his soul.

As darkness came on, the beauty of the landscape faded. Jasper scanned the horizon. He saw no sign of the local residents. Landing at Mill Bay had been a good choice. It was nearly in the open sea and not in sight of Dale village and Carew Castle. And this tiny bay within the larger bay could not even be seen from the cliffs above.

Jasper had chosen this place because he knew it. And because here were his people – those he had governed and those he had loved. Still doubt nagged at him. Were they still his people? Would they remember him after all these years?

He feared they would not. But he guarded his anxiety closely. Not even Henry, whom he loved dearly, knew the depths of his uncle's fear.

Movement continued around him as the troops organized. Through the confusion, Jasper sought out the slight form of his nephew. At last he spotted him outside the center of activity gazing toward the cliffs.

Jasper walked toward where Henry stood transfixed. His concern for his nephew waxed great at times. So introspective, was Henry. Too much so. All those years alone, though well cared for by the Herberts, left Henry unable to become close to anyone. Should they succeed at this campaign, Jasper wondered what kind of relationship his nephew might build with the late King Edward's beautiful daughter, Princess Bess.

As he approached Henry, his nephew fell to his knees and whispered the psalm, *"Judica me Deus, et discerne causam meam."* He lowered his face to the ground and kissed it, before getting up. Though Henry had not yet noticed his presence, in tandem uncle and nephew made the sign of the Holy Cross. So moved was he by Henry's reverence, Jasper could not speak.

Henry saw his uncle and whispered, "We shall prevail."

Jasper nodded and swallowed the lump in his throat. "Come – we must make preparation to enter Dale. We know not how we are to be received at Carew Castle."

They were startled by a voice behind them. "Send these Franks back where they came from, Jasper and Henry Tudor. You have no need of them. Wales shall rise and fight fearlessly by your side."

Peering through the darkness, Jasper recognized a broad-shouldered man with rough features standing a short distance away. It was the chieftain Rhys ap Thomas who greeted them.

The large man bowed low. "Carew Castle welcomes you, my countrymen."

****

John Morton stood in the shadows near where Lady Anise slept. His journey through the vortex had left him shaken, so he rested a moment before making his next move.

The lady slumbered fitfully on a narrow cot. Morton had convinced the men at the door to let him in, lying that he had come at Margaret's behest to give Anise a strong sleeping draught.

It was imperative she make no noise when he woke her.

Perhaps he could rouse her by sending a sliver of awareness from his ring to hers. Morton focused his will upon her, but could not sense her ring. How could that be? It was the method Glendower had used to find her.

From his coat, Morton retrieved the powerless ring he had taken from the dungeons of Brecknock Castle. If he was to exact his revenge, the bishop must convince Anise to give up her ring for this one containing no magic.

Of all the rings Morton had forged, only the one he wore possessed the magical properties enabling travel and empathy. No one yet realized he had mastered it. Its mate – the original ring of power forged by Glendower – was worn by both he and Anise, but on different planes of existence, thus blocking Glendower's corporeal existence.

Going through with the marriage to Glendower would cost Anise her life. But would Anise see the wisdom of relinquishing the only shred of power she owned? Would she grasp that his plan would save her?

For the only way to get rid of Glendower was during the wedding ceremony. The moment the old wizard gave his ring to Anise, and she gave her powerless one to Glendower, his spirit would no longer be bound to earth. Glendower would be flung back into the netherworld from which Morton had called him. And if the marriage succeeded? Then the union of flesh and spirit would be made permanent when Glendower took Anise to his bed.

Anise's continued existence would be unnecessary. If Glendower did not kill her, Morton knew Margaret would.

Lady Stanley was no stranger to murder. Perhaps a glimpse at Margaret's ruthlessness would be just what Anise needed to convince her to throw in with Morton's plan.

Anise stirred. Morton crossed the room to her bed. Covering her mouth with his hand, he whispered, "Do not cry out. I won't harm you. I'm John Morton, Bishop of Ely. I will help you."

The lady became quiet. When she nodded, he took his hand from her mouth.

Her voice low, she asked, "Aren't you Lady Stanley's lover? Why would you help me?"

"I'm to perform your wedding ceremony."

"That's bloody marvelous. That won't help me at all. What do you really want?"

This was not going to work – those outside the door might hear them. Morton made a decision. "We can't talk here." He grabbed her shoulders and threw them both into the blackness of the vortex.

His ears shattered with the howling winds as Anise struggled against him. If she got free here, she might be lost forever. Morton concentrated on their destination and when he opened his eyes, they had arrived.

Shaking off his disorientation, Morton felt along the damp stone walls, drawing Anise along beside him. He perceived her fear, and extended his heightened senses to discover what other people may be nearby.

Yes, we've found the place.

This pleased Morton – his control of the ring had improved.

Shivering, Anise pulled her nightclothes around her. Morton untied his cloak and threw it over her shoulders. "We are safe. How do you feel?"

"How do you think?" she bit back. "What happened?"

"We're not at the Lathom tower anymore. I've used the ring – *my* ring – to bring us to a different tower."

Morton shuddered at the memory of the last time he had been here. He was loathe to relive it – but there was no choice.

"And why did you do that?" Anise snorted. "Not that I'm complaining, really."

"We shall be alone for some time. We can talk freely." He stopped short of telling her the real reason they had come.

Anise leaned against the wall and folded her arms. "You said you wanted to help me. So talk."

****

Margaret railed at the mist overhead. "You left out the part about how she would gain power after the wedding!"

"You never asked, Lady Stanley."

Margaret's fury raged hotter. "'Tis true then? You might not be able to kill her?"

"Do not underestimate me. She will wear a ring, yes – but she does not know how to control it. Through our connection, I shall do with her as I please."

This from a wizard who was trapped in a cloud without a body. Margaret suppressed the sarcasm rife on her tongue. "She will be able to fight you."

Glendower laughed. "A shadow of a female against the great warrior wizard of Wales is like an ant beneath my thumb. I created the ring. She cannot think of defeating me."

Margaret remembered the frightened look in the Lady Wynford's eyes. Yet the woman had also displayed surprising determination and spirit. "It's a ruse, Owain. She's stronger than she appears."

A low rumble in the tower walls began until the walls around her shook. "You doubt me?" roared the wizard.

Margaret fell to her knees. "I do not doubt you, but only play devil's advocate!" To remain in Glendower's favor was the only chance she had to gain power. She must not endanger her son.

The cloud above growled. "I shall crush the wench, absorbing her soul with the ring's power. She will struggle – oh, she will fight for her life – but t'will be as a hare struggling in the jaws of a wolf. When the two rings merge, I shall be the dominant one. After I take her to my bed, and my manifestation on earth becomes permanent, I shall discard her corpse to her own time. Balance will be restored to the world and the Great Glendower shall be Prince of Wales and King of England."

King of England? Margaret quailed beneath the wizard's proclamation, but she summoned the courage to ask the one question that mattered to her. "You will not desert my son?"

"Henry Tudor shall be victorious because Welsh blood runs through his veins – and because I allow it. But his dominion over the land shall begin and end with me."

Glendower's laughter froze Margaret's blood. *What had she done?*

CHAPTER NINETEEN

Though she clutched Morton's cloak around her, Anise shivered. From behind an abutment, they peered into a room lit only by the hearth, the red embers casting an eerie glow upon the stone walls. Unaware of their visitors, two boys slept peacefully in a shared bed.

Anise could hardly believe she was here. This was the Tower of London and those children were Edward IV's sons – the "Princes in the Tower." Somehow Morton had used the ring to carry them to this place in time – *if only he would teach me that trick* – to the night the princes died.

The bishop had described what was in store for her if the marriage with Glendower took place. He was convinced if she gave up her ring, the old wizard could be defeated. What Morton did not know was that the ring she wore did not have a shred of power, and that Richard had the real ring.

What would the bishop do if he found this out? Would he send someone to Richard's court to get it back? That ring was the only chance of survival Richard had. Anise could not risk his losing it.

She'd have to play along. The ring was her only bargaining chip. Morton would expect her reluctance to part with it. "You might think that giving you my ring is my best hope. But it's all I have for protection. What if Glendower realizes I don't have it anymore, and kills me on the spot?"

Morton had his answer prepared. "'Tis a risk, I'll give you that. But if you keep the ring and go through with this, you'll not survive the wedding night. If Glendower doesn't kill you, Margaret will."

"Margaret? You must be joking – that old bag of hot air?"

"The Lady Stanley is not one you wish to cross wills with, m'lady. She doesn't fight fair."

There was a footfall on the stairs. With a sudden motion, Morton pulled Anise deeper into the shadows, eliciting a gasp of surprise. He breathed into her ear, "For the love of Jesu, keep quiet."

A sound came from the other side of the door. As the bolt was drawn back, the unthinkable crossed Anise's mind. *Richard?* Why else would Morton bring her here? She watched with bated breath.

The door opened. Three men entered. One ignited the torch on the wall. The two princes sat up in bed, clutching one another in fear. The oldest boy cried, "I demand to know who disturbs us!" He did his best to speak with authority, but his voice shook.

"They've come to kill us, Ned," said his brother quietly.

"Silence the brats." It was a woman's voice. And it belonged to Margaret Beaufort, Lord Stanley's wife and Henry Tudor's mother.

Anise grabbed Morton's arm in relief. *Not Richard!*

The children screamed when the men approached the bed. "No one but us to hear you." With two swift blows, the boys were knocked to the floor. With the force of a bear crushing a squirrel, one burly man punched the youngest child in the jaw. Anise heard bone crack.

"Dickon!" The oldest prince threw himself in front of his brother to shield him.

"Don't kill them!" shouted Lady Stanley. "I need them alive – for now."

The men did not hit the boys again. The princes stopped struggling as they were gagged and bound, as if they'd been expecting this.

Anise sank against the wall, nauseated. She glanced at Morton to find his eyes fixed on the gruesome spectacle. She grabbed his sleeve. Edward's sons did not have to die! She put her mouth his ear. "We can save…"

Morton put a hand over her face before she could mutter another word. His grip was like iron. Anise gave up fighting him. She had no choice but to watch the scene play out before them.

"Bring them to the hearth." Margaret's voice was like ice. The men laid the boys out side-by-side before the fireplace, as if for slaughter.

Anise realized with horror that's what it was for.

The youngest prince stared with wide eyes at the Lady Stanley.

He recognizes her!

Margaret approached the hearth. "Stoke the fire!" One of the men picked up the iron and poked the embers into a blaze. She stood over the bound children. "Leave me."

Anise stared transfixed, wanting to turn away but unable to. The firelight flickered over the doomed children's faces. Lady Stanley gazed at them, a demonical hunger in her eyes. The door slammed, leaving her alone with her victims. "Do not fear death, Your Graces. I promise to make it quick."

Anise did not know how the knife came to be in Margaret's hands. The witch held it before her with fingers curled lovingly around its carved handle. The narrow blade had a lethal point. When the princes saw it, they struggled against their ropes.

Anise could not escape Morton's grip, his hand held firmly over her mouth.

The Lady Stanley kneeled before Ned and ran her finger over the knife. "Be pleased, my children, for your deaths shall not be in vain. Your self-righteous uncle will accept his blame and hold it dear."

Margaret pressed the blade against the eldest prince's throat. The edge bit in and a trickle of blood trailed onto his collar. He whimpered.

The flames threw a light over the witch's demonic face. Her lips curled into a smile. "He who usurped your power, Edward Plantagenet V, shall pay for his mistake. You are avenged!" With a deft motion, Margaret Beaufort slashed the blade through Edward's throat. His head fell back limply and blood gurgled from the jugular as the boy's heart fought through its final pulsations. A thick red puddle formed around the killer's knees.

Anise stared in mute horror as the Lady Stanley dipped her fingers into the gaping wound and put them to her mouth, tasting her work. Gall rose in Anise's mouth and she gagged against Morton's hand, but he did not let go.

Her repulsion was replaced by shock when Edward's corpse caught fire. A few feet away, Margaret watched the dead prince become engulfed in flames, an expression of rapture on her face. When the fire died down, Lady Stanley raised the knife and took a step toward the youngest prince, who stared in wide-eyed fear.

Anise could fight the nausea no more. The odor of burnt flesh brought the contents of her meager supper into her mouth. Her stomach cramped and she doubled over just as Morton shoved her into the howling vortex.

****

In his dream, Richard had lain with Anise again. Now the memory of it followed him about his duties and would not release him from its grip.

They were in bed at Middleham. Richard always knew peace at the childhood home that had become his adult haven. This contentment pervaded the dream. Yet it was odd – for as so often happens within the confines of slumber, past and present merged.

He had returned to her after a journey so long, he could not remember its purpose. *She* stood before him in her nightdress, enraptured at his sudden appearance. She was beautiful in the firelight. Richard gazed at her, longing in his heart. In her eyes, he recognized her desire for him. They had no need for words.

He went to her and caressed her shoulders. She pushed his hands toward her breasts, and his loins tightened. When their lips came together, he felt her nakedness beneath him, and knew they had found their way to the bed. Her hands ran over his back, over his hips. She reached lower and opened like a flower as he thrust into her.

Saying her name, he awoke with a start. It was not his wife, Anne, he had called for. It was Anise.

A tap came at Richard's door, rousing him from his thoughts. He nodded to his page, who stood near. He must keep his mind clear – there was England to think of.

Francis came in and Richard's heart lightened – until the bitter memory of their last meeting came to mind. He turned his will to the ring. Using it had become second nature. He perceived the viscount's nervousness.

"How go the preparations in Southampton? Is the navy ready?" he asked coolly.

Their estrangement chafed the viscount. *He should have thought of that before aligning with Stanley*, thought the king with bitterness.

"Henry Tudor will find no purchase on England's southernmost shores, Your Grace." Francis bowed his head in deference – an uncommon gesture between them when they had been friends.

With a curt nod, Richard tried to be indifferent of the hurt he sensed in Francis. He found he could not stop caring. Too long had Francis been his friend. Despite his friend's lies, Richard could not help wanting to mend fences. If he had not been King of England, he might have given in. But his duty was to his country. Betrayal could not be brooked.

Francis folded first, his voice low. "Might we speak alone, Dickon?"

Richard strengthened his resolve, preparing for another lie. He dismissed the page, who closed the door behind him. Not wanting Francis to guess his inner conflict, the king went to the window to stare down at the sprawling countryside.

Francis could not bear this. "Don't turn your back on me, Dickon." The plea caught at Richard's heart.

The viscount came to where Richard stood, inserting himself into his peripheral vision. The king felt his childhood friend's inner turmoil and recognized it as his own.

Francis bowed his head. "Sweet Jesu, I have betrayed you – as you know." He hesitated. "When I came to Nottingham and learned of Stanley's vile behavior, I knew I had been duped. Yet that is no excuse for the betrayal of my king – and my dearest friend." Francis kneeled before Richard, his words ringing with regret. "I know you cannot forgive me. I am brazen to ask, but Dickon – I do ask." His body shook. "I surrender my life to your will."

Richard felt Francis' agony – and could not deny his affection. Swallowing the emotion gathering in his throat, he grasped Francis by the arm and urged him to stand. They stared at one another, unable to speak. At last, Richard broke the silence, his voice rife with certitude. "We have all been manipulated by Stanley. Would that I had put his head to the block as hastily as I

had Hastings'. Your life remains your own, Francis. I only pray you choose to serve me for as long as I need you – and I *do* need you, my friend, more than ever."

They embraced as brothers and put their differences aside. It was the first time in years Richard had won back what he thought was lost forever. At last, he had done something right.

****

The murders had knocked a hole through Anise's heart. Morton, incensed that she would not yet agree to his plan, returned her to her cell, and what remained of a night that refused to end.

"My plan is your only chance." Morton faded to transparency before her eyes. "You have an hour before I return, before I seek another way to defeat Glendower. And *you* will be on your own."

"I need more time to think!"

"There is no time left." Morton vanished.

Anise sank upon the cot. She might have no choice but to go with Morton's plan. But as soon as he had her ring, he would know it was as useless as the one he meant to give her to trick Glendower. What would he do then?

Their journey through the howling hell of time had shaken her, and witnessing that innocent child's murder had left her sickened. Morton's threats, the fear of her own death, and her desperation to save Richard overloaded her thought processes. She did not know what to do.

In despair, she wept. This place of no hope, she had been here before – lived it, breathed it. The uncertainty, the ultimatums, the everlasting night. When had that been? A memory stirred, but she could not call it forth. Odd how she had forgotten its existence when now it felt as familiar as home. Shivering with dread, she sat curled upon the cot, staring at the black window at the top of the room, waiting for the light.

****

Morton arrived before dawn. One moment she was alone, and the next he had materialized from nowhere. Her eyes smarted from the light cast from his lantern. He gazed at her with eyes that were yellow pools of reflection. Darkness took hold inside her.

"If you resist, you must die." There was steel in his voice. He withdrew a leather strap. "I cannot let you live now you know my plan."

Anise stared. She did not want to die.

"Dawn approaches. I cannot allow you to marry Glendower, one way or t'other. Your decision which."

His threat sounded to her very depths. From there stirred a memory. Anise had felt this terror before. Ignoring Morton, she found herself dropped front and center into a horrible, frightening place. It was the well from which sprang her illness, the source of her anxiety, the reason for her panic attacks.

It was her mother. *"If you tell anyone, I will send you to an orphanage!"*

"It was you! I know it was you! I saw…"

Morton leaned in to peer at her. "What is wrong with you?"

His words disrupted the memory. She stared at him. For that moment, she had remembered a sliver of her childhood. She could not shake the feeling, and did not want to.

But it had gone. And Morton was still here, threatening her life.

Anise had no choice. "I'll go along with your plan. I'll switch the rings. But we have to do this my way."

Morton looked at her as if she'd gone mad. "You are in no position to make demands."

"Use your head," she argued. "Glendower is able to detect my ring. So if I walk into that ceremony without it, he's going to know right away that I don't have it."

This logic undid Morton. He shrugged. "No matter. I will protect you by directing the power from my ring around you, like a cocoon. I think it can be done. I haven't tried it, but—"

She looked at Morton squarely. "You have no idea, do you? What if it doesn't work, this cocoon thing?"

"Well, I..."

Anise narrowed her eyes. "Here's what we're going to do. I will swap the rings – but I must go into that wedding wearing the real thing. It's the only chance we have to fool him." She knew what Morton did not – that she wasn't wearing a ring of power at all. But Morton's papoose of power idea? Anise did not like the sound of that.

"How will you change my ring for yours during the ceremony, when Glendower will be focused on you the entire time?"

Anise nearly shouted, "Who's conducting this ceremony?"

Morton appeared confused. "You know I am."

"Then come up with a diversion," she snorted. "As soon as Old Smoky looks away, I'll do it."

The corner of the bishop's mouth twitched. "Of course. You make a good strategist, Lady Anise." He opened the pouch on his belt and withdrew a ring. "Give me your hand."

She clenched her fist – she was prepared for his tricks – and showed him the ring. He held his imitation up to it. "They are like enough."

He pried open her hand and put the powerless ring into her palm. "There is much risk in this plan. I must work out the details of the... diversion."

Before Anise could reply, Morton was gone.

****

On the eve of the ceremony, Glendower lingered as a mist over the spires of the ruptured tower. The consequences of his plan troubled him. Loathe as he was to admit it, the Lady Stanley may be right. He was not certain he could dispose of his bride once they had wed and consummated the marriage.

Just as civil marriage unites male and female into a single entity, the laws of alchemy dictate that the "conjunctio" is the only way to restore balance to a man's soul and thus attain immortality.

Yet because the ring's power and its bearer's spirit are intertwined, the contract of matrimony must be entered into by both parties willingly. Wresting the ring from its owner would break the contract. Anise must accept him of her own free will, or Glendower would remain incorporeal forever.

Her choice would be marriage – or death. What better way to convince her?

But how would destroying her after the contract was made affect the union?

Glendower did not know.

With this marriage, he journeyed into the unknown. After the rings had been exchanged, he did not know the nature of their coexistence. Does the power of one dissolve, giving way to the other? If so, which survives? Would he have power over his wife, also a bearer of a ring, or would their powers be equal? Would the power of both rings diminish?

Such a risk! But what choice did he have? He knew no other way to solve this conundrum and return to earth as a whole man.

Margaret's doubt of his powers had not pleased him. Though she made for him a fine partner in subterfuge, Glendower could not keep his mind from the attributes of his beautiful bride. Anise was comely, young and desirable. How long it had been since Glendower had taken to bed a wench of such tender years? With such pleasures within his grasp, he was loathe to trade them for an old shrew.

But if he did not kill Anise, Margaret would never cooperate. Yet she was Henry Tudor's mother, and must remain alive. The wizard needed that hapless boy to be crowned king. Through Henry, Glendower could wield his rightful power and exact vengeance against England for suppressing his Welsh homeland.

Glendower's bride would have to die.

****

Richard reread the letter from his mother. He could not ignore the truth any longer. He could not deny what he had done. Despairing, he sank into his chair behind the desk.

Caxton had told Anise's story to Cecily Neville, who had accepted it without question as the truth. His mother rarely misjudged a situation this significant.

Her words settled heavy on his soul.

She has been sent by God to prevent the evil descending upon us. She represents hope that the reign of the Plantagenets might continue. My dearest son, I pray to Our Lord that thou hast not cast her away, for her enemies lie in wait for her. Behold the evidence! She is thy salvation, Richard.

Richard held the wrinkled parchments Anise had given to Caxton, and he to Cecily. The evidence could not be argued, she said. The pages contained not witchcraft – but prophecy. In them, the course his life would take was revealed.

Take counsel from these words, or England is lost. You are lost.

So it was true. His decisions over the past two years had caused only suffering and pain to himself and his country. In the end, his actions would have been for nothing.

He had no choice but to believe as Cecily, his mother, bade him.

Richard studied the pages, similar in quality to those of the book he had burned. The printing consisted of the same odd lettering, only this text had not been rendered into verse. He remembered how Anise had admitted removing some pages from Master Shakespeare's book – the pages that were not poetry, but those that described actual historical events.

His facility with the bastardized English had improved, but it was still with some difficulty that he read, "Historical Background and Sources – Richard Plantagenet was born on Oct 2, 1452, at Fotheringhay in Northamptonshire, where one hundred and thirty-five years later..."

Richard blinked and read the sentence again. "...where *one hundred and thirty-five years later* the last Tudor was to execute her rival, Mary Queen of Scots."

The last *Tudor?*

Taking a deep breath, the king considered this: The last Tudor. It read *Tudor. Not Plantagenet.*

He lay down the pages and reached for the wine, pouring some into his cup. After the spirits had steadied his nerves, he picked up the parchment again. His eyes fell upon a different paragraph.

It was a tale of battle, recounted dispassionately:

As Richard, with a small group, charged for Henry Tudor's standard, Stanley and his men swept down upon his rear. Surrounded and unhorsed, Richard III died swinging his ax. Polydore Vergil, Henry Tudor's official historian, felt compelled to record, "King Richard, alone, was killed fighting manfully in the thickest press of his enemies." The last Plantagenet died fighting.

The king's hands trembled and sweat broke out beneath his clothes. He groped for his wine cup. Sweet Jesu, he had just learned the circumstances of his own death. And for the first time, he understood what Caxton had sensed when he held the book while wearing the ring.

Truth.

He stomach soured with the wine, but his eyes sought more details – more truth.

Stark naked, despoiled and derided, with a felon's halter about the neck, the bloody body was slung contemptuously across the back of a horse. As it was borne across the west bridge of the Soar, the head was carelessly battered against the stone parapet. For two days, the body lay exposed to view in the house of the Grey Friars close to the river. It was then rolled into a grave without stone or epitaph. At dawn on the day of the battle, there had been no chaplains present to perform divine service for the king, and so the greatest fear of a soldier of his day came to pass for Richard III. He went to his grave unshriven.

Despoiled. Unshriven. Damned. He buried his face in his hands. But he could only shield his eyes from the words, and not his mind from the certainty of his fate, now that he knew it.

As this realization settled upon his heart, Richard recalled how his mother always eased him unerringly to the truth. But this time, it was too late. If he had read these pages before denying Anise, before sending Caxton away, would he have still disbelieved them? Richard did not know.

If this was not proof he was damned, then what was?

He wondered how many weeks were left him on the earth. Was there still time to atone for his sins and seek mercy from God?

A knock came upon his door, voices accompanying it. Shaken from his despair, the king composed himself. "Enter."

Francis stood with members of his counsel. "Dickon, there is news."

A nobleman clothed in the raiment of Wales came forward. He was Richard Williams, constable and steward of Pembroke Castle. "Four days ago I received word that Corston Beacon was alight. As the Haven lies on t'other side, it can mean but one thing, Your Grace."

Richard's words seemed to hang in the air. "Henry Tudor has come."

CHAPTER TWENTY

Cecily Neville drifted like a spirit through the halls of Berkhamsted. It would be *Matins* soon, but there would be few joining her for prayers at the chapel. Tonight she would pray for the soul of her last living son, and her dearest. The duchess knew she would not see Richard again. Henry Tudor had made his landing in Wales. The battle would be soon.

She had given her leave to the castle guard to join the king's forces at Nottingham. Cecily knew the futility of their mission, but could not prevent their going. And Richard would be heartened by their loyalty.

And so, there was no one about tonight, except for her ladies-in-waiting, some of the holy brothers and the household staff. Cecily was alone. That was well, for this night she preferred solitude.

Cecily paused at the door of the chapel. The thought of Richard brought a smile to her face. She was not ready to pray for the safe deliverance of his soul into God's hands – for she did not want to give him up.

Silence pervaded the castle, its mute echo pounding incessantly upon her ears. After hearing of the Tudor's landing, Cecily could not sleep but a few winks without being awakened by horrible dreams.

She had found peace within the tenets of the Church for many years and even came to believe that faith had healed the scars she suffered from the violent deaths of her family. But when the knowledge of Richard's imminent death unfolded before her, demons of doubt had returned.

Driven from slumber by these devils, Cecily sought communion with God as a way to thaw the place in her soul that threatened to ice over once more.

Surely, God's love would renew her faith, as it always had?

Yet something inside her would not let her enter the chapel.

The chimes of Matins had not yet been struck. Perhaps a walk in the garden would dispel her reluctance. The sweet scents of blooming lavender had oft before soothed her spirits. She ought to send for her lady, Isabel, before going out, but was not in the mood to keep company with someone so unscathed by life.

As she walked, Cecily dwelt upon Richard and his fate. She thought of Anise, who came from a time far distant in the future. She wondered if her son had heeded her advice and read the pages Caxton had brought her.

If so, would he act on these prophetic words? Cecily was not sure. Richard had inherited the stubbornness of his father.

She thought he might not, after all. For she felt more than ever that she'd never see him again.

Cecily looked up and realized she had wandered beyond the garden and stood now at the gatehouse. The evening was warm and pleasant, and she spotted the trees beyond the curtain walls. Suddenly, a fierce longing rose in her to escape the castle confines and walk in the woods.

The moon waxed large, throwing a gentle light over the land. She felt safe enough and would not be gone for long. It would lift her spirits and free her from this dark mood. She knew she could slip past the view of the guard manning the gates. Cecily felt adventure rise up within her. Dare she chance it?

Before she knew it, she stood on the grassy plain overlooking the castle, her home. How strange to see the darkened structure from here, without detail or inhabitants. She set off toward the wooded glade, away from Berkhamsted. She would not stay out long.

There was something about a particular copse of trees drawing her toward them.

She stopped to catch her breath, and looked around her in surprise, suddenly aware of her surroundings. The last she remembered, she had been walking in the garden – but something had pulled her this direction.

Gazing into the woods, she realized where she was: the pagan altar.

It was here that Richard had found Lady Anise lying unconscious.

Cecily crossed herself. She was a daughter of God – why would she be drawn here?

From the corner of her eye, she saw something on the ground reflecting the moonlight. Stooping to pick it up, she recognized it: Richard's ring. But no – not Richard's, nor Anne's, nor Anise's – but one like it.

How many are there? she wondered. Without a thought, she slipped it on. Lights flickered near the altar.

****

As they stood on the upper floor of the tower, torchlight reflected off the broken ceiling overhead. Anise glimpsed the forest through a crack in the partially collapsed wall. A stone cross, cracked through the middle, stood propped in the corner.

This had once been a chapel. How fitting.

Stanley held Anise's wrists firmly behind her back. Her arms had begun to ache. Margaret stood to her right, her face hard as stone. Standing behind a makeshift altar, Morton faced her. In his hands he held a small book.

The groom had yet to appear.

The bishop glowered at Stanley. "Release her."

Margaret protested.

Morton smiled indulgently. "Without her consent, the marriage is invalid."

She *could* refuse. Catching Morton's eye, she knew she could not back out now.

Stanley let go of her arms. She rubbed them, but did not try to run. Anise felt queasy. She would have to go through with this.

"It's time to begin." Perspiration beaded on Morton's forehead. He looked at her hand. Anise's eyes followed his. She was wearing what the bishop thought was Glendower's ring. But it was no more powerful than the fake one he'd given her to switch at the crucial moment.

What would happen if Glendower figured it out before they exchanged rings?

That's simple. He'll kill us.

Anise exhaled with impatience. "Let's get this over with."

Morton's voice quavered. "We have gathered here before God and his angels and all the saints, in the sight of the church, to join together two people, this man and this woman…"

Anise fixed her eyes on the ceiling and noticed a white mist gathering. *What man?*

The bishop had told her what to expect, but as the cloud grew larger, she began to feel sick. The mist expanded to fill the entire circumference of the tower. Unlike a normal cloud, this one glowed eerily with light that came from somewhere within.

How did anyone expect her to marry *this?*

When Anise caught Morton's glance, she saw him nod. The diversion he'd planned would be occurring soon.

Their plan would work. *It had to.*

The mist – *Glendower* – descended. Anise felt its cold moisture settle around her. Its particles condensed into something resembling a human figure. Anise recognized the *thing* that had visited her at Kenilworth. Her flesh, her bones, her soul shuddered.

"…that they may become one body, and so that these two souls may live in the faith and the law of God, and together be found worthy of eternal life."

Dammit, Morton – where's the diversion?

At the moment she thought it, there came a noise from the ground floor.

"Any man who can show just cause why they may not lawfully be joined together, let him now speak…"

An ominous rumble shuddered all around Anise – and she could make out words, "Who dares interrupt?"

She froze. *Glendower!*

She shivered as the cloud churned up and away from her. "Take care of it, Morton!"

Morton jumped. "Yes, Master! I will be but a moment."

As the bishop headed for the stairs, he glanced at Anise's hand as she fumbled in her pocket. While actually swapping the rings was not necessary – since Richard had the one Glendower was after – she still had to convince Morton she was playing along.

But before Morton attained the stairs, Glendower screamed, "What treachery is this? This woman doesn't have my ring! I sense no power anywhere near her!"

Morton came back in an instant. "I-I don't understand, Master! I see it right there on her hand!"

"That isn't the ring, you fool! It's a fake! If I exchanged rings now, I would be destroyed! Or is that what you were hoping?"

The bishop quailed at this, his face stricken with fear. Anise anticipated his next move.

Morton abandoned her, accusing viciously, "You tricked me!"

Throughout this exchange, Stanley crept closer to the stairway that led from this madness, and slipped down it. But Margaret had not moved, taking in the scene with nerves of steel, a smug expression on her face.

Glendower's mist swiftly gathered around Morton. Stumbling backward, Anise escaped with a cry from the cloud, which condensed and shrouded the bishop from view. The tower walls shook, nearly knocking Anise from her feet.

"John Morton. You have betrayed me!"

"Owain – it wasn't me!" Through a part in the mist, Anise saw that Morton had fallen to his knees. His arms were raised in supplication to his master.

"All is not lost yet. If you wish to live, hand your ring over to that woman – *now*!"

"My ring, master? But…"

"Do as I say!" keened Glendower. "This *will* work! *Do* it!"

Margaret stepped between Anise and the churning mist. "Owain, think about what you are doing! Give me the ring so that the two of us, worthy of power, may rule together."

The cloud boiled angrily. "I long to lie with beauty and youth, not the ancient flesh of a hag!"

His hands shaking, Morton held out his ring to Anise. As if by its own accord, it flew into her hand.

Immediately, she sensed the power trailing up her arm. She had a ring – one with power. Now she might be able to escape!

Yet her feet would not move. She was bound to the spot she stood, unable to break free of the force holding her there.

Glendower laughed. The mist coalesced into human form, and the wizard took his place beside her. "I will take you to wife, my harlot. Morton, continue the ceremony!"

The bishop had staggered to his feet. "M-master – you must remove your ring, to be ready for the exchange." His voice shook.

Lady Stanley protested, "It's me you should wed!"

"You cannot marry, have you forgotten? You have a husband."

Margaret was flung back against the wall.

Anise watched in horror as Glendower removed the ring, glowing gold on his misty finger. "Get on with it, John. Do it now."

Morton murmured, "Wilt thou have this woman to thy wedded wife, to live together after God's ordinance in the holy estate of Matrimony?"

Anise wanted to scream, to cry, to stop this madness. But her voice was frozen, her soul ice, as she gazed into the glimmering mist.

"Wilt thou love her and keep her in sickness and in health, and, forsaking all others, keep thee only unto her, for so long as ye both shall live?"

With each word, the cloud grew more substantial. As Glendower regained human form, Anise stared in horror upon his face, consisting only of gleaming bone, decayed flesh and the eyes of a demon.

The face of death!

The wizard consumed her beauty with his gaze – and smiled. "I will," he whispered.

Anise screamed. When Morton turned to her, she gaped. "Help me!"

He merely looked at her, outmaneuvered as he was. "Wilt thou have this man to thy wedded husband, to live together after God's ordinance in the holy estate of matrimony? Wilt thou obey him and serve him, love, honor, and keep him in sickness and in health, and, forsaking all other, keep thee only unto him, so long as ye both shall live?"

A compulsion welled up within her. Her lips formed the words, and her tongue moved unbidden in her mouth. That *thing* was forcing her to answer! Anise fought the urge with all she had. *I will not consent! I love Richard!*

Morton's words shook fearfully. "Wilt thou, Lady Anise? Answer!"

Anise averted her gaze from Glendower's terrible face. His eyes burned through her, compelling her. She could resist no longer. "I-I will."

Morton turned to his master. "Taketh the lady's right hand and repeat after me..."

Glendower had substance enough now to secure her hand in a vice-like grip. Morton's litany disintegrated into white noise.

Anise's traitorous tongue spoke the words implanted in her mind. "...and thereto – I give thee – my troth."

In a voice that echoed with death, Glendower intoned, "With this ring, I thee wed, with my body I thee worship and with all my worldly goods I thee endow..." The wizard forced his ring onto her finger. He did not release her, but pried open her palm in search of Morton's ring.

When he snatched it from her hand, Anise's mind filled with static and the world went black. Within moments, she crashed back to consciousness, her ears pounding from Owain Glendower's agonized scream.

Then silence. Anise was splayed on the floor with the Lady Stanley crouched beside her laughing. "Owain Glendower, thou shalt not have trifled with Margaret Beaufort!" The tower shook dangerously around them. Morton was nowhere to be seen.

And everything went dark as Anise tumbled into the vortex.

****

Richard woke in a sweat, sheets binding his limbs. He never could remember the dreams that smothered him in doom, but had them whenever he slept. This night he had conferred late into the night with his Privy Council on how best to rebuff Tudor's landing in Wales. No decision could be made, no matter how they debated. At last, upon Francis's urging, Richard had retired to his room.

The night was uncomfortably warm. Although nearly Matins when he went to his bed, Richard did not fall asleep until his mind was exhausted and his thoughts incoherent. He woke now with a shudder, realizing it had not been the dreams that had awakened him, but a burning sensation in his hand.

The ring!

Its blaze of angry power rushed up his arm. What was this all about?

After several minutes, his arm began to ache. His breathing grew more labored as the ring's sorcery took its toll on his body. The king stared at the ring as the thin light of dawn filtered through his window, but his eyes saw nothing.

He closed them – and his heart leapt. He saw *her*.

Her black gown ripped to the knee, her hair flying about her face, Anise called to him. "Richard... help me!"

"Anise." She was there, so real he could have touched her.

Darkness swallowed her. A hollowness filled him. She was gone. He knew it with a certainty he could not explain. Wherever Stanley had taken her, she had been alive – until a moment ago.

His arm stopped hurting, but he felt the aftershocks of the ring's power. This had not been a dream.

Anise was lost to him forever.

Soon he may join her. How long had he fought to survive? It did not matter, now that all he'd loved was gone. A sense of the eternal enveloped him. He knew his death was near – that time was short. He no longer feared it.

What had been impossible now seemed within reach.

Richard felt more capable than he had in years. He had a strength Henry Tudor did not – the strength to die.

I shall bring you with me, cousin.

If neither of them lived, England would be better for it. Richard had named his nephew John de la Pole as heir to the throne. John would make a good king and an honorable one. The country would continue to thrive under Plantagenet rule. The descendent of bastard slips would not inherit the kingdom.

Dawn was breaking when the knock came. For a moment, he waited for his page to answer, but remembered he'd dismissed the boy in the middle of the night. Richard pulled on his robe. "Who's there?" His sense of purpose renewed, he felt no weariness.

Francis entered. "There is a matter of great import which needs dealt with, Dickon."

Richard opened the door and found Sir Richard Ratcliffe, one of his councilmen, in the outer apartment. Richard said to him, "Send for my attendant, Sir Knight, so that I might dress and join you in my office." Ratcliffe left.

"What has happened?"

He hoped for word of Anise – but knew it would not be so. The kingdom was threatened, and one woman's welfare would not seem important to Francis. It should not weigh so with him either, he knew.

Francis's expression was grim. "Stanley's son attempted to flee last night. We caught him, but when he was questioned, he let it slip that his uncle, Sir William, intended to support Tudor."

Richard was not surprised. "What of his own father?"

"George insisted his father would remain true to the crown. But news from that quarter is not encouraging. Thomas answered your summons with the excuse he wouldn't be joining us – yet – because he suffers from sweating sickness. He said he'll be there when need arises."

The king frowned. "We must consider our options."

"We dare not trust him, Richard. Without the Stanleys…"

Richard nodded. "Without the Stanleys, we are outnumbered."

****

The tower shuddered on its foundations. The earth shifted beneath Morton's feet, and he realized he should flee. Great boulders broke free from the building and crashed nearby. Death would find him instantly, if he was unlucky.

An odd calm enveloped him. Morton knew luck – and something else – was with him.

The rocks came down in an avalanche, scattering around him until the only clear ground was the small circle in which he stood.

Dust raised by the tower's destruction obscured his view. Many trees had been crushed; broken branches lay all about him. At last the tower's throes of death ceased. The air cleared and dawn's light filtered through.

Morton stood unscathed amid the ruins.

Glendower was dead. Morton, the inadequate student, had vanquished the great Welsh wizard. For the first time in his life, the bishop knew his own power. He had remained calm in the face of death and defeated it.

His master was no more. Yet Morton knew his debt to Glendower had not yet been fulfilled. With the knowledge of the ring, his teacher had ensured Morton's long life. In return, Morton must see to it that Henry Tudor became king.

Not that his hatred of Richard Plantagenet had anything to do with it.

Shaking free of his reverie, the bishop stepped outside his circle of protection – and heard human noises coming from the forest. A ways into the woods, beyond the rubble, he spotted the Lady and Lord Stanley catching their breaths. Covered in dust, the lady that Morton had once loved looked no better than a charwoman. When Lord Stanley got to his feet, he brushed his fine clothing carefully, with nary a glance toward his wife, who was doing the same.

They deserve each other, thought Morton with contempt. He left them to their own devices.

Once Margaret comprehended the damage she had done to her son's cause by knocking the ring from Anise's hand, the lady would agonize over it. That must be punishment enough – for now.

Henry Tudor would prevail because the bishop would make it happen. Glendower had prophesized that Morton would wear the archbishop's red robes. But Morton must earn Henry's favor without the Lady Stanley's assistance. Margaret must never again be allowed influence over his life.

Morton realized he must not go to Henry too soon. Tudor would be far more grateful if the bishop showed up at the eleventh hour and provided the supernatural assistance the young man was counting on.

In the meantime, Morton could make his plans comfortably in his house across the sea.

He glanced at Margaret one more time. The familiar ache for her had deserted his heart. If he could not have love, then he would seek power. In the end, it was far more satisfying – for it did not betray.

Satisfied with this shift in priorities, Morton turned his thoughts toward Flanders.

Though he no longer wore the ring of power, it mattered not – its magic had been absorbed by its maker. And Morton realized, *I have surpassed my master.*

Without another thought, he fell into the blackness of the vortex and went home.

CHAPTER TWENTY ONE

Anise screamed, but no sound could be heard in the dark vacuum of time. Her journey with Morton through the vortex to witness the prince's murder had lasted only seconds. But here and now, time stretched to infinity, and she drifted without thought or sensation through the vastness of eternity.

It was familiar, this place. She remembered running in fright, someone at her heels, and then stumbling down stairs, into the blackness – and falling forever. Night and shadow filled her. Anise embraced the darkness, where there was no sensation, no sound, no sight.

This was death.

And this was life – her existence flashed through her mind in disjointed fragments: caring for her invalid and ungrateful mother, struggling against ever-present panic, being bullied at school, pushing past the tears, braving out college and losing her fears in drama, sobbing her eyes out, struggling to fit in, forcing herself to hold it together, missing her Dad.

Dad.

Anise gasped into consciousness. *I remember!*

She knew where she was. And she knew what had happened.

Hearing a loud pop, and seeing Daddy buckle over. Momma screaming for Anise to get out of the way. Matthew fighting with Daddy, who pulled a gun before he fell to the floor. Another loud pop, and seeing Momma fall, tears streaming.

"Momma, don't die! I promise I won't tell anyone! Just please don't die!"

After that, time fell into suspension, physical awareness subsided, and Anise rested, existing only as subconscious thought. When her mind awakened again, comprehension dawned at last.

Don't tell, don't tell, don't tell how Matthew rushed in too late to stop Gwendolyn from committing murder. How Matthew fought with a dying man, a man vowing to take his wife to hell with him. And how the bullet flew wild from Daddy's pistol and caught Momma in the back.

"Don't tell anyone that I shot your father," Momma whispered. "All they'll remember me for is murder."

Anise wept. Momma was dying. She would have promised anything to save her. Where was everyone? Where were Matthew and Dom?

"Don't tell, honey, please don't tell."

Anise heard the police sirens.

She remembered all of it now. Anise had given up her childhood memories to protect her mother. In her strange, formless existence, there were no tears. She did not think she could ever cry again.

Her mother had not died, but Anise had lost her.

Anise had lost everyone.

And now I've lost Richard, too.

Richard had needed her and she, him. They filled the emptiness in each other and somehow they had healed the grief. When everything and everyone else she had ever known was gone, Richard was there. He saved her – then abandoned her. Then saved her again.

Now that he believed in her at last – she could not save him.

Maybe I still can, with Glendower's ring. I only have to learn how to use it.

She had the power of the gods at her fingertips. Time had no meaning. She *could* change things – change them for Richard. For Dom. For herself. She had time on her side.

But how to get where she needed to be? How could she learn to use the ring if she had no idea how to begin? How had Morton done it? Maybe if she…

Like the sudden dying of a gale storm, all went still.

When she opened her eyes, she found herself sprawled on the living room floor in Matthew's farmhouse. To her left, she saw her tote bag and its scattered contents.

A man stared at her from the center of the room – her brother, Dom. He had grown from Anise's gauzy childhood image of him into an adult.

On his finger, he wore the ring.

****

Cecily moved closer to the pagan altar so she could see, murmuring a hasty prayer for protection. As the light grew stronger, a mist arose. Within it were shrouded, but insubstantial figures, and Cecily knew she was witnessing an enchantment. Through a break in the gloam, she recognized the Lady Stanley, crouched on the floor of a ruined tower, her face twisted with laughter. Cecily shuddered. So the rumors were true – Margaret was a sorceress. *That woman had carried Anne's train at Richard's wedding.*

Beside Margaret was her foul consort, Bishop Morton. Cecily recognized another woman – this one in a black dress. It was the Lady Wynford, staring in horror at—

Cecily gasped – it was an abomination from Hell, a ghoul with the countenance of death and bone, reaching for Anise. Unable to look away,

Cecily grasped a nearby tree for support. *That the poor girl should die by that creature's hand —*

But Anise stood up to her attacker. The ghoul opened his mouth and screamed – the sound echoing through the silent woods – and vanished in a cloud of smoke.

The enchantment faded and was gone.

Her heart racing, the duchess hugged the tree for support, its rough bark biting into her cheek. The morning haze evaporated beneath the rising sun, which cast dappled shadows across the sandstone altar, turning it into a harmless pile of stones.

When her breathing returned to normal, Cecily's gaze fell to the ring she had placed on her finger when she first came to this unholy place.

The ring! She hastily removed it and stuck it in her pocket.

Cecily returned to the castle, hoping no one had missed her. On the way, she spoke a prayer for Anise's soul – and one for her son.

****

Silence enclosed the darkened storeroom where she had found the ring that night of the dress rehearsal. Through the window of the farmhouse, Anise heard the soft sound of rain pattering on the roof and a dove cooing a haunted song. Reaching for the switch beside the door, she flipped it on, and light washed over the clutter. *So they'd finally turned the power on.*

The brightness of the sun at the flick of a switch. *How strange.*

She immediately went to the shelves. There were history books here. Lots of them. There had to be something about fifteenth century England. She pulled a book from the shelf and cracked it open. Turning to the index, she found "Richard III" and went through the page numbers until she found what she needed: the details of his final days.

August 18, scouts brought word that Henry Tudor's host had lain outside the walls of Lichfield the evening before...

August 19, Richard came down from his eyrie on the rock of Nottingham and took the southeast road to Leicester...

August 20, Richard mustered his host...

August 21, the royal army formed along the route, trumpets resounding, Richard on a white courser, a commanding sight in his full armour, bearing a golden crown upon his helmet that friend and foe alike might know that the king was going forth in battle...

The descriptions painted images in her mind until she thought her heart might break. She forced back the tears. This was no time to cry.

Down the Swine's Market swung the troops, over the bridge across the Soar. As the king crossed, his spur momentarily scraped against the stones of the bridge. An old woman that some believed a seer cried out, "Turn back, Plantagenet! The foot that strikes the stone shall be your head next crossing." And indeed, as Tudor's troops reentered the city after the battle – triumphant and drunk with bloodlust, conveying Richard's naked body carelessly upon the back of a mule – the head of the dead king was, in the press of beast and man, crushed against the stones of the bridge.

Anise felt sick. That Richard should die with so little honor. Was it even possible to save him from that? She knew she had to try. As she was memorizing the details she had just read, she heard a footstep behind her.

"Anise, what are you doing? You can't change history."

She shrugged. "Who says?"

After the journey through time and the shock of seeing her brother again, Anise had picked herself off the floor and flown into his arms. "I'm sorry I didn't remember you before."

He'd brushed a strand of hair from her eyes. "It's not your fault."

"You're so much taller."

Dominic laughed. "You, too, Sis."

He'd told her how he had discovered a box from the U.K., delivered to the farmhouse months ago, with her tote bag and the ring inside. A note explained it had been found at an archaeological dig at Berkhamsted castle. The team in charge found her driver's license inside and sent the box to the address on it.

Dom had used the ring to call her back to him.

Anise had told him about Richard, and what she meant to do.

He stared askance. "You what?"

"I love him."

They had argued about it for an hour. But Anise was determined.

Now, as he stood in the storeroom trying to figure out how to stop her, Anise lifted her chin. "I have to go."

"Please, think about this! We've only just found each other."

"I have to save Richard."

Dom went over to her. "I won't stop you. I only want you to be safe, and to come back."

He leaned in to hug her – but Anise had already stepped into the darkness.

CHAPTER TWENTY TWO

Stanley's horse beat the ground with its hoof. The lord patted it on the neck and watched the preparations going on around him. "I wish to be off, too, Joachin."

Around him, his men organized the equipment required for a march of several days followed by battle. They needed to hurry. It would be a miserable trek, if the heat of this day was anything like the day before, with sun scorching the ground, streams dry, crops withering around them – and no rain in sight.

Just after dawn and it was already hot.

Stanley patted Joachin on the nose, set foot in stirrup and swung astride. From a short distance away, someone called his name.

"Thomas – wait!"

At the sight of her, he reined in. She appeared much wearied by that foolish plot she'd attempted with the hapless Morton. The bishop's body had not been found in the ruins of the tower. If his luck held, Stanley would never again lay eyes on the man who'd cuckolded him. He hoped Morton was dead, fried to a cinder in the Glendower's last wrath. And if Anise had not survived, all the better. Since her appearance, everything had gone wrong.

Margaret refused to speak of it, as if ashamed. In the end, it would be him, Thomas, Lord Stanley, and his brother, William, who would determine Henry Tudor's victory.

Stanley gloated over Margaret's failed plan. Yet he could not deny he still had feelings for her. Her regal beauty moved him, as a majestic oak shows its autumn colors before succumbing to winter's starkness.

"Margaret." The tenderness of his own voice surprised him.

Her expression softened to one he recognized from their courtship. "I could not let us part in anger."

She fashioned the words to touch his heart – he knew this. He would not allow her satisfaction so easily. "Do I care?" he replied coolly. "Nothing has changed between us – as you would have it."

"What if it has?" After a hesitation, she added, "You are going off to battle. And I want to know – I need to know – it hasn't always been so bad between us. I don't want you to believe…"

He finished her sentence, " — that you never loved me?" He released a short laugh. "You hope I don't know that you only ever loved Edmund Tudor? That you still love him, though he's been dead for two and thirty years? Don't worry Margaret. I won't throw you to the wolves. It wouldn't be politically astute."

Stanley studied her face, once so beloved to him. Her hurt expression was as false as her intentions.

She would not give up. "I came only to offer a kind farewell. I shall pray for your safe return. I do care for you, husband."

He wished he could believe her sincerity; she was such a deft liar. And yet her words tugged at his heart.

His tone softened. "I ride to uncertain battle and know not if I shall return. Should I not, remember me well – or as well as you can."

"That I shall do. And should you prevail, send my deepest affection to my son."

The truth at last. She wants confirmation of my allegiance. Well, she shan't have it.

"But surely, dear heart, you realize I fight on the righteous side of our sovereign, King Richard."

Margaret considered him with an implacable gaze.

When Stanley heard a shout and saw his troops were finally moving, he was relieved. At last he could escape this woman he both loved and loathed. When he spurred his horse, Margaret smiled. He could not fool her. She knew he'd fight for her son.

****

Darkness settled upon them as heavily as the fear in Henry Tudor's heart. He and a dozen of his bodyguard stood uncertainly at a crossroads, their mounts impatient to be off.

"I know now where we be, Your Grace," said Henry's knight of the body. "Tamworth lay in that direction." He pointed to a road.

"That's the way we just came," snorted another.

But in truth, none of them had any idea which was the right way to Tamworth. Mostly Welshmen, they were unfamiliar with this country, and Henry proved a poor leader.

Jasper and his troops had probably arrived at Tamworth hours ago. Why had Henry ever insisted on falling behind the main army that morning to travel by himself? He knew Morton would not appear, although that was the excuse he gave his uncle for lagging behind. In truth, Henry had given up hope on receiving magical assistance. Something had gone terribly wrong with his mother's conjuring.

Henry had trailed behind the army for another reason – a reason no one else knew and he prayed they never found out.

He was scared.

Visions of doom had haunted him as they traveled the roads of this hostile country. He was terrified of dying in battle, his head crushed with a mace or his throat slashed with a broadsword or else trampled to death beneath the crush of men and horse.

Though he never let on to anyone else, and especially to his war-hardened uncle, the concept of dying – no matter how noble or righteous – made him physically ill. And as he marched through England – a land that was his and not his – Henry could not help thinking that these miserable hours on the road might be his last ones on earth.

So he'd bade his army to go ahead to Tamworth. He would keep a small body of men to guard him. Jasper had been angry. It was too dangerous for Henry to travel with so few to guard him. It was foolish for him to wish for Morton's help. They would prevail without magic.

His uncle so protested his nephew's decision, that Henry was afraid he had figured out the truth. Yet Henry knew Jasper loved him too much to believe him a coward.

Henry insisted – if he traveled apart from the main army, Morton may come. If magic could be procured for their cause, it would be a great asset. Publicly, Henry insisted he must fall back to think – there were many things to consider by the man who would be king.

In the end, Henry got his way. Jasper would not embarrass him in front of the troops.

Now here he stood at an uncertain crossroads, night falling, lost and alone but for a few staunch Welshmen, loyal to their kinsman – the only thing standing between himself and disaster.

How would they treat him if they knew he was a coward? What would they do if they learned the only reason he'd stayed behind was to give himself the chance to run away?

His call to greatness had not diminished. But death? He could not bear the thought.

How would he, Henry Tudor and unproven in battle, ever survive? If he knew nothing else, it was this: he was nothing like his warrior cousin, Richard.

Dafydd ap Llwyd, the miller-now-soldier, interrupted Henry's thoughts. "Your Grace, I have a bit of sense when it comes to the choice between ways." He pointed at their road to the left. "That be the road to Tamworth."

Henry considered the direction Dafydd pointed. Still he pondered the greater question. Could he risk death as this man seemed to do so effortlessly? Dafydd had already proven his bravery when he left home and hearth behind to join them on this campaign, knowing he might never return to his family. A simple man with simple needs, Dafydd had become devoted to Henry. Even Henry's poor excuse at Welsh – which he spoke with such a taint of the French that he often had to repeat himself – did not seem to make any difference.

What mattered is that Dafydd wanted what Henry wanted.

Freedom.

Freedom from those who believed themselves superior, in Dafydd's case, the English. In Henry's, all those who had oppressed him for years. Only if he was king, could Henry escape.

Damn Richard Plantagenet and the rest of the Yorkists who spat on his Welsh bloodlines.

Henry hated his cousin, the general – the king – who rode into battle without flinching at death, who meted out bloody punishment to those who opposed him – who won every battle he led men to.

May Richard burn in Hell.

Henry heard the horses of his guard growing restless. Out of the lengthening shadows, Dafydd's voice came again. "Which road, Your Grace? Soon it may be too dark to find our way."

Squinting in the direction the Welshman pointed, Henry decided. "Yes, kinsman, I believe you have chosen rightly. There, do you see?"

Dafydd gazed down the road. "Some huts," he affirmed with a nod. "A village, perhaps. There we might ask the way to Tamworth and find shelter for the night."

Relieved, Henry called out to his men to make haste.

****

At last they were moving. Now there would be no more waiting, perched upon the great rock of Nottingham. Tudor had chosen his direction. Soon it would be over. Soon this summer of slow torture would be done with.

One way or another, Richard would be at peace.

It was with such thoughts that the king rode ahead on his horse, White Surrey. Those loyal to him were near – Francis Lovell, Richard Ratcliffe, Rob Percy – as he traveled through the streets of Leicester and the Swine's Market. Soon they would leave this town for some patch of land that would be remembered ever after as a place of death.

For a moment, he thought of Anise, who had brought to him, in the pages from the history book, the name of that place of battle.

Bosworth Field.

Even if he believed in the truth of this, what could he do? Certainly not turn his army back because he believed an accused witch. After such a gesture, England might crown Tudor without a fight, thought Richard grimly.

What had Anise told him that he did not already know in his heart? He'd already suspected that Stanley would support Tudor, that Percy would not fight. And of course he always considered the possibility of his own death – what knight riding into battle does not already have half a mind on heaven?

After studying the pages of history, Richard knew if he should die, England would not languish without Plantagenet – but, indeed, become even more powerful under Tudor reign. Nor would the bloodline be lost – for it would pass on through Ned's daughter, Bess. England would prevail, as it always had done, and become one of the greatest nations of the world.

He no longer dwelled on his poor decisions of two years past. And he did not lie to himself about his motives. If he lived, what happiness would there be? For what he regretted most was not being with *her* again.

A shout issued from the scout who rode ahead. They had nearly come to the bridge. The army must thin its lines to cross it. The call harkened through the ranks, so that those to the rear knew to fall back.

Richard spotted the bridge, their only passage westward over the River Soar. It was narrow, and at both ends gathered the men and women and children of Leicester, cheering the army and straining to catch a glimpse of the king.

White Surrey struggled into the bottleneck, the press of citizens and armored men and horses forcing Richard close to the wall. As the bridge opened onto solid ground, Richard's spur caught on the stones of its left side. At last on solid ground, he heard a woman wailing. He glanced back and saw her – a madwoman, her hair awry, her gaze intense, her voice shrill: "Turn back, Plantagenet! The foot that strikes the stone carries its master to misery."

As White Surrey carried him far from the bridge into the wide streets, Richard wondered if he'd imagined it – and knew he had not.

****

Inundated by more advice than he could stand, Henry Tudor waved his hand in dismissal. Although the sun had dipped below the horizon an hour ago, the tent was still unbearably hot, and perspiration ran disagreeably down his back. Henry hated to sweat. And there stood the Earl of Oxford, so condescending of Henry's lack of experience, telling him how they would easily defeat the king's army, which was twice the size of theirs.

Despite Henry's obvious frustration, Oxford prattled on. "We can't count on the Stanleys, Your Grace. They have made overtures, 'tis true, but..."

The battle would take place on the treeless hill called Redmore Plain, not far from Market Bosworth and south of Stoke Golding, the village outside of which Henry's troops had made camp. To the east rose Ambien Hill, where the royal army now made ready. Scurriers had informed Jasper that William Stanley's army camped to the north, and to the southeast, his brother, Thomas Stanley. If both Stanleys chose to support the king, Henry's forces would be crushed between.

Henry did not need the Earl of Oxford rubbing this in.

"My stepfather will not betray our hopes," insisted Henry. "So often has this battle been played out before me that I feel I have fought it ten times over. Tomorrow we shall know. I want everyone to get out, except for you, Uncle."

It maddened Henry that Oxford looked at Jasper for confirmation of the order. He could not see Jasper, but suspected his uncle offered the earl a discreet nod. Oxford bowed and quit the tent.

Henry breathed with relief and crossed the room to sit on a trunk. This pretense at leading an army exhausted him. But he could not let Jasper know how afraid he was. "Would that we might be at tomorrow's end and know the outcome."

Although this might have been interpreted as fear by those unfamiliar with battle, the war-weary Jasper understood completely. "Aye."

A moment later, another joined them in the tent. "I have seen the morrow's end," said the voice, as if emanating from Heaven. "A Welsh king shall once more sit upon England's throne."

Then they saw him. First the black robes became visible, then the face, bearing a self-satisfied expression.

Morton.

Henry gaped. At first he thought it must be an apparition. He turned to Jasper to affirm he was not seeing things, and saw his uncle looking much aghast.

"Are you surprised?" asked Morton lightheartedly. "Did I not assure you I would come?"

Henry went to the bishop and touched his sleeve. He looked into Morton's eyes – and smiled. "Bishop – we have been expecting you."

CHAPTER TWENTY THREE

Anise fought like hell to get to Richard Plantagenet.

Through the blackness of time, she turned her will to finding him. And through the ring, she discovered where he was and what he was doing. She did not have to know his history to know his mind: he was going to sacrifice himself to bring down Henry Tudor.

In the vortex, time had no beginning or end. Anise must find a moment before the battle when she could communicate with him without distraction. When she could tell him what was going to happen – and let him know that he had not lost her. That if he lived, there was a chance for them.

That he did not have to lose everything.

With her acute perception, she followed his linear movement through time along the path to his death. She knew he still wore Glendower's ring – but did not know the extent of its power or that it offered salvation.

When Anise approached, she could not get through to him. He was as real to her as an old vignette photo – clear at the center, but with the blurred edges acting like a barrier, keeping her away.

Anise knew from Morton that she and Richard could not exist on earth together while they both wore the same ring. *Except under one condition.* But Anise was not trying to manifest into a corporeal body. She only needed to talk to Richard. Why couldn't she turn herself into a mist as Glendower had?

Anise followed him, finding him alone again and again, perfect opportunities for her to tell him what he needed to know: the night before the army left Leicester when he was alone in his room at the White Boar, when he dined alone in the town of Kirkby Mallory, on the eve before the battle, kneeling in his tent in prayer.

Anise trailed him as far as the battle, and lost him in the fray. She traced his timeline backward and forward. Not once could she break through.

She could not even figure out how to tell him she was there, no matter how she shouted, "Richard, can you hear me? Richard!"

The longer she stayed in the time vortex, the wearier she became. She was not a powerful wizard like Glendower. She did not know how to hold her own in the vacuum between the years. If she stayed here much longer, she would diminish to that senseless state of the dead.

Even as she thought this, her willpower ebbed away as she called for him, *"Richard,"* but his name had become a whisper in her soul.

****

The door of the church was scored by centuries of use by the simple people of his parish. Richard ran his fingers along the scars just as Francis caught up with him. "Dickon. The hour grows late. This, of all nights, you must rest."

"I've learned to do without rest. What I haven't learned is why God has forsaken me. This I must know before I die."

He looked up at the exterior of the old church. Small and squarely built, it had been put up by the Normans long before a Plantagenet ever wore the crown of England. A corner of his mouth quirked – *and doubtless it would remain so long after.*

"Perhaps here I will find it. I cannot be swayed from this, friend."

Francis sighed, recognizing Richard's stubbornness in full force. Grasping the large iron ring at the center of the door, Francis pulled. It opened with a groan.

Within, the walls glowed, bathed in the light of a multitude of candles. Stretching to the ceiling were the colored glass windows that in daytime colored the interior of the church, but at night receded into shadow. The vicar hovered near the altar, his face anxious. He had faced a steady stream of knights who had come this evening to make peace with God.

Other than the priest, the church was empty. Richard nodded to Francis, who stayed by the door to keep others out. The king did not want to be disturbed.

Under the vicar's watchful eye, Richard kneeled before the altar. The priest consecrated the bread and wine, ministering to his king who, in the eyes of Deus, was but a mere mortal.

But Richard could not open his heart to God. Even now, forgiveness would be denied.

Why have you deserted me, Lord?

Richard spoke the prayer that gave him the most peace: *"De beato Juliano. Cum volueris pere res afflictos relevare captivos redimere in carcare positos..."*

But he could not concentrate. The memorized words flew from his mind like startled birds. And though he knelt before God, Richard could only think of Anise.

Forgive me, my love – I judged you by my own besmirched soul. I accused you when you were without guilt. My ignorance brought you only suffering – 'tis this I abhor most of all. Dear Anise, wherever you are, know that even hours before my death, I would give up my kingdom to be with you.

A sense of peace flooded his soul, causing him to gasp. He sensed Anise nearby. Was he imagining it? Or had she heard his thoughts? He choked back a sob. "Anise?"

Richard remembered he was not alone. He looked at the vicar and saw the priest staring fearfully at something to Richard's left.

He followed the man's gaze and knew why he was frightened. In the aisle, a mist had gathered. Glowing with an otherworldly light, it spread out before him.

Richard's senses expanded as the power of the ring thrummed through his arm. Opening to its insights, a presence filled him up.

Her presence. *Anise.*

Richard got off his knees and rose to his feet. His pulse raced as he watched the mist take human form, and now recognized her face at its center.

In his mind, he heard her speak – but could not make out the words.

He sensed her struggle. She wanted to tell him something. He could feel she was weary. And she began to fade.

Don't leave me, Anise!

He thrust his arm into the glimmering mist, reaching for her – and caught hold of a hand that wavered between two worlds, one moment solid and the next, spirit. The shock of her presence filled him. She could not come to him, but was confined in some place that would not let go.

Where in God's name was she?

Richard's mind numbed to everything but Anise – and at last he heard her.

So... tired... cannot go on... must tell you...

She was giving up. Her exhaustion coursed through him. Richard was losing her. *I must not... lose... her.*

Clinging to the tendril of mist, using what power he could glean from the ring, he fought for her. He pushed back the weakness that sapped her strength, lending her his will and his strength – and his love.

As her spirit rallied, the otherworldly light grew brighter. He could discern her features more clearly now, her eyes hollow with weariness, her full lips, her dark, flowing hair.

She said his name, not in his mind only, but spoken aloud, "Richard."

From the corner of his eye, Richard saw the vicar backing away in terror.

Anise tried to speak, but no words could be heard. Richard concentrated, opening his heart, drawing her into himself. Her thoughts, her emotions, her soul, joined his.

He knew the eternal blackness she experienced, and sensed her weariness. Without words she told him – she could not hang on. She had tarried too long in *that place*.

If he let go now, if he lost her, it would be forever. She could not return.

Then all became clear. Richard knew how to save her – to save *them*.

Clinging to her insubstantial hand for all his life, he shouted to the vicar, "Marry us!"

The priest held up his hands, shaking his head. "N-no, Your Grace – 'tis *evil!*"

"You fool! 'Tis a miracle! If you don't marry us, she will die!"

Still the priest refused.

Richard was furious. There was no time for this! With his right hand, Richard felt for his scabbard, and made ready to draw his sword. "Do you deny your king? As I am your sovereign Lord, I demand you marry us, or be cut down upon this altar."

The vicar's eyes widened. He stared between his king's poised hand and the apparition. As he began the litany, his voice trembled. "We are gathered here, in the sight of God... to join together this man and this woman."

For what seemed an eternity, the priest rambled, voice clumsy with fear. "Wilt thou have this woman to be thy wedded wife, to live together after God's ordinance in the holy estate of matrimony? Wilt thou love her, comfort her, honor, and keep her in sickness and in health and forsaking all others, keep thee only unto her, so long as you both shall live?"

Anise was fading. Richard's heart filled with fear. Desperate to hold on, he whispered, "I will!"

With trepidation, the priest turned to Anise. She had become more solid than spirit, but appeared as a bride of the netherworld in her black dress. He spoke fearfully, "Wilt thou have this man to be thy wedded husband, to live together after God's ordinance in the holy estate of matrimony? Wilt thou obey him and serve him, love, honor, and keep him in sickness and in health; and forsaking all others, keep thee only unto him, so long as ye both shall live?"

Anise became whole. The mist evaporated. Richard looked upon her face and into her eyes. His heart was full as she said, "I will."

Anise was with him now – but Richard sensed how weak she was. The danger remained. She could still slip back to the place he had saved her from.

The priest hurried to finish the ceremony. "Repeat after me…"

Once the king was united with Anise before the eyes of God, Richard knew all in the world would feel right. He was as certain as he had been the first time he had said these vows – to Anne.

"I, Richard Plantagenet, take thee, Anise Wynford, to my wedded wife, to have and to hold from this day forward, for better for worse, for richer for poorer, in sickness and in health, to love and to cherish, till death us do part, according to God's holy ordinance." His voice was thick. "And thereto I plight thee my troth."

Anise returned the oath without hesitation. "I, Anise Wynford... take thee, Richard Plantagenet..." A few times she faltered, and the vicar quietly reminded her of the words.

"...And thereto I give thee my troth." Her voice grew thin.

From his hand, Richard removed his ring – the ring that had brought them together and had torn them apart – and now would join them once more.

Without waiting for the vicar, Richard began, "With this ring, I thee wed, with my body I thee worship, and with all my worldly goods I thee endow: in the name of the Father, and of the Son, and of the Holy Ghost..."

He took her hand and slipped the ring onto her finger.

With wonder, he watched as the solid ring melded smoothly with the spirit ring, until there was one. Anise gazed at him, love shining in her eyes. She took the ring off – but did not take it off – and she slipped it onto his left hand.

And then there were two. But in truth, there was only one.

Anise slumped against him in exhaustion. Richard caught her in his arms and cradled her head against his shoulder.

In a frightened whisper, the vicar pronounced, "You are now man and wife." By the time king looked up, the priest was gone.

Richard draped Anise's arm over his shoulders and lifted her easily into his arms. She moaned softly and he felt her breath on his throat. Richard kissed her forehead. "You are safe now."

He carried her to the door where Francis waited. Their eyes met. He had witnessed all.

The viscount pushed open the door, and they went out into the warm night. Feeling Anise's body against his own made Richard's blood to rush like wildfire through his veins. He followed Francis through camp toward the royal tents. Most of the men slept, unaware that Richard passed them. But some looked in wonder upon the king as he carried a woman to his tent on the eve of battle. Concerned only for his bride, Richard paid no heed to the whispers that followed him. Knowing his friend's mind, Francis entered the tent first and upon finding the king's knight of the body in residence, hurriedly bid him to sleep elsewhere and return at dawn.

The king caught Francis' glance as he left the tent. In his friend's face, Richard saw no censure. He nodded in thanks.

Gently Richard settled Anise across his cot and lay beside her. He put his face close to hers and saw her eyelids flicker. Unable to help himself, he brushed away a strand of her hair and kissed the corner of her mouth. She sighed. "Richard."

"My bride – how do you feel?"

Anise found his hand and squeezed it. He kissed her and pulled her close. When she opened her mouth to him, his loins tightened. He pulled away. "You are too weak."

She wrapped her arms around him. "Don't go. I need your strength—"

Her words stoked his passion. His mouth eased along her throat to her collarbone as her hands entwined in the hair at the nape of his neck. With her breath falling warm against his ear, he sensed her need.

Surrendering to his desire, he found the laces of her bodice and undid them, slipping his hands beneath the cloth to cup her breasts. When she moaned, he silenced her with his mouth, their tongues kneading together. His skin afire at her touch, Richard got up to undress and found his hands shaking. He helped Anise take off her gown, and fell upon her, an urgency to be inside her driving him. He ran his hands over her stomach and took possession of her breasts. Anise released a whimper and shifted beneath him, opening to him.

Groaning her name, Richard crushed his body onto hers, gasping as he entered her. *Sweet Jesu, how long he had wanted this – wanted her?* Knowing this was only her second time, he tried to be gentle, but could not. Anise did not seem to mind, but met his thrusts with equal abandon.

"Richard," she cried, urging him deeper, her insides clenching against their shared friction. Through his ring, Richard felt her passion wash over him in undulating shockwaves. Anise arched against him, her fingers digging into his back, crying out in pleasure. His mind narrowed to the sensation of their bodies merging as one. Instinct claimed him, and without thought, Richard took her for his own. Anise clung to him, riding the crest of his passion until he exploded inside her.

The storm past, their desire spent, Richard and Anise lay quietly together, limbs entangled. He reached to caress her cheek and found moisture there. "What is it, my love?" But he thought he knew.

He barely heard her whisper, "Tomorrow."

Richard prevented more words as he captured her mouth. When they parted, he wiped her tears. "Don't cry. All I wished for was to have you with me again."

But she wept for a long time afterward and Richard could do nothing to comfort her. And so, cradling her against his chest, he held her close until sleep found them.

****

As Anise pushed aside the tent's heavy flap and peered into the darkness, the acrid smell of extinguished fires assaulted her nostrils. As far as her eye could see, men lay sleeping. Yet within the hour, all would come alive as they prepared for battle.

She glanced once more at Richard, her heart full. She could hardly believe he was her husband. They had married – it seemed more like a dream than a memory – and they both wore the ring.

It pained her to leave him. To wake with him this morning, to feel his lips on her throat, his hands on her body, would have been the greatest of pleasures.

But this was not an ordinary morning. Richard would die today if she did not do something about it.

If I can't change history.

There must be a way.

Anise went outside, abandoning the illusory tranquility of the tent. She considered entering the vortex long enough to discover exactly how

Richard's fatal ride down Ambien Hill unfolded. But before when she'd tried to locate him during the battle, her perception was disrupted by the confusion of so many emotions swirling in one place.

Anise wondered if he would listen to her if she told him, "Whatever you do, don't go after Tudor yourself."

She could not risk it. Until now, history had marched on regardless of what anyone knew. Simply telling him would not change his actions in the press of battle.

If Richard was to survive the day, Anise would have to be the one who stopped him. She had to be by his side; it was the only way.

Anise wandered through the sleeping men, using her ring to locate Francis Lovell. When she found him, he was not asleep. He was surprised to see her. Still fully dressed, he got out of bed. An attendant was with him, and the viscount sent him away.

His expression was not kind. "I should kneel to thee, my lady, now wife to my king – but I cannot."

The words found their mark, but Anise knew she must find a way to convince him. "I don't want you to kneel. I want you to help me save Richard. Don't we both love him?"

"He is my dearest friend." His gaze pierced her. "But when I look at you, I see only his doom."

Anise began to feel panic. "I'm from the future. I know what's going to happen. Don't you believe me?"

"Do I believe that my king, my dearest friend and the most honorable man I know, will be struck down in battle by the son of a bastard who playacts at being sovereign?" Francis shook his head. "How can I believe such a thing without my heart breaking? But after what I witnessed last night, how can I not believe? I don't deny what my eyes have seen. You love him. Still I cannot help but think you bring Richard's terrible fate with you."

Anise protested, "It's history! I didn't have anything to do with it."

"Then Richard is doomed," said Francis gravely. "We are all doomed."

"I said it *happened*... but maybe it doesn't have to happen."

"If Dickon is destined to die, how is it possible to prevent it?"

"Because I'm here. I might have changed things already. Maybe I can do something about this."

Francis studied her. "If 'tis my help you need, then you have it."

Relief went through her. "Thank you."

The viscount sighed. "All that can be done must be done, even if it is at your bidding, my lady."

This exasperated Anise. "I wish you would trust me." She remembered something else she'd learned from her history books. She remembered Francis Lovell's fate. "Do you want to know what happens to you after the battle?"

Francis' eyes widened. "Do you know?"

"It's not good."

"Tell me."

Anise nodded, averting her eyes. "If I fail today… if Richard dies and Henry becomes king, there will be an uprising to put Richard's heir on the throne."

Francis whispered, "John de la Pole, his nephew."

Anise's stomach felt hollow. "You'll be there, Francis – with an army, fighting against Henry. Richard's heir is killed, but you escape. But whatever you do, don't go to Minster Lovell."

"It's my home," insisted Francis. "I could hide there. I know a place…"

Anise interrupted, "Don't go there. Don't hide in the secret vault in the cellar. You'll be trapped there. You'll starve to death."

Francis went pale. "No one knows of that room but me." He did not speak for a long time. Finally he asked, "What can I do to help you save Richard?"

Anise took a deep breath. What she had in mind she was not even sure she could manage.

"I need armor and a horse. I'm riding to battle with you. And we can't tell Richard."

Francis gaped. "If he finds out I've done this, he'll kill me."

"And if you don't, he'll die. I have to be there when *it* happens – I mean, when it's *about* to happen." Anise's voice sounded surer than she felt. She knew how to ride a horse, but she was hardly a master equestrian. The physical demands alone might do her in.

Francis bowed slightly. "Wait here.

CHAPTER TWENTY FOUR

The thin light of day shone through the tent flap and glinted off the king's armor. Richard's knight of the body and two squires tended him, buckling his harness of Nuremberg steel and fastening the greaves about his legs. At his waist hung his sword.

His mind checked off the preparations for battle. For a moment, he thought of Anise. She had been gone from his bed when he'd awakened just before dawn, but Francis had come to him with assurance she would be kept safe. Richard wished he could go to her, but he knew he must concentrate on the problem at hand. He refused to think he would never see her again. Henry Tudor might not live through the day, but Richard intended to. He must – now.

The viscount stepped into the tent.

"Have you brought the chaplain?" Richard did not believe he would die, but repenting of his sins before battle was a necessarily precaution.

"There are no chaplains to be found in the camp," said Francis. "Word of your... of what happened at Sutton Cheney last night—"

Richard sighed. "The vicar, of course."

"Some of the men are frightened, too," said Francis in a low voice. "They fear your actions have displeased God."

Richard's mouth quirked up at one corner. "'Tis not the first time men have believed that. Come on –'tis time."

Outside, all was as it should be, the ranks of armored men astride their mailed horses, awaiting the king's command. If men feared he had doomed them, they did not show it. As he and Francis moved through the troops, Richard often heard his name spoken with respect.

He joined the small band assembled of his household – five score of his most trusted knights. They quieted their mounts, tightening their plate and saddles. Richard looked upon them, the Knights and Esquires of his Body – Sir Richard Ratcliffe, Sir James Harrington, Humphrey and Thomas Stafford, his faithful Constable of the Tower, Sir Robert Brackenbury, his secretary, John Kendell, his childhood friend, Sir Robert Percy – and others, their faces hidden by their helms but their colors informing him who all was present.

Before him also stood John Howard, Duke of Norfolk. The king had fought with Norfolk against the Scots; Richard trusted him utterly. He was a capable general and loyal to York.

Howard bowed to his king. "Your Grace, word came last night from Lord Stanley and his brother, Sir William. Both refuse to come. Thomas says he will serve you better staying where he is, for his army lies between you and the enemy. I would have told you last night, but when I learned…"

The enemy camp lay to the west of them, skirting the edges of Redmore Plain. Last night Richard had seen their campfires and calculated that their numbers did not match his own forces by half – yet his calculations had included the armies of the Stanleys.

Norfolk looked at Francis. Richard recognized the worry on the duke's face and nodded. "You have done all you could. I sent for Stanley again this morning."

Even now a messenger approached them. The man hesitated before addressing the king. "Your Grace, Lord Stanley is not of a mind to join you. He says even though you hold Lord Strange as hostage, he has other sons."

Even without hearing it from Anise, Richard had known Stanley would betray him. For years, Francis warned him against Stanley, but Richard had granted him land and titles, just as his brother Edward had done. Now Stanley held all of Lancashire and commanded a formidable army.

Richard sought for his sword. Stanley would not go unpunished for his disloyalty – his son was under guard nearby. "Let George Stanley be executed for his father's treachery." His words were hard and his voice held no mercy. He pointed to two of his men. "Do it now."

Those around him objected. "Your Grace! Do not jeopardize your soul before battle," cried Norfolk. "With no chaplain to absolve you…"

"Let the battle decide," said Francis.

Stanley's defection must not be allowed to distract him. Richard calmed his anger. "When York has triumphed, Stanley's son dies. Bring my helm!" Francis brought it, the king's golden crown circling its rim. Richard caught his friend's gaze.

"I advise against it, Dickon. If you wear the crown, the enemy shall mark you easily."

He donned the helm. "I lived a king, I shall die a king."

White Surrey was brought to him and, with the aid of his squires, Richard mounted the great horse. Behind him, his knights vaulted into their saddles.

Richard shouted, "Sound the advance!" Norfolk's trumpets blared, relaying the call. Battle cries of the enemy rose above the din, shouted out in Welsh and French, as if the field lay in foreign lands.

White Surrey leapt forward as Richard's army ascended the ridge. From the top of Ambien Hill, he watched his archers spray volley after volley upon the rebel troops climbing toward them. The sharp explosion of the royal artillery assaulted his ears before dying away. Agonized shouts of the first wounded assaulted his ears. Near the bottom of the hill, Oxford's vanguard swept around the swamp, crashing into the royal ranks. The clash of steel, the cries of death, the scream of horses, arose with the dust on the breeze. All was confusion.

Richard pivoted in his saddle to assess his artillery. A faulty cannon had exploded upon his men, spraying them with fire and propelling chunks of steel into the ranks. The mortally wounded screamed for a priest. Richard's conscience panged, his heart pierced by their cries, that he could do naught for them. His gaze fell on the fighting at the bottom of the hill. A mace crushed the head of a foot soldier while a hailstorm of swift arrows sang scores of men to their deaths. Horses crashed into the lethal spikes Norfolk's army had set against the enemy, impaling themselves and the knights who rode them.

Richard watched from the crest of the hill with his regiment behind him. When Norfolk's center gave way, he commanded a detachment of reserves to strengthen it. The center held and won ground against the enemy, driving their army inward. With satisfaction, Richard watched Oxford's left flank crumble. Trumpets shrilled and Oxford's men fell back, assembling around the banners of their leaders. The fighting paused, the two armies catching their breaths and glaring at one another across the field.

So far, Tudor's main army held back. *Waiting to see how it would go*, thought Richard. If things went ill for Tudor, did he think he could escape?

"He's there, Your Grace!" It was one of Richard's men – a knight known for his keen sight. "I see Tudor—" The knight pointed. The king's eyes followed his line of sight. "He has a small force with him. Can you not see his banner? The dragon of Cadwallader?"

Across the distance – beyond Oxford's army, past Lord Stanley's troops lying hunched and ready for their leader's cry to battle – the king spotted the enemy standard. Beneath it, he knew, stood Henry Tudor. The thrill of battle surged through him. *So close.*

And so foolish.

In his hesitation, the Pretender had allowed the main battle line to shift away from him; he was unprotected except for his guard of twenty foot soldiers and his knights of the body.

Norfolk's trumpets broke the silence, and the two armies crashed together with a clash of steel. A breeze blew over Redmore Plain, carrying the odor of blood from the field. With Richard's battle sense guiding him, he saw his chance to finish this fight. As long as the Tudor held back, it might be accomplished. Richard glanced at his personal guard. They could charge through the gap between Oxford's army and Tudor's, cutting the Pretender down where he stood and ending Tudor's campaign.

For good.

It was a great risk. His household ranks numbered only a hundred or so. They would have to charge in front of William Stanley's army, and battle a body of troops twenty times larger. Then Richard would have to fight his way to Tudor before anyone realized what was happening.

Richard could cut down this Welsh pretender by his own hand. A single deadly blow would win the day from this unworthy cousin of tainted bloodlines. The Tudor's troops would scatter, knowing their cause lost, and the fighting would be over.

Richard might have a chance to begin his reign again, ruling England with a new queen – and this time sparing no traitors.

As he called his household together, a cry rose through the ranks. "Norfolk is down! Norfolk is down!"

Richard's breath caught in his lungs. *John Howard – slain! How so?* He swallowed hard and leapt to action, ordering Northumberland to join the fray. He ordered it again. *What defiance was this?* Henry Percy's troops did not stray from their perch on the opposite side of Ambien Hill.

Ratcliffe cried, "Percy's refusing to fight! Let us flee, Your Grace! 'Tis just one battle, more or less."

But that would leave Tudor to fight another day. "That I cannot do!" Richard shouted to all who would hear. "Please God that I do not take one step backward! Either Tudor dies this day or I do – like a king!"

With no time to lose, he found Francis and pointed out Tudor's standard. Having heard Richard's refusal to retreat, Francis nodded, knowing there was no stopping his king when he had his mind set. Richard's knights of the household rallied around him.

The king looked from one to the other with a full heart. None but these would he trust for this mission. "Sirs – Henry Tudor lies within our sight. Death to him ends his cause forever. Will you ride with me?"

His knights surged forward, awaiting his command. Richard's battle-ax was thrust into his hand. Richard spurred White Surrey forward and rushed down the slope.

****

Anise's armor felt like a steel trap. The suit belonged to a squire who'd fallen ill before the battle and was the lightest armor Francis could find. Anise had torn swaths from her dress to pad the suit, turning it into a roaster.

She rode a small gelding Francis had scared up for her, trained for battle, but still small enough for her to ride comfortably – that is, if she had not had to wear this stupid helmet, the only way to hide her identity.

So far, she'd kept up with Richard's household troops and now stood with them at the top of Ambien Hill. An uncanny hush fell over the battlefield. Anise patted her horse, whose name was "Prudentio." Francis told her it was Latin for "foresight."

At the trumpet's call to battle, chaos had fallen upon the land. Anise swooned at her first sight of blood – a foot soldier disemboweled by a sword thrust, his intestines spilling at his feet. Existence descended into nightmare. All around her, there were fallen horses frothing blood and dying men everywhere, crying for their mothers. If it came down to having to use her sword, Anise knew she was goner. She could lift it, but had no idea how to wield it in battle. If she had not been wearing the ring, she'd have lost her nerve entirely. As it was, she used it to guide her through the fray and steer her from harm's way.

A half hour into the fighting and both sides fell back for a moment's reprieve. Richard, who had been fighting battles since he was a teenager, sat confident amidst his element of war, his dark hair falling over the steel plates at his shoulders. White Surrey stamped the ground impatiently and nickered at Prudentio. As the king calmed his horse with a soft word, he looked at Anise, causing her heart to race with anticipation of his recognizing her. *Should he use the ring...* But Richard's attention was drawn away by a cry from his ranks.

Norfolk was slain and Northumberland held back. Richard motioned Francis to him. Anise reined in closer to Francis. Staying close to him had kept her an easy distance from the king – close enough for when the moment came. *And then what will I do?*

Her eyes followed the direction Richard pointed. "I'll cut him down where he stands. Are you with me?"

And Anise remembered the dream. *Or maybe it was a vision... or a future echo.* But it had been exactly like this – she had been armored, chasing a white knight, fearing she was too late.

The knights of Richard's household rallied. Anise spurred her horse after Francis. He'd forgotten about her!

"Richard, stop!" she screamed, not caring now if he knew she was here. It was too late.

Francis handed the king his helm with its gleaming royal crown. Another knight passed an ax into Richard's hands.

Anise cried out, but the battle raged again, and no one heard. There was no way she was going to stop Richard from trying to kill Henry.

White Surrey jumped as Richard led the charge. Anise spurred her horse after him, losing all bearings in the violent gallop down the slope, her teeth clattering, the armor gouging her flesh, and the helmet rattling her brain. A cloud of dust rose, obscuring her view. When she could see again, she discovered Prudentio had somehow kept up with White Surrey – and they rode even with Richard's flank.

In front of them, Tudor's men blundered into one another, scurrying for their horses. A moment later, Richard's men slammed into Tudor's foot soldiers, who were caught by surprise.

A knight bore down upon them, his mace whistling at Richard's head. Its spiked ball grazed the king's visor and the attacker pivoted on his horse, moving in for a second strike. Richard was faster, burying his ax in the man's skull. Anise was so close that the knight's blood sprayed over Prudentio's mane. Pulling his weapon free, Richard reeled back in the saddle. The knight fell from his horse, dead. Richard spurred White Surrey back into the fray, his arm working like a madman, cleaving his way in single-minded fury to the center, hacking all in his way.

Anise wrestled her sword from its sheath. Wielding it with terror and pure adrenalin, she spurred her horse after Richard and rode in his wake, protected by his murderous shadow.

She could see nothing through her visor but a sea of red washing over them. When she realized what she was looking at, she knew the moment had come. The crimson she saw was an army of soldiers crashing into the flanks of Richard's army.

Anise heard Francis shout over the din, "'Tis Will Stanley!"

Richard cried, "Hold him back! I'm going for Tudor!"

Francis paused too long to go after him; Richard was gone. With his fellow knights, the viscount turned to stand against Stanley's forces.

In the confusion, Anise nearly lost Richard. Thrown off balance by the onslaught, her horse fell behind White Surrey as the king hacked his way toward his target. As she struggled to catch up, the ring warned her, *Danger at your flank!*

Prudentio pivoted as a blade whistled by her ear. She tried to wield the sword and nearly called on the ring to take her away – but if she abandoned the fight now, she'd lose Richard forever.

Dear God, what can I do?

The steel gauntlet around her hand grew hot with the ring's power and the sword lightened in her hand. As the knight charged her again, Anise reeled her horse around to face him, and drove the blade hard into his shoulder. With a scream, the knight grabbed his arm and fell upon the neck of his horse. Covered in his blood, Anise spurred Prudentio forward.

Where is Richard? In a panic, she tried to catch a glimpse of him. *Damn this helm!*

There he was! He and White Surrey bore down on his enemies, his ax rising and falling, pummeling those who stood in his way, pushing forward to his goal.

The dragon of Cadwallader rose before him.

Anise sensed Henry Tudor's fear before she caught glimpse of his slight figure spurring his horse cruelly to get away from the flailing madman.

She sensed another presence that sent shockwaves through her. *Morton!*

The wizard appeared at Tudor's side – and vanished. Anise felt helpless, knowing he was helping Henry with magic. *How am I going to fight that?*

Richard drove White Surrey into Henry's banner, slamming his ax into the head of the standard bearer. The man's face froze in shock as his knees crumpled. Another blow and he rolled away dead. Richard turned to find Tudor. Their eyes met, Richard's full of righteous anger, Henry's rife with terror. The king raised his ax over his cousin's head.

Anise dug her spurs into Prudentio's sides and leapt headlong into the fray – and at that moment realized: *Morton is controlling this!* An invisible force knocked her forward. By the time she yanked back on the reins, it was too late – she barreled into Richard. White Surrey stumbled, knocking his blow off the mark and sparing Tudor's life. Like the red sea crashing onto the rocks, Stanley's forces collided into them, forcing her and Richard apart. From the corner of her eye, Anise spotted a Welshman raising his halberd – but it was too late. With terrific force it fell on Richard, smashing his helm but not penetrating it. Richard lost his ax, but drew his sword to fight off Stanley's red demons. Pivoting in his saddle, the king fended off blows from all sides.

Anise galloped to his side, shaking with exhaustion. "Richard!"

White Surrey howled. Anise fought nausea as she watched the horse gutted. The dying animal sank to its knees, carrying Richard with it. "Treason!" the king cried. "Treason!"

Screaming, she tumbled from her horse. Confusion and death in an ocean of crimson washed around her as steel crashed into steel. She tripped over the dying horse and forced her limbs to work, crawling toward Richard. Blow after blow fell upon him, who lay before her covered in blood, his helmet missing, his armor smashed. Still he fought, striking blindly with his dagger, the only weapon left him. Anise flung off her helm. "Richard!"

A knight aimed for his chest. With a cry, she threw herself in front of the sword, her body absorbing the shock. Pain shot through her as she sustained more blows. Fighting unconsciousness, she threw her arms around Richard. Her vision blurred. With the last of her strength, Anise dragged them into the blackness.

This time, she welcomed the numbing of her senses. The vortex howled in silence around her, but Anise was not afraid.

Because she was not alone. One in particular seemed familiar. *She* – Anise sensed it was female – was terrified. Another being was chasing *her*. Anise wanted to reassure the frightened thing that *she* was safe – that no real harm could come to *her* in this place.

But Anise knew, somehow, things were *not* right. There *was* something here, in the vacuum between years, that wanted to consume *her*. And soon *she* would be no more.

Who was this poor lost soul?

Focusing her will, Anise employed her heightened perception to discovering who *she* was —

Ah, now that's a funny thing. Time had no boundaries here. All moments existed at once, overlapping in endless loops. Anise had been here before just as she was here now.

She's me!

But who's the aggressor?

And soon that, too, made itself clear.

Glendower.

You will not prevail, he told her, beginning to feed on her soul.

But Anise said, *I have already won, Glendower – you'll see.* Then *she* joined *she*, and together they became strong and drove the evil from them.

And *she* who did not yet know love nor a brave heart, blundered to the moment of her journey's beginning, where a man on a white horse would find her.

A man on a white horse.

Now she must find her journey's end – and she found it at the house near the edge of the woods.

Anise had come home.

A great noise accompanied her as she fell from the darkness onto the sweet, damp lawn in front of her father's house, a canopy of stars lighting her way.

But what was that crash? Who was this metal man next to her?

CHAPTER TWENTY FIVE

Anise came to. She and the metal man were sprawled in front of the farmhouse. Pain wracked her body. It was several minutes before she remembered what had happened.

The Battle of Bosworth Field.

She was unsure how many wounds she'd sustained after throwing herself between Richard and his fate – but it had to be half a dozen, at least. Somehow, she pulled herself to her knees.

Although Richard still wore armor, Anise found herself in that same black gown Marilee had designed for the play. And it was not even in tatters.

What's going on here?

Anise crawled to Richard and pressed her fingers to his throat. He was knocked out cold – but he was alive. She stroked his bloodied face, smoothing the wet hair from his eyes. With a kiss on his temple, she thanked God.

Now if she could only get Dom's attention. He was a doctor.

Blood covered the remains of the king's armor. Parts of the suit had been stripped from him. The right arm piece was missing, but he seemed to have no injuries. His face and head were also unscathed. *How odd.*

Anise got to her feet and made it to the front door. Pounding on it, she cried at the sight of her brother, and caught hold of his arm, pulling him after her. "You have to help him. He might be dying – I can't tell."

Dominic knelt beside the fallen knight as Anise stood helplessly by. She could not stop shaking. Her brother looked at her with concern. "Are *you* all right?"

"I don't know how it's possible – but I think I'm just bruised from the battle."

Dom stared at her. "The battle?"

"I'm not kidding!" Anise knew how crazy it sounded. "Look at what he's wearing!"

Dom's eyes ran over Richard. "Help me get this off." He started removing the shattered metal.

Anise tried to assist, but her hands were trembling. "He's not moving! Why isn't he moving?"

"He's in shock. We'll get him inside and warm. But we have to get this armor off. Calm down and help me."

Anise nodded. "I know something about it. I was wearing some, too." She found the fasteners and undid them while Dom set the broken metal out of the way. Between them, they got Richard into the house and onto the couch.

"He's not in immediate danger. Find some blankets and I'll get a fire started."

By the time Anise returned with blankets, flames blazed in the hearth. Dom had retrieved his black bag and held a stethoscope to Richard's chest. A blood pressure unit was lying nearby. Her brother glanced at her. "I realize he's medieval – but who is he?"

Anise swallowed hard. "His name is Richard. He's my husband."

Dom stared at her. "You *married* him?"

"Don't look at me like that. I had to. It's a long story. Why isn't he waking up?"

"I don't know. His vitals are good. He doesn't have any injuries."

"None?"

Her brother shook his head. "None of that blood was his. He's just exhausted, I expect." I'll give him some epinephrine, though." He pulled a hypodermic from his bag and administered the shot. Then he looked at Anise. "Your turn."

"You're not sticking me with anything. I've had enough puncture wounds to last me a lifetime, even if you can't see them."

After a quick examination, he pronounced her bruised.

"Is that why they pay doctors all that money?" asked Anise, but her heart was not in it. She went back to Richard. "He's still not waking up."

"Give it a few minutes."

After some more waiting, the king moved his fingers. Anise leaned over him. "Can you hear me, Richard?" A faint moan escaped him. "I think he's trying."

"It might take a while for him to come out of it," said Dom. "Be patient, Sis."

Anise sighed. "I wonder if there've been any consequences."

Her brother raised an eyebrow. "What do you mean?

With a snort, she said, "I mean, I changed history. He isn't dead. But he isn't there, either."

A bemused expression crossed Dom's face. "Isn't *where*, exactly?"

"1485. You'd think it would have had *some* effect on the world."

"What are you going on about? One man can't be that important. You said his name is Richard?" Dominic's eyes widened. "What *have* you done, Anise? Richard *who*?"

Anise lifted her chin. "I don't regret it."

"Richard *who*?"

"Richard Plantagenet."

"The Lionheart?"

"Not the Lionheart! I said 1485. It's Richard III – you know, *crookback*," she whispered.

"You're kidding?"

"What Shakespeare wrote was all lies. I love him and I saved his life." Anise almost laughed at Dominic's look of astonishment.

Richard opened his eyes and blinked. "Anise? It's so bright – what is this place? Heaven?"

Anise kissed his forehead. "Home."

****

Richard's eyes watered and his limbs were heavy, but the angel smiling down at him was comfort enough. "What happened?"

"You're safe."

The battle – he remembered it now. Being in the thick of fighting, the charge at Tudor, Stanley's men overwhelming them – White Surrey's scream. The last memory pained him. His horse had been a good and faithful companion and should not have died so heinously.

Richard looked around him. There were rows of tiny flowers covering the wall and the ceiling gleamed as bright as the summer sky. "Is this real or are we dead?"

"We're alive." Anise said quietly. "We're in my time now. The twenty-first century."

He had trouble following her meaning. His thoughts fell back to familiar ground. "Did York win the day?"

"You're exhausted, Richard."

This irked him. "I want to know."

"Tudor did." After a slight hesitation, she added, "Since you're here, I think he must have."

It was as he suspected. "It's what was prophesied."

Surprise flickered over her face. "Those pages you read?"

Richard nodded, struggling to take it all in. "I remember you, at the last. You were there."

Anise smoothed his hair. "I was."

"Then we were dead – but we're not. By… witchcraft?" Richard looked into her eyes. He meant not to accuse, but to understand.

Anise squeezed his hand. "With the ring. But I should say 'rings,' because now there are two."

"Two rings." Richard remembered. "We're married."

Anise smiled and kissed his forehead again. "Sleep… you're tired. I'll be here when you wake up."

The king closed his eyes. "As you wish, my queen."

EPILOGUE

The troops surged over the bridge into Leicester, their cries drunk with victory. "Hail, hail, King Henry!"

The armies of the Stanleys and Northumberland swelled his ranks to a great force. Henry rode tall in the saddle, exalting in the praise – and despising the press of the people so close around him. He felt alone among the crowd, though he rode among men who admired him. Even Morton's magic could not shield him, for the bishop had vanished after the battle was won.

He thanked God for Jasper, who kept the hordes from carrying him away.

At the front of the procession, Henry's men dragged along a mule bearing "Richard's" body. Henry made sure the face was mutilated beyond recognition. Fear pierced Henry's heart as he thought on it. *That despoiled corpse isn't Richard's.*

He remembered that moment of destiny with the clarity of crystal: the raging madman bearing down on him with ax in hand and death in his eyes, Stanley's hesitation – *may he well remember it!* – nearly costing Henry's life, and Morton's sorcery that made Richard's horse stumble before his weapon found its mark.

In my skull! Henry felt sick at the memory of that terror. That battle would be the only fighting he saw – that much he vowed.

Henry recalled seeing his cousin fall beneath a dozen weapons, in his heart comprehending Lancaster had prevailed against all odds. Then suddenly realizing Richard had not died. He knew, for he had seen, not as one involved in the action, but as a bystander watching and praying for deliverance.

Richard had not died!

A miracle, an apparition, an angel sent from God – Henry knew not what it was – had appeared from nowhere in the guise of a woman and carried Richard away in her arms.

Richard's armor was the only thing left of him – that, and the crown of England.

The body flung across the mule? No – that was not his cousin.

The procession grounded to a halt. Jeers rose in his ranks and Henry strained to see what the commotion was about. Then he saw the shingle outside the inn – The Whyte Boar – and Henry's anger flared. He spurred forward.

The innkeeper stood outside his business, staring at the crowd.

"What mean you to exhibit this treasonous display before your king?"

The man looked at him askance. "Are you speaking to me?"

Henry seethed. "Take down that sign. For I hearby demand that no white hog shall ever disgrace these streets, henceforth!"

The innkeeper barked back, "Who is he that so does make such demand?"

Henry's face went hot. *How dare he question me?*

Jasper pushed to the front of the crowd. "King Henry of England does so command you!"

"What jest is this?" the man cried. "I know none but King Richard as my sovereign lord."

Henry could scarcely restrain himself. Had he not dated his reign from yesterday, the day before the battle? "Richard Plantagenet and all who fought with him are traitors to this kingdom! You are guilty of treason and will pay the price!"

Jasper tried to intercede. "Henry, this isn't right – he doesn't know!"

Ignoring his uncle, Henry nodded to three knights, who seized the startled innkeeper and dragged him to the nearest tree where a rope was being slung over a branch.

His wife emerged from the inn and screamed as her husband was hauled up by the neck, gasping his last breaths, his limbs jerking in death.

Henry cared nothing for the life of one so insignificant. He'd made his point. Traitors could not be tolerated.

"Cut down that sign, and let us be gone."

As they moved on, Henry plotted. He needed his mother here. She had spent much time at court and could advise him. Morton, too, must come. Henry would have the bishop close to him. His sorcery would be of much use to the new king.

The queen dowager, Elizabeth Woodville, must be told of Henry's intent to fulfill the bargain he made with her long ago – his claim to the hand of her daughter, Bess – Edward IV's eldest daughter. They would marry as soon as Henry arrived in London.

Through their offspring would York and Lancaster be united at last – and Henry's claim assured. In triumph, he cried, "Ride on! The road to London is long and there is much to be done!"

****

Richard leaned back in the wicker chair, the morning sun warm on his face. The porch of the farmhouse had become his favorite place – except for the bed he shared with his wife. These "modern" clothes, as Anise called them, were comfortable, though ugly and strange.

For the fortnight he had been in "the twenty-first century," Richard had done nothing but lounge and read. His life as king, with its worries and sleeplack, seemed a lifetime ago.

He wondered what kept Anise, who had gone to town for "more goodies" for him to try. The food and drink in this century astonished him. It did not rot or spoil. There were fruits and vegetables of all kinds the year 'round. And many new delights had been invented – coffee, tea, chocolate, champagne.

The common folk of this country – which he had not even heard of – worked less and lived better here than those of the noblest blood from his time. Few took the sacrament now and "Christians" worshipped in so many ways Anise could not name all the sects.

Richard learned of inventions that seemed more like witchcraft than science. Those took much getting used to – especially the "TV," with its noise and flickering pictures.

Still, if he made it silent, he could see this wondrous new world without leaving the house. It did not surprise him that it was full of fear, death, lies, and betrayal – only that men had found new methods of torment.

"Don't believe everything you see on there," Anise had told him.

But the one thing he thought least likely, she assured him was real: flying machines called "planes." Anise had taken her brother to "catch one" today. It would carry him through the skies to lawyers for the settlement of Dominic and Anise's inheritance – an issue Richard thoroughly understood.

Dominic would get Richard an "I.D." – Anise said he must have these "traveling papers," as she explained it, if they were going to get married.

"But we are already wed," Richard protested.

"We have to do it again here."

Richard spent hours reading. At first he looked at the pictures, for this strange new English he found difficult to read. He only wished he could show Master Caxton. Will would have been

proud to know his printing hobby persisted and that English had become the language of the world.

Mostly Richard read histories. It galled him that the Tudors had seized power, but he was proud that Plantagenet survived in the bloodlines of the present-day queen. He compared what he learned to William Shakespeare's versions, whose plays were written during the era named after Richard's great-grandniece, and survived to this day.

Reading Shakespeare reminded Richard of his family and friends, so long dead. He missed his mother. And Francis.

He heard Anise's car and looked up. She drove the conveyance onto the gravel and got out. She was beautiful in the immodest frock she called a "summer dress" – but he had little trouble getting used to looking at her clothed so provocatively.

She came up the stairs and tossed something at him. Catching the shiny packet, he examined it enough to see it was something called "Twinkies."

"More goodies?"

Anise laughed. "The modern man's vice. You can enjoy them while you're reading this." She sat beside him and withdrew a book from a bag.

His smile faded. "Redmore Plain."

"It goes into more detail about the battle – they've used forensics, a kind of science, to figure out what happened."

Richard did not like the quiver in her voice. "What did they find out?" When she did not answer, he opened to the page she had marked.

A dozen weapons smashed through his armor. In the midst of his foes, alone, he was beaten lifeless to the ground, leaving his kingdom and his fame to Henry Tudor.

Richard's eyes sought hers.

"Keep reading."

...so said the reports. Yet there are other versions, mostly discounted, insisting that by the time Tudor arrived to claim the crown, plucked from Richard's

battered helm by Lord Stanley, the body of the dead king could not be found. Contemporary writings found later maintain that the mutilated body buried at Grey Friars in Leicester was not the body of the king at all. DNA evidence bears this out."

"So they've figured it out?"

Anise nodded. "Sort of. As much as they ever can."

Richard caught her gaze. "We could tell them."

"We can't." She was adamant. "They'd think we were crazy."

"Don't you think they would like to know?"

"Richard." Anise watched him twisting the gold ring on his finger. "What are you thinking?"

He glanced up. "I could go back. And this time..."

Anise flinched at his words. She shook her head, fear in her eyes. "Don't even suggest that. Don't even think it."

Richard regretted frightening her. "I won't ever leave you, Anise. I shall remain in your world and love it the more, for 'tis yours."

Her eyes flickered with relief. "It's yours, too, now – because this is the world where your child will be born."

Richard stared. "What are you saying?"

Anise looked him in the eyes. "Your heir."

Richard's tongue would not work. No words sufficed.

ABOUT THE AUTHOR

Karla Tipton cut her literary teeth on gothic romances, Edgar Allan Poe and the vampire soap "Dark Shadows." Long before there were sparkly vampires roaming through the cultural consciousness, she wrote about ordinary women time traveling through history and falling in love with powerful men of myth and magic. "Genre-bending" came naturally. Despite publishing industry advice to find a genre and stick with it, Karla shamelessly mixed it up, blending history, paranormal, time travel, fantasy and mystery into her novels. When she became fascinated with Richard III, she made a research trip to England, so she could lend authenticity and historical detail to her novel about a romance between a modern woman and her favorite medieval king.

"Rings of Passage," a time travel romance set in medieval England, is Karla's first published novel. Time travel and magic are also at the heart of the project she's just wrapping up, "Dangerous Reflections," a romance about a twenty-first century post-graduate student and an Edwardian-era wizard.

Karla is a member of Romance Writers of America, and her writing has earned top honors in several RWA chapter competitions.

When not at her government job or writing novels, Karla plays guitar in a classic rock band.

FRANK STEINWACHS PHOTO